OBLIVIONGATE

OBLIVIONGATE

BOOK THREE OF THE SOULMIST SERIES

HELEN GARRAWAY

Published by Jerven Publishing

Cover designed by MiblArt

eBook ISBN: 978-1-915854-15-5

Paperback ISBN: 978-1-915854-16-2

Hardcover ISBN: 978-1-915854-17-9

A CIP catalogue record for this book is available from the British Library.

Sign up to my mailing list to join my magical world and for further information about forthcoming books and latest news at: www.helengarraway.com

First Edition

*For every reader who joined me on my writing journey
and loves my books.
Thank you for your support, your enthusiasm,
and your desire for many more!*

ALSO BY HELEN GARRAWAY

<u>Sentinal Series</u>

Sentinals Awaken

Sentinals Rising

Sentinals Justice

Sentinals Recovery

Sentinals Across Time

Sentinals Banished

Sentinals Destiny

<u>SoulMist series</u>

SoulBreather

DragonBound

OblivionGate

<u>Standalone</u>

Harmony

CONTENTS

ANGELICUS
PURONIA
CITADEL
CHECKPOINT
DESTINE
INN
BASRIL
TYRAL
CROSSROADS
MINE
SERAPHIM CASTLE
SHANDRA'S DEN
RENSOR
JINNEL
MERAPOL
FALLIR
EIDOLON

1

KIARA – OBLIVION GATE, EIDOLON

Kiara drifted through the silent halls of the Oblivion Gate. She couldn't ignore the feeling that she wasn't alone and someone was watching. Flickers caught the corner of her eye, but when she looked, no one was there.

Not knowing what else to do and still trying to adjust to her new reality, Kiara concentrated on exploring the empty chambers. They were breathtakingly beautiful. A green glow illuminated the high ceilings and washed over the smooth stone walls. Elegant reliefs decorated the corners and columns lining the doorways, leading into darkened alcoves and concealed spaces.

Arched doorways led off in a maze of corridors and passages. It would be easy to get lost, though she wasn't concerned; it wasn't as if she would starve to death. She was already dead. She shivered as a chill flashed through her at the thought. It was weird how she still felt things, even though her body didn't exist and she was an ephemeral mist floating above the shiny floors. She was disappointed to see that she didn't even have a reflection.

The only time she seemed to have any substance was when she was with Mav. Something about him helped to anchor her, but then he always had. Mav was the one person who had believed in her and her abilities without question. He had never treated her like a child but always as an equal, as someone he trusted.

Kiara straightened her shoulders. Even in death, he had made her his Gate Wraith. He had given her purpose at a time when her world had been shattered. He had been there for her, and she wouldn't let him down.

Continuing down the corridor, she gasped as a majestic room opened before her. At one end, a grand staircase rose in an elegant curve, splitting into two branches halfway. It was a gorgeous room and completely empty. She wasn't sure what furnishings would suit such a picturesque room.

Choosing the darkened doorways beneath the stairs, she ventured deeper into the halls. She was surprised to find a spotless kitchen, its storerooms filled with various types of fresh produce. Someone was cooking for people who ate, though there was no sign of them. Where had they gone? And who were they?

Leaving the kitchen, she found more stairs, utilitarian in nature, that led down into darkness. Kiara floated down the steps and along corridors until she entered another large space and halted with a gasp. Green flames flared in the torches on the walls and lit a complex matrix of metalwork, cogs, pulleys, and chains. Her gaze followed the linkages, and she revelled in the complexity, delved into the chains and the joints, and winced at the signs of rust and neglect.

Why had such complicated machinery been allowed to become so atrophied? She paused. What was it supposed to do? Was this the Gate? Part of it? Whatever it was, it had not been used in decades. Was there another? Where had all the soulless gone in the meantime?

She frowned and traced the links, following the pattern, and saw the result. The wall was supposed to slide open, though the wheels were rusted solid and wouldn't move any time soon.

There had been a container of grease in the kitchen. She headed back down the corridors, eyeing the torches that flared and died as she passed. Was someone watching her? How did they know she was here?

At the first attempt of picking up the pot, her hand passed right through it. She hissed her breath out. She was here for a reason, and that reason was to look after the Oblivion Gate. "I'm here to help you, blast it," she muttered and tried again. This time, her fingers seemed to brush against the pot as they passed through it, and something inside her quickened.

"I'm a Gate Wraith," she said and concentrated on the clay vessel.

"What…is a Gate Wraith?" The deep voice grated on her ears, rough and fractured.

Kiara stiffened. Peering around, she said, "The one who will grease these wheels if I can pick up this stupid pot."

"Why do you need to grease my wheels?"

"Because they are rusted."

"Why do you care?" The voice was slow and dejected.

"Why do I care?" Kiara twisted, searching for whoever was speaking, but she couldn't see anyone. "That's complex machinery. You have to look after it. How could you allow it to get into such a state?"

"I didn't have a choice."

"Of course you have a choice. Who is responsible for maintaining it? Where are they?"

"I don't know."

Kiara spun again, peering into the shadows. "Who are you? Where are you?"

"Why does it matter?" The voice faded as if the speaker were leaving.

"It matters because Mav asked me to help maintain the Oblivion Gate. He asked me to be his Gate Wraith, and I said yes."

"Mav?"

"Yes, Mav. Deus Demavrian." She stared at the pot and scowled. "If I am dead, how do I make myself more solid?"

"You are dead?"

Kiara rolled her eyes. "Duh! Can't you tell? I'm a ghost. A spirit. Not real."

The chuckle was raspy as if the person weren't used to being amused. "You look real to me."

"Who are you?"

"I am the Oblivion Gate."

Kiara froze. "The Oblivion Gate?" she whispered.

"Yes. And you look solid to me."

"I do?"

"Yes. Why are you here? You are not like the others who roam my halls."

"I told you. Mav asked me to be his Gate Wraith. He wants me to look after you."

"Why?"

Kiara scowled at the ceiling. "Why? Because you are the Gate! The soulless pass through you. Mav will help you look after the people of Eidolon."

Silence. After an extended pause in which Kiara thought the Gate might have withdrawn, he said, "Kaenera is the Gate Keeper, and he doesn't care about anyone except himself."

"Not anymore. Mav defeated him."

"He what?"

"Mav defeated him. Kaenera isn't dead, as far as I know, but he lost all his power, and Mav inherited it. Mav's a really good guy. He's an Archdeus. No, a Deus now. Though he doesn't have a soul. He's been living in Eidolon for years. Mav needs to become the Gate Keeper, however that works."

"A new Gate Keeper?"

"Mmm." Kiara focused on the pot again and placed her hands on either side of it.

"You have to *believe* you can pick it up. It's all in the power of the mind." The Gate snorted. "You haven't got much else left to work with!"

"Believe in myself. Mav believes in me, and so should I." Kiara tightened her grip and nudged the pot away from her. She exhaled, concentrated, and tried again. She picked the pot up. "Yes!"

"What are you going to do with that?" the Gate inquired. His voice had grown smoother the more he spoke and now vibrated with a deep timbre. Kiara thought it was a nice voice.

"Which bit hurts the most? We'll begin there."

"Start with the wheels. They really ache."

Kiara returned to the complex wall of machinery and, kneeling on the floor, rubbed grease around the joints. "Who else is here?" she asked after a while. "I haven't seen anyone."

"Few stay. Kaenera's people come and go. Dybbuks usually."

"How do dybbuks differ from wraiths?"

"Dybbuks are the soulless who died and whom Kaenera bound to him, refusing to allow them to pass on. Wraiths are those who died but chose to stay here."

"Are there many wraiths?"

"A few. Kaenera was never interested. He always ignored us."

"I don't understand. How can Kaenera ignore you? He

was the Gate Keeper. How did he pass the soulless through you?"

"He didn't. That's why most of my mechanisms are seized. I've only managed to keep the small gate open."

"The small gate?"

"The one I assume you tried to go through."

"The one with the flowers?"

Another moment of silence. "Flowers?"

"Yes. The trellis had green vines and pink flowers."

"No, it doesn't."

"It did when I was there."

"That's not possible."

Kiara shrugged and continued working. "Do you want to see if you can rotate the wheels so I can reach other bits?"

A deep groan echoed through the hall, but the wheels didn't move. Kiara wedged her shoulder against the bracket and tried to rock the frame, but it wouldn't budge. "Let me add some more grease," she said, panting heavily.

It wasn't until she was slapping on more gloop that she realised she had been able to brace against the structure. It had been solid, and so had she. She smiled as she worked. They tried again, but the mechanism was seized tight.

"Do you have any tools? Wire brushes? Looseners? Spanners? Oil?"

"There's an old box in the sub-basement. I'm not sure what's in it."

"Can't hurt to look," Kiara replied. "Show me the way."

2

SOLANJI – EIDOLON

Staring out over brackish heath, Solanji scowled at the layer of mist suffocating the land of Eidolon. Beneath the murky gloom, the fields extended in all directions, surrounding the small homestead. Rubbing her hands down her leather trousers, she was glad she had changed out of the golden robes Mav had found for her. He insisted she had every right to wear the garb of an archangel, heartsworn as she was to him and a SoulBreather to boot. No one with any sense would try to say different.

Since Mav's ascension to Deus, she knew they were both adapting to the changes. He had many new powers he had yet to learn to control, and she was sure she had gained some in the backlash. Her ability to "read" soulmist had sharpened. In fact, if she concentrated, she didn't have to touch the soulmist at all. It was almost as if she could read minds.

Something else to talk to Mav about. Was this her innate skill or one she was gaining from him via their bonding? She thought it might be due to Mav's new status as a god.

She was torn between staying in Eidolon to comfort her little brother and going to Puronia to support her heartsworn. Demavrian, the man she loved and had exchanged oaths with, was more important, or so said her brother, Brennan. But she'd heard the quaver in his voice as he'd said it and saw how he'd lifted his chin in an effort to appear nonchalant.

Her brother needed time and support to recover from being soul-stripped and banished to Eidolon. Time to recover from the harrowing experience he suffered when he had tried to escape from the slave camp with some other kids and seen one of them, Bailey, nearly strangled to death while trying to help him. Bailey *had* died, according to Mav, but Mav had managed to resuscitate him and bring him back. Solanji shivered. Bren still had nightmares about it, which was the reason she was here with Bren and not with Mav. But Mav had suffered some life-changing events himself, and she should be with him.

Brennan was still skittish and uncertain after his ordeal. Understandably clingy, seeing as he had been abducted from his family and home, he was still adjusting to losing his soul and recovering from the hardship of being sent to a slave camp. He was only nine, and if she were being honest, he was coping reasonably well. The company of ten or so other children his age who had also been incarcerated and worked almost to death had helped to keep him occupied.

The presence of an enormous dragon had also helped to distract him from brooding on his recent experiences. Said dragon was currently rolling about in the dust like a frolicking, oversized vemlow pup, her iridescent scales gleaming in the dull light.

Vemlow's, or vems as they were often called, roamed the forests in packs. Occasionally, a pup would be abandoned, and if you were patient enough, they could be trained to help guard the livestock. On rare occasions they became domesticated and could be very loyal companions.

Xylvin's rider, Ryvalin, a stocky woman with a very dry sense of humour, threw her hands up in the air and stalked off, complaining about dragons who could never stay clean. An excitable group of youngsters who were fast losing any fear of the beast were slowly moving closer, their eyes huge and voices high as they argued about who would touch her first.

Solanji shook her head and smiled at them, knowing Xylvin would never harm any of them.

Her visit with Mav to see her mother and explain what had happened to Brennan hadn't gone so well. She grimaced as she remembered her mother's reaction. Relief that her son was alive had been replaced with anger at his treatment, and then she had been overwhelmed by the news that Solanji had married a god, that she was the only SoulBreather in existence and had a dragon familiar. Maybe she had dumped too much information on her mother at once. Mav had soothed her mother's stressed nerves, and Solanji still wondered if he had used his persuasive powers on her even though he'd sworn he had not.

The hinges of the door squealed as it opened behind her, and she turned to face it. A young girl smiled at her as she pushed her blonde, flyaway hair out of her face. The smile didn't reach her deep blue eyes, and her sharp face was gaunt, a result of her recent incarceration in the same slave camp as Brennan. Shandra was the eldest of all the orphans. She was calm and collected, her responsibility for the other kids giving her a certain weight that hadn't lifted with Solanji and Ryvalin keeping her company.

Dark shadows swirled around her in place of the golden soulmist people usually had; a shadowsoul. Somehow, Mav had given his fledglings shadowsouls, the same as his. Only, he didn't know how he had done it, another thing he needed to figure out. She wished he could give Brennan a shadowsoul; at least then, he could return to Angelicus and go home.

No. That was *her* job. She needed to find Brennan's soul in all the hundreds, no, thousands of souls stored in the citadel. The soulless couldn't survive in Angelicus for more than twenty-four turns of the timepiece. Only those with soulmist could live in Angelicus—another reason why she should be in Puronia. She should be searching the citadel for Brennan's soul so she could return it to him and he could go home.

"Has anyone plucked up the courage yet?" Shandra asked, gesturing at the dragon.

"All talk so far."

Shandra laughed, and Solanji was glad to hear it. There had been little laughter in the last week, such a contrast to her previous visits. All the children had been scarred by their experiences.

She wished her mother had agreed to come to Eidolon to see Brennan, but she had been petrified by Solanji's golden dragon, Ellaria, and more terrified of the idea of visiting Eidolon. Solanji huffed under her breath. Ellaria was a fraction of the size of Xylvin and not at all threatening.

Rubbing her face, she joined Shandra at the bench on the veranda. "How are you doing?" she asked as she sat.

"Fine," Shandra said as she always did.

"Ryvalin or I could take you to the citadel to see the others if you wanted."

"I can't leave the little ones."

Solanji thought it was time she did. She and Mav had found a new house mother to care for the orphans—an older couple, grey haired and comfortable. They had never been able to have their own children, but they showered affection on the youngsters, and after a month, the children began to respond. The kids shouldn't be the responsibility of a girl barely seventeen.

"They need a bit of stability for a while, something they know," Shandra said as if reading her mind. "Too many changes at once would upset them."

"You must miss Kerris, Muntra, and Bailey," Solanji said, naming the other fledglings currently in Puronia.

"Of course I do. But I know they are safe with Mav." Shandra's lip trembled, and Solanji knew it was because of Kiara, the one member of their little family they had lost in the slave compound. Kiara had died in an explosion she had set that went wrong, and now she was a wraith lingering in the halls of the Oblivion Gate. Mav said she was his Gate Wraith, and she would help him look after the Oblivion Gate. Solanji wasn't quite sure whether she believed him. She didn't think the fledglings believed Kiara was still in the Gate, either. They never spoke of her.

A squeal of laughter made her look over her shoulder. The kids had brought buckets of water from the stream and were now washing the dragon. Well, the bits they could reach, such as her very long tail and her snout, which was lying flat on the ground.

Xylvin's eyes were half-lidded, and she rumbled with pleasure as the children scrubbed. Solanji spotted her brother scratching Xylvin's eye ridge, and she smiled. His face wore a peaceful expression as he leaned against her. He looked tiny beside the dragon, and Solanji's stomach fluttered at how vulnerable he seemed next to the dragon's bulk. Her vision misted, and she hurriedly blinked back tears. She had nearly lost him. "Now, that is not a sight you see every day," she said.

"They will miss her when she leaves."

"They'll have the chickens and goats to look after," Solanji replied.

Shandra huffed. "No comparison."

Solanji chuckled.

Mrs Bridges came out of the house with a hessian bag and a bowl in her hands. "There you are. Would you mind shelling these beans for me?" Her gaze landed on the dragon, and she paled. "Why are those children near that beast?"

"Xylvin is harmless," Solanji said. "The kids are having fun."

Mrs Bridges shuddered. "It's unnatural. It will be better for all of us when they leave." She shoved the bag at Shandra, placed the bowl on the table, and shuffled back into the house, muttering under her breath.

Shandra watched her go and then sighed. "Maybe it is time for new beginnings," she said as she emptied the sack on the table and began shucking beans.

Solanji leaned forward to help, but she was interrupted as her familiar, Ellaria, appeared beside her. Ellaria was a glowing golden dragon who made the veranda creak as she landed on the wooden boards with a soft thud. She was daintier than Xylvin, more ethereal, with softer spines and flowing tendrils, and a fraction of the size, but she still had a considerable weight to her.

"Mav needs us," Ellaria said without any preamble through their mind link.

She stood and glanced over at her brother. He was still engrossed in the dragon, but Xylvin had raised her eyelids and was watching Solanji and Ellaria. "Tell Brennan I'll be back soon," Solanji said, and Ellaria must have reassured Xylvin because the immense dragon closed her eyes again. Ellaria draped herself around Solanji and they disappeared.

Shandra blinked at the empty veranda, shook her head, and then continued shelling the beans.

3

DEMAVRIAN – CITADEL, PURONIA

Deus Demavrian strode up the central nave in the Assembly Hall and, with a swirl of his brilliant white robes, sat in his seat on the dais. The heavy material tightened as it wrapped around his legs like a noose, and he resisted the urge to straighten them. It was the first time he had worn the robes of a Deus, but he wanted to make a point, no matter how ostentatious they were.

Trying to conceal his wince as another soulless pleaded for sanctuary in his head, he glanced around the chamber. His cherubim, Adriz, stood behind his shoulder in place of his Captain of the Host, Ryvalin, who was still in Eidolon. It was time to recall Ryvalin from babysitting duties. He needed her knowledge and experience in the forthcoming fight with Kaenera.

Adriz was a large, muscular woman whose purpose in life was to keep him alive. She was feared by all in the citadel, having proved her prowess with any weapon many times. With the number of suspicious gazes on him, he was glad of her presence behind his shoulder.

Amaridin strode up the aisle with his partner, Valerian,

beside him and Ziriel, his Captain of the Host, following him. He grinned at Mav before taking his seat, and Mav relaxed a smidgen. The sight of his brother so happy was still a little unnerving.

Averdeus appeared in a flash of white light, and Mav shook his head at his father's dramatic entry. The galleries were filling, angels and administrators alike eager to hear what would be debated today. Mav knew they wouldn't be so keen once he'd said his piece.

Would they support him in his fight against Kaenera, though? That was the question. Until he claimed the Oblivion Gate, he was vulnerable. As a new god getting used to his powers, this was the obvious time for Kaenera to attack.

Mav's muscles tensed, and his chest tightened. Unease made his breath stutter, yet there was no apparent threat. He flexed his fingers and tried to breathe evenly as he observed the room. Tall ceilings arched overhead, and heavily laden chandeliers cast a soft glow from above. Crystal inclusions in the white marble floors glittered in the candlelight.

He recognised most of the archangels and some of the seraphim, but none of the fledglings and few of the councillors or administrators. In the last fifty years, during his and his father's absence, many posts had changed hands, and he no longer knew who held power. Felather had tried to bring him up to date, but the lack of familiarity with the people involved made it difficult to associate the right details with the right person.

Mav's head was already full of other people's memories, and making sense of more information was proving challenging. The one thing Felather had been sure to tell him about was the shift in control from the ruling Deus to the archangels and the Assembly. Serenia had seen to that, and the Assembly were reluctant to hand the power back.

Averdeus eyed Mav for a moment. Mav hoped his father didn't notice the gleam of sweat on his skin. Nausea swept through him, and he swallowed. His father touched his shoulder, and the need to vomit eased. Mav concentrated on breathing in and out.

Exquisite white wings flared, and Averdeus turned to the room and raised his hands. He waited until silence fell in the Assembly Hall. White feathers surrounded Averdeus, and he seemed to glow. "Much has happened since I last stood in this chamber," he said, his voice reaching the farthest corner of the room with ease. "We grieve the loss of many friends in our absence and the damage to our citadel, but our heart is warmed by the return of our son, Demavrian, to the citadel's embrace."

Mav flinched at his father's words. He could not stay. His future was bound with a different entity—if he could find it. The Oblivion Gate was the key to him defeating Kaenera for good, but he couldn't do it alone.

"We are heartened by the knowledge that Demavrian has ascended, that he will hold the Oblivion Gate and welcome the soulless of Eidolon as they take their final journey, a journey we all must take one day. But to protect that right…"

Mav's attention drifted as another soulless took up residence in his head, pleading for passage through the Gate while his father's voice droned on, until he was suddenly aware of an expectant silence. His father had turned towards him, his eyebrows rising as Mav stared at him. Heat warmed Mav's cheeks as he realised he had missed his father's introduction.

Grimacing, he stood and faced the chamber. He took a step forward, almost tripping over his robes, and a low titter made him grit his teeth. Too many had witnessed his fall from grace. It was easier to believe him fallen and irrelevant.

"As many of you saw, here in these chambers, I defeated

four counts of Apologia, proving my innocence of all accusations." Mav gestured at Averdeus. "As you can see, I did not murder my father." Angels shifted in discomfort at the reminder, their wings rustling. "I reft Kaenera of much of his power and severed him from the Oblivion Gate, but the threat he poses to all of us has not been nullified. He wants his power back, and he won't stop until he has it."

"You are Deus," a slender archangel stated. His soft white wings fluttered behind him. "You killed Kaenera and took his power. Stop creating threats where there are none."

"My brother is not dead," Averdeus said, glaring at the angel.

"Then how did Demavrian become Deus?"

"You were there, or so I'm told," Averdeus replied, holding the angel's gaze. "You tell me."

The angel shrugged. "I know what I saw. Demavrian cleaved Kaenera in two and he disintegrated."

"But there was no corpse to dispose of," Mav said. "Kaenera will tend to his wounds and rebuild his strength. We need to strike before he has a chance to recover."

"Strike at what?" an officer of the Heavenly Host demanded, stepping away from the guards lining the hall. His uniform was immaculate, and his broad shoulders filled it well.

His name is Lynen, Mav thought. Lynen had risen through the ranks quickly, an able swordsman and an astute strategist, and he now led the division of the Heavenly Host responsible for the security of the citadel. Too arrogant and quick to judge, Felather had said.

"You struck him down, and he fled; he cannot return to Angelicus," Lynen continued.

Mav frowned. "Why are you so sure he cannot return?"

"Kaenera only gained entry because the citadel was dormant. The citadel is revived. Averdeus is back. Even if

Kaenera lived, he would not be allowed to enter." Lynen glanced at the nodding councillors behind him.

Mav noted that Lynen hadn't counted him in their defences. "We must work together to protect all of Angelicus and Eidolon, not just the citadel."

"We have never stopped protecting Angelicus, you are the one who deserted your post." Lynen held Mav's gaze and then turned his back on him and returned to his position by the wall.

Amaridin rose. "Demavrian never deserted his post. Circumstances beyond his control forced him into Eidolon."

"We are not repeating Apologia," Mav snarled as memories of being chained like a criminal replayed in his mind. His shadows leaked, and he fumbled to restrain them.

A portly, red-faced angel stood—Councillor Gineray, Mav thought—and stepped down into the nave. His gaze swept around the seated assembly, careful to avoid the angels on the dais, and he clasped his hands behind his back. Raising his chin, he said, "Kaenera is no longer a threat. You defeated him. We have more important topics to discuss. I would suggest that removing the divide would be more of a threat to our safety than Kaenera. It is a preposterous idea. Eidolon is lawless. We do not want them coming here with their total disregard for authority."

Voices rose in agreement, and the debate began. Averdeus gripped Mav's shoulder. "Leave it for now. They are not ready to listen," he murmured. "I'd forgotten how intractable the council could be. Amaridin will work on them."

"By the time they are ready, it will be too late," Mav ground out between gritted teeth as he watched Lynen side with the councillor. That man would not support Mav, no matter the topic. Maybe his old friend Julius, a captain in the Heavenly Host, could persuade him to pay attention.

The ache in Mav's head spiked. Rubbing his temple, he flared his shadowy wings and, with a thought, changed his white robes to a dark grey. His shoulders dropped as his discomfort eased, and the chamber fell silent.

Mav glared at them. "You have become isolationist, elitist. This angelic council is here for the good of the people, *all* people, souled or soulless, not for your comfort. Until you look around you and see how our world is changing, you will remain vulnerable. Kaenera is not interested in the good of anyone. He is only interested in what he wants, and I took it away from him. I would suggest that if he ever manages to get it back, you will have more to worry about than an artificial divide which should never have been put in place to begin with!"

Mav stomped down the steps, and Adriz followed. His shadows trailed around him as he left the hall. Once the doors shut behind him, a hubbub of voices rose. He briefly closed his eyes. Amaridin could deal with them. He returned to his rooms.

The citadel's heartbeat thumped, triggering yet another spike of pain in Demavrian's temples. He slumped over his desk, holding his head. His fingers curled into his hair, and he pressed the heels of his palms into his eyes and groaned. Head pounding, he swallowed the rush of saliva as nausea swept through him, and he lurched to his feet. Staggering across the room, barely able to see his way, he clipped the doorframe to his bed chamber, sparking a dull ache in his arm. He made a sudden dash to the bathing room, just in time to vomit down the toilet.

Heaving up his lunch, he hugged the basin and laid his cheek against the cold stone. His skin was so hot that he was surprised it didn't sizzle. He dragged off his jacket and pulled at the laces to open his shirt, flapping the material to waft a bit of air over his heated body.

Another spike of pain stabbed through his head, and he groaned into the basin as he retched up bile.

"Mav?" Cool hands touched his forehead.

When had Solanji arrived? He hadn't heard the door, but then his head was down the toilet, and his ears were buzzing.

"You're burning up!" Solanji exclaimed, and she disappeared and returned to pat a damp cloth against his skin. She wiped his face and flushed the toilet, clearing some of the vile stink.

He slumped, unmoving, his eyes closed. Solanji was supposed to be in Eidolon with her brother, Brennan. Ellaria must have felt his distress and rushed her back. He was sure she would be hovering over him soon as well. Wherever Solanji went, her dragon familiar went, too. It didn't matter that all three of them were bound together with the citadel. Ellaria was Solanji's.

"But we both love you, so that's all that matters," Ellaria murmured in his head, and he winced.

"What's the matter?" Solanji asked.

"Pounding headache," Mav replied.

"Let's get you up. Ellaria, go and fetch Felather."

Mav didn't think Felather would be able to make a dent in the pain squeezing his head so tight, but he allowed Solanji to lever him off the floor and over to the bed. He flopped on the mattress and rolled on his side, away from the bright sunshine flooding the room. "Too bright," he mumbled. The swish of the curtains shutting soon followed, providing some blessed relief, and he moaned in appreciation.

"Here, drink. It will help clear your mouth." Solanji pressed the edge of a glass against his lips, and he opened them enough for her to carefully dribble in a tart juice, which cleared the crud from his mouth.

As Solanji rubbed his back with one hand while threading her fingers through his hair with the other and her soulfingers through his shadows, he relaxed under the soothing caresses. His head settled for a moment.

The door opened, disturbing him. He tried to lift his head, but it was too heavy, and his mouth flooded with saliva at the sudden movement. So, instead, he relaxed back onto the pillow and drifted. His head still ached, but not so badly.

"Mav?"

His scribe, Felather, was standing over him. More cool hands touched his heated skin.

"Mmm?"

"Do you still have a headache?"

"Mmm."

"And the light makes it worse?"

"Mmm."

"Do you still feel sick?"

"If I move." Even to his own ears, his voice sounded slurred.

"Drink this; it will help with the pain and nausea."

Mav drank the vile liquid Felather offered, and he gagged. It set his head thumping, and he lurched up. Felather steadied him.

"Sick," was all Mav was able to say before he vomited everywhere.

It took far too long to clean him and the bed up, but finally, he was tucked back into fresh, cool linen with a scarf wrapped around his eyes to block all light and a damp cloth on his forehead. Felather gently massaged his temples, and he drifted off again.

· · ·

"It's a severe migraine," Felather told Solanji in a hushed voice. "Keep the curtains closed; don't let him take the scarf off until we get the pain under control. No bright lights, no mind speech, and speak quietly. Loud noises will set him off again. He should only drink water for now and only small sips. I'll be back with a more suitable draught for the pain. He should sleep for a turn or two. I'll be back before he wakes."

"Do you know what's causing it?" Solanji whispered.

Felather shrugged. "He's been under a lot of strain. His body is still recovering from major trauma and a huge influx of power. It could be anything. I'll speak to his father; he may have some idea of what is happening."

"Can you make sure no one tries to mind speak him?" she asked.

Felather nodded. "I'll warn them." After a glance at Mav, he squeezed her arm and silently left. Solanji followed him out of the bedchamber and closed the curtains against the brilliant sunlight in case Mav did wake up and ventured out into the main living area.

Solanji stood in the doorway and watched Mav sleep. She was afraid to enter the room as she might disturb him. His face was paler and not so flushed, but he was still sweating. He hadn't said he was suffering. Her lips tightened. That was one thing she and his oathsworn agreed on: Mav had to stop hiding the pain he was in. How were they supposed to help him if he didn't tell them?

At least his knee no longer bothered him. The flush of divine power flowing through Mav's veins had healed all his injuries and removed his scars—those that were visible. Solanji frowned. So, what was causing his migraine?

Ellaria manifested behind her, a slight disturbance in the air, and Solanji joined her in the main room of their chambers. The dragon had once been a golden tattoo on her forearm, but now she was an ethereal, golden creature with curved horns on her head, razor-sharp teeth, and soft spines down her back.

The dragon landed on the floor with a dull thud and flipped her wings back. She was as tall as Solanji, though a quarter of the size of Xylvin, the dragon currently babysitting her brother. As light and airy as Ellaria seemed, she was solid and heavy.

"How is he?" Ellaria asked, her voice a soft caress in Solanji's mind.

"Sleeping. Felather said we mustn't try to mind speak with him until his headache eases."

"I should have been keeping a closer eye on him." Ellaria sounded contrite.

"We both should have. I've been too engrossed in Brennan." Solanji rubbed her temples, which were also aching. *"Mav has so much more to contend with."*

"We need to convince him to let us share his burden. He doesn't have to do everything on his own."

Solanji sighed and sat in one of the comfortable armchairs beside the fire. Ellaria curled up in front of the flickering flames, basking in the heat and blocking most of it. Her snout inched closer to the burning wood even as Solanji watched. The dragon breathed on the fire and the embers flared.

"Ellaria, he's a Deus now. Shouldn't he be able to heal himself?"

"I don't think this is a physical affliction."

"What do you mean?"

"He's the Oblivion Gate Keeper. Thousands of soulless are clamouring to pass through the Gate every day. He doesn't know how to deal with it. I imagine those soulless are weighing heavily on his mind."

"How do we find out how the Gate works?"

"We can't. There is no one to teach him unless you count Kaenera, but I wouldn't trust a word that snake says."

Solanji shivered at the vicious bite in the dragon's voice. Kaenera was Mav's uncle and had been the previous Gate Keeper until Mav had defeated him and absorbed all his power. However, Kaenera was not dead, and Solanji knew they hadn't heard the last of him.

There was a tap at the door to their chambers, and she looked up from her contemplation of the flames. The door opened, spilling light into the darkened room, and Solanji rose with a gasp of surprise as Mav's father entered with Felather behind him.

Averdeus was a slight man with blond hair swept off his classically handsome face. His brilliant blue eyes sparkled with intelligence, and the aura of the man was nearly over-whelming. Solanji frowned. Why didn't Mav have a similar aura?

"Because it is new. He is growing into it," Averdeus replied. "Which, no doubt, is part of the problem." He strolled over to the bedchamber and peered in at Mav. "Felather, why don't you escort Solanji to dinner? I'm sure she hasn't eaten yet."

"But…" Solanji didn't get the chance to protest. Felather grabbed her arm and tugged her out of the room. Ellaria vanished, leaving Averdeus frowning down at his son.

"Now, this won't do," he muttered and leaned down to touch his son's temple. He hissed his breath out. "No wonder your head hurts."

"Demavrian," Averdeus said as he shook son's arm. He waited a moment and shook him again. "Wake up, son. We need to talk."

Mav stirred and stretched. "What time is it?" he asked and pushed the scarf off as he rubbed his face.

"No idea, but it's still light, so not too late. Solanji is getting something to eat. Are you hungry?"

"No." Mav shuffled up the bed and leaned against the pillow.

Averdeus inspected him. "You need to claim the Gate, son."

"Claim it?"

"Yes, you are carrying an influx of soulless, and you need to let them go. When you defeated Kaenera, you took on his mantle, his power, and those he had not passed on. You have quite a backlog weighing you down."

"Is that why my head is pounding?"

"How long has it been hurting?"

"It's been gradual, building over the last few weeks."

Averdeus tutted. "You should have said."

"It was just a headache," Mav replied with a shrug.

"You know that's not true. You need to claim the Gate so you can release the soulless. You need to pass them on so you can take on more. It's a constant process."

Mav groaned. "Constant?"

"Of course. Someone dies every minute. You can't hang on to them; you have to let them go, and to do that, you need the Gate. The longer you leave it…well, your pain will only get worse." He gestured at Mav with an elegant hand. "You can't afford to be incapacitated like this with Kaenera out there plotting your death."

"Gee, thanks."

Averdeus chuckled and then became more serious. "Amaridin needs to step up and claim the citadel. You can't hold both, as you now know. They are opposing forces, light versus dark, and you are the battleground."

"Without the citadel, I would be dead," Mav protested.

"And without you, the citadel would still be dormant, so you are even and have no need to feel guilt."

"I don't want to break my connection. I only just came back." Mav pondered for a moment, a frown creasing his brow. "I don't even know how to break it."

"Yes, you do. Amaridin can't take the citadel until you release it and claim the Gate. You won't lose your connection completely. You are bound to Solanji and Ellaria, and they will still be connected to the citadel. One person is not meant to hold both. The burden should be shared."

Mav leaned forward. "I don't know how to claim the Gate or where it really is. The only times I've visited, I haven't physically been there."

"You are not going to find it here. The Gate is peeved that you are here and not there."

"And where is there, exactly?"

"That is for you to discover." Averdeus smiled, but he didn't put much effort into it, and he wasn't surprised when his son squeezed his arm in sympathy. Lethargy pulled at his limbs like heavy robes, and his bones ached with anguish and loss.

"Father."

"My time here is over. After all that has happened, I don't think I can walk these halls and be content. I failed your mother, and I need time to come to terms with that. It is up to you and Amaridin as to how you proceed. If I stay here, I may do something I regret, and I do not want to make matters worse."

"Maybe *you* should deal with Serenia," Mav said. "It may give you some closure."

Averdeus shook his head. "No. Her crime was just as much against you, if not more. She took your mother and your life. I think you have more to avenge than I do."

Mav exhaled and then winced, his lips tightening as he rubbed his temple. "Father, please don't make any rash decisions. I've missed you, and you need to spend time getting to know Valerian and Solanji. There is still much for you here. We need you, especially after the council's response to me today. They are not going to listen to anything I have to say."

A flush of warmth eased the chill settling in Averdeus' chest, and he leaned forward to kiss his son's cheek. "You'd be surprised. Your parting speech shook a few of them. Rest for now. I won't leave without saying goodbye."

4

DEMAVRIAN – CITADEL - PURONIA

Later that afternoon, Mav sat behind his desk and frowned at the parchment in front of him. The only way he had thought of to sever his connection to the citadel was for Solanji to do it, and he knew she would not be happy about that. At the same time, Amaridin needed to claim it. Mav was sure Amaridin's partner, Valerian, wouldn't be too pleased about that, either.

The logistics threatened to give him another headache as he mulled over the best way to approach Solanji. At least he would still be bound to her and Ellaria and, through them, to the citadel. Surely, that would reassure her?

One step at a time. Claiming the Oblivion Gate was the priority. He needed to offload the soulless before his head exploded. Added to that, his fledglings were in some disarray, and he needed to speak to all of them and reassure them. He had palmed them off to the tutors while he tried to assimilate the changes wrought on his life, and that wasn't fair to them, either.

He rubbed his temples. Make a list. Get the worries out of his head and onto paper. That might ease one ache.

Reaching for a quill, he realised the holder was empty. Pulling open the drawer, he searched for another. Unable to find any spare quills, he tried to remember where he'd last seen one. Felather had used his quill last; he must have taken it with him.

Twisting his lips, he pictured Felather's leather folder with all his papers and pens—he had enough pens already without taking Mav's—and he gasped as the wallet appeared on his desk. Tentatively, he poked it with his finger. It was solid. Flipping the folio open, he stared at it. It was definitely Felather's. Felather would be pissed when he couldn't find it. Had Mav really called it to him?

Picturing the book on his nightstand, he imagined it on his desk, and his breath caught as it appeared next to the folio. He picked it up. It was the same book he was reading, and he did not doubt that if he went and looked, it would no longer be where he'd left it. Was this one of the powers his father had mentioned? He could call things to himself with his mind?

Staring at the leather wallet, he wondered if he could return it, but after considering his options, he thought it safer not to try. Maybe he would experiment later when Solanji was with him.

He picked up a quill with trembling fingers and, after taking a deep breath, began writing.

The door opened, and Solanji and Felather entered the room. Mav lifted his head, bracing for their recriminations, as he was not supposed to be out of bed. He was not disappointed, and he sat back with a rueful smile on his lips.

His heartbeat quickened as he met Solanji's concerned gaze. Those golden robes did suit her. The soft folds of material gathered around her slender form and made her brown skin glow, warm and vibrant. Dark brown curls tumbled loose over her shoulders, and his fingers twitched, eager to touch the silky strands.

"Mav, you are not fit to be working!" Solanji exclaimed as she came around the desk. "You should be resting!"

"What is the point of me easing your pain if you cause it to happen again?" Felather scolded.

Mav shrugged. "It's not going to get any better." He tapped his temple. "According to my father, I am collecting soulless. I am supposed to release them into oblivion, and I can't do that until I pass the citadel to Amaridin and claim the Gate."

"What's involved in claiming the Gate?" Solanji asked.

"I'm not sure. But I need you to help me pass the citadel to Amaridin."

"Me?"

Mav decided to be blunt. "You need to sever my connection to the citadel."

"Absolutely not!" Solanji replied.

Ellaria popped into the room and thumped onto the floor. She looked at Solanji, her faceted eyes whirling, and Solanji waved her arm.

"He wants me to sever his connection with the citadel. I won't do it! That's what started this whole mess!"

"Then my head will explode," Mav said with an apologetic smile. "Seriously, though, I will still be connected to you and Ellaria and, through you, to the citadel. I just won't have a direct link. Amaridin needs to host that."

"But you are the cornerstone."

"I *was* the cornerstone. Now Amaridin will be. I need to be the cornerstone for the Oblivion Gate."

Solanji stared at him as Felather picked up his leather folder from Mav's desk. "I don't remember leaving this here." His lips pursed as he frowned at Mav, his mind obviously not on the folder. "Does that mean we'll be leaving the citadel for good?" he asked after Solanji remained silent.

"Of course not, though the majority of my time will need to be at the Gate, especially at the beginning while I'm learning all its vagaries."

"But I need to be here," Solanji protested, "learning how to be a SoulBreather and how to return souls. I need to search for Brennan's soul."

"Fortunate that you have Ellaria who can transport you around then, isn't it? Because I am very much hoping you'll call the Oblivion Gate home."

"If you can find it," Felather said with a scowl.

Mav shrugged. "Next time I visit, I'll have to go outside and see if I can get any bearings. I have to go to the halls and search for the connection anyway."

"Not without me, you won't," Solanji snapped.

Mav smiled. "I'd never go anywhere without you, my love." He reached out, clasped her arm, and pulled her into his lap. He twisted his lips. "Certainly not into the halls of the Oblivion Gate. I need your insights and skills to help me find the path."

"We're all going with you," Felather said, and from the expression on his face, Mav knew he wouldn't be able to persuade his oathsworn otherwise.

"Thank you," he murmured, relieved they still wanted to follow him into the craziness that was about to descend on them. It never seemed to stop.

"I need to speak with my fledglings first, make sure they are settled. At least Bailey is out of the infirmary now, which will make Muntra happy."

"Adriz was complaining that he hasn't made it to the training ring yet."

"It's only been a few weeks. Give them a chance to adjust. They've never seen anything like Puronia before."

Felather shrugged. "You know Adriz."

"Let them get settled, and then I'll talk to them about their options. They are all journeymen or women material. We just need to help them reach their potential."

"You really intend to build a home in Eidolon?" Felather asked.

"Of course. I can't help the people if I'm not there."

Solanji tapped the parchment on his desk. "You haven't got very far with your list. Shouldn't dealing with Serenia be a higher priority? Until you do, you won't get rid of those vendetta stones."

"Possibly," Mav said, his fingers drifting to the two stones at his throat, "but I can't deal with Serenia until I've claimed the Gate. That is my immediate objective." He exhaled, thinking about all the things that could go wrong before then.

The red vendetta stone was Athenia's, the SoulBreather before Solanji. Mav had gained it as he had held her dying body in his arms. Athenia's murderer, the former archangel Serenia, was now incarcerated in the cells below the citadel, waiting for him to execute her sentence. The blue stone had something to do with the people of Eidolon, though what, he wasn't sure.

Drumming his fingers on his folio, Felather frowned at Mav. "Whereabouts in Eidolon *is* the Gate?"

"I'm not sure. I'm hoping I'll get a sense of it once we're in Eidolon." Mav rubbed his temple. There was so much he didn't know and so many people depending on him.

Felather's sceptical expression summed up how he felt. There was a lot of hope involved, but it was all he had.

A soft tap on the door preceded one of his fledglings, Kerris, sliding in through the gap and shutting the door behind him. Kerris froze as he caught sight of them seated around the desk.

"Shouldn't you be in class?" Mav asked, smiling at the crafty expression flitting across the boy's face. Kerris was smart, a scribe in the making. Felather would have his hands full with him.

"I'm just going back, but we've got the afternoon off in a couple of days, and I wanted to ask whether Shandra would be able to come here," Kerris said in a rush. "We all miss her, and it doesn't seem fair she's the only one not getting to see the citadel and Puronia."

"We can certainly speak to her and see if she wants to visit." Mav glanced at Solanji. "Weren't you going back to stay with Brennan?"

"Yes, for the weekend. I can ask Shandra for you then and bring her back with me if she agrees."

"Then that is what we'll do. In the meantime"—Mav pointed at Kerris—"I expect you all to be exemplary students." He opened a drawer and pawed at its contents for a moment. "And as you have a free afternoon coming up, I have no doubt that you'll want to visit the market and sample the wares. Ah-ha!" He found what he was looking for and opened a small drawstring bag. He hefted it, took a few coins out, and then tossed the bag at Kerris, who caught it. "Don't let the pickpockets get it."

"You mean we can…?"

"Go and explore. But stay out of trouble!"

Kerris flashed Mav a brilliant grin and scampered out the door.

"Was that wise?" Felather asked, staring at the door as if he were going to call Kerris back.

"They've survived on their own for years. You should be more worried about everyone else," Mav said as he leaned back in his chair. "That will keep them from worrying about Shandra. But first, Solanji, please. Will you transfer my bond with the citadel to Amaridin?"

"You've only just got it back. Do you truly want to give it up again?" Solanji fidgeted with the papers on his desk.

Was he sure? The need to bond with the Oblivion Gate stirred in him. Its power simmered, calling to him through his veins, and he knew he would never understand all its secrets without bonding to it. If he didn't commit, then why would the Gate? "Yes, I'm sure."

Solanji exhaled. "Then get your brother. We might as well get it done before I change my mind."

Mav stood and leaned over his desk to kiss her cheek. "Thank you, my heart."

She flushed, a small smile hovering over her mouth. "I expect more than a peck on the cheek in thanks."

Grinning, Mav moved around the desk and pulled her into his arms. "I think I can manage that."

Felather rolled his eyes and stood. "Please," he said, shielding his eyes. "Make sure you're still dressed when I return. Amaridin will not be impressed if you're not."

Mav laughed. "Amaridin won't mind. After all, he has Valerian."

Felather blushed beet red and fled.

Solanji hugged Mav tight. "Still, he has a point. Decorum is the word," she said as she kissed him. "You can thank me in more detail later."

"If you insist." Mav kissed her back, forcing her lips open and tugging her closer. Their bodies fit perfectly as she moulded herself to him. He shivered as she caressed his shadows.

"Mav, are you sure about this?" She leaned back to peer into his eyes.

"Yes. The sooner, the better. I need to claim the Gate so I can offload these soulless. My headaches are only going to get worse if I don't."

Solanji pressed her lips together and nodded. "Very well.

You do realise you might react the same way to the severance as you did before?"

"I'm hoping you and Ellaria will keep me grounded this time. I will still be connected to you, and I know what will happen. I'll still have my shadowsoul, so it's not like last time."

The knock on the door heralded the arrival of Mav's brother, and there was no time for any more discussion.

5

SOLANJI – CITADEL, PURONIA

Amaridin strode into Mav's apartment in a billow of pale blue robes, and his partner, Valerian, followed him. Solanji inspected them closely as Felather backed out and shut the door. Both men were blonde and tall, but Valerian was slightly shorter and broader across the chest and shoulders. His robes were a pale grey, and they shimmered in the shaft of sunlight penetrating the gap in the drawn curtains.

Amaridin frowned. "Why is it so dark in here? You should let the light in."

"Demavrian has been living in the shadows for more years than I have; we both need time to adjust to the sun," Valerian said in a soft voice. He strode past his lover with his hand outstretched. "Demavrian, it's so good to see you."

Mav grinned and shook his hand.

Solanji was surprised when Valerian tugged him into a hug.

"It's good to see you, too," Mav said. "I couldn't believe it when I heard you had split with my brother."

Valerian released Mav and stepped back to Amaridin.

His hand sliding down Amaridin's arm in reassurance. "It was not by choice, I can assure you."

"I'm glad you are all recovered from your ordeal. You haven't met my wife, Solanji, have you? She was a member of the party who found you."

"Then I am doubly happy to meet you." Valerian's pale blue eyes sparkled as he shook Solanji's hand, and she tensed, almost expecting a hug. "Congratulations on snaring my future brother-in-law. I am glad to be able to call you sister."

Solanji smiled. She was going to like this man. His golden soulmist curled around him, leaving him only to quest towards and tangle with Amaridin's soulmist, which was more agitated.

Mav gestured to the sitting area. "Please, sit. Would you like a drink?"

Amaridin shook his head. "Let's get this over with."

Solanji rested her hand on Mav's arm and frowned at Amaridin. "Do you not wish for the transfer to take place? If not, now is the time to speak."

Valerian clasped the back of Amaridin's neck as if he were soothing a nervy calope. "He does. We understand the need. But Amaridin is unsure of what it will mean."

"You will become the cornerstone of the citadel instead of me. Your connection will be closer to the citadel than it is for others. You'll feel its heartbeat." Mav shrugged. "There is little difference other than that. The citadel may try and communicate with you on occasion, mainly through images. But you will be the foundation."

"See, there is nothing to worry about." Valerian sat on the sofa and tugged Amaridin to sit beside him. "We would like to request…" Valerian paused and licked his lips before looking at Solanji. "*I'd* like to request that you bind both of us to the citadel."

Solanji raised her eyebrows as surprise flitted through

her. She looked at Amaridin, who nodded. "I agree. We will not be separated again. What we do, we do together." He gripped Valerian's hand.

"Very well," Solanji said as her brain churned with ideas of how to do it. "You'd better sit as well, Mav. *Ellaria?*"

Their golden dragon manifested and dropped with a thump to the floor, and Amaridin flinched. Valerian stroked his arm and then left his hand on Amaridin's thigh, and Amaridin slowly relaxed.

"What an amazing creature," Valerian murmured as he watched the golden dragon preen. She flipped her wings tight against her body and possessively curled her tail around Mav's leg as she leaned against him. Solanji knew she was loving the attention. Mav patted her head and scratched her eye ridge. She rumbled deep in her chest.

"This is Ellaria, my familiar," Solanji said. "She helps with the soulbreathing. Now, Ellaria will help Mav, as I believe he will feel the effects of this much more than you will. He is losing his connection to the citadel, which can be unnerving. You, on the other hand, are strengthening what you already have, and you will be sharing the burden he currently carries on his own." Solanji silently cursed herself for not insisting that Mav let her share the load. Maybe she could get him to share the burden of the Oblivion Gate? Would he? She didn't know.

"Right. To start with, I need to sever Mav's link to the citadel." She stroked his shadows, searching for the scintillating connection she had created. He shivered under her caress but remained silent. *"Ellaria? Please support him. I think this may hurt."*

"Of course," Ellaria replied and she laid her head in Mav's lap as he continued petting her. *"Make sure you don't sever our bond."*

Solanji followed the golden threads twisted into Mav's

shadows. *"I bound us all together. What if I can't separate Mav's connection to the citadel from ours?"*

"You will," Mav's said, his voice low and assured.

That was easy for *him* to say, she thought, as she searched his shadows, following golden strands until she found what she was looking for. Mav's eyelids had dropped to half-mast as she searched, her soul fingers brushing through his shadows. She found a thicker cord, made up of three twisted strands: one red-gold, Ellaria's; one gold, hers; and one strand of black shadows. It burrowed deep inside Mav as if hiding, sheltered, and protected.

Mav clung tight to the connection, even though he didn't realise it. Rooted deep inside him, the citadel was part of him, part of his history. Solanji suddenly doubted this was the right path. Surely, she didn't have to sever the link completely, only transfer the part of the citadel that Mav sustained?

The more she searched, the more entwined the cord became. Her soul fingers became entangled, and Mav groaned, his grip tightening around one of Ellaria's horns. Solanji muttered under her breath and untangled herself. Where did it connect to the citadel? Maybe she was approaching this from the wrong angle. What if she followed the connection from the citadel to Mav?

She reached for the citadel, now a scintillating tapestry of threads and patterns. Her binding bloomed, clear and bright, and the citadel welcomed her. Would the citadel welcome her after she'd severed it from Mav? Maybe she ought to explain to the citadel what she was doing. But how?

"Images," Ellaria said.

"What images? How do I imagine severing Mav?"

"Show Mav on his own, supporting the citadel, and then replace the image with Amaridin and Valerian holding hands. Two is better than one."

Solanji tried as the citadel filled her head with sunlit images of Puronia as it shared its joy at being connected again. It stilled as she offered the image of Mav and then replaced it with Amaridin and Valerian. She then pushed an image of Mav with the thread joining them cut, and the citadel panicked. The building trembled beneath them.

"What is she doing?" Amaridin hissed.

"What she needs to," Mav said, his voice slurred.

Solanji hurried to show an image of the connection being tied into Amaridin and Valerian. *"You won't be alone,"* she soothed. *"You'll have two angels instead of one."*

The citadel settled and threw panicked images at her. It wanted to know why.

She responded with visions of Kaenera and the battle in the citadel hall. The citadel knew why.

The citadel pondered for a moment, and then the building shivered. *Acquiescence,* Solanji thought. A golden thread glowed brighter than those around it, and Solanji reached for it, gasping as tingling power flooded through her. Mav held this all the time? She followed it down into Mav's core and, careful to avoid the threads joining him to her and Ellaria, she snapped it in two. Mav convulsed. Oops, she should have warned him, but it was too late now.

Ellaria curled around Mav, crooning in his ear, and Solanji concentrated on collecting the threads from Amaridin and Valerian, binding them together, and then she wove the bound thread into the citadel's scintillating golden thread and into the overall weave.

She was conscious of the citadel watching with interest as she tied off the final knot and withdrew herself from the soulmist. She inspected it for a moment, but she knew the connection was sound.

Reverting to herself, she smiled at the astonished expressions on Amaridin's and Valerian's faces; they were sitting even closer together. Her smile faded as she realised Mav was laid out on the floor, his face pale. She dropped beside him and extended her soul fingers.

"Mav? We're still here. You are not alone, I swear. Ellaria and I are still here. We're still connected."

Silence. *"Ellaria? Weren't you talking to him?"*

"He was fine, and then he just shut down."

Solanji trawled her soul fingers through his shadows and caressed their connection, trying to stimulate it back to life. She knew she hadn't severed their link, so why was it so dull and lifeless?

"Is he alright?" Amaridin's voice was right by her ear, strained and concerned. He gripped his brother's hand. "Demavrian?"

"He's adjusting," Solanji said, hoping that was true. Adjusting to the emptiness that he would need to fill with the Oblivion Gate.

Amaridin began rubbing Mav's hand between his own. "He's freezing." Then he hauled Mav's upper body into his lap and hugged him. His voice shook. "Demavrian? Don't you leave me again."

Solanji focused on soothing Mav's shadows while Amaridin rocked his body, muttering endearments and curses in turn. Solanji found that she was beginning to like Amaridin a little more. Maybe under his cold exterior, there was a nice man. There had to be for Valerian to be so steadfast in his love for him.

When Mav's eyelashes fluttered, Solanji exhaled in relief. Glazed amber eyes stared up at Amaridin in confusion. "Amaridin?" Mav whispered.

"Oh, thank goodness. You scared the shit out of me," Amaridin mumbled in return, his voice muffled as he buried his face in Mav's hair. Solanji thought it was to hide the tears streaming down his cheeks.

"We're still bound, you, me, and Ellaria," Solanji hurried to say as Mav's gaze found hers.

"I don't feel right," Mav said out loud.

"I severed your connection to the citadel, Mav. That's why you feel off-balance."

He slowly nodded, his gaze sharpening as if he were searching for something deep inside. His eyes glistened as tears gathered when he couldn't find it.

"I'm so sorry, Mav," Amaridin whispered. "I didn't know what you had lost until now. You need to go and claim the Oblivion Gate. You'll feel more balanced once you are bonded. It will fill the empty spaces."

Solanji snapped her jaw shut. She hadn't expected Amaridin to understand what Mav was experiencing. Valerian chuckled, and she realised he had seen her reaction.

"He's not as dense as he makes himself out to be," Valerian said, rubbing the back of Amaridin's neck before he kissed his cheek.

Mav sat up out of Amaridin's embrace and cleared his throat. "Everything went to plan, then?"

"Looks like it," Valerian said. "You need to rest, Mav. You're still looking pale. Maybe we could all have dinner tomorrow night?"

Mav nodded, and Amaridin helped him to his feet. "Steady?" Amaridin asked as Mav swayed.

"Yes. Just takes a bit of getting used to."

"I can imagine," Amaridin said. "It's like a warm embrace bolstering you." He winced. "Sorry, that was thoughtless of me."

"It's fine. I'm glad it worked."

"We'll see you for dinner at seven in our apartments. Rest for now, Mav," Valerian said and tugged Amaridin towards the door.

Amaridin resisted and pulled Mav into another hug. "Are

you sure you're alright?" It was the most concern Solanji had seen Amaridin show for his brother.

Mav hugged him back and sighed out his breath. "I will be."

Amaridin gave him a searching glance and then nodded. He smiled at Solanji, and she nearly gasped out loud. His smile transformed his face; it was as if he were lit from within. She could finally see the real Archdeus, and he was breath-taking. "See you tomorrow evening at seven," he said and left with Valerian, their hands tightly linked and shoulders bumping.

Felather entered and closed the door behind them. Then he looked from Solanji to Mav expectantly. "Well?"

"Well, indeed," Mav said, collapsing in the chair and covering his face with his hand.

Felather was beside him in an instant. "What's the matter?"

"Nothing you can solve, Felather. I'm just tired. I might nap before dinner." Mav heaved himself back upright and ambled to his room, shutting the door behind him.

"He's not alright. Did something go wrong? I thought Amaridin and Valerian looked really happy when they left."

"They are. Mav is adjusting to losing the citadel."

"Shouldn't you be in there with him? He shouldn't be alone."

"He shut the door," Solanji pointed out. "Maybe he needs some time on his own."

"You're kidding, right? He's just lost an important part of himself. Are you really going to leave him to struggle on his own? Just because he says he wants to be on his own, it doesn't mean he should be."

Felather had a good point. Solanji flexed her fingers. *"Ellaria? Did he say anything to you?"*

"No. You should go to him. He is sad."

At that, Solanji hurried over and entered the bedchamber without knocking. Mav lay on the bed, a darker shadow in the dim light. "Mav? Darling?" She moved over to the bed and lay down beside him. "Oh, sweetheart," she murmured as she kissed his damp cheeks. Extending her soulmist fingers, she caressed his shadows as she stroked his skin. She drew him into her arms and held him, sliding her leg between his so she could hug him tighter.

If she could have filled his empty spaces, she would have, and she told him with lips, and touch, and whispered endearments. Relief flooded her as he finally began to relax under her ministrations. The rigidity in his body gave way with a tremor as more tears flowed down his cheeks, and Solanji held him tight, binding her soulmist into his shadows, joining them wherever they touched, until he relaxed in her arms and exhaustion dragged him into sleep.

6

KAENERA – EIDOLON

The castle in northern Eidolon had been useful, secluded and concealed as it was. Kaenera stood on the open ledge halfway up the mountain and scowled down at the shadowed valley, not seeing the hidden beauty or feeling the edge of the bitterly cold wind whipping through the bare cavern.

He snarled deep in his throat. He should have known better. Centuries of planning and years of moving his pieces into position, and he had everything in his grasp. Kaenera clenched his fist. And then…Demavrian! A flash of pure, unadulterated fury burned down his spine, clearing the debilitating fog in his head for a moment.

He'd had everything in place.

If he ever got his hands on that woman, Serenia, wherever they had stashed her, he would take great pleasure in shredding her into tiny fragments.

Spinning away from the edge, he inhaled the faint tang of blood and fear. Yes, there was still a memory of Demavrian's incarceration in the cavern. Chains still hung from the ceiling, the only evidence of his suffering. His blood had soaked into the rock and would never leave. Demavrian had been afraid, desperate, almost ready to give up, teetering on the edge of the abyss, and Kaenera had been ready to catch him; just one last nudge was all he'd needed.

But Kyrill had brought a SoulBreather instead of a SoulSinger, and Kaenera had erred, waiting too long for the exquisite pleasure of Demavrian's final capitulation and had let them escape. He salivated at the thought of getting both the SoulBreather and Demavrian. The SoulBreather would be the icing on the cake.

He could taste Demavrian's downfall, so long in the planning. And now Demavrian thought *he* would be the Gate Keeper. Foolish boy. The Gate was Kaenera's. He would reclaim it, or he would destroy this petty world and everyone in it.

Rotating his shoulders against the ache gathering in his muscles, Kaenera stopped in the middle of the cavern. Stretching his arms wide, he flared his wings and sent his senses questing, searching for Demavrian. Nothing. He must be holed up in the citadel. But he wouldn't stay there for long. He wouldn't be able to resist the people of Eidolon. Kaenera smiled. And Demavrian would be bogged down by the soulless he was currently collecting.

Massaging his neck, he ignored the sullen throb, the result of searching for Demavrian. His powers might be weak, but he still had some. The fact that he needed to use them judiciously riled him.

Kaenera folded his wings away, ignoring the tattered edges and fading colours. His wings had lost their shine when he had lost the Gate and were now a dull grey. He had misjudged the importance of his connection to the Gate, and he would get it back.

But now was the time to strike, before Demavrian had a

chance to assimilate his new state. He had to keep him off balance and draw him out of the citadel.

Another flash of rage sped through him, shattering the thought. His own stupidity had caused this situation. He had allowed those peons to play their games, and it had cost him his. He knew he should have destroyed the citadel, and the thought made him grind his teeth. But he had been amused. Entertained. It had been so long since anything had filled him with pleasure, but the anticipation of the tantalising reward at the end had kept him occupied, too distracted to prepare for the unthinkable.

He didn't know how Demavrian had stolen some of his power, stolen the Gate. To compound the frustration, he had made the mistake of stashing the one thing that could destroy them all in the Oblivion Gate. He should have used the Aeora sigils to bring Demavrian to his knees, but he had hesitated. It had felt too heavy-handed. And now they were stuck in the Gate, and he couldn't reach them.

Kaenera narrowed his eyes at the chains, imagining Demavrian writhing in agony, his skin shredded and blood-streaked, his body shuddering under the constant flaying. A pain eased in his chest, and he breathed a little easier. He had caught Demavrian once; he would catch him again.

Stealing the sigils had been his greatest triumph, right from under Averdeus' nose. Kaenera's laugh was harsh. He doubted anyone even knew they were missing. No one in their right mind would ever use them, so no one thought about them. It was unlikely Demavrian had even heard of them, let alone knew what they could do. Averdeus had been adamant that they be buried, both physically and in the tomes of history.

Using a weapon no one could anticipate or defend against was genius. The sigils were a relic from a destroyed world, a magic no one would believe existed. Averdeus had bound the glowing symbols in a small, iron chest and tried to hide them. Kaenera had to get the box back, but how? Ideas fluttered, and he plucked one. It was simple. He would reclaim the Gate first. Demavrian wouldn't know how to keep the Gate ephemeral. He would have to choose a physical location to anchor the Gate in order to enter it properly.

Soon, Kaenera thought. He had weapons. He just needed to instruct them. As soon as he knew where the Gate had landed, he would transfer his people inside.

But first, he would prepare. Kaenera cast his mind out across Eidolon. Ignoring the throbbing pain in his temples, he flung a fine web of thoughts over the landscape and slid his fingers down its whisper-thin skeins; they would warn him when Demavrian tried to claim the Gate. Demavrian would be at his most vulnerable. That was when he would strike.

Swaying, he steadied himself against the stone wall. It was ridiculous! Using such a small piece of his power shouldn't have affected him at all, but a slight hissing filled his ears, and his vision greyed at the edges.

He had to get the sigils. It was the only way he would win. Kaenera grimaced; the muscles in his face resisted, but his lips twitched. And he would have a backup plan this time. Demavrian wouldn't know which way to turn.

Demavrian thought he could "save" Eidolon and its people? Well, he would have something to say about that!

This time. Kaenera flexed his fingers and scowled at their ineffective shape. This form was so constricting. He hissed his breath out as he struggled to grow some pointed claws. Once he had his talons in Demavrian, this time, he would never let go.

7

———

MUNTRA – CITADEL, PURONIA

Before the first streaks of dawn had stained the sky, Muntra was up and running around the training ground. He hadn't wanted Adriz trying to rouse him to disturb Bailey's first uninterrupted night of sleep outside of the healerie. Bailey was still nervy and easily upset—understandable after all he had suffered.

While creeping out of the fledgling hall, Muntra had frowned at the sight of Bailey curled up in a tight ball, his pale face hidden beneath the bunched-up covers. In contrast, Kerris was flopped over his bed like a weeping willow, his long brown limbs draped over the edges and nearly reaching the floor, his sheets twisted around his middle.

With it being so much warmer in Puronia, Muntra would have expected Bailey to be pushing off his blankets, stretching out, and questing for a waft of air. But no. He was barely visible, and that was another thing to worry about.

Making his way to the citadel training arena, Muntra began running around the perimeter. The warm burn of muscles working as he ran was a familiar sensation. He had missed his daily runs around the homestead. He sighed, admitting to himself that he missed the soft embrace of the dim light of Eidolon. The brilliant sun beat down on him, unrelenting and revealing his inadequacies. He felt exposed, and he didn't like what he saw. No wonder he was losing Bailey. Why would Bailey want him? He had failed in the one job he had so badly that Bailey would be scarred forever.

He was so immersed in his misery that he didn't notice when Adriz joined him on the training ground.

"Don't exhaust yourself before we've even started," she called from the centre of the ring, and he jerked his head up. "Knowing when to stop is just as important as the running."

Muntra slowed and veered into the middle to join Adriz. He acknowledged her words with a nod before he bent over, gasping for breath. He hadn't noticed he was pushing his limits while running, but stopping brought it home. The air burned his throat all the way down to his gullet.

Adriz offered him a waterskin, and he took a grateful gulp. "I didn't notice the time," he gasped.

"How long have you been out here?"

Muntra shrugged a shoulder.

"A good soldier knows how to conserve his strength, not waste it. I see we'll have to start with the basics."

"The basics sound like a good place to begin," Muntra agreed. He knew nothing about anything.

"I'll talk. You listen while you stretch out, or you'll be stiff tomorrow."

"Yes, ma'am," he murmured, planting his foot so he could lunge.

"Good. You will run no more than ten laps of the ring in the morning. You will stretch out before and after each run and drink plenty of water."

Muntra nodded. All stuff he knew.

"I want to know what's going on up there," Adriz said as

she poked his forehead with a stiff finger. It hurt, and he scowled at her as he rubbed it.

"What do you mean?"

"Why are you trying to punish yourself?"

"I'm not!" he exclaimed, shocked at the accusation.

"Oh, I think you'll find you are. Why?"

Muntra shook his head in denial.

"Very well. We'll speak of that later. What do you know about hand-to-hand fighting?"

Inhaling a sharp breath, Muntra said, "Not much," and he cringed at the evil smile that spread over her face.

"Let's see what you do know. Try to take me down to the ground." Adriz widened her stance and beckoned him forward.

Blowing his breath out, Muntra stared at her. She was solid muscle, and he knew he would fail. There was no way he would be able to shift her centre, and the way her eyes gleamed, she knew it. Common sense told him it was a waste of time, but an inner voice said, *Try. At least try.*

He raised his fists and rushed her. Before he knew it, she had twisted him onto the ground, locking his arm in a painful hold behind him. He had no idea how she did it. He tensed, his face pressed into the sand until she released him.

Standing, he flexed his shoulder. "How did you do that?" She had moved so fast!

"A combination of blocking and control. You'll soon learn. Let me show you." Adriz slowly demonstrated how she had blocked his flailing arms, pushing him away as she rotated and slid her hand down his arm to apply pressure while locking him in the hold. After that, she had him practising the blocking moves for the rest of the session.

"Enough. We'll continue in the morning. Same time, same place. Go shower and then join your friends in class."

"How do you move so quickly?" Muntra asked. For such a large woman, she was light on her feet.

"Core strength and practice. If you train with me every day, you'll find you can control your body much easier. But it will take time. So, every day, without fail."

Muntra nodded. "I'll be here."

Clapping him on the shoulder, Adriz grinned at him and then left.

Muntra rubbed his forearms. They ached from the battering she had given him. He was sure he would be bruised, but it was worth it if he could learn to move like her.

He hurried to the showers to clean up and change, eager to join Bailey and the rest of his family for first meal.

It wasn't right. Solanji hated the unnatural silence that had descended over Mav. She knew severing him from the citadel had been a bad idea. She had sent Felather to collect all the fledglings to join them for first meal in the hope they would jog him out of his melancholy. Adriz arrived first, and after giving Mav a keen inspection, she filled in the silence with a report of her activities.

"I never thought I'd see the day when the citadel guards were complaining about missing Xylvin," Adriz said as she sat at the table.

She glanced at Mav from under her lashes, her brown eyes concerned. After a glance at Solanji, who gave a small shrug, she continued. "I was stopped no fewer than three times today by people asking me when they would return to the citadel. Mav? When will they return?"

Mav didn't answer, lost in some introspection of his own. Adriz leaned across the table and gripped his hand. He jerked, and his confused gaze lifted to Adriz. He looked around the room as if only just realising he was sitting at the table. Clearing his throat, he said, "Sorry. What did you say?"

"I was asking when Xylvin and Ryvalin will return; they are missed."

"They'll have to get used to it. We are moving to the Oblivion Gate, and they'll be coming with us."

"I thought we agreed you would discuss things with us first? And we'd make decisions as a family," she said, her voice quiet.

Mav ran his fingers through his hair, his hand visibly trembling. "I know. But I thought it was obvious we'd have to move to the Gate. I *am* its new Keeper."

"I wasn't arguing about the if; I was concerned about the when."

"When I find out where it actually is, we'll move. I need to start searching for it today." He swallowed and looked at her with some uncertainty. "Will you come with me?"

Adriz stared at him in open shock. "Of course I will. As if I'd let you go to Eidolon on your own!"

"And so will I," Solanji said, gripping his other hand. "I said we'd do this together."

Tears rose in Mav's eyes, and he nodded. "Thank you."

Adriz watched him, a frown creasing her brow. "What's happened?"

Oh, God. Solanji's heart stuttered. Mav hadn't told Adriz that today was the day he'd intended to sever himself from the citadel. She was going to be furious. Solanji cleared her throat and squeezed Mav's hand. "I severed him from the citadel today."

"You did what?" Adriz screeched as she launched to her feet, and Mav visibly flinched. She was around the table in moments, hauling him upright. She stared into his eyes. "You idiot," she snapped and embraced him tight. "Why didn't you tell me? I would have been here for you."

"I…" Mav was interrupted as the door opened and Felather entered with his fledglings. Felather halted on the threshold, his eyebrows rising.

Adriz turned on him. "Did you know?" she growled through gritted teeth.

Felather stared at her in momentary confusion, and then he tensed, looking from her to Mav. "Umm…"

"It's not his fault," Mav said. "This was my decision. It had to happen sooner or later."

"'Later' being the operable word," Adriz replied as she glared at Felather.

Wincing, Felather ushered the fledglings in as if they would be a barrier against her ire.

Mav stepped out of Adriz's grip and smiled. "Bailey, I'm glad to see they released you from the infirmary. How are you feeling?"

"Much better, thank you. I'm to go back if I suffer any chest pains or breathlessness. Otherwise, I should be fine."

Mav hugged him. "That is good to hear." He glared at Kerris and Muntra. "Don't drag him all over Puronia when you visit. He needs to build up his strength."

Solanji relaxed as Mav's behaviour became more natural, and they sat around the table. "How are your lessons going?"

Kerris groaned, and Muntra laughed.

"You are supposed to be a scribe. I thought scribes liked learning?" Mav asked as he transported a jug of bannoe and a plate of warm rolls from the kitchen and placed them on the table. It was fortunate that the cook kept a supply ready.

"But adding up columns of numbers seems so pointless."

"Not when you're managing an angel's finances," Felather said. "You have to be able to add and subtract to ensure that a merchant isn't overcharging you or you are not overspending and driving your angel into debt."

Kerris gaped at him. "Then why don't they give us real examples that make sense?"

"They will. You just need to learn the formulas first. They'll give you more complex solutions to solve once you've got the basics."

"They should have said so," Kerris grumbled as he reached for the jam pot, and everyone laughed.

After a while, Adriz pointed her knife at Muntra. "Muntra did well training, today. I expect to see him in the training ring at dawn tomorrow."

"Dawn?" Mav protested. "Give the lad a break."

"He's had a break. I've left him alone so he could be with Bailey, but now that Bailey will be in class, it's time to start Muntra's training."

Bailey nodded. "I've got to catch up on the classes anyway."

"You will not be rising at dawn," Mav said, his twinkling eyes belying his stern expression. "You will be sensible and get a good night's sleep."

Bailey gave him a sweet smile of agreement, and Mav relaxed.

Solanji silently patted herself on the back. The fledglings were what Mav needed.

Comments flew back and forth, and she squeezed Mav's leg under the table when he grinned at her. He gave her a smouldering glance, and her mouth went dry. After that, Solanji barely kept up with the conversation.

8

DEMAVRIAN – CITADEL, PURONIA

Mav's chambers were eerily silent once his family had left. He sat at his desk and let his mind wander. A moment alone to savour. Solanji and Ellaria had gone to meet the SoulSingers. Solanji wanted to recruit them to help her identify the souls in the citadel, but they would be back in time for the evening meal with Amaridin and Valerian.

Beautiful, haunting halls with impossibly high ceilings and iridescent walls rose around him, and he blinked. A soft green glow emanated from the walls, and as he walked, the torches in the sconces flared to life with green flames that chased away the darkness.

The light was dim, soothing after the glare of Puronia, and Mav relaxed into the subtle warmth and gentle shadows. He knew that these magnificent, if deserted halls, were the Oblivion Gate.

His footsteps echoed in the silent halls. The floor shone as if it had been polished that day, and his steps faltered as he saw his shadowy wings in the reflection below him. He realised he had instinctively flared his wings and relaxed at the rightness of it all.

Breathing deep, he stopped and rotated at a junction where the corridors split into four arches, each leading off into darkness. They would lead him deeper into the halls, but he needed to find the exit so he could identify where in Eidolon the Gate existed.

Choosing one of the arches at random, he strode down the corridor. More lamps filled with emerald-green flames flared into life as he walked, lighting his way.

A flurry of cool air swirled around him, and he smiled. "Kiara?"

"Mav! I'm so glad you're here. You are not going to believe what I found." The young girl who had died in the slave camp in Eidolon manifested beside him, kissed him on the cheek, and grabbed his hand. He stared at her hand as she tugged him towards the archway on his right. Cool fingers clasped his. He didn't question it; he just followed her.

Her strawberry-blonde hair was as translucent as the rest of her. He could see through her, but he could feel her touch.

"Where are we going, Kiara? Have you found the Gate?"

"Yes, he is eager to meet you."

"He?"

"Well, I don't know if it's a he, but I find it easier to speak to him if I think of the Gate as a person. It seems rude to call him an it."

"You can talk to the Oblivion Gate?"

"Of course. How else is he going to tell me what needs fixing? The previous Gate Keeper didn't care for him at all. It's taken me since you were last here just to grease all his wheels. Some of them had seized up. You are already in his good books for giving me to him. He can't wait to meet you."

Mav floundered for a moment, trying to comprehend all the information she was throwing at him. "I'm glad you were able to help him. But I'm not sure I'm ready to meet him. After all, I'm not really here."

Kiara's laugh rang out, and he smiled. "Of course you are here." She flashed him a cheeky grin. "You are looking much better. I love your wings; they are so pretty."

"Thank you."

"I want to show you the Gate. You were right; the mechanism is quite amazing."

"I haven't claimed the Gate yet. I'm not sure how I'm supposed to."

Kiara chuckled, and the sound resonated in his bones. It wasn't that he heard her voice: he *felt* her voice within him. He wasn't convinced they were actually speaking out loud, or even speaking at all.

"Knowing you, you'll find a way. You wouldn't be here otherwise. I haven't actually met him, either, but I found some of his mechanisms."

"Mechanisms?"

"The stuff you said I need to help you with." She stopped abruptly, and he stumbled, trying to avoid her.

"Mav." Her voice was a low whisper.

"What's wrong?"

"You need to be careful. There are others here."

"Others?"

"Yes. I keep catching movements in the shadows, but they won't show themselves." She shrugged. "Or I just can't see them. I'm not sure what I am supposed to be able to do in this form." She gestured at her translucent body.

"I'm so sorry, Kiara. I never meant for you to be trapped here."

"I'm not trapped. It's all just so different and…" Her voice faltered. "I'm all alone."

Mav swept her into his arms and hugged her. "You are not alone. I just need to finish some stuff at the citadel, and then I'll be here all the time. I won't ever leave you on your own. I promise."

Kiara snuffled into his shoulder. "It's always better when you are here. I feel more…real."

Mav rubbed her back. "That's because you are real. You're my Gate Wraith, and between us, we will claim the Gate and help the soulless." He smiled into her hair. "You'll be glad to hear Bailey has recovered and is out of the healerie."

"I'm glad."

He released her and grinned. "Show me this mechanism and what you've discovered in the halls. We'll need to map the place out and find rooms to sleep in and somewhere to cook meals if we are going to live here."

"I found rooms you could use. And Mav…I found a library!"

Mav had begun to walk down the passageway, but at that, he halted. "A library? Why would Kaenera have a library?"

"It's a big library. Covers many floors. The Oblivion Gate is larger than you would think."

Mav frowned. "I suppose that's to be expected. We keep thinking it's just a gate. But the citadel is much more than a gate. Why wouldn't the Oblivion Gate be the same? Be careful, Kiara. Who knows what Kaenera used this place for."

Kiara laughed. "I'm already dead, Mav. I have no soul. What can they do?"

"I don't know. But let's not make it easy for whoever is lingering in these halls. Be discreet and be safe.

Pursing her lips, Kiara nodded. "Alright. I will take care, but they may not even be able to see me."

"True, but they might. And we don't know who they are nor what they intend." He ran a hand through his hair. "I think I need to claim the Gate and clear any lingering threats before I bring the others here. I don't want to drop them into a battleground."

He started walking again, following Kiara as she flitted ahead. More halls opened onto a large room Mav would have called a ballroom in any other building. At one end were tall double doors, and opposite them, an elegant staircase rose from the centre, split into two branches midway, and curved up the walls. It was beautiful.

"Is this an exit?" Mav asked, strolling towards the doors. He twisted one of the doorknobs, but the doors remained locked. "Kiara, do you know how to open the doors?"

"No idea," Kiara replied. "I don't think I could leave these halls anyway."

"I need to find out where we are. The Gate must be situated somewhere."

Kiara wrinkled her nose. "I'm not sure where we are. No one ever mentioned actually seeing the Oblivion Gate that I remember. Does it matter?"

"Well, I need to give Ryvalin and Xylvin directions. They'll not find us if they don't know where we are."

"Maybe once you've claimed the Gate, you'll know more."

"Maybe." Mav slowly climbed the stairs, following Kiara deeper into the building. Balconies wended their way around the upper levels of what Mav decided to call the ballroom, and doors lined the landings, opening into empty rooms. None were furnished, though torches lit the chambers with a green glow every time he opened a door.

"Those would be ideal bedchambers," Kiara said, leading the way to a pair of wooden double doors. "But this…" She pushed them open, and Mav's jaw dropped as he halted on the threshold. Shelves covered the walls. Bookcases stood in regimented rows, and every single shelf was filled with leather-bound books.

Mav ran his fingers over the spines of the books on the shelf nearest him. He stopped and pulled one out, flipping it open. Unfamiliar words filled the page, but as he stared at them, they slowly resolved into a language he understood. He flipped back to the front and read the first page. It was a very early copy of the history of Eidolon. He snapped the book shut and moved on, tucking it under his arm as another title caught his attention.

Opening it, he inhaled as the letters danced on the parchment and then solidified. It was a book of poems, about Kaenera.

Out of the shadows, our Lord appears.
Bend your knee before his might,
Exalt in his presence. Bathe in his glory.
Know that death is all he reveres.

Mav snapped the book shut and went to place it back on the shelf, but he hesitated. He needed to understand Kaenera as much as possible. Someone had written these poems, maybe even Kaenera himself. He was egotistical enough to praise himself. He tucked the book under his arm as well and continued deeper into the room.

The collection rivalled that in the citadel. The centre of the room was empty as if you weren't supposed to linger and read. The lack of tables and chairs or study booths felt wrong.

Mav stood in the middle of the library, thinking of his favourite armchair in his rooms. A comfortable chair, a good book, a glass of basinthe, and he'd be happy. He stared up at the vaulted ceiling above him and wondered who had created this amazing library.

Kiara's gasp drew his gaze back down, and his breath caught. An assortment of chairs and tables surrounded him, but right next to him was his own chair with the side table and a glass of amber liquid waiting for him.

"Well, this is nice," he murmured, placing his books on the table as he sat down. He gestured at the chair beside him. "Kiara, have a seat."

"Do you think we should?" she whispered.

"The Oblivion Gate wouldn't have provided chairs if he didn't want us to use them." He glanced around and smiled when he saw the sofa on one side. His mother had introduced him to the joy of reading curled up on a similar sofa, safe in her arms. The sight of it relaxed his tense muscles. "I think the library is saying hello."

"How can the library say hello?" Kiara asked.

Picking up the crystal glass, Mav sniffed it and then sipped the viscous liquid. He smiled in appreciation at the smooth taste of basinthe and then, leaning back in the chair, opened the history book. "The citadel is a sentient building. I'm sure the Oblivion Gate is as well."

"Did the citadel library welcome you like this?"

Mav hesitated, his glass hovering in the air as he frowned. "No, it doesn't." He sipped his basinthe and inspected the book in his lap.

"Mav, what are you doing?" Kiara asked, perching on the edge of the leather chair set at an angle towards him.

"Making myself at home, as requested."

Kiara glanced around her uncertainly. "Do you think it's the library welcoming you or the Oblivion Gate?"

Mav shrugged. "I doubt the library is separate from the Gate. I would think it is all one entity, but I expect we'll find out soon."

"I've been searching for a book on the Gate's design," Kiara said, still uncertain. "Maybe if you ask, it will give it to you."

"And a map," Mav murmured. He formed the thought, and a book flew off the desk and landed on a table.

Kiara leapt up and hurried over to check. "Yes!" she exclaimed. Sitting at the table, she began to read. She was unfolding a larger piece of paper when Mav felt a gentle touch against his mind.

Mav tried to extend his thoughts in greeting but met empty space. This was nothing like the citadel, whose embrace had warmed his soul. But then, he no longer had a soul; he had shadows. He concentrated on his swirling shadows, trying to extend his awareness, tentatively seeking the entity reaching out to him.

He bumped into something, an unexplained resistance, and he spun as he found himself in a small chamber with a chandelier hanging from thick chains embedded in the ceiling. Emerald-green flames flickered in the glass spheres, which were suspended from the circular wooden frame. They grew brighter as he watched. Low benches carved from smooth black stone followed the curved walls, and he recognised the wrought-iron gate set into the wall. He came to a halt in front of the gate and stared at the delicate rosebuds entwined in the latticework, curling this way and that.

A flicker in the shadows made him swing around, but the halls were empty. He turned back to the gate, remembering sitting on a black stone bench with Bailey, persuading him not to give up but to live.

Mav exhaled, the strength of his relief at Bailey's choice surprising him. Had it been that close a call? Maybe it had. No one was sitting on the benches in the hallway today, and no one was waiting for his judgement, just empty hallways and smooth stone walls.

He touched a flower bud, which promptly bloomed, and then the gate swung open. The sudden spike of agony and unrelenting pressure in the back of his mind nearly brought him to his knees.

"Mav?" Kiara's voice was soft and by his ear.

The excruciating pain *had* brought him to his knees; he was sprawled on the floor, and Kiara was kneeling beside him.

"I-I need to release the soulless," Mav managed to utter. His head pounded as the soulless clamoured to pass through the Gate.

"Then let us help you," Kiara murmured.

An overwhelming presence hovered just out of reach, coaxing Mav to step across the threshold.

"Kiara?" Mav struggled to get on all fours and swayed as nausea ripped through him. "I need to be able to return. I can't pass through the Gate."

"You are the Gate Keeper. The Keeper of the Shadows. You can go wherever you want."

Mav held his head as he sat back on his heels. His head thumped, and he swallowed. "Kiara, please…"

"Trust me, Mav." Kiara's presence swirled around him.

"I don't know enough about the Gate to take that step. *Ellaria? Are you there?*"

"*Mav?*" Ellaria's voice was very faint. "*You've stopped breathing, and Adriz is in a panic.*"

"The only way you will find out is to take the step. There is no other way, Mav." Kiara met his eyes, and his breath caught against the sadness he saw. "This is the only way you will learn. You have to trust us."

Could he? Could he trust a… a…he didn't even know what to call it…him. Pain spiked behind his eyes, and he hissed his breath out. Kiara would not deliberately lead him astray, but she was so young. And yet, she had already built a relationship of some sort with the Gate. If Kiara could, then he should be able to as well.

Gingerly, he climbed to his feet and swayed as he threw a thought back at Ellaria. *"Tell Adriz and Solanji not to worry. I'm about to shed the soulless."*

The awareness grew stronger as he stepped towards the Gate and then through. It was as if he had entered a storm. Winds buffeted him, tearing at his clothes, at his shadows, at his wings. He stood there and let the storm scour him, stream through and around him. His shadows swirled and flapped, but they coiled back around him as the winds dropped.

He felt lighter and more clear-headed than he had in weeks. His mind was empty, the clamouring weight gone, and Mav realised the soulless had passed on. The Gate had been searching for the soulless to lead them where they wanted to go.

"I don't know where I am," Mav said in that weird, non-vocal way he communicated with Kiara.

"Welcome, Keeper of Shadows. Welcome to the Oblivion Gate," a deep, resonating voice said.

The voice did have a male feel about it. Mav could understand why Kiara had labelled the Gate a "he". The voice had a deep timbre.

"Is the Keeper of Shadows not the same as the Oblivion Gate Keeper?" Mav asked.

Mav sensed amusement—not a chuckle as such, but a definite lightening of the air. "Kiara assures me you can manage both."

That would be a no, then.

"Can you tell me what is expected of the Keeper of Shadows and the Oblivion Gate Keeper?"

"I could. But are you here to claim me?"

"Do you wish to be claimed?"

There was a short silence. "I would prefer not to be… reclaimed by the one before."

"If I don't claim you, he will."

"I know." The voice was more of a sigh.

"I would prefer to support you in what you need to do. I would claim you, but only to protect you. We would be a partnership to serve the soulless of Eidolon, performing the duties expected of us."

"You would do that for me?" A ripple of uncertainty stirred the air.

"Yes."

"Even though you know nothing about me?"

"I am shadowsouled. I belong here, wherever here is. I feel it every time I visit. This is where I'm meant to be. I believe you will fill the void that sits within me, and together with my family, we will bring life back to your halls."

"Your family?"

"Just as I know nothing of you, you know nothing of me. We both have much to learn."

Mav waited as a sense of heaviness surrounded him. His heart thumped loudly in his chest, and he cringed at what his oathsworn were going to say to him when he returned—if he returned.

"I need to warn you that Kaenera, the previous Gate Keeper, will try to claim you back."

If a gate could snort, then Mav was sure that's what it would have felt like. "You'd better claim me, then," the Oblivion Gate said.

9

DEMAVRIAN – OBLIVION GATE

The halls of the Oblivion Gate trembled, a deep vibration as if it was settling after some major disturbance. Mav twisted around in concern, but a swirl of calming energy soothed him. Within the Oblivion Gate, a green mist rose around him, obscuring the surroundings.

"You have not been well," the Oblivion Gate murmured. "That won't do."

"How do you know that?"

"I'm not sure. I sense something is not quite right."

"I will be better now that you took all the soulless I had been carrying."

"That is good. If you truly intend to claim me, then you will have to become me."

"I don't understand."

"Unlike the citadel, I don't primly sit on top of a mountain. I am currently contained within this space because that was what *he* wanted. Though I've never had physical halls before, you are already changing me. My physical appearance is how you see me."

"I'm doing what? How can I change you when we have no connection?"

"I don't know." The Gate sounded dubious. "You are different than what I have experienced before. Everything feels more...solid. I think, if you so desire, we could be all of Eidolon."

"To what purpose? I would prefer to be more hands-off. The people of Eidolon should live their lives as they wish."

"Kiara said they were not doing a very good job of it on their own."

"That's because Kaenera has deprived them of the freedom to do so. I intend to set them free."

The air swirled again. "And me?"

Mav exhaled. "Well. You *are* the Gate. Between us, we need to pass the soulless onwards. Can you even leave"— Mav waved his hand—"wherever you are?"

"I don't think so. It's been so long that I'm not sure."

"Do you want to roam Eidolon? What would you do?"

"I don't know. Reacquaint myself with the world, see what is behind the clouds. It has been a long time since I've spoken to anyone. Maybe I could help you with your plans." The Gate's voice rose with excitement. "I could even walk these halls you've created."

"If you want to walk the halls or explore Eidolon and see what you could do to help the people in the meantime, I'm good with that."

"You would let me roam? Freely?"

"Is there a reason I shouldn't?"

"No. My purpose is to provide a path to oblivion for those who die without a soul. I do not cause their death; I am merely a conduit. But I would like to do more. I will observe and then discuss my thoughts with you."

"Excellent. Now, how do I claim you?"

"You have to open yourself to me."

Mav's hair lifted on the back of his neck, and he shivered. Why he was so uneasy about bonding with the Gate when he had once been bonded with the citadel, he wasn't sure. He supposed it was because he knew so little about the Gate. He didn't actually know that much about the citadel; it was just that he had been bonded since he was a child, so it felt natural.

"You do not wish to open to me?" the Gate asked, his voice tentative.

"I do. It's just not so easy to drop your defences when it comes down to it."

"Kiara says you will honour and respect the Gate. You will honour *me*. I promise I will honour and respect you in return."

Mav concentrated on opening his mind and dropping his defences. His shadows unravelled, rippling around him as if preparing to embrace someone—and that was what it felt like, a warm hug. It was like coming home to a place he belonged, that had been waiting just for him, that was just as eager to embrace him as he was to embrace it.

Until fire seared through their bond, ripping away the scintillating connection. Mav collapsed, and all the lights went out.

Kaenera watched his frail web of sensors and chewed his knuckle as anxiety gnawed at his concentration. He tried to observe the gaps, but his gaze flitted between them all, unable to keep still. He had sent his dybbuks out to the areas he could no longer reach. His mind was dulled by the lack of connection to the Oblivion Gate and all of Eidolon.

Muttering curses under his breath, he ranted about Demavrian. How had it even been possible for that boy to steal his power, his position, everything? His head pounded as fury swept through him, and he closed his eyes until he remembered he was supposed to be watching.

How could he not have realised how important the connection to the Gate was? He had assumed he controlled all of its power, but no, the Oblivion Gate accounted for over half. Half!

It was untenable how weak and confused he felt, like his mind had been muffled by something and he was struggling through a suffocating pile of cloth just to breathe. But he couldn't wait. He had to get that box. It was the only way he could defeat Demavrian now.

His web rang with vibrations, and he lunged for the connection. The Oblivion Gate would be his again. He would trap Demavrian inside, and he would go no further.

Slashing at the links flaring across his web, he opened the way for those who would do his bidding. He sent a stream of flames into the consciousness he sensed, but after the initial flare, it died. Not enough! Panic rushed through him as he hissed his breath out. This was his only chance, and he tried to fan the fire, but someone, or something, doused it.

He lost the connection and he howled as he drew himself back. Now, he was reliant on his dybbuks, and he railed against the injustice of having to depend on those feeble peons.

Flames turned Demavrian's tentative link to the Oblivion Gate into fiery liquid. Agony followed the flames, and he flinched back as molten fire burned through his defences, burned through *him*. He was open, and vulnerable, and dying.

"*No!*" the Oblivion Gate screamed, and a shower of

cooling liquid quenched the fire, solidifying their connection deep within Mav's bones, deep within his shadowsoul. His shadows surrounded him like a defensive barrier, and Mav gulped down cooling air and concentrated on collecting himself. Slowly, he rebuilt his mental defences, blocking the probing attacks. His body trembling, he patted himself down, shuddering as he realised he was physically in the Gate, wherever it was. Adriz would have been frantic when his body disappeared from the citadel.

The Oblivion Gate had protected him, still protected him, but at what cost? His nerves were on fire, his skin sensitive, but he had never felt stronger, more complete. Awareness hovered behind his eyes, and he embraced the sensation of being more. More everything.

Mental defences in place, Mav inhaled and searched around him. Whoever had attacked, and he had no doubt it had been Kaenera, had done so both on the metaphysical plane and in the physical halls. He had been caught unaware, too wrapped up in the excitement of claiming the Gate. He wouldn't be caught a second time.

Mav searched the shadows of the Mechanism room. "Kiara, are you here?" For a moment, he was fumbling in the dark, and then his connection to the Gate flared, and he saw everything. Every intruder, every threat. He sent some of his shadows racing through the corridors, determined to clear out anyone who should not be here.

Scorching heat reached for him, and he slid to the floor as he retreated. His shadows scoured the halls, and dybbuks exploded into dust in their wake as they raced down passages, and through what seemed to be solid walls.

Wraiths huddled in the library; a presence there was protecting them. Mav frowned. Who was strong enough to protect anyone from him? His shadows streamed down either side of the library but not within it and continued on.

The Gate itself looked fine, but he knew there was damage somewhere because their connection had dulled from the first scintillating experience and was now a low throb. Shadows swirled around him as if scenting the air, and he encouraged them to find the presence that had been so welcoming but was now absent. Worry gnawed at him. Had the Gate taken the brunt of the attack?

Instead, his shadows found a breach, an invasion that slashed through his senses, and it burned. It was so painful that it was as if real flames had scored his skin. It didn't make sense. Was the connection he had made to the Oblivion Gate damaged?

It had to be; the gash was like a wound on his body, one that pierced his skin. He had to be connected to the Gate, and Kaenera was trying to destroy his connection. His shadows flared and filled the breach, binding the wound tight, and he inhaled a shaky breath.

Trying to ignore the pain, he concentrated on the intrusion. Someone was inside who shouldn't be. A brief thought, and he called his sword to his hand as he ran down a side passage, drawn deeper into the building, towards the pulsing core. He skidded around a corner and hissed his breath out as his shoulder slammed into the wall and new fire flared under his skin.

Blinded by a brilliant light, he shielded his eyes, and the image of a shattered casing and a shadowy form hovering over it was followed by agony coursing through his veins. He dropped to his knees, gasping for air. "I'm coming," he muttered through gritted teeth.

Blindly, he charged towards to the form as it straightened from its crouch. The box fell back to the floor with a dull thud, and steel met his sword.

He stared into the dark eyes of a woman, who snarled at him and stabbed at his side with the knife she held in her other hand. He blocked her thrust, shoving her back, and they circled. As desperate as he was to check whatever damage she had done, he couldn't take his eyes off her. She would kill him if she had the chance; he could see it in the way she moved.

"How did you get in?" If the halls of the Oblivion Gate were his projection, created from his imagination, how could anyone else find them?

The woman laughed and lunged for him as he hesitated in confusion. He parried the strike and danced to the side, observing her immediate response. Not giving her time to balance, he rushed her, swirling the cloak he had called to him to foul her blade and thrust his knife into her stomach. She blocked his blow and tried to push him aside, sliding her own knife down his ribs.

He ignored the sting and wrestled the woman to the floor. She was as slippery as a piece of soap, sliding out of his hold and twisting herself around him. Who was she? Wrapping his legs around her torso, he twisted into a reverse hold. The strain across his back was agonising, but he knew it was twice as painful for her. Her breath hissed out in a weird groan as she struggled. He tightened his hold, and she moaned. Leaning back, he increased the pressure until she went limp.

Exhaling a painful breath, he waited for a moment and then released her. He knew she wouldn't be unconscious for long, so he called the belt cords from his robes, and bound her wrists and feet, and then slowly rose. Pain twinged through his side, and he clamped a hand over the slash. His senses sank into his skin, and he roughly knitted the edges of the wound together. He would fix it properly later.

"Oblivion Gate? Are you alright?" he called as he crouched beside the shattered casing. He needed a better name. "Oblivion Gate" was so awkward.

The container was two hand's breadths wide and deep. Whatever material it was made of shimmered in the dull light. He reached for the connection he had begun to build with the Gate and requested more light. The green glow emanating from the walls increased, and he inspected the box.

He had never seen anything like it. Flaming red sigils swam under the surface, taunting him as they twisted and turned. He had no idea what it was, and he couldn't make out the symbols. With his connection to the Gate strained, there was no way to find out. The woman had been able to pick the box up, so he rested a tentative finger on it.

Images of carnage and destruction burned into his mind, and he snatched his finger away with a gasp. Rising, he retreated.

Standing over the woman, he inspected her face. She wasn't a beauty, but she caught the eye with her angular cheeks and dark eyes. A sudden concern hit him. Had she been alone? Had the attack only been on him and the Oblivion Gate?

"Solanji? Are you alright?"

"I'm just fine. How about you?" He winced at her sharp tone. *"What happened? Adriz called us to the citadel, but we lost the connection with you when you disappeared."*

That would not have gone down well. Mav was surprised she was so calm. *"I'm sorry for scaring you. Someone attacked the Oblivion Gate. I instinctively called my body to me. I'm unhurt, but I can't reach the Gate."*

"Ellaria says an oppressive weight is pressing down around you. She thinks the intent was to block communications. It must be targeting the Gate. I'm surprised we can still speak, to be honest. She went to search for the cause."

"I found one intruder. Why don't you join me down here? Maybe you can tell who she is, because she won't speak to me." Mav trans-

ported Solanji to him and grinned at her squeak of shock as she appeared beside him. He liked this ability to move things and now people. He idly wondered what his limits were.

"How did you do that?" Solanji asked with a scowl. She peered around and patted herself. "Where am I?"

"In the Oblivion Gate."

Solanji swallowed and then glared at him. "However you did it, you'd better bring Adriz here before she eviscerates you."

"Ah," Mav said and called Adriz to him.

She appeared and staggered, hands flailing to catch herself. "Demavrian!" she exclaimed in relief.

Mav winced. "Sorry, Adriz. You're in the Oblivion Gate. We've got a bit of a problem." He motioned to the woman on the floor.

"We are going to have a long discussion when we get home," Adriz growled. "About friendly warnings and considerations for others."

"I thought you'd rather be here than not."

"That is beside the point. We can speak mind to mind, you know. A warning wouldn't go amiss."

"Kaenera's blocking communications," Mav said, wincing as Adriz glared at him.

"You spoke to me," Solanji said.

Mav frowned. "I did, didn't I? Not sure how."

"You stopped breathing, and then you disappeared," Adriz said. "Felather was about to lose it when you brought me here. Maybe you could see if you can send him a message and reassure him?"

Knowing Felather, he would be panicking. Mav sent him a thought: *Felather. I've claimed the Gate. We'll return soon and explain all. Adriz and Solanji are here with me, so don't worry.*

"Don't worry?" Felather shrieked, and Mav winced as he pressed his temple.

"We'll speak later. I don't have time to explain now."

Solanji grimaced at him. "Well, whatever this barrier is, it isn't affecting you, is it?"

"That is, if the intent is to block."

"You said you can't reach the Gate," Solanji said. "I imagine he was the target, not you. They wouldn't know you were here."

"I'm not so sure," he said, staring at the woman. "Can you skim her thoughts?"

"Not while she is unconscious. She's soulless, so I can't read her soulmist."

"I think she was trying to steal that box. Don't touch it; it burns."

Solanji raised an eyebrow. "Speaking from experience, are you?"

Mav shrugged. "She smashed the casing, and when I caught her, she was lifting it out of the shards. So, she could touch it."

"It looks alive," Solanji said as she knelt to inspect it. "Did anything else happen when you touched it?"

"A blur of images, though I didn't really see what they were."

A low moan drew their attention back to their captive. Crouching beside her, Mav held his blade across her throat, and she stilled. "What did you do to the Oblivion Gate?"

The woman glared at him and then tried to twist out of her restraints. "You won't live much longer. Your death is imminent."

"She's not alone; there is another," Solanji reported. *"She is terrified that if she fails, Kaenera will kill her and make her a mindless dybbuk. Her fear is off the scale. Be careful, Mav. She is desperate."*

"Your threats are meaningless. Why does Kaenera want that box?" Mav growled as the building shuddered.

The woman's eyes widened.

"She believes it belongs to Kaenera, though she's not sure. She was told to wrap it in an iron mesh before she touched it. The mesh will contain the sigils."

"What do the sigils do?"

The woman glared at him; her lips clamped tight.

"They can be used to subsume the Oblivion Gate…" Solanji said. *"Or the citadel, or even the whole world."*

"Where is your companion?" Mav asked their captive. "The one trying to suppress the Gate?"

The building trembled again, and a pressure Mav hadn't realised was affecting him eased. A sharp pain pierced his temples, and he closed his eyes as a new soul arrived and the man's memories spooled through his mind. He sighed.

The woman snarled, and then she stiffened as a golden dragon appeared and dropped a limp body on the floor.

"Apologies, Mav. I broke his neck. He wouldn't drop the barrier," Ellaria said as she landed. The body collapsed in on itself, leaving a small pile of dust that swirled for a moment and then faded from view.

"I assume that was your companion, Steraf?" Mav asked. The man's memories lingered in his mind, and his shadow weighed heavily on his chest. "You've both been very busy."

The woman's face paled.

"Her name is Ana, and she was once a local proctor," Solanji said. *"He was her partner. Seems they both ended up on the wrong side of the Justicers."*

"So, Ana. What to do with you?"

Ana flinched. "How…?" She bit the words off as she glared at Ellaria and Solanji. "The SoulBreather? You let her out of the citadel? Foolish." She clamped her mouth shut.

"Why is that foolish?" Mav asked. "Maybe we should just send you back to Kaenera and let him enact his punishment?"

Ana's face paled. "Please don't. Kill me and pass me

through the Gate. I would prefer to die than live an endless non-life."

"Is that what he's been doing? Creating dybbuks instead of passing people on?"

Ana bit her lip and nodded. "Please don't send me back."

"Depends how helpful you are. How did you get here? How did you even find us?"

Ana shrugged. "Kaenera's been really quiet, but a week or so ago, he went berserk. He kept yelling that the Gate was his. Ever since, he's been watching for some signs that only he can see. No idea what. 'Some disturbance in the air'," she said, like she was quoting. "The next thing I know, he's all excited about the Gate being grounded, and I turn up here."

"Grounded? Do you mean by physically being in a location?" Was this all his fault? Had his perception of the Gate as a physical building put them all in danger? "Do you know where Kaenera is?"

Ana tensed as she stared at Mav.

"She's trying to block her thoughts. I think she knows, but I can't quite read her," Solanji said.

"He's here in Eidolon, isn't he?" Mav asked.

"Yes," Solanji said. *"Somewhere cold and bleak."*

The image of a stone cavern with blood-stained chains hanging from the ceiling made him shudder, and Solanji gripped his arm. *"I'm here with you,"* she whispered as the sensation of Ellaria wrapping herself around his body reassured him.

Mav rotated his neck, trying to relieve the sudden tension. "But he's weak. Or he would have come himself."

"Yes," Solanji said again.

"You are not alone," Ellaria said. *"I'm here."*

"Demavrian?" the Oblivion Gate's voice was faint.

Mav stiffened and then held up his hand as his muscles

relaxed under Ellaria's body heat, infusing him with warmth, love, and reassurance. "I can hear the Gate."

"Oblivion Gate? Where are you? Are you injured?"

"You must accept and seal the bond. Please, I misjudged him."

"Kaenera?"

"Yes, he is stronger than I thought. You said you had defeated him. I thought we had…time to connect. I had to block our connection so the attack wouldn't incapacitate you, but you need to accept it."

"I thought I had already accepted it," Mav replied. *"I know we are connected."*

"The bond exists and is stronger than I would have thought, but you need to formally accept the bond to seal it properly."

"We need a better solution than blocking. We will be more effective as a team."

"I know. I'm sorry. I panicked when they attacked. I should have known better. I was distracted by our bonding. It won't happen again."

"We were both distracted; it will be life-changing for both of us. But please don't ever block me again. No matter what. You have to trust me to have your back, as I need you to have mine."

"Please forgive me."

"Of course I forgive you. This is as new for you as it is for me. Unfortunately, we haven't had time to figure out how to work together, let alone bond. Is there any way to hide our location? We don't want any more of Kaenera's people finding us."

"I've put up a barrier. No one should be able to enter."

"How do I claim you?"

"It would be better if you came to the heart. Kiara will show you where to go."

"Mav? " Solanji said as she wrapped her arms around his waist. *"Are you talking to the Gate? None of us can hear him."*

Mav tried to swallow against the sudden dryness in his throat. *"Yes. We were just discussing how to finalise the bond."*

Mav redirected his thoughts to the Gate. *"First, we need to deal with our intruder. We need to move Ana to a cell or somewhere you can restrain her. She was trying to steal a box of weird sigils for Kaenera."*

"Is the box secure?"

Mav tensed at the concern in the Gate's voice. *"If by 'secure' you mean the sigils are still in the box, then yes. She smashed the casing."*

"Whatever you do, don't open it." After a moment, the Gate said, *"She's one of Kaenera's trusted. Does his dirty work. Turned up with her friend a few months back. None of Kaenera's people ever last long. She knows nothing about the Gate, and I'd prefer it stay that way."*

"Me, too. Safer for all of us." Mav rubbed his eyes and shifted awkwardly as his side twinged. *"Is there somewhere we can lock her up for now? Can you make sure Kaenera can't contact her? We can decide what to do with her later."*

"Transfer her to the sub-basement. There are some cells down there."

The Gate gave him the image, and Mav transported her to the cell before withdrawing his presence. This new skill of moving people around was very useful, though tiring. A wave of lethargy swept through him. Maybe he had reached his limit.

"Mav? Where did she go?" Adriz asked, spinning around.

"Don't worry. I just transferred her to a cell, somewhere we can keep her locked up and out of Kaenera's reach."

"Since when can you…"

"I'll explain later." Mav rubbed his eyes.

"I'll secure the box," the Gate said. *"If Kaenera wants it, it's probably best he doesn't get it."*

"Fine, though I expect you to tell me what those sigils are," Mav said to the Gate and then exhaled as he hugged Solanji. "Now that we have a base, we need to protect it."

"I have increased the protections around the halls. You'll know if

there are any breaches in the future. Only people you invite will be allowed entry. I am sorry. I didn't realise we were so exposed," the Gate said in a small voice.

"Please forgive me," Mav replied. *"It's my fault for making you solid. I wasn't aware that previously, you didn't have a physical presence. Maybe we should revert back to what you were before."*

"I like this form. I want you to live here with me." The Gate hesitated. *"I promise I will protect you if you bond with me."*

10

DEMAVRIAN – OBLIVION GATE

Mav was amazed that he still hadn't completed the bond with the Gate. It seemed like he already had a connection. "First, I need to claim to the Gate," he said aloud, his head aching from keeping the two conversations straight. "We need to go to the heart."

"Are you sure it's safe?" Solanji asked as Ellaria released Mav and dropped to the floor.

"I thought you had already claimed the Gate?" Ellaria asked.

"We were interrupted. We didn't seal the bond. It's now or never. Kiara? Are you here?"

A swirl of cool air rippled around him as Kiara appeared, her form rippling like the breeze over a pond. "Mav! I'm glad you are here."

"You need to show me to the heart."

"Who are you talking to, Mav? What heart?" Solanji asked, her gaze flicking around.

Adriz stiffened and gripped Mav's shoulder. "Who else is here?" she demanded.

"There's a presence," Ellaria murmured, her tongue tasting the air.

"Kiara is here with us. I'm assuming you can't see her?"

"No," Solanji and Adriz said at the same time.

Kiara glanced around her. "I think it's best if we don't reveal where the heart of the Gate is until you've spoken to the residents."

"What residents?" Mav asked.

"There are some others here," Kiara said, "supposedly looking after the Gate, but they are not doing a very good job of it. I'd sack them all."

"There are residents? Where?" Adriz asked.

"I need to claim the Gate," Mav said, running his fingers through his hair. "I don't know who these others are."

"Then we'll do it here," the Oblivion Gate said, urgency edging his voice. *"I had not thought about the others. Drop your defences and claim me now. We are out of time."*

Mav exhaled and then gritted his teeth. Closing his eyes, he opened himself up again. The Gate greedily swarmed through him, filling all his empty spaces. He caught his breath at the strangeness of another awareness within him, an awareness that was much more cognizant than the citadel had ever been. The Gate had an intelligence, and although they were rusty from lack of use, Mav didn't expect it to take long for him to flex his mental muscles.

Mav tried to relax as the Gate rifled through his memories, slowly watching Mav's experiences over the last half-century.

"I accept your claim," the Gate said, his voice resounding through the halls. "You are a worthy Gate Keeper, and I am honoured to bond with you. In return, you will know all that I know, see what I see, and speak in my voice. Welcome, Keeper of Shadows and Gate Keeper to Oblivion."

A deep, sonorous echo of a gong resonated through Mav

and throughout the halls. He inhaled as a wave of…He wasn't sure what swept through him. It left him tingly and with a sharper awareness of much more than his immediate surroundings.

"The Gate is open to you. Protect the Shadows."

Mav staggered, and Adriz braced him. A beat pulsed through the hall, followed by a second. Chest fluttering, he placed both hands on Adriz's shoulders and stared at her as his body vibrated with the beat, which faded as his heart aligned to the slow rhythm.

"Mav?" Adriz asked, worry etching her face.

Warmth embraced Mav, and his wings flared. The Oblivion Gate filled him, surrounded him, was him. His shadows swirled, taking on the greenish hue that the Gate exuded, gilding his black feathers so that they gleamed with an iridescence more forest green than black.

Mav's sight blurred with double vision as if he saw through two pairs of eyes. Then his sight cleared, and the mist dissipated, revealing a complex mechanism of cogs, chains and pulleys.

He tensed as the Gate's explanation crystallised in his mind and he understood all the workings, the connections, the sheer beauty of the Oblivion Gate. The Gate was not just a conduit; it also sustained the barrier between life and death. The Gate was the doorway to the shadows, and he was the keeper.

Mav frowned. Shadows? What shadows did he need to protect? How was the Keeper of Shadows different from the Oblivion Gate Keeper? What more was expected of him?

Information on the Aeora sigils, the glowing symbols in the box that Oji had secured, flowed through his mind, and he froze. He now held what? Mav began to shake as he understood the destructive power held in that small box—a box Kaenera knew about and wanted.

A flash of horror chilled Mav to the bone, and he shuddered. Kaenera had come so close to retrieving the sigils. He could so easily have stolen the power to destroy them all.

"Oblivion Gate, the Aeora sigils are secure, aren't they?"

"I promise. No one will find them except you," the Gate replied.

A frantic tugging on Mav's arm made him veer drunkenly towards to the right.

"Mav? Are all you alright?" Solanji's voice was tinged with fear as he tried to collect himself.

Adriz tightened her grip on him, and he took a deep, steadying breath. Knowledge jostled for attention, overloading his brain. There was so much history, information, and wonder mingling with the horror.

"Give me a minute," he said, ignoring the fact that his voice was slurred. *"Thank you,"* he murmured to the Gate. *"I thank you for your trust. I won't betray it."* The vow bound them tightly, deeper than any bond he had experienced. A sense of completion settled within him as if, in all the years of his life, he had been missing some essential part of himself and never knew it.

"Is this the bond you had with Kaenera?" he asked. If it were, then Kaenera would no doubt be struggling to deal with the fallout of losing it.

"Not as deep, nor so complete. He never opened himself to me the way you have. Kaenera wanted absolute power. He wouldn't share himself the way you have. He never allowed me to manifest as you have done. Thank you for your trust, Demavrian. I won't betray it." The Gate hesitated a moment and knowledge bloomed with Mav. There would be no way to break this bond except by death. The searing pain of their initial attempt to bond had fused their vow so deep within Mav, they would never be able to separate it.

"I'm sorry," the Oblivion Gate whispered. *"I never intended*

to make it irreversible." The Gate faltered as he felt the flash of fear that sped through Mav.

"*It is not your fault. Maybe Kaenera did us a favour. He cannot undo what has been done, and I've never felt so complete in my life. This is meant to be. It feels right. It is ours.*"

"*Ours,*" the Gate repeated, and relief percolated through Mav.

Solanji was hugging him, cursing under her breath in a constant litany, her voice edged with terror. It didn't help that she and Adriz were holding him up. Ellaria had wrapped herself around his leg, and the heat from her scales penetrated his clothes, grounding him.

"*You went away again,*" Ellaria murmured.

"I'm here," he said, trying to ease their concern. His arm tightened around Solanji. "Please, my love, give me a moment. I need to talk to the Gate."

She stopped squeezing him and exhaled. "You can have one minute," she said, her voice quavering, and she kissed him on the lips.

Mav tried to concentrate on what the Gate was saying, but he hadn't quite grasped what had happened. "I still don't understand how these halls come from me," he said aloud.

"You see so clearly," the Gate replied. His deep voice echoed in the hall, and Solanji stiffened, staring around her as she searched for where the voice was coming from. "What you see around you is how you perceive me. If our bond were ever severed, this would all disappear."

"Are we still anchored in Eidolon?" Mav asked, his awareness spreading through the room, venturing down the hallway, closer to the mechanism Kiara was so excited about. "Still physically present?"

"If you wish it so."

"I get to choose?"

"You are the Gate Keeper."

"But we are safe? You have protections up? Kaenera won't be able to enter?"

"You will always be safe in our halls," the Gate vowed.

The rightness of that statement permeated into Mav's bones. Their halls. His halls.

"I'd like you to meet my heartsworn, my wife, Solanji." He embraced Solanji. "Dear heart, I want you to meet the Oblivion Gate."

"It's a pleasure," Solanji said, staring up at the ceiling.

"The pleasure is mine," the Gate replied. "Are you going to live here with us? Mav would like you to." Eagerness bled into his tone, and Mav smiled as he rotated his shoulders, easing the stiffness.

"I live wherever Mav lives. And there are probably some others who will live with us as well, along with some dragons. This is my familiar, Ellaria."

"Dragons?" the Gate said. "I haven't seen a dragon for a long time. Dragons are always welcome. Ellaria, be safe in our halls."

"This is Adriz, my cherubim, guard, and oathsworn. A member of my family." Mav indicated Adriz.

"Adriz," the Gate repeated.

"I'm not calling you Oblivion Gate," Mav said. "I'll call you OhGee, or maybe Oji for now, but if you have a preferred name we should call you by, please let me know."

"I will consider it. I have never had a personal name before."

Ellaria released Mav and raised her snout, scenting the air. *"You are the building? Similar to the citadel?"* she asked in delight as she folded her wings against her back.

"Much more than the citadel," Mav replied. "I think the citadel has grown lazy. I'm sure she could do just as much as Oji can."

"And you." Ellaria stared at Mav accusingly. *"What have you done? You look different."*

Solanji grabbed his arms and inspected him. "She's right. You look younger and yet not. I'm not sure what it is."

Mav shrugged. His fingers fumbled for the vendetta stones, and he slid them back and forth on the cords around his neck. "I just claimed the Oblivion Gate. Of course I'm different. Let's not worry about it now."

Kiara solidified beside him and then launched herself at him. "You did it! I can see you are the Gate. I knew you could do it." She released him and patted herself. "I'm solid," she said in surprise.

"I can see her. I can see and hear a ghost!" Adriz said, her face paling.

"I'm Mav's Gate Wraith," Kiara said proudly.

"You will be able to appear in that form now, if you choose," Mav said. "I think Shandra and the others would prefer you to be solid, though." He swayed as his vision greyed out for a moment, and Adriz steadied him.

"Are they coming here? To live with us?"

"If they want to," Mav replied, slipping his arm around Solanji's waist as Ellaria curled a possessive tail around his leg. "This is my heartsworn, Solanji. You remember her, don't you? Ellaria, her familiar, and Adriz, my cherubim.

"Of course. Hi, Solanji, Adriz." Kiara grinned at the golden dragon. She extended a hesitant finger and rubbed Ellaria's eye ridge. "You are beautiful." Ellaria leaned into her hand and crooned.

Solanji smiled. "I am very interested in finding out what a Gate Wraith is, but it's lovely to meet you again."

"You had us worried when you went away and we couldn't reach you," Ellaria murmured.

"I'm sorry," Mav replied. *"Hopefully, we won't have a problem communicating anymore now that I've claimed the Gate."*

"They are afraid you'll disappear again," Oji said in surprise.

"You can hear us?" Ellaria asked, equally surprised.

"I can hear what Mav can hear."

"We love him and want to make sure he is well," Solanji replied.

"Then we all have the same objective."

"That is good to know," Solanji said with a smile. "So, Oji… May I call you Oji?"

"I hope you will," Oji replied.

"I look forward to getting to know you better."

"I can show you around our new home," Kiara said.

"Tomorrow," Oji said. "Demavrian needs to rest. He is exhausted. And I need to check the halls for repairs."

Kiara's face fell. "Oh, Oji, I'm so sorry, I should have thought. I'll help you. We'll soon get things fixed."

Solanji inspected Mav's face and frowned as she smoothed his cheek. "You do look tired. We'll push Amaridin's dinner to tomorrow night. I'm sure he'll understand."

Mav leaned into her palm and almost fell over. "Good idea." Now that Oji had mentioned it, exhaustion dragged at his limbs. He was struggling to keep himself upright. His bones ached, and when he remembered that the bond had been fused within him, he wondered why he was surprised. His shadows were also overly excited, still swirling around him in enthusiasm. He was surprised Solanji hadn't mentioned them.

As if she heard him, Solanji reached for his shadows and soothed them. "Yes, well done," she murmured as they settled at her touch, and a flush of warm satisfaction spread through him.

11

DEMAVRIAN – OBLIVION GATE

When Mav transported Adriz and himself back to his rooms in the citadel, leaving Ellaria to transport Solanji, they were met by a roomful of upset people.

His brother, Amaridin, hauled him into his arms and gripped him tight as Felather demanded, "What do you think you were doing?"

Mav raised an eyebrow at him over Amaridin's shoulder. "Claiming the Gate," he replied as if the question were unnecessary.

"Felather contacted me when he lost you," Amaridin said, "but I couldn't reach you, either."

"I thought we agreed you wouldn't go on your own," Felather snapped.

"I didn't intend on doing so. One moment, I was sitting at my desk, and the next, I was walking the halls of the Oblivion Gate."

"You should have returned as soon as you claimed the Gate."

"We were attacked. I called Adriz to me as soon as I

could. Felather, please, I am not deliberately leaving anyone behind."

"Called? How?"

"I don't know. I think of something, and it appears. It's happened a couple of times. It seems I can transport things and people from one place to another."

Felather frowned at him, and then his brow cleared as he shrugged. "Well, you are a god. I suppose you must be able to do some weird stuff."

Mav chuckled and collapsed in a chair, aware of Oji observing the room through his eyes just as Mav was aware of the Gate and all within it—even those shadows flitting through the corridors, who didn't think he saw them. He needed to check them out as soon as possible. He couldn't move his family in if there was a threat inside the halls.

"How did Kaenera find you so quickly?" Adriz asked as she squeezed Felather's shoulder.

"No idea. But I am bonded to Oji now. I am the Gate, so Kaenera can't get in, and I'll know if he tries."

"Oji?" Felather asked.

"The Oblivion Gate. Can't call him that all the time, so he's Oji."

"And you've claimed it?" Amaridin asked.

"Yes, and he's a him, and he is aware."

"What?" Amaridin exclaimed. "How?"

"I don't know." Mav frowned. "It may be because Kaenera never bonded properly. He controlled; he wasn't a partner. But then, why is the citadel dormant? Surely, the citadel should be even more active? I was fully bonded, but I've never spoken to it. It's always communicated through images." He grinned at his brother. "Something for you and Valerian to investigate."

Amaridin nodded. "We will. You should rest. Your body must be exhausted with what you're putting it through, especially as Felather said you stopped breathing and then disappeared"—he waved his hand—"without any warning!"

"We were hoping to move dinner to tomorrow, Amaridin," Solanji said. "Mav needs to assimilate the Gate."

"Of course." Amaridin gave his brother a searching inspection and then went to the door. "Rest. I'll see you tomorrow for dinner, and we can discuss more then."

Mav rubbed his face. "A chance would be a fine thing," he muttered under his breath as he moved towards his desk

"Now that you've claimed the Gate, what about Serenia?" Felather asked as he collapsed in a nearby chair. "You need to deal with her as well."

Mav sat in the chair opposite him and grimaced at the mention of the archangel who had joined forces with Kaenera and betrayed all of them. She was currently incarcerated in the citadel, under Amaridin's watch, but Averdeus had decreed that Mav had to pass her through the Oblivion Gate.

"I need to understand the Gate a little more before I start passing people through it. During the bonding, the Gate took all the soulless I had been collecting, so at least my head is a lot better."

"That is good," Adriz murmured handing him the drink she had poured. She slumped into another chair and sipped from her glass. "Is the Gate secure?"

"As much as it can be. Oji has it locked down, and it only seems to become physical when I am there. I make everything solidify for some reason."

"And Kaenera won't be able to access it again?" Felather asked, leaning forward to rest his arms on his knees.

"Oji assures me that he won't be able to."

"This bonding," Adriz said slowly. "What does it actually mean?"

"It means the Oblivion Gate and I are one. What one

sees, so will the other." Mav paused. "It's quite weird. I can see the Gate, and I know exactly where all the wraiths are, including Kiara." He grimaced. "Or those who are left. I cleared a few out who had harmful intentions." He smiled. "Kiara's back in the engine room."

"How many wraiths are there?" Adriz asked.

"There are about six left. I scoured all the others out of the halls."

Felather scowled. "Scoured?"

"When Kaenera attacked, I sent my shadows off scouting. They cleaned out the undesirables, those who had ill intent against me or the Gate."

There was a short silence. "You know, you can be quite scary at times," Felather said eventually.

Mav smiled. "I have no doubt I am about to get much scarier as I learn what being the Gate Keeper and the Keeper of Shadows really means."

"Keeper of Shadows," Felather murmured. "I'll research it." He looked around the room and then observed Mav for a moment before rising. "I'll keep the fledglings occupied tonight. You've had a tough day, Mav. You need to rest, and make sure you have a good night's sleep."

"No rising at dawn," Adriz said with a grin. "We won't be leaving for Eidolon until after Muntra's training session anyway."

Mav was quick to agree and finally closed the door behind them. He exhaled slowly as he turned around and rubbed his eyes. Exhaustion swept through him, and Oji watched from behind his eyes with interest.

Solanji closed the distance, pressing him up against the door. Her grin was pure mischief as she traced his cheekbone and then stroked his beard with gentle fingers. He shivered under her touch, and a fire flared in his gut.

"So," she purred, "I believe you still owe me a thank you."

"I believe that is so," he murmured against her lips, his exhaustion draining away as a flare of desire flushed through him. Solanji smiled as he demonstrated he was a willing participant in whatever she was planning. She trawled her soul fingers through his shadows, and he shuddered.

"If you thank me well enough, I can assure you, you'll sleep really well."

"Oji? I need some privacy," Mav said.

"Oh, yes, of course. My apologies."

Smiling at Oji's flustered response, Mav's chuckle was sinfully low. Twining his fingers with Solanji's, he led her across the room and into the bedchamber. There, they helped each other undress until she pushed him onto the bed and climbed on top of him.

"I thought I was supposed to be thanking *you?*" he said as he kissed her smooth brown belly. His shadows curled around them, a soft caress against her silky skin, and he groaned as she extended her soulfingers to pet them. Heat pooled in his groin, a need demanding attention. Mav shivered beneath her, and his aura leaked. He couldn't help it, and he became *more*, surrounding her, filling her. He could taste her, a smoky, burnt vanilla, so smooth and rich that it made his mouth water.

She leaned down to meet him, her breasts rubbing his chest as she ground against him, and he moaned into her mouth. "I think we can thank each other," she said as he trailed hot kisses down her neck and stroked his callused fingers down her back and over her buttocks. He gripped them as he pressed her tighter against him, his pulsing erection leaking and slick as she slid against him.

Solanji gasped as he suckled her nipples. His fingers sliding into her heat, and she arched her back, craving more.

She whimpered when he removed his fingers, but his throbbing erection soon filled her in their place, and his breath caught as her heat encased him. She sank down on him, eager for him to fill her, and he moaned beneath her as she clenched him, pulling him deeper. He was fully seated within her, and he never wanted to be anywhere else. His stomach muscles tensed, and he teetered on the edge as exquisite sensations rippled through him as she began to move, riding him. She leaned back and slowly undulated, arching her back so he could enter her easily. His thrusts quickened, his core tightening as his fingers caressed the place where they joined, and she sucked her breath in.

"So beautiful," he whispered, his voice a husky growl as he pumped his hips. She rode him as hard as he thrust into her, his fingers moving in sync and bringing her to the edge.

Her moans vibrated through him, bringing him closer, and he growled, "Solanji!" and his heat flooding her brought her to her climax as she bent over him, forcing her tongue into his mouth, plunging deeper as heat pulsed through them as they rode out their orgasms. Shadows spiralled around them in a dizzying dance, and he felt invigorated. Their bond swelled with an exquisitely painful overload of all that he had become, yet she absorbed it all and offered back to him her love. Warmth embraced him, filled him, sheltered him.

Solanji flopped over him, kissing his shoulder, his chest, his neck, whatever skin she could reach. He moaned in response, his skin sensitive to her touch. He didn't want her to ever stop; he needed her like the air he breathed.

She raised herself and glared down at him. "You are mine," she said.

Mav's lips twitched. "Most definitely."

Solanji wasn't satisfied. "You are mine first. Before everyone else."

"Always," Mav replied, pulling her head forward and rising to kiss her. He held her gaze. "Just as you are mine, bound to my heart, entwined with my shadows, oathsworn, consort, and lover. You are so perfect," Mav whispered, and as he collapsed back on the bed, she followed him down and relaxed in his embrace, chuckling against his skin.

"It takes two, you know, and I would say you are amazing. You can thank me like that any day."

He nuzzled her neck, his fingers caressing her back, drifting lower and making her shiver. "It will be my pleasure."

She sighed into his chest and tightened her grip on him, and he smiled at the thought that she was as unwilling to move as he was.

"We need to clean up," Mav murmured after a while, and Solanji whined. He laughed and slid out of her with a low hiss of breath.

"I suppose," she said, inhaling the scent of him and nuzzling his neck. "I don't want to move."

Wrapping Solanji in his arms, he dozed for a moment, but he knew they needed to clean up. He climbed out of bed and returned with a damp cloth to wash them both with, and then he smiled as she sighed and wrapped herself around him again.

He revelled in her warmth, her breath on his neck, and then he relaxed. His breathing evened out, and he slept.

12

———

DEMAVRIAN – OBLIVION GATE

The next morning, Mav returned to the Oblivion Gate with Solanji and Adriz. Oji had searched the halls and declared all secure.

"Even the wraiths?" Mav asked as he hugged Solanji tight against his side. Her presence grounded him. "What do we know about them?"

"Not a lot," Oji said. "I don't remember them being residents, nor where they came from. Wenson says they look like Kiara does to him, but I disagree. The other wraiths look nothing like Kiara."

"Who is Wenson?" Mav asked.

"Wenson is the librarian."

"And how do they differ?"

"Kiara is a constant glow in my perception. I know where she is; her presence feels right. She is part of me, and I would be sad if she left. She is part of the Oblivion Gate like you are."

Mav paused on the landing as he digested Oji's words. "And Wenson is not part of you?"

"I'm not sure. Cook isn't, but Wenson seems more solid,

like we have a connection of some sort, only I don't know what it is. But that may be because I don't remember him."

"We have a cook?" Solanji asked.

"Yes, you'll find him in the kitchens. He is there now."

"So, they are living in your halls," Mav said. "They are physically present."

"They exist, but they are not part of me. They are not here to serve… No, that is not the right word." Oji fell silent for a moment. "I don't know how to explain it. You and Kiara *want* to be within my walls. You want for me to exist. You make me real. I have no connection to the other wraiths."

"Are they something Kaenera planted? One of his unwilling wraiths?"

"I don't think so. We cleaned out those with malevolent intentions. Those left chose to be here."

"We need to know for sure."

"Which is why I called you. I believe they are not Kaenera's tool, just someone caught between."

"Between what?"

"Between the ephemeral gate and the real gate you have created. You have made them real by making me real."

"You mean they were ghosts, wraiths like Kiara, until I grounded you?"

"I think so, though they are not as substantial as Kiara. From what Kiara has said, I think you make her solid. I think it is her connection to you that grounds her, whereas the cook, for example, has no such connection, so he is more wraith-like.

"The difference is that the dybbuks are those who died and were bound to Kaenera, prevented from crossing. He controls them, and they have no free will. Once Kaenera releases them, they will cease to exist, but the wraiths are bound to the Gate and will remain here until *they* choose to pass through. Some have passed, and some you cleared out, but others are still here."

Mav rubbed his temples. Somehow, he thought unravelling all the complexities of Eidolon would give him a constant headache. "Very well. Let us meet the cook and Wenson."

They entered the kitchen, and Mav searched the empty room for the cook. He sat at the table, patting the seat next to him for Solanji, and then made himself comfortable and extended his awareness. Releasing his shadows, he let them explore the kitchen. Adriz stood by the door, arms folded, inspecting the room. Mav grinned as Kiara appeared and stared at him in bewilderment.

"When did you arrive?" she asked, wrinkling her nose. "Where's Cook?"

"I'm sure he'll be here in a moment," Mav said, and the air beside him rippled.

The cook appeared and scowled at Mav. "What do you want?" he asked, his form solidifying, revealing a small man with a receding hairline and hazel eyes flashing with anger. The cook bustled to his workbench and began pulling out pots and small sacks of herbs.

Mav leaned on the table and said, "I wanted to ask you when you first arrived here. Have you been here as long as Wenson?"

"Oh no. He was here before me."

"But you cooked for Kaenera?"

Cook paused. "I think so."

"You're not sure?"

"I don't remember. It's hazy. The only thing I know for sure is that everything became clearer when you took over."

Mav grinned. "Well, I am glad to be of service."

Cook frowned at him, and then his face lightened, and he suddenly smiled. "I'm not sure why, but I like you." He slapped a jug of bannoe on the table with a couple of mugs. "I'm glad to be cooking again."

"I'm happy to hear you say that. The Gate is only going to get busier. I am afraid we are going to tax your patience."

Cook waved his hand. "Give me as much warning as you can."

"I'll try, but I am at war with Kaenera. Unexpected things may happen."

Cook stared at him. "You give me a warning when you can. Unexpected events are exceptions."

Mav smiled. "I promise I will warn you when possible and order in advance. Do you have a personal name, or do you prefer to be called Cook?"

Cook stared at him in surprise. "I am a cook."

"You are also a person," Mav said. "You are more than just a cook."

"Cooking is all I am."

"It doesn't have to be," Mav replied.

Cook's gaze became vague as he obviously trawled through his memory, and then he looked at Mav in amazement. "I remember!"

"Remember what?" Mav asked.

"Who I am."

"And who is that?"

"Cecil. I lived in Struira, in the north of Angelicus. I owned a restaurant until…"

"Until what?" Mav asked.

"Until an angel falsely accused me of poisoning them and I lost my license, my restaurant, my soul. I lost everything."

Mav internally winced. It seemed there was a streak of corruption in Angelicus that everyone ignored. "What was your restaurant called?"

"Ambrosia."

Somehow, Mav was not surprised. From his own hazy memory of Angelicus, he was sure Ambrosia had been one of the best-rated restaurants in Puronia. He would check. But he had the feeling someone had been skimming off of the best businesses in Angelicus over the last few… He didn't know how long. He wondered who it was.

"When was this?"

Cecil rubbed his chin and frowned.

"Do you remember the date you first started your restaurant?

A beautiful smile spread over Cecil's face. He looked so much younger, full of possibilities, and Mav's heart ached at the knowledge that it had all been stolen from him. He had no doubt some people deserved to be soul-stripped and cast out, but he also knew that some good people had been exploited, and it seemed Cecil was one of them.

"It was fall, a time when all the orange and amber colours flourished. We decorated the restaurant with a range of seasonal plants. It was really effective, evoking that smoky, misty atmosphere. I'll never forget it."

"How long ago?" Mav prompted.

Cecil confusion returned. "I don't know."

"Was Averdeus in the citadel?"

"Oh yes! He and Malena came often. They loved my revelia."

Mav internally winced at the mention of his mother's name. But that was centuries ago. How long had Cecil been here?

"Do you remember when Kaenera took over the Oblivion Gate?"

Cecil hesitated, and the sparkle left his eyes as he folded in on himself.

"I didn't mean to distress you."

"No, no, I know. I don't remember." Cecil paused and

then sighed. "There is much I have forgotten. But I know the day you arrived and claimed the Gate. Everything came into focus. Felt right. I am so glad you are here."

"I am, too. This place seems like home. I feel comfortable here."

Cecil nodded.

"Is there anything you remember about the Gate when Kaenera ruled it? Any odd sites? Places that didn't feel right?"

Cecil thought for a moment and then shook his head.

"I'm worried Kaenera hid entrances to the Gate, ones only wraiths could use."

"You mean like Clarence?" Cecil asked.

"Who is Clarence?"

"One of Kaenera's dybbuks, though he roamed the halls like a wraith at times." Cecil stared off into the distance. "Clarence was here for years. He was Kaenera's right-hand man, always poking his nose where it wasn't wanted. Ana was more recent. Don't know about any doors or such."

"I want to confirm that Kaenera didn't leave me any surprises."

Cecil laughed. "Even if he did, it wouldn't bother you."

Mav sat up. "Why do you say that?"

"The Oblivion Gate is awake. Fully aware." Cecil tapped his nose. "You bonded with him."

"But so did Kaenera."

Cecil tutted. "He wishes. Anything Kaenera left will reveal itself to you. The Gate watches, and the Gate Keeper? He sees everything. And the Keeper of Shadows rules over all."

"The Keeper of Shadows? I'm not clear on the difference."

"You would be if you thought about it. The Gate is a conduit. The Keeper of Shadows decides."

Mav rested his chin on his hand as he stared at Cecil. "Decides what?"

Cecil snorted out a laugh. "Everything. If the Gate feels right to you, then there is nothing you need to worry about."

Mav leaned back in his chair. "I'm not sure that helps."

"If you use your shadows right, nothing can surprise you." Cecil turned back to his stove. "How many for dinner tonight?"

Mav's shadows returned to him, unperturbed and quiescent. He rose. "I am sorry, but we are unable to stay for dinner tonight."

"What's the point of a kitchen if it doesn't get used?"

"We will have need of you soon, I can assure you," Mav said.

Kiara grabbed Solanji's hand and eagerly towed her out of the kitchen and down the hall towards the staircase. "I can show you around. I know the perfect room for you and Mav. There's space for everyone. Do you want to see the library first?"

Adriz shadowed Mav as he followed them.

Exploring the halls, Mav was aware of Solanji observing him. He knew his appearance hadn't changed except that he was keeping his wings flared and they had gained a green glow similar to that of the walls. He felt more relaxed, more assured. It was like he had found the answer to something, and he thought that maybe he had.

"Figured out what is different yet?" he asked as he slid his arm around her waist. She leaned into him.

"I think you've regained the confidence of the youthful general."

Mav nodded. "I feel right. As if everything is as it should be." He looked around him. "I'm where I am supposed to be."

"Then that is where we should all be."

"It will take some time for us to improve conditions here in Eidolon."

"Eidolon has its own beauty. Be careful what you change."

"Don't worry. I am not going to make any sweeping changes. I am hoping everyone will help. But first, we need to make sure the Gate is secure before we bring the family here. I want to explore every part of it so I know where everything is."

"That's good because we need to get the fledglings into a routine. Most of that will be at the citadel, to begin with, so if you have a reason for delaying bringing them here, that will go over much better."

"I want them here, but I need to make sure Kaenera didn't leave any nasty surprises."

"Wouldn't Oji know if he had?"

"I'm not sure. It doesn't sound like Kaenera shared everything with Oji."

"Then, at a minimum, Adriz should always be with you. You shouldn't be here on your own."

"He has no choice," Adriz said from behind them. "I am not leaving him."

Mav flashed her a grin. "I wouldn't have it any other way. It's also time Ryvalin and Xylvin came to help us."

Adriz nodded. "I agree."

He paused as Kiara pushed open a tall wooden door.

"This should be yours and Solanji's room, Mav."

Mav entered the chamber and looked around. A suite of rooms greeted him, similar in layout to his chambers in the citadel. "I agree," he said as he walked deeper into the rooms. He stopped by the far wall in the room he was mentally calling his study and placed a hand on it. The wall shimmered and then began to clear. It settled into a transparent floor-to-ceiling window overlooking the headland at the end of the beach.

"It's perfect," Mav said.

"It is now," Solanji agreed, joining him at the window. "What a view."

It was truly stunning. He could spend all day just watching the birds wheel above the waves. A slick, dark head bobbed in the water, and he squinted at it. Its sleek body breached the water, and he relaxed. It was a seal or something similar.

"Oji, these will be our rooms. I'll use this room as a study." He cocked his head at Solanji. "Do you want to work in the other room, or would you prefer a dressing room?"

"I'm not one to worry about clothes. An office will be a better use."

Nodding, Mav returned to the main living area and peered into the room that would be the bedchamber, with an adjoining bathing suite. "Let Oji know what you want. He'll furnish it for you. There's plenty of furniture in storage."

"I'd be glad to help," Oji said.

"How do you know that?" Adriz asked.

"Know what?" Mav asked.

"That there are beds and desks and stuff available in storage."

Mav wrinkled his nose. "I just know. It's like I think of what I need, and the answer pops up." He sensed a flash of uncertainty from Solanji. "What's the matter?"

"Nothing."

"There's definitely something bothering you; I felt it."

"Is Oji everywhere? Even with us in our bedchamber?" she asked via their mental connection.

Mav chuckled. *"He understands the concept of privacy."*

Solanji relaxed. *"Good. I don't like the idea of constantly being watched."*

"I don't think he is watching us. It is more of an awareness. He is the building, so he knows what is happening inside himself. But he can absent himself when required."

Mav smiled at Kiara's excited chatter as she led them through the halls, pointing out further bedchambers for Felather, Adriz, and his fledglings. There would be more than enough room for all of them.

"We need to return to the citadel," Mav said. "But we will come back very soon, and then you can give us the grand tour," he added quickly as Kiara's face fell. This was home. They would all work together to make it perfect.

He tensed at the spike of pain shooting through his head as a soulless took up residence. Someone else's memories spooled behind his eyes and settled.

"We need to figure out how to manage the arrivals," Oji murmured to him alone. *"That hurt."*

"I think that, along with a check of our defences, needs to be at the top of the to-do list," Mav replied. If Oji felt his pain, he was quite sure he would feel any attack on the Gate. The thought was worrisome. He could only hope Kaenera was as affected by the loss of his connection to the Gate as when Mav had been when severed from the citadel, but there was no guarantee.

"Agreed," Oji said.

Solanji leaned against Mav and pecked a kiss on his cheek. "Ellaria and I will go and get Shandra and meet you at the citadel. It's time we reunited our family."

"Thank you." Mav hugged her. "We'll all be glad to see her."

Once Solanji and Ellaria had left, Mav returned to his chambers in the citadel along with Adriz and started working on his plans to relocate to the Gate. He stopped when Solanji arrived with Shandra.

Mav rose from his chair as Shandra rushed into his arms exclaiming, "Mav!" She hugged him.

"My dear girl, it is so good to see you. Welcome to the citadel."

"I'm so happy to be here at last," Shandra replied, her voice muffled in his shirt.

Mav rubbed her back. "The boys have been eager for you to arrive."

Shandra raised her head. "I thought they'd be here with you."

"They're causing havoc in the city, but they'll be back for supper."

Shandra laughed. "You let them loose on their own?"

"They'll be alright," Mav said as he released her.

Solanji wrapped an arm around Mav's waist. "Ryvalin wants to come home. She's bored."

Mav chuckled. "Only Ryvalin would view a peaceful break as boring."

"I'm glad it has been peaceful. It's what those kids need." Solanji said. "Shandra, let me show you to the dormitory. You'll have a bedchamber to yourself, but you'll share the facilities with the boys, so you can catch up with them for supper. Mav and I won't be able to join you tonight, but we'll see you for first meal."

"We'll speak more tomorrow," Mav promised.

Shandra flashed him a smile as she followed Solanji out of the room. Once the door shut, Mav sat behind his desk, steepling his fingers. He had called his father, but he didn't know if Averdeus would appear.

His father had been…"unreliable" was the word Mav would use. Averdeus had been devasted to learn that Serenia had killed his wife, Mav's mother. To make it worse, he had not even had an inkling of Serenia's plans, let alone been able to protect his family from her machinations. As a result, he had left to nurse his wounded pride in private, leaving Amaridin and Demavrian to tend to their world. Demavrian didn't think he would return except to help them defeat Kaenera.

Mav could understand that deep sense of failure. If anything ever happened to Solanji, he would never forgive himself.

He was, therefore, surprised when his father did appear, not even two turns after he had requested his presence. The fact that he had responded so quickly, meant that the box of sigils was more of a threat than Mav had realised.

Mav rose and walked around his desk and straight into his father's arms. His father had never been that demonstrative, not until his brother had tried to kill his son. Mav inhaled the scent of his father, associating comfort and security with him. The only time he'd ever seen him falter was when he'd found out what Kaenera and Serenia had done. Seeing his father shatter had been a shock, and he offered him unstinting love and belief in return.

Averdeus released him. "Demavrian. I wasn't expecting your call. What has happened? Is Solanji alright?"

"Solanji is fine, Father." Mav took a deep breath. "We have a new issue. Kaenera attacked the Oblivion Gate. He was trying to retrieve the Aeora sigils."

"That's not possible." Averdeus paled. "How do you even know the name?"

"Father, I was there. I saw the box. Oji said they were the Aeora sigils."

"Oji?"

"The Oblivion Gate. I have claimed him, but Kaenera tried to steal the box while I was there."

"He couldn't! They are safe, buried far from here. No one knows where they are."

"I suggest you check because when I touched the box, I

saw death and destruction. And the sigils were like a burning flame swirling under the surface. Kaenera believes they can kill a god or the whole world. Is that true?"

Averdeus paced away and back. "Yes, it's true. That's why I had them hidden, buried. No one should know where they are."

"Oji said Kaenera stored them in the Gate and wants them back."

"No, that can't be right." Averdeus' expression was haunted. "I can't have failed that as well."

"Father, you need to check if the sigils are where you left them." Mav gripped his father's arm and gave him a slight shake to stop him from pacing.

Averdeus nodded, his gaze distant. "It will take me a while. I put multiple protections in place. I don't see how Kaenera could have found them."

"Then come with me to the Gate and see what is stored there."

Averdeus stared at him. "I'm not sure I can enter the Oblivion Gate. Let me check my safe spot first. If I can't find them, we can see if the Oblivion Gate will allow me entry. But Demavrian, pray that this it is not needed. The Aeora sigils should never see the light of day."

"They haven't yet, not while they are concealed within Oji. Is there a way to get rid of them?"

"No. That's why I had them buried. They are the only thing that could destroy you or me—or Kaenera."

"So, I could use them to kill Kaenera?"

"Demavrian, no one should use them. They would obliterate whatever is in their vicinity. Everything! Including the wielder."

"Then why would anyone create them?" Mav asked with a frown. "What is their purpose?"

Averdeus shook his head. "They are an abomination left

over from another world. I confiscated them to prevent this from ever happening. Kaenera must be mad if he thinks he can use them. The sigils would destroy everything; there would be nothing left for him to rule."

"I don't think that would be a deterrent for Kaenera. He was furious when I defeated him. I've never seen such unadulterated hatred. He would gladly sacrifice everything to destroy me and all I love. He wants the Gate back, and he'll do anything to get it."

Averdeus ran his hand through his hair. "Then you'd better make sure you have your protections in place. We can't afford for him to regain the Gate." He gripped Mav's arm. "And I don't want to lose you."

Mav grimaced. "You won't. I promise."

"Very well. I'll check to make sure the sigils are still concealed. Pray that they are."

Mav stared out the window for a long time after his father left. Somehow, no matter how hard he prayed, he didn't think his father was going to find them.

The door opened as Solanji returned. Her black eyes twinkled. "Your newest fledgling is somewhat overwhelmed by the citadel."

"Not surprising," Mav replied, pushing the worry of the Aeora sigils to the back of his mind. "I'm glad she's here, though. You'd better freshen up. We need to go and meet Amaridin and Valerian in a turn."

13

DEMAVRIAN – CITADEL

Mav twirled the glass between his fingers, his attention drifting as Solanji and Valerian discussed souls and soulmist. He struggled to repress the flinch as another spike of pain stabbed his mind. Memories flashed past as another soulless took up residence, and he gritted his teeth.

"I think I see where they are coming from," Oji murmured in his head. *"Maybe if I block the synapse, it will divert them. They have to pass through you. After all, you are the Gate Keeper, but it shouldn't incapacitate you. I'll work on it."*

Deliberately relaxing his clenched jaw, Mav took a sip of his wine and concentrated on what Valerian was saying.

"I think the SoulSingers will be glad to have a change in their responsibilities. I always said soulstripping was barbaric, and fortunately, Averdeus agrees. Amaridin will make an announcement in the morning."

"I'll need some help to match the souls with those who were soulstripped," Solanji said. "There are so many souls in the citadel that I don't know where to start."

"I'm sure we can provide the details of those who were

recently soulstripped.," Valerian said. "The SoulSingers should be able to assist in identifying them, and then you can return their souls to them."

Solanji exhaled, and Mav suddenly realised how worried she had been. He had been so caught up in his own problems that he hadn't noticed hers. "That would be a great help," she said.

Mav twined his fingers with hers, and she flashed him a smile. He squeezed her hand and said, "That would relieve some pressure on you. Returning souls will be exhausting enough."

Solanji shrugged. "I haven't done anything yet. The sooner we can start, the better. If we can reduce the number of souls, I'll have more chance of finding Brennan's soul. He needs to go home."

"Agreed," Mav murmured.

Valerian lifted his face as Amaridin paused beside him. Amaridin dropped a kiss on his lips and then refilled his glass. It was so unaffected and natural that Mav smiled as he watched them.

His brother's relaxed demeanour was in such contrast to the uptight Archdeus he had met a few weeks before. Valerian's presence completed him, and Amaridin had bloomed under his partner's attention. With the release of the constant strain he'd been under, he looked much younger, and he wore a permanent smile.

"When are you two getting heartsworn?" Mav asked. "I'm surprised you haven't already, to be honest."

Amaridin twisted his lips. "Father wants to make a big deal of it. He's planning a ceremony, the full regalia. He's inviting everyone." His voice rose, and Valerian stroked his arm, calming him. "He was kind enough to let us pick the date, so we chose the seventeenth, two weeks from now. That should keep him occupied with preparations and out of our hair."

"Amaridin would prefer a private ceremony," Valerian said with a smile.

"But Father won't hear of it." Amaridin glared at Mav. "Especially as you ran off and tied your knot in secret."

Mav laughed. "I must admit I was grasping at life while I could."

"As you should," Valerian agreed. "Your situation was unprecedented. We can only be thankful you met Solanji when you did."

Mav's fingers spasmed around Solanji's hand, and she rubbed his knuckles while her soul fingers caressed his shadows. His tight muscles relaxed under soothing ministrations, and he shoved the memories of Kyrill's torture chamber from his mind.

Valerian leaned forward, his eyes narrowing. "What haven't you told us?" he asked.

"About what?" Mav replied.

"About you," Amaridin said as he sat opposite him. "You've changed." He smiled sadly. "And don't tell me it's because you're now a Deus. You were different before. Quieter. More restrained. Even your oathsworn were worried. They never leave your side." He shrugged. "They still don't; I know Adriz is outside in the corridor."

"That's understandable, don't you think?" Solanji said when Mav stayed quiet. "They've only just found him after nearly fifty years. They are going to be a bit overprotective."

"It's more than that," Valerian said, his expression betraying his concern. "Out of all of us, you aged the most. I am glad to see your appearance has reverted nearer to what you used to look like, but why did it take so long?"

"I said that was what was different. You are the youthful general," Solanji said.

Valerian nodded.

"I'm not that person anymore," Mav said.

"You could be," Amaridin coaxed. "Oh, that reminds me. I have something of yours." He rose and crossed the room to the desk. The wooden slats rattled as he opened the cover and rummaged in the cubby holes.

"No. That person was idealistic, believed anything was possible, thought he knew it all," Mav replied, watching his brother. He had no idea what Amaridin could have of his.

"You're a god. Of course you can do anything," Valerian said gently, a small frown creasing the skin between his brows.

"The person I used to be didn't value life the way he should have. Eidolon taught me much in the years I was there. I took my life for granted. Living a life of luxury in Angelicus shields us from reality to a degree. Oh, I know that in council session, we discussed how we could improve life for the soulless." Mav waved his hand. "But we didn't understand what would really make a difference to these people. We assumed we knew what they wanted. We don't."

"And what do the people really want?" Valerian asked.

Mav stared at him for a moment. "Safety. Family. The ability to work to sustain themselves without being exploited. To us, basic rights. To the people of Eidolon, an impossible dream." He swallowed the lump growing in his throat as he thought of his fledglings. His vision misted, and he was aware of Solanji sliding her arm around his waist. He leaned into the offered comfort.

"The people of Eidolon have lost everything, from their souls to the sun and everything in between. Most are just waiting to die. They believe they are worthless and unwanted. They want their endless misery to end. How do you reverse such ingrained beliefs? Beliefs that we reinforced with the Divide."

As Amaridin returned, he said, "There was a valid reason for creating—"

"Not really," Valerian interjected.

Amaridin handed Demavrian a gold signet ring. His ring. Mav hadn't even thought of it in decades. When he had awoken in Eidolon, it had been gone. He'd assumed someone had stolen it and thought nothing more of it. He hadn't missed it, but now that it had been returned, he realised it was part of his identity. Of who he was. Deus Demavrian.

"How did you get it? I thought it was lost," Mav said in a low voice.

"I believe it was confiscated when you were arrested. With your reinstatement, the Host administrators apparently found a record of it as they updated your paperwork. They sent it to me."

"I'm surprised they kept it all these years."

Amaridin grinned. "You know the Host, good at following the rules when they choose to."

"They should have given it to me."

"I think they weren't sure what your reaction would be."

Mav huffed out a laugh. They were afraid of him now? "I wish it were as easy to return to the Eidolons all that they lost—and to remove that artificial divide we created."

"Demavrian is right," Valerian said as Mav rotated the ring, admiring the swirling D engraved over the wings in the background. He slid it on the little finger on his left hand. "Creating a natural structure, a sheer escarpment, and leaving the Eidolons stranded at the bottom was a pretty obnoxious move."

"Who were we protecting, and from what?" Mav asked, rubbing his throbbing temples. "You know, my head is crammed full of other people's memories, and they are not happy ones. There is strife, loss, pain, and grief. A sense of despair and despondency. There is no purpose, no hope in Eidolon, but they don't want to take that final step and end it all because they fear the Gate Keeper." He rolled the blue vendetta stone, hanging on a leather cord around his neck, between his fingers. The stone was smooth from constant rubbing, as was the red stone next to it.

"Why do you still have two of those?" Amaridin asked. "How did you gain two vendetta stones?"

Mav held up the blue one. "This is for the people of Eidolon. The red one is for Athenia."

"Athena's murder has been solved," Amaridin objected. "You're the one who proved Serenia was behind all the scheming and her death."

"But Serenia's sentence has not been carried out yet, not until I pass her through the Oblivion Gate."

"Then you need to get on with it and stop wasting time." Amaridin sighed and raised his eyebrows. "What are you still doing here?"

Mav grimaced. "Having dinner with you."

"Idiot," Amaridin said with an affectionate glance at him. "You know what I mean. Why aren't you off fulfilling those vendetta stones? That should be your objective."

"Defeating Kaenera is my objective, even if the council doesn't see the threat. I can't protect my family, the Gate, nor the people of Eidolon until I deal with him."

"But not by yourself," Solanji murmured from beside him. She was still caressing his shadow soul, and it felt like a warm soothing hug encompassing him.

"True," he replied, wanting to sink into her arms and forget everyone and everything else. "I need help."

"Then we'll help you," Amaridin said with a sharper edge to his voice. "Whatever you need, you ask for it. I'll make the council see reason."

At that, Mav sat up and blinked at his brother.

Amaridin scowled at him. "I'm not losing you again, Mav, so don't let Kaenera gain the upper hand. Tomorrow, you return to the Oblivion Gate, and you make sure it's yours."

"A toast," Valerian said as he raised his glass. "To the new Oblivion Gate Keeper."

"The Oblivion Gate Keeper," the others repeated as they clinked Mav's glass. They were interrupted by a loud knock on the door.

Adriz opened the door, and Felather stepped into the room. "Sorry to disturb you, but we've got trouble. Mav, you're needed at the guardhouse."

14

BAILEY – PURONIA

Bailey stared at the beautiful blue sky. Everything was so vibrant and colourful in Puronia; it was almost overwhelming after living in the predominantly grey palette of Eidolon. His stomach clenched as he remembered the rain and the mud, the blood and the pain. He swallowed. Living in the constant fear of being attacked or worse was draining, as were the memories which would not leave him be. He shoved the horrible memories away and said in a rush, "When do you think Shandra will arrive? I miss her. She should be here with us."

"That, I agree with," Kerris said.

"She won't leave Brennan or the kids for long," Muntra added.

"She might for a few days," Kerris replied. "Ryvalin and Xylvin are there, after all. Shandra should see Puronia. She can't decide whether to stay in Eidolon or move here without at least experiencing it."

"Move here?" Muntra asked.

"Well, if Solanji can flit back and forth, I don't see why Shandra can't," Kerris said.

"Mav's already done so much for us; it seems a little ungrateful to keep asking for more," Muntra said.

"I think Mav would be insulted if you said that to him," Bailey murmured, squeezing Muntra's hand. "We're his fledglings. He wants us to be happy. Shandra being here would make us happy."

"I've already asked him," Kerris said. "I'm sure she'll be here soon."

"Good." Bailey sighed out his breath and closed his eyes. It seemed an effort to open them again until memories of sitting outside the Oblivion Gate flashed through his mind. His heart racing, he stared at the sunlit streets, the stone buildings, the *life* filling this busy city.

"We shouldn't have explored so much. You're tired," Muntra whispered.

"No, I'm fine. There's something else we need to discuss." Bailey pinched his lips for a moment and pushed the words out. "I miss Kiara as well." There, he'd said her name out loud.

Muntra stiffened and tried to pull his hand away, but Bailey tightened his grip. Kerris curled up like a stray cat claiming its spot and began plucking blades of grass, one after the other, his head bent.

"I do," Bailey said, trying to keep his voice soft. "We never mention her, and it doesn't seem right. I miss her cheeky grin and her never-ending chatter."

Kerris smiled, his attention on the grass. "And how she'd always take things apart and improve them."

Muntra remained silent.

"She made me a knife to protect myself with," Bailey whispered, his voice not so steady.

"You shouldn't have needed it. I should have been there," Muntra said.

Bailey struggled to continue, ignoring Muntra's self-recrimination. Memories of Kiara shouting at him to go back flashed through his mind. He had left her there all alone. Abandoned her. "Once Shandra has seen the city, we should all go and visit Kiara at the Oblivion Gate."

Kerris and Muntra tensed and then exchanged concerned glances.

"Did I tell you I heard her when I was sitting outside the Oblivion Gate? She was yelling at me to go back."

"You went where?" Muntra exclaimed, his face paling. "Tell me you didn't."

The city landscape blurred as Bailey stared at it, and he swallowed before whispering, "Wasn't as if I had a choice."

"Of course you had a choice!" Muntra shouted, lurching to his feet. "You would have left me…us?"

"No!" Bailey's heart shredded at the expression of horror on Muntra's face. Everything he said, Muntra took personally. "I hadn't intended on leaving you. I was just so tired, and I found myself sitting on a bench outside a wrought-iron gate. Mav said it was the Oblivion Gate."

"Mav was there?" Kerris asked, watching him intently.

"Yes. He said I shouldn't be there."

"He was right about that," Muntra snapped. Hurt still coloured his voice, and Bailey flinched. Kerris scowled at Muntra.

"I said Kiara shouldn't be there on her own, and he said she wouldn't be because she would be with him, looking after the Oblivion Gate. He wanted me to help him from the side of the living."

"Bailey. I am so sorry, but Kiara is dead. She's already passed through the Gate," Kerris said gently, leaning forward to rub Bailey's leg.

"I know she's dead, but Mav said she was going to stay and help him look after the Gate."

"Kiara is at the Gate?" Muntra asked.

"Yes. Once Shandra is here, we should get Mav to take us so we can go and see her."

"Wait a minute. You saw the Oblivion Gate?" Kerris asked, awe tinging his voice.

Muntra kicked his foot.

"What?" Kerris frowned at Muntra.

"Bailey should never have been in the halls, let alone near the Gate."

"It was a lot smaller than I expected. A metal gate with latticework and flowers," Bailey said, drifting off into his memories.

"And you are not going back there. Wake up." Muntra shook Bailey, and Bailey's eyes snapped open. "Promise me you won't go back to the Oblivion Gate without me."

"We'll all go through it one day."

"But not anytime soon. Promise me, Bailey."

Muntra's distress penetrated his awareness, and Bailey's gaze sharpened. "I promise I won't leave you," he said quickly and leaned forward to kiss Muntra on the cheek. "I promise," he said again, and some of Muntra's distraught expression eased.

Then Muntra buried his face in Bailey's neck and shuddered.

Bailey hugged Muntra tight as tears dampened his skin. "I'm sorry," he whispered into Muntra's hair. "I'm so sorry."

Kerris cleared his throat. "You'll miss the sunset," he said, staring up at the sky.

Bailey wiped his eyes and stared in wonder at the brilliant colours stretching across the sky. On the horizon, a deep, virulent orange blazed as the sun crept lower. The orange sky was streaked with crimson and bled to swathes of yellow and then a pale blue that deepened the higher he gazed. "I would never have believed it if I hadn't seen it," he breathed.

"Doesn't seem real, does it?" Muntra whispered, sitting

close enough that his breath stirred Bailey's hair. Bailey leaned into his comforting bulk.

"Why doesn't the sun shine in Eidolon?" Kerris asked, a clear whine in his voice.

"We'll have to ask Mav. Maybe he can make it so it does," Bailey said. He fidgeted for a moment, his legs dangling over the edge of the grassy bank they were seated on.

"I could watch this forever." Muntra wrapped his arm around Bailey's shoulder, and Bailey struggled to repress the flinch. He couldn't help it. It wasn't Muntra he was afraid of; it was being touched. His heart sank as Muntra dropped his arm. Muntra must have felt Bailey's slight withdrawal. He was glad it was getting dark and Muntra couldn't see his flushed face.

"I think a sunrise might be even more spectacular," Kerris said as he looked around them. "Um, guys. We've got a problem."

Between one moment and the next, the orange ball of fire sank below the horizon, and complete darkness descended. After a brief pause, Muntra asked, "Did anyone think to bring a torch?"

Silence.

"I guess not. Do either of you know the way back to the citadel in the dark?"

"As long as we are going up, we can't miss it," Kerris said.

"What's that up in the sky?" Bailey asked as he peered above him in awe. "Is that a spray of lights? How do they stay up there?" He fell silent, and then said, "Is it safe? It's so...so...endless."

"I don't know," Muntra's said from behind him, his voice tense. "This is the first time we've been out when it's dark."

"They're called stars," Kerris said. "It's perfectly safe; it just is. You can see them because the sun set. Felather said they are always there but we can only see them when it's dark." He glanced around and exhaled. "We'd better get back, or we'll be late for supper. I'm starving."

Now that Kerris mentioned it, Bailey realised he was hungry, too.

Climbing down from the grassy bank and onto the path was simple. However, the maze of city streets defeated them. Every time they took the road leading upwards, it turned away from the citadel and confused them even more.

By the time they reached the citadel gates, they were exhausted, and the gates were firmly locked. The guards stared down at them from their lofty heights, and the boys retreated.

"How do we get in?" Bailey whispered, his heart fluttering in his chest.

"Once the gates are closed, they won't open them again until morning, according to the other fledglings," Kerris said.

"Maybe we could climb the wall?" Muntra muttered as he followed the stone barrier around the corner.

"It's far too high, and there are no footholds," Bailey said.

"We need a rope," Muntra said.

"Where are we going to find a rope?" Bailey asked, laying his hands flat on the curtain wall as he peered upwards. "We can't climb this."

Kerris snapped his fingers and darted off. He was soon back with a coil of rope over his shoulder.

"Where did you find that?"

"The well."

Bailey wrinkled his nose. "You took the rope from the community well? How are people going to get water?"

"I'll return it in the morning. Muntra, I'll climb onto your shoulders and between us, we help Bailey climb up us to the top. He can then tie off the rope so Muntra and I can climb over."

"What about the citadel guards?" Bailey whispered.

"As long as we're quiet, we should be ok. They concentrate on the gate."

"And you know that because…?" Bailey asked.

"That's what I heard. We'll be fine."

Bailey doubted that, but he was exhausted. He tied a noose at the end of the rope and coiled it over his shoulder. "Alright. Let's do this. I want to go to bed."

Muntra widened his stance and cupped his hands. Kerris stepped into them and then onto his thigh and then onto his shoulders. Balancing against the wall, he beckoned to Bailey. Sighing, Bailey stepped into Muntra's hands and let him lift him up, and then he carefully climbed up Muntra. Kerris hauled Bailey up beside him, and Muntra clamped his hands around Kerris' calves to steady him.

Bailey clung to Kerris. After a precarious wobble, he hissed his breath out and, gritting his teeth, stepped into Kerris' hands and then onto his shoulders. They all swayed, and Bailey yelped as he wedged his fingers into a crack in the wall to anchor them. "Never again," he muttered under his breath as his stomach cramped and he breathed in the tang of stone.

"Ow, that's my ear," Muntra grumbled.

"If you'd stop moving, it would be much easier," Kerris hissed in reply.

"It's not me that's swaying; it's you. I'm solid as a rock here, but you'd better hurry up."

"Will you both shut up?" Bailey whisper-shouted. "Do you want us to get caught?"

The top of the wall was still just out of his reach. Bailey stepped on Kerris' head and pushed up, teetering for a moment as Kerris cursed him under his breath. Kerris gripped his ankles, and once they'd steadied, he uncoiled the rope and tried to flip the noose over one of the jutting crenelations. He missed and had to coil the rope back up.

"Any time now would be good," Kerris said through clenched teeth.

Bailey was successful the second time.

Pushing off Kerris, Bailey climbed up the rope and, with some effort, over the top of the wall. Squirming through a gap in the crenelations, he landed with a thud in a breathless heap on the parapet walk. He cringed as a metal pole clattered to the ground, the clang echoing in the silence.

A loud curse from below had him peering down through a gap. Below him, Muntra and Kerris sprawled on the grass, groaning. "Sorry!" he whispered. When he had pushed off Kerris, they must have overbalanced.

"Throw us the rope!" Kerris shouted, trying to keep his voice low but not really succeeding.

Bailey shook his head and threw the rope over the side.

Kerris clambered up the wall and grunted as he levered himself over the top. They were both leaning over the wall, encouraging Muntra as he climbed, when someone cleared their throat behind them. Bailey froze, his stomach dropping, and then he turned around. He shuffled closer to Kerris at the sight of a stooped, grey-haired man flanked by two guards. The man was incongruously dressed in his nightshirt and a thick cloak.

"Kerris?" Bailey asked as he gripped his arm. He couldn't prevent the tremor in his voice.

"It'll be alright," Kerris murmured, stepping in front of him.

"I think this must be a first. People breaking into the citadel? Are you that desperate to see an angel?" the elderly man asked, his voice breathy and low. The two guards scowled at them over his shoulder.

"No, sir," Kerris replied. "We got locked out. We were just trying to get back in."

The man raised an eyebrow. "By climbing over the wall? How novel."

"This would have been so much easier if Xylvin were here," Muntra said from behind them. "She would have given us a lift," he continued as he heaved himself over the wall. "Appreciate your help, by the way." His voice died away as he realised they had company.

"And who are you to know Xylvin by name?" the man asked. "Though I grant you, she would have been a better solution than the pickle you now find yourselves in. Breaking into the citadel? From the racket you were making, I'm amazed the guards didn't hear you. I heard you."

"Our apologies if we disturbed you, Master," Kerris said quickly. "We did not mean to wake you."

"Of that, I am sure. Only foolish people want to be caught when breaking and entering, and you don't strike me as foolish. Noisy but not stupid."

"We're not trying to steal anything. We're just trying to go to bed," Bailey said indignantly.

"Interesting. So, you belong here? Who do you look to?"

After a moment of silence and fearful glances, Kerris deflated. "We're Deus Demavrian's fledglings."

"Mav is going to kill us. So is Adriz," Muntra muttered.

"Demavrian?"

They were interrupted as the citadel's guards stormed up the steps to the parapet. The walkway was suddenly crowded, and the elderly man chuckled. Then he coughed.

"You shouldn't be out in the damp air with that cough, sir," Kerris said as a citadel guard clamped a hand on his shoulder.

The man didn't reply, just watched the fledglings as they were marched off to the guardhouse. "The captain of the guard has some explaining to do. Children defeating his defences. Whatever next?"

"You should return inside, Master Xabier," one of his guards spoke from behind him.

"Yes, yes, don't fuss. I want to speak to Demavrian. Send him a message for me."

"Yes, sir."

15

———

KAENERA – CROSSROADS, EIDOLON

As Kaenera watched his troops silently approach the Crossroads, splitting up to surround the raucous tavern, which blazed with light in the misty drizzle and the sprawl of merchants' tents, he held his calope still in the shadows and slowly smiled.

The Crossroads were a couple of leagues from the Divide and were the main meeting point, the place where the people of Angelicus and Eidolon truly met and mingled. After days of hard bargaining, the merchants collected within the tavern, drank the piss-poor ale, and swapped stories before heading home to Puronia.

Kaenera couldn't send a clearer message to those who thought they ruled. His failed attempt on the Oblivion Gate would not stop him. Grinding his teeth, he ignored the recent humiliation. His calope shifted beneath him. He had to send a message as quickly as possible. He was not defeated. Nothing was out of his reach, but he'd lull them to begin with, make them think his focus was on Eidolon, that his gaze only fell on retrieving the Oblivion Gate.

Raising his hand, he brought it down in a sharp chopping motion, and flaming arrows seared across the night sky. They thudded into the wooden roof, and small pockets of fire slowly burned through the panels. A cry of alarm was swiftly silenced as his dybbuks rushed forward, with one group cutting down anyone who peered out of their tent and the second troop storming the tavern.

Screams faded into low gurgles and the aroma of spilt blood drifted in the air.

Dybbuks kicked in the tavern's front door and poured into the building. More screams pierced the darkness, and Kaenera leaned forward, eager to see the occupants rushing out of the back door like terrified frellers searching for the nearest burrow.

He only wanted those with the intelligence to try and escape; the rest, his dybbuks could slaughter. The back door slammed open, and desperate men rushed out and straight into his trap. Nooses dropped over their heads and cinched tight, cutting off airways. They were not so smart after all. Men dropped like felled trees and Kaenera's dybbuks swarmed all over them.

His captives were quickly trussed up as they tried to regain their bearings. Sacks were tugged over their heads and tied in place, disorienting them even more. It didn't take long for them to be loaded on a wagon and taken away, more recruits to his cause.

Thick smoke coiled into the air, and the crackle of flames grew louder as they took hold. The fresh tang of blood mingled with the acrid stench of the burning tavern. Beams sagged and with a huge roar, the roof collapsed.

Buildings weren't constructed to last in Eidolon. If Kaenera had his way, he would burn them all to the ground and start again. His buildings would last.

He dismounted and handed the reins off to a nearby

dybbuk. There had been little resistance, not that he thought drunken merchants would put up much of a fight.

Shadows flickered in the light of the fires as tents went up in flames. Bodies were dragged out of the collapsing tents and piled in front of the tavern. Some moved feebly, but none rose.

Beasts squealed as they were herded out of the pens. They didn't have time to herd all the animals back to his garrison, but the smaller animals could be loaded up on wagons while the rest were slaughtered.

Kaenera's calope stirred nervously as blood gushed from slit throats, coating the soil with an ever-growing puddle of red liquid. He wanted the ground to be drowned in blood, and animal blood would work just as well as human.

The dirt squelched beneath his boots as he crossed to the growing pile of bodies.

"Help me," a low voice moaned, and Kaenera paused. He bent over the dying man and stroked his cheek, smearing blood over ashen skin. Kaenera inhaled the scent of his fear, of his pain. The man wore worn boots and frayed clothes, and under the tang of blood, Kaenera detected the aroma of livestock. A farm worker. Soulless.

"I only help those who help me," he said and unsheathed his dagger. "Know that you die in agony so that you may be my messenger." Hovering over the man, he bared his teeth. "Give my regards to Demavrian," he said and plunged his blade into the man's chest. The man screamed as Kaenera slowly cut his chest open and wrenched his heart out.

Rising with the blood-drenched organ in his hand, Kaenera searched the yard. As the soulless died, they should come to him, begging him to pass them through the Oblivion Gate or swearing their allegiance if they could just serve him and exist for a bit longer, but none were waiting for him to gather into his arms.

Kaenera clenched his fist, squishing the bloody organ between his fingers, warm and slick but no longer beating. They had all gone to Demavrian. He hoped Demavrian struggled to cope with them all. Flinging the remnants away from him, he returned to his calope. Mounting, he surveyed the massacre, and satisfaction filled him.

There hadn't been enough time for Demavrian to understand the Gate yet. He wouldn't be able to pass the soulless through easily. And the screaming agony of death would only make it worse. The soulless would be like a punch to the gut.

When Demavrian realised what had happened, Kaenera would be victorious once again.

All that would be left were death and destruction.

Demavrian couldn't be everywhere at once.

He wouldn't be able to protect everyone.

This failure would hurt.

16

DEMAVRIAN – CITADEL

Mav took a deep breath before knocking on the chamber door. He hadn't seen Xabier since he had returned to Angelicus. A mistake, maybe, but he'd hardly had time to think since he'd been back. Xabier had been one of the elder councillors, once custodian of the citadel, and a good one at that. Even though he was now retired, he still held influence, a fact Mav had forgotten in his haste to prove his innocence.

And of course his fledglings would stumble across him. They were a magnet for trouble. He should have known.

The door creaked open, revealing a dim interior. He passed through the outer chamber and entered the well-lit room. A hollow cough greeted him, and Mav frowned. He stepped through the doorway, and his frown deepened at the sight of Xabier huddled in an armchair, a shawl draped over his shoulders, his wispy grey hair framed his thin face. Lines creased his skin and crinkled around his eyes.

"Xabier, it has been too long, my friend. I wasn't aware you've been unwell."

Xabier waved his hand. "Why would you? You've had

your hands full, from what I hear." He peered up at Mav. "And still do, I think."

Mav smiled as he bent over and clasped Xabier's hand. "It's certainly not peaceful. Is there anything I can do to ease your discomfort?"

"I'm just old. Age gets most of us mortals in the end. Sit down. I'll strain my neck peering up at you."

Mav sat in the chair opposite and accepted a cup of bannoe when offered it by one of Xabier's attendants. He took a sip and then smiled at Xabier. "You wanted to see me?"

Xabier nodded. "Your fledglings. They intrigue me."

Mav raised an eyebrow. "Intrigue?"

"It's not often you get woken up by the sound of someone trying to climb over the curtain wall."

Lips twitching, Mav leaned forward to put his cup on a side table. "They are certainly adventurous."

"Determined, I would say. But I don't understand why they had the need."

"I haven't spoken to them yet. I thought I'd let them stew in the guardhouse while I chatted with you."

"Don't leave them there too long," Xabier said, his face wrinkling in concern.

"I won't. I'll retrieve them as soon as we've finished."

"I wanted you to know that they would have made it in if I hadn't caught them. There were no guards on the parapets, and there should have been."

"The guards have become lax," Mav said and then sighed. "In more ways than I would have thought possible. I don't understand why."

"You underestimate the influence of your generalship. Once, there were consequences for failures. You held them accountable. You need to reinstate that practice."

"Amaridin will have to reinstate the practice. Now that

I've claimed the Gate, Eidolon will take all my attention. There is much to put right there as well."

"Make sure you influence him, then, before you leave. And don't doubt it; you will be missed. You've been missed these last five decades."

"I would suggest my father was missed more."

Xabier waggled his hand in a "maybe" gesture. "It is unfortunate Lynen is the captain of the guard. He is resistant to suggestion."

Mav lips pinched, and then he exhaled. "He doesn't like me. I know that much. I'm hoping he'll listen to Amaridin or Julius."

"He shouldn't need convincing." Xabier tutted, and then his gaze grew piercing. "Where did you find your fledglings?"

"In Eidolon, of course. They each have their own contribution to make. If I can keep them alive long enough, that is."

"They won't make it easy," Xabier said with a laugh, which descended into a coughing fit.

Mav took the glass of water one of the attendants brought over and waited for Xabier to catch his breath. "I was going to suggest they come to you tomorrow and apologise for disturbing you, but if you are not well enough, they can come another time."

"I don't have much time left. Tomorrow is fine. I'd like to speak to them."

"I'll send them up about fourth turn. Give you time to rest. I can ease the tightness in your chest if you would just relax for a moment."

Xabier waved him away. "Don't fuss. I hate fussers."

"It's not fussing when I can do something to help you feel better. I would not leave you suffering unnecessarily."

Scowling at him, Xabier suddenly capitulated and leaned back in his chair—a sign, Mav thought, of how unwell he was.

"Do your worst," Xabier said.

Mav observed him, from the pallor of his skin to his breathlessness. He placed his hand on Xabier's chest and sent his senses skimming through his body. He internally winced at the congestion clogging the man's lungs.

"Have you seen a healer recently?"

Xabier didn't reply.

Breaking down the congestion, Mav encouraged the excess fluid out of Xabier's lungs and into his digestive system so that he could pass it naturally. He waited as Xabier took an easier breath and then another. Mav persuaded his body to drowse, and the tension in Xabier's frame relaxed. "You need to rest. Drink plenty of fluids. I'll send the healer to check on you."

Xabier grabbed Mav's wrist. "I still want to see your fledglings at four."

"As long as you agree to rest until then."

"If you insist," Xabier said with a sigh.

Mav caught the eyes of Xabier's attendant, and the man nodded.

"I'll leave you to rest, then. I'll see you again soon."

"Make sure you do," Xabier replied, his eyelids already drooping.

Mav rose. Xabier would sleep and feel much better for it.

Crossing the room, intending to leave for the guardhouse, Mav stiffened as a wave of soulless bombarded him, and he gasped for breath under the onslaught. The souls were anguished. Images of death and carnage filled his mind, and he shuddered.

"Demavrian? Are you alright?" Xabier's voice was faint. Mav braced himself against the wall as image after image of broken bodies, slaughtered livestock, puddles overflowing with blood, the burning tavern. He recognised the

Crossroads and pushed himself upright. Acrid smoke filled his lungs, and he choked. Then he saw Kaenera.

Devilish eyes, gleaming with hatred, stared down at him as the blade plunged into Mav's chest, and agony swept through him along with the whispered words, "Give Demavrian my regards."

"No," Mav moaned, somehow on his knees as strong hands held him in place. He clutched his chest, expecting to see blood spurting everywhere, and his vision was drenched with blood.

"Hold him." Xabier's voice came from a distance. "Demavrian? Can you hear me? Get Felather, quickly."

More soulless bombarded him, too many to count, and he panted for breath. He was on fire, yet he was freezing. His body hurt, his head was on the edge of exploding, and all he could see was blood.

His heart throbbed in time with his head, and he gritted his teeth as he regained control of his breathing.

"Mav?" Oji whispered through his mind, and Mav winced. *"What was that?"*

"Too many soulless dying at once," Mav managed to reply before he was manhandled into a chair.

Gentle fingers rubbed his temples, cool against his over-heated skin. Felather was here. "Just sit a moment. Collect yourself." Felather's voice was a soft caress.

"I'll kill him," Mav mumbled as darkness clouded his vision.

"Not right now," Felather soothed. "Don't try and move. Catch your breath."

"I need to…"

"No, you don't."

Mav stiffened and glared at Felather. "Yes, I do. Kaenera just massacred everyone at the Crossroads."

"If everyone is dead, then there is no point rushing

anywhere," Xabier said from behind him, his voice harsh. "And going on your own would be suicide."

Mav swivelled to glare at Xabier, and then he swallowed as he noticed his shadows swirling around him. He slowly reined them in and took a deep breath.

"You need to send a troop to investigate and confirm while you rescue your fledglings," Xabier said. "The Host are just loitering here. Amaridin can spare them. You cannot be dashing off to deal with everything yourself. You'll only wear yourself out." He gestured at Mav. "You are in no fit state to fight anyone, so delegate."

"He's right," Oji said in his head.

Mav stared at Xabier and then gave him a tired smile. "Fine. I'll go and speak with Amaridin. Felather, would you go and retrieve our fledglings from the guardhouse?"

"Of course," Felather replied, giving him a searching inspection.

"I'll be fine," Mav said. "It was just a shock. That many soulless arriving all at once was unexpected. I'll ask Xylvin to go and check the Crossroads."

"That is an excellent idea. I'll meet you back in your chambers."

Leaving Xabier's rooms, Felather descended the stairs and headed for the guardhouse. Arriving at the stone building, he paused on the threshold and inspected the occupants. He focused on remaining calm when it was obvious Mav's fledglings were not present, which meant the guards had locked them in a cell. Normally, he would have let that slide as a just punishment, but seeing as the fledglings were still new to the citadel, vulnerable, and had not offered any violence, he was prepared to take offence.

"I am Scribe Felather. I understand Deus Demavrian's fledglings are here," he stated as he entered the room. "I don't see them. Have you already released them?"

The guards all stiffened but remained silent.

"Well? Are you going to tell me what you've done with them?"

"They're in a cell."

Felather stared at the guard who had spoken. "A cell? Three boys were such a threat that you couldn't contain them?"

"They attempted to attack the citadel," another guard said, belatedly adding, "sir."

"Rubbish. They were unarmed, wearing fledgling attire, and I am quite sure they told you they looked to Deus Demavrian. Otherwise how would you have known to send him the message?"

"Captain Lynen said to lock them up."

"Well, I am here now, and I suggest you unlock them."

"Are you prepared to pay their fines?"

"Fines for what?" Felather demanded, unable to keep the edge from his voice.

"Damages."

"For?"

"They stole the community well rope to scale the walls."

"And no one stopped them? They could have been seriously injured if they fell."

The guard shrugged, and Felather's ire ratcheted up a notch. "I see. And where is the captain?"

"Doing his rounds."

"I am not waiting for him. So, they owe damages for one rope. Anything else?"

"No, sir."

"Tell me how much they owe, and then you can take me to these dangerous criminals and release them into my care."

Felather dropped enough coins on the table to cover the fine. "A receipt."

Once he had the piece of paper securing their release, he followed the guard down the steps, shivering as recent memories intruded. His anger grew when he found the fledglings incarcerated in separate cells. The guards hadn't even locked them in together. "Bailey first," he said. "That one."

The guard flicked a nervous glance at him and hurriedly unlocked the cell. Felather entered, hissed his breath out, and gathered the little bundle of misery in his arms.

"You're safe now," he murmured in Bailey's ear. The boy snuggled closer while Felather waited for the guard to release Kerris and Muntra.

"Did they hurt him?" Muntra demanded, worry clouding his expression. "He wouldn't answer me."

"We haven't touched any of them," the guard replied, jutting out his chin.

"But you've done enough damage all the same," Felather said as he climbed the stairs, the fledglings close behind. He didn't stop when he reached the guardhouse, and the guards let him go after one look at his furious expression. "You two alright?" he asked over his shoulder.

"Yes, Felather."

He relaxed slightly at their subdued responses. At least he only had the more sensitive Bailey to worry about for now.

Bailey stirred in his arms. "There were too many of them," he said, his voice shaking.

"Too many what?" Felather asked. As he strode down the hallway, staff skittered out of his way.

"Memories," Bailey whispered.

Felather exhaled. Bailey's latent cherub skills were waking. The cell would have been mental torture for such a sensitive lad as him. The terror and fear of previous inmates, including Mav's, would have seeped into the stone. "Are the memories still crowding you?"

"No, but they were horrible, and I can't forget them." Bailey shuddered.

Felather tightened his arms. Mav should have given them their journeyman designations. If he had, they might have been treated more sympathetically, though Felather had a feeling that, in this instance, it wouldn't have made any difference. "I'm so sorry, Bailey. They should never have incarcerated you in a cell."

"Not your fault. We shouldn't have embarrassed the guards."

Felather grimaced. Bailey had understood the reason for the guards' extreme reactions. His empathy was growing stronger by the day. Sero, the cherub Mav had asked to mentor Bailey, would have his hands full.

Bailey sighed into his neck. "You can put me down now. I feel much better. You are so comforting. Thank you."

"My pleasure," Felather replied as he set him on his feet and steadied him. Bailey hugged him and then went to hug Muntra. He clung to Muntra's hand as they walked the last few corridors to Mav's rooms.

Once they were inside Mav's chambers, Felather sent for hot bannoe and supper. While they were eating, Mav arrived, and he hurried to check that they were alright and ask what had happened.

Felather observed him. Mav still looked pale, but he was hiding his recent shock well.

"Any news from Xylvin?" Felather asked, though he thought it was still too early.

Mav shook his head and frowned at his fledglings. He asked in some bewilderment, "Why didn't you bang on the gate and request entry?"

"We thought it was too late and the guards wouldn't open it," Kerris said.

"Did you try?"

The boys exchanged sheepish glances.

"Of course you didn't." Mav sighed. "You thought it would be much better to break into a highly defended fortress. Are you sure you are not hurt?"

The boys were quick to put Mav's fears to rest. Only their pride which was dented.

"Tomorrow, Felather will explain the rules of entry so you don't find yourself in this predicament again. I think it best if you avoid the captain of the guards. I have spoken to Master Xabier, who is expecting all three of you to present yourselves in his apartment in the East Tower at fourth turn. You have apologies to make. Do not be late."

Felather added with a scowl, "You also need to pay for the new rope for the community well. You ruined the other one. I'm amazed it didn't snap under your weight. You could have been seriously injured!" Not only had the rope stretched, leaving it dangerously thin, but the guards were armed with crossbows. The boys could have been killed.

"It seems you cannot be trusted on your own," Mav said. "You will not leave the citadel without an escort. Apply to Adriz or Felather as needed.

"You should also know that if you had returned as promised for supper, you would have seen Shandra, who arrived today. Instead, you left her to eat her meal on her own, deserted on her first night in the citadel. When you see her tomorrow, I think you also owe her an apology." At their distraught expressions, Mav refrained from adding anything further.

Once they finished their supper, he said, "Go and get cleaned up and go to bed. First lesson tomorrow, without fail, is with Felather."

Three very dejected boys left his study, and Felather suppressed a relieved grin as he watched them go. Solanji entered not long after and was soon followed by Adriz, and he relaxed as they discussed damage control.

"I was going to suggest they avoid Lynen, but I think it may be better if they at least apologise," Mav said.

Felather frowned. "Would that not call attention to the guards' lapse, though? I'm not sure what our fledglings would be apologising for. It's the guards who should be apologising to them."

"I'll think about it. It might help alleviate some of the ill feeling."

"It would put our fledglings in a vulnerable position."

"But *I* will be with them," Mav said. And no one in their right mind would say he was weak.

17

FELATHER – CITADEL

The next morning, Felather stood at the front of the chamber that had been allocated for the fledglings' lessons and silently inspected them one by one. "I'm disappointed in all of you. Mav trusted you to be responsible."

"We wanted to see the sunset," Kerris muttered to the table.

"Then you should have asked for permission. You knew Mav expected you back by supper."

"We got lost," Bailey said in a small voice.

"So, I need to teach you how to navigate Puronia as well as how to knock on a door and ask for entry?"

The boys squirmed under his critical gaze.

"Your behaviour reflects on Demavrian. He is your sponsor. He is responsible for everything you do." Felather took a deep breath and controlled his voice. The boys were penitent enough, but they needed to understand the consequences of their behaviour. "He's had to smooth things over with Captain Lynen, the guards, and Master Xabier. Demavrian has enough to deal with, without you causing extra work for him."

"We never meant—" Muntra began.

"But you still did, anyway," Felather interrupted. "First thing this morning, I was replacing the rope you stole from the well. People were complaining they couldn't get water. More complaints that Demavrian will have to deal with."

"We would have taken it back, but the guards confiscated it," Kerris said.

"We're sorry," Bailey whispered, his shoulders drooping.

"It's not me you need to apologise to. It's Demavrian, Master Xabier, and the captain of the guard, whom you have managed to completely humiliate. I doubt he is going to look kindly on you for the foreseeable future." *And that could be a problem,* Felather thought. "Once you've apologised to him, I recommend you keep out of his line of sight. He will not do you any favours."

With that thought in mind, Felather began to pace. "You are having lunch with Demavrian. After that, he will escort you to the captain's office. You will return here for map-reading lessons. There will be a test afterwards. At four, Demavrian will escort you to Master Xabier's chambers." His lips twitched at their downcast expressions. He doubted they would have much appetite for lunch.

A shadow hovered in the doorway, and Felather beckoned her in. He relaxed and grinned at the boys. "But first, I think it's time you met your new classmate. Shandra, welcome to Puronia!"

Chairs scraped as the boys leapt to their feet, and Shandra was engulfed in happy hugs.

Felather leaned against a desk and watched the reunion with a small smile on his face. After a moment, he clapped his hands. "Back to lessons. Please sit. You can chat at lunch."

Once they were all seated, he twisted his lips and said, "I can't believe you didn't try to knock on the door first before trying something so dangerous as to climb over the wall. The guards could have killed you."

"You did what?" Shandra gasped. She glared at Kerris as he sank lower in his seat. "I leave you alone for a few days, and you start doing crazy stunts like that. Why?"

"We couldn't get in. I was told that once the gates were locked, you would be refused entry."

"First lesson. Do not believe everything you hear. Check with someone you trust. That is me, Adriz, Solanji, or Mav."

"Or Sero?" Bailey asked.

"Or Sero," Felather said. "Second lesson. The citadel is a political minefield. Everyone is out for something. They will only offer advice if there is something in it for them. Do not assume it is well meant or true."

Shandra raised a hand. "I don't understand. Why is everyone so selfish?" She gestured at the citadel around them. "They have so much already."

Felather shrugged. "That's politics. It seems that people everywhere are prepared to step on others if it means they can achieve their goals. The possibility of power goes to people's heads."

"It doesn't go to Mav's head," Shandra said with a scowl.

"Which shows that it is possible to behave with more consideration for others. Take note. Lesson three. Mav is your sponsor. Your behaviour reflects on him. Think twice before causing him more trouble."

"I'm never leaving the citadel again," Bailey mumbled.

"Yes, you will. Because at dawn tomorrow, I will take you all to see your first sunrise."

"You will?" Kerris stared at him in shock.

Felather smiled. "It was our error. Of course you want to see the sun rise and set. For us, it is normal; for you,

Angelicus is a wonder you need to explore. If you stay out of trouble, we'll show you more."

The beaming smiles of his charges rewarded him. He nodded. "Good. Then, let's start with the citadel regulations. This is not a prison, and you should be able to come and go as you wish."

Felather kept them working until the timepiece turned twelve, and then he escorted them back to Mav's chambers for lunch with him and Solanji. Felather grinned at them and then left.

Mav had deliberately asked for a light lunch of pastries, vegetables, and bread, but judging from the way the boys were playing with their food, their nerves were getting the better of them. Mav gave up trying to get them to eat properly, realising he should have taken them to Lynen first thing. Only Shandra ate a proper meal, exclaiming over the dishes.

"Bailey, do you think you could replicate this dish? What is it? Root vegetables in a honey glaze? They are so sweet!"

Bailey smiled at her and shrugged before looking back down at his plate.

"That's enough. Lynen is not going to eat you," Mav said with some heat. "We're going now, just so you will all lighten up." He threw his napkin on the table. "Solanji, ask the kitchen to keep the food warm for us. They'll be hungry later."

"Of course," she replied, watching the fledglings with some sympathy.

"I'm coming with you," Shandra said, standing as well. "The guards need to know there are four of us and we stick together." And then she ruined it by saying, "Even if you are idiots!"

Mav tried not to laugh, especially when he caught Solanji's eye. "We'll be back soon."

"I'll be with Sero if you need me."

Mav nodded. Sero was helping Solanji search through the citadel, trying to match some of the lost souls to the register, though the souls were agitated and not easy to identify.

Mav kept the visit short. He didn't even give Lynen time to say anything except to acknowledge the fledglings' apologies, leaving the man in no doubt of his opinion as he pinned him with an icy glare.

"We apologise for any inconvenience we caused by our ill-considered actions," Kerris, the self-proclaimed spokesperson, said. He seemed determined to prevent Bailey from even speaking to the man.

"We never meant to cause any harm," Muntra added.

"We will knock on the gate if it ever happens again," Kerris said.

"But it won't," Bailey said, his voice a faint whisper as he stared at the floor.

"I'll make sure it doesn't," Shandra said with a firm nod.

Mav glared at the man until he flushed and stuttered, "Apology accepted." Then Mav bundled the fledglings out of the room.

Exhaling, Mav said brightly, "Well done! Come with me. I need to show you something."

He led the way through the courtyard and down the curving road towards the city. The fledglings exchanged glances and followed. After many twists and turns, Mav stopped outside a small brick building with windows that extended into the street. Jars of lumpy shapes filled the window.

He grinned at them. "This will be your new favourite haunt!" he said with a mischievous gleam in his eye.

"Why?" Bailey asked, his depressed demeanour lightening a little bit at Mav's excitement.

"This is the Emporium. Come inside and let me show you," Mav replied as he opened the door and entered. "Meri? Is that you? Where's your mother?"

The plump, grey-haired woman behind the counter gasped, and her jaw dropped. "Demavrian? Dear Lord above. Gerry! It's Demavrian!" she shouted over her shoulder as she hurried into the main shop. Her blue eyes sparkled with joy. "I thought we'd lost you! It's been so long. We've been hearing the most terrible stories about you. Ma was right worried."

"Well, you can ignore most of them, I'm just fine," Mav replied as he hugged her. He smiled ruefully. "It's been longer than I realised." The last time he had seen Meri, she had been a lissom young woman with vibrant auburn hair.

"This used to be my favourite shop when I was your age," he said to the fledglings.

"And when you were older," Meri said. "I am so happy to see you. Ma is long retired, but I married Gerry and we've got three of our own now."

"That's wonderful. I am so happy for you. These are my fledglings. Shandra." Mav pulled the girl forward, and Shandra smiled and offered her hand to Meri. "Bailey, Kerris, and Muntra."

"It's a pleasure to meet you," Meri said, shaking Shandra's hand.

"These are your new best customers, only they have no idea what you sell or what they'll like. They've never tasted anything like this before."

Meri's eyes widened. "How could they not…?"

"We're from Eidolon," Bailey said in a whisper.

Meri smiled at him and gently cupped his face. "Then you are in for a treat!" she replied. She clasped his hand and tugged him forward. "Which do you prefer? Savoury or sweet?"

"Sweet."

"Nuts or fruit?"

"Fruit."

"Bitter or smooth?"

"Nuts or fruit?"

Bailey hesitated. "I don't know."

Meri smiled. "Then let's find out." She placed two white dishes before Bailey, and the fledglings crowded around, eager to see what she was doing. "Try this." Meri sliced a thin sliver off a beige-coloured bar and lay it on the dish. Then she sliced a darker bar with red lumps in it and put that on the other.

She watched Bailey intently as he nibbled the first one, and she laughed at his surprised expression. "Mmm, that is so creamy."

"Try the other."

"Oh!" Meri nodded in satisfaction. "It's like a berry exploded in my mouth."

"That is a dewberry. Best picked at dawn and combined with my dark alvo, it is exquisite."

"Exquisite," Bailey repeated as he popped the rest of the alvo in his mouth.

"That's Demavrian's favourite," she said with a smile. "It's called Dewberry Delight." She gave Mav a slice, and he moaned with pleasure.

"God, it's been so long," he mumbled, flushing as Meri cackled.

"So, you'll need plenty of dewberry. Who's next?" She laughed as the fledglings jostled to be first. She handed both

Bailey and Mav a package tied with a purple ribbon and then smiled at Shandra.

"Savoury," Shandra said immediately. "I don't like things too sweet."

Meri nodded. "Try this. The saltiness combined with the alvo is a surprisingly tasty combination." She placed a pale blue slice on the plate. "And try this for contrast. Cheese can work really well."

Shandra broke off a piece of the blue slice and slapped Kerris' hand away. "It's mine," she said as Meri chuckled.

"There have been wars fought over Meri's alvo," Mav said, peering in his bag and selecting another piece.

"Mmm," Shandra said. "I never tasted anything so delicious." She broke off a piece of the yellow slice and wrinkled her nose. "No, I prefer the blue one."

"Salted alvo for you then. Though try this." Meri offered her a knobbly brown cluster, and then offered the others one as well.

Shandra bit into it and froze. An expression of pure joy spread over her face. "What is that?" she asked.

"An alvo cluster. It has cream, salt, and core nuts."

"I love it."

"So do I," Kerris said. "I thought I'd like sweet."

"I expect you will need to sample something different each time you visit. Tastes change over time, though dewberry has always been the best," Mav said from behind them. "We'll take a couple of bags of the cluster, but let them each choose one flavour for themselves."

"So, Kerris, you like sweet?" Meri asked.

"Yes, though not fruity."

"Hmm, try the Flirtby. Cream base, mallows and biscuit."

Kerris' eyebrows rose as he stuffed the rest of the alvo in

his mouth. Meri laughed. "Flirtby for Kerris. How about you, Muntra?"

"I don't know," Muntra said.

"He loved the silk berries, but we rarely found them," Bailey said. "I used to preserve them for him, so he could at least get a taste now and then."

"Silk berries? Good choice! You will love this. I call it Angel's Gift. I named it after you, Demavrian." She placed a multi-coloured slice on the dish and waited. Muntra picked it up and shoved it in his mouth.

"You did?" Mav asked.

"Yes, something rare and beautiful."

"I don't remember it."

"You wouldn't. I created it when you went missing. A way to remember you. It's one of my best sellers." She handed him a slice.

Mav's groan drowned out Muntra's. "That is amazing. Solanji will love it. Add a couple of bags to the pile."

Meri did as asked and then found a larger bag to put them all in.

"Everyone chosen one?" Mav asked before placing a large number of coins on the counter. "Meri, thank you."

"My pleasure," she replied, scooping the coins into her hand.

"We'll be back," Bailey said, and the other fledglings reinforced his promise.

The return journey to the citadel passed quickly, helped along by the fledglings swapping their alvo to try other flavours.

A much happier group entered Mav's rooms than had left. "Don't eat them all at once," Mav said as he retrieved his packages and the ones for Solanji.

"We won't," the fledglings chorused as they happily left for their map reading lesson with Felather.

18

FELATHER – CITADEL

Felather scowled at his excitable students. He'd expected them to be a bit dejected. Sniffing the air, he caught a sweet aroma and his ears detected the rustle of paper. "If you don't give me a Dewberry Delight right now, you will regret it."

Bailey laughed. "Mav's got them. He took my bag as well by mistake. He'd better not eat them all."

"I wouldn't guarantee it. He could never resist them. I imagine he's reawakened a long-forgotten craving. What *do* you have?"

"Alvo clusters?" Muntra offered.

"That will do," Felather said and plunged his hand into the bag. He sighed out a breath. "Mav took you to the Emporium?"

"Yes. We met Meri," Muntra replied.

"She is a genius. She concocts such amazing flavours, and they are all so moreish."

"We've only tried a few, but I would agree," Shandra said, popping a cluster in her mouth.

"Right. Then let's find the Emporium on the city map so

you can find it again," Felather said, unfolding a large map of the city of Puronia.

By the time fourth turn approached, the fledglings knew every street in Puronia. Felather was impressed. They had paid attention, asked astute questions, and passed his test easily. "So, fourth turn, you are visiting Master Xabier. I thought it might be good to give you a little of his history so you'll know what to expect." Felather paused.

"We have to apologise to him as well, don't we?" Kerris asked.

"I'm not sure. From what Mav has said, Xabier was more intrigued than annoyed. You have to understand that Master Xabier has been retired for about ten years. I would say he is a little bored. After all, he used to run the whole citadel."

"He did what?" Shandra asked.

"Master Xabier was a custodian. He was responsible for ensuring that the citadel ran smoothly, from making sure the staff did their duties, to ordering supplies, planning meals and events, and more."

"He did all of that?"

"Very successfully for many years. I'm not sure what caught his eye, but be attentive. Fledglings would kill for the opportunity you have. He wants to meet you, and he's never met any other group of fledglings."

"Isn't that going to cause more ill will towards us?" Kerris asked.

"Only from those who don't know better. The people worth knowing will be impressed."

"Good to know," Muntra murmured.

"Right. Make sure you arrive by fourth turn. Off you go."

Felather watched them leave. Shandra's arrival had balanced the little family, and they all instinctively supported each other. He cleared up the papers and left the chamber.

Mav had some Dewberry Delights, and he was determined to get at least one.

Kerris straightened his tunic, checked that his companions were ready, and knocked on the wooden door. It opened immediately, and Kerris recognised the man as one of Master Xabier's guards from the night before.

He cleared his throat. "My name is Kerris, and we,"—he indicated behind him—"are Deus Demavrian's fledglings. We understand Master Xabier wanted to see us."

The guard raised an eyebrow but stepped back as he opened the door and gestured them in. Kerris peered around him as he entered. The room was very orderly. Leather-bound books were stacked on a bookshelf. A cabinet made of red burnished wood had many shallow drawers which hid its contents. A low table had a bowl for knickknacks, but other than that, the room was devoid of anything that would help them understand the man who lived there.

"Go on through. He's expecting you," the guard said, closing the door behind Muntra.

A single lantern hung from a metal bracket, casting a golden glow over the antechamber. Kerris weaved through the furniture and continued into the next room, warmer than the first. More lamps lit the area, and a roaring fire explained why it was so hot.

Kerris assumed the elderly man seated near the fire felt the chill. He seemed frailer than the previous evening.

"Don't loiter. Come in, all of you," Xabier said, beckoning them forward.

"We're sorry we disturbed you yesterday, Master Xabier," Kerris said, once everyone was seated.

"You didn't. I was already on the parapet. Unfortunately

for you, that's where I take my evening walk. I didn't expect to find some fledglings trying to break into their home. It was quite entertaining."

Kerris flushed.

Xabier tutted. "No need to be embarrassed. It's the guards who were delinquent in their duty."

"We apologised to the captain earlier. He didn't seem pleased."

"I told Demavrian it was a waste of time."

"I expect that was why he barely let us get the words out before he bundled us out of there," Bailey said. "It wasn't much of an apology."

"I need to know," Xabier said with a smile. "Why didn't you enter via the gate like most people?"

Kerris squirmed in his seat. "It was my fault. The gates were locked, and I was told the guards wouldn't open them. I thought we had missed a curfew. The only way to get in was over the wall."

"Who told you the guards wouldn't open the gates?"

"One of the other fledglings."

"Do you have proof that they said this, or is it just his word against yours?" At Kerris' expression, he nodded. "No proof, then. Be very careful about inflicting any revenge. If you're caught, Mav won't be able to protect you from the consequences, and he has enough problems already."

"There will be no retaliation," Shandra said. "We have too much to do to worry about immature fledglings. The boys know better now."

"Ah. We haven't met," Xabier said, peering at Shandra. "You didn't climb the wall."

"No, sir. And if I'd been here, those idiots wouldn't have, either," Shandra replied, glaring at the boys.

"So, you are the common sense, I see."

"I have to be. Keeping twenty kids under control would have been impossible without rules."

Xabier's eyebrows rose. "And why would you be responsible for twenty children?"

Shandra shrugged. "We're orphans. We had to fend for ourselves. It was easier if we did it together."

"It was Mav who found us and taught us what to do," Bailey said.

"Without him, I doubt we'd be here," Kerris agreed. He stared at his hands. "He was the first person to ever give me anything and didn't expect something in return. Eidolon is difficult enough without a place to sleep. He helped us set up Shandra's house when her pa died. Other kids found our signs, and we grew."

"Signs?"

"We knew where desperate kids would end up." Kerris twisted his lips. "It's where we went."

"So, we set up a system for others to find us," Muntra murmured.

"And there were no adults to help you?"

"Only Mav, but he couldn't stay. Someone was hunting him, and he didn't want to bring them down on us. We couldn't convince him to stay with us." Muntra shrugged. "But they found us anyway."

Xabier grunted. "So, you were already under his wing in Eidolon. He's just formalised it now. But if you are from Eidolon, you are without souls, are you not? How is it you are still alive?"

The fledglings exchanged worried glances, and Kerris bit his lip. Mav had said to answer Xabier's questions, but this was a topic they rarely discussed.

"Nothing you tell me will go any further. You are just amusing an old man."

Shandra narrowed her eyes. "There is nothing old about you, no matter how you appear."

Xabier laughed.

"We're told we all have a shadowsoul like Mav does," Bailey said, "and they act the same way as normal souls."

Xabier whistled. "He continues to surprise." He frowned at Kerris. "So, you're Kerris. With your eloquence, I would assume you intend to be a scribe?"

Kerris nodded. "Felather is mentoring me."

"Good." He observed Bailey. "A gentle soul like you must be a cherub." His gaze moved to Muntra. "And by the size of you, a cherubim, I assume?"

"Yes, sir," Muntra replied.

Xabier's gaze rested on Shandra.

"I want to be a custodian, like you were," Shandra stated. "I am going to be Mav's custodian at the Oblivion Gate."

Kerris gasped. "When did you decide that?"

"This morning. As soon as Felather told us Master Xabier had been a custodian, I knew that was what Mav needed. He can't run the Oblivion Gate and manage all his other responsibilities as well. I am going to help him."

Bailey slowly smiled. "What a great plan, especially as Kiara is there waiting for us. I love it."

"But we're still fledglings; we've got to finish our training," Kerris said. "And anyway, you only just got here. Are you sure you want to go back to dreary Eidolon?"

"We can learn just as well in Eidolon as here, and Mav is a Deus. Eidolon won't always be dreary if he doesn't want it to be."

"What if Felather and Adriz want to stay here?" Muntra asked.

Shandra laughed. "You seriously think they are going to let Mav out of their sight? Of course they will go to Eidolon with him. Sero as well, I expect."

"When did you meet Sero? You've only been here two days," Bailey asked with a frown.

"He came to say hello last night. Like Master Xabier, he wanted to know what had happened to us in Eidolon."

Kerris glanced back at Xabier. He had forgotten he was there. Xabier's eyes were bright, and he was very focused on Shandra.

"I'm not sure who was the lucky one here," Xabier said. "Demavrian for finding you or all of you for finding Demavrian."

"It's simple. Without Mav, none of us would be here. I would say we are the lucky ones," Bailey said firmly.

Xabier nodded. "I have one more question. Who is Kiara, and why is she in Eidolon and not here with you?"

Bailey leaned forward and smiled. "Kiara is one of us, but she died in Eidolon in one of the slave camps. She is Mav's Gate Wraith. She is maintaining the Oblivion Gate for him, and she's waiting for us to go home."

Xabier stiffened in shock as Shandra gasped.

"I would love to meet her."

Bailey's smile widened. "I am sure that can be arranged."

19

SOLANJI – CITADEL

S olanji wanted to be with Mav, but she knew she needed to give him space. He was acclimatising to enormous changes within his body and his life. Her heart shrieked at her to be by his side, to observe every change and make sure he was still the man she knew and loved. But she needed to trust him, to allow him room to adjust, and she should learn how to manage her soul-breathing skills.

There was a citadel full of souls unfairly severed from their people, and she needed to return as many as she could. It would help her feel like she was doing her bit, earning the right to stand beside Demavrian as his heartsworn and consort.

She huffed out her breath as she hurried up the stairs to the citadel library. Sero was supposed to be meeting her there, though she had no doubt the cherub was still stealing the jam pots left over from the morning meal.

Reaching the library, Solanji pushed open the heavy door, slipped through the gap, and, leaning on the door, shut it again. Lamps flared to life, their yellow flames throwing out a warm golden glow that gradually spread to reveal the tall wooden stacks and the books lined up in regimented rows.

Solanji inhaled the musty aroma of parchment and ink, and the tension flowed out of her. She hurried to the botany section and pulled Athenia's book off the shelf. Athenia had been the SoulBreather who had inadvertently started this whole crazy mess. If Serenia hadn't murdered the only SoulBreather in existence before Solanji, Mav would never have been stranded in Eidolon without his soul and would never have been caught and tortured by Kyrill and Kaenera.

Sitting at the large table in the centre of the room, facing the beautiful oil painting of Mav and Athenia, she placed her hand on the cover, took a deep breath, and opened the book. Slowly, she began turning the pages, reading the messages Athenia had left for her.

Solanji's throat tightened as she wished she could have met the woman who had been such a close friend of Mav's and who knew so much more about soulbreathing than she ever would. The fact that Athenia had died in Mav's arms was so distressing, and a tear trickled down her cheek and splashed on the book.

She wiped her cheeks and then the parchment and, sniffing, turned the page. Hesitating, she turned the page back and lifted it in front of the candlelight, squinting at the letters illuminated in the flame's light. Where her tear had smeared the ink, a new phrase was visible.

Beware In Absentia.

Solanji frowned as she read the words again. How had they appeared? What did Athenia mean? It was definitely a warning, but against what? She caught her bottom lip in her teeth as she racked her brains for a meaning, but she came up empty.

Solanji leaned back and took a deep breath. She could do this. She *would* do this. She was a SoulBreather, like Athenia. Possibilities swirled, and she reached across the table and pulled a roll of parchment towards her.

Athenia was warning her to be careful. When would she be absent? Solanji mulled over how she perceived souls. Even when she saw the soulmist, she was still conscious and aware, distracted maybe, but she could be more careful. While searching for souls in the citadel? Would that make her vulnerable? If so, how could she protect herself?

Maybe she shouldn't try to do it on her own. She should wait for Sero, no matter how tempting it was to reach for the citadel now. The need to find her brother's soul burned within her, and she curled her fingers.

The library door opened, and low voices disturbed the silence.

Solanji would reunite the soulless with their souls where she could. She just had to ask them who they were. Deep in her bones, she knew it was that simple. She didn't have to make it difficult.

Resting her chin in her hand, she observed the painting. The painter had caught Athenia's inner beauty, the joyful expression in her eyes as she gazed up at Mav, the youthful general. Even now, it was obvious that Mav was a different person from the one in the painting. He no longer had that carefree confidence, and yet, with his bonding to the Oblivion Gate, there was a suggestion that he was recovering some aspect of his previous stature.

Solanji wrinkled her brow. She was annoyed she couldn't put her finger on what had changed, but something had.

Willing Athenia to be more specific, she dropped her gaze back to the book, turned the page, and kept reading.

Her concentration was broken as Sero perched on the table, one leg crossed over the other, his chin resting in his hand as he watched her. His blond curls glowed like a halo and his vivid blue eyes sparkled. "You know," he said, "it is extremely dangerous in this day and age to be so focussed on something that you don't notice anyone approaching you from behind you. There are nefarious people who could come along and steal your soul."

Solanji grimaced. "The very reason I was waiting for you before I tried to contact the citadel." She indicated the book and flipped back the pages. "Athenia is being cryptic."

Sero chuckled, and his tiny golden wings fluttered as he leaned forward to read the text. "Angels love puzzles."

"I am not an angel," Solanji said.

"No, but you are heartsworn to one, so get used to it."

Solanji exhaled. "Will you watch my back while I try and contact the citadel?"

"Of course, though we might be safer using Mav's chambers."

"I need their help," Solanji said, glancing at Athenia and Mav.

"It's just a painting," Sero said.

"Is it?" Solanji asked.

Sero raised an eyebrow and then stared at the picture more closely.

"You know, I never thought about it until now," Solanji said, "but Athenia's soul must be somewhere in the citadel. With Averdeus missing, there was no one to pass her onward, and he would have said if he had passed her on."

"Do you think you could find her?" Sero spun towards her, his eyes bright.

Solanji squeezed his arm. "I don't know, but I'll certainly look."

"Do you think that might be the reason Demavrian still has the vendetta stone? Her soul is waiting for us to find and release her. It's not Serenia's death that would be closure for her."

"I think that is more likely," Solanji replied, her voice soft as she watched him. "From what you've said, Athenia was full of life. She would not linger for a murderer's execution."

"Should we tell Julius? He was her life partner."

"Maybe we should wait until I find her soul and then we ask her?"

Sero choked on his words. "Y-you think we'll be able to speak to her?"

"I don't know. But she was a SoulBreather. If any soul could speak to me, it would be hers. I'll start looking this afternoon."

Sero swallowed and stared at the painting.

"But first, let's see if I can find Brennan," Solanji said and placed her hand on the book to ground her. She reached for the citadel. Sunlight surrounded her, warming her skin, kissing her cheeks in welcome, and as the glare subsided, she walked along the corridor lined with doors. She stopped at the door labelled with a B. Today, she would find Brennan's soul, and after that, she would find the next one.

Pushing the door open, she released the scroll in her hand, allowing it to unroll as it dropped to the floor. Quill poised, she smiled. "Right, you lot! Line up. Time for a roll call." The swirling souls stuttered to a halt and shivered.

"Where's Brennan?" Solanji asked.

The agitated soul mists undulated, and then, after a moment, they slowly parted, and two swirls of golden mist ventured forward through the gap. They weaved in a pattern, one dependent on the other as they swirled around each other. Solanji's heart jumped in her chest and set off on a race all of its own. How could it be so simple? All she had to do was ask! She smiled. "Brennan. Who have you found?"

Images flashed through her mind as her brother introduced his friend, Bailey. Solanji's breath caught. "Bailey?" Why hadn't she been searching for Mav's fledglings as well?

A flurry of details was impressed upon her. Bailey shyly offered that he was originally from a homestead south of Puronia. He shared images of a vibrant farm, his favourite tree, baking cakes, the comfort of his mother's arms, and then the unimaginable horror of his parents being attacked and killed in front of him. The memory burned in Solanji's mind, and she found it difficult to associate it with the shy and innocent Bailey she knew. He didn't remember anything else.

Solanji knew this was her Bailey, and her heart broke for him. The fledglings rarely spoke about their pasts, and now she understood why. She doubted Bailey even remembered Puronia, being so young when he was abandoned in Eidolon.

Solanji held out her hand and drew their soulmists within her.

She had twenty names, along with their details listed on her scroll, when she became aware of an insistent tugging, and she glanced behind her. Losing her connection with the citadel, Solanji shuddered as the library solidified around her.

Her cheeks were wet, and she hurriedly wiped the tears away as Sero hovered beside her. Solanji closed Athenia's book. "I found Brennan's soul and Bailey's."

Sero rose into the air, his golden wings fluttering. "You did? How?"

"A bit of organisation. And a pointer from Athenia." She patted the book.

"That is amazing news. When will you return them?"

Solanji rolled up her scroll. "After I visit the Justicers and give them my list. They can check their register. If they can find the area these people were abandoned in, maybe I can return their souls."

"I'm coming with you. Maybe I can help."

Solanji smiled. "You would do that? Help me search?"

"Of course! If we can return just one person to their family, that would be a success."

"In that case, you are welcome to come with me." Solanji returned Athenia's book to the shelf and then paused in front of the oil painting of Mav and Athenia. "I want that painting hung in the Oblivion Gate."

Sero fluttered beside her. "I'm sure Amaridin would give it to you if you asked."

"The youthful general," Solanji murmured.

"He was beautiful."

Solanji laughed. "You obviously haven't seen him recently."

Sero narrowed his eyes. "What do you mean?"

"You should drop by and visit. You may be in for a pleasant surprise."

"What has he done now?"

Solanji shrugged as she tugged open the library door. "Claimed the Oblivion Gate."

"He didn't!"

Stopping in the middle of the corridor, Solanji frowned at him. "And why are you so surprised?"

"I'm not surprised that he's done it, only that he did it so quickly. I thought…"

"Thought what?"

Sero exhaled. "That Kaenera would have made it more difficult."

"Oh, he's trying. Believe me, he's trying. As much as I need you, I think Mav could do with your help at the Gate. There are some residents lurking in the shadows, and he won't let any of us stay there until he discovers who they are and whether they mean harm. Any chance you could help him with that?"

Sero began to fly down the corridor. "I'm not sure I want to know the history of the Oblivion Gate."

"If you don't help him, Bailey will." Solanji sighed as she followed him. "No matter what we say, Bailey is determined to move to the Gate with Mav."

Sero spun in the air and glared at her as his tiny wings flapped in agitation. "In that case, I suppose I have no choice. I can't let my student venture where I'm not prepared to go."

"No, Sero. I didn't mean it like that. I wouldn't want you to go in unprepared, nor for anyone to see a terrible history they can't unsee. Maybe ask Mav for a little of Oji's history first so you know what to expect." Solanji tapped her temple. "I understand that Mav has it all up here now. You just need to tease it out of him."

She brushed her hair out of her eyes and started walking again. "We need to move to the Gate, and sooner rather than later. Mav is more comfortable there. We should be with him, but he's worried it's not safe for the rest of us." She bit her lip. "He shouldn't be doing everything by himself. He needs his family around him."

Sero's glare softened. "Not a truer word said. Very well. I will visit him and see what I can find out."

"Thank you, Sero."

"That doesn't mean you can slack on cataloguing those souls. We can ask the scribes to help match your lists to the records."

"That would help. There are so many souls."

"And Amaridin can't pass the souls on if their host is still alive," Sero said thoughtfully.

"It's going to take years to sort them out."

"It will keep the SoulSingers out of trouble, then. You know what they say about idle hands."

Solanji stared at him with some suspicion. "I don't think I want to know."

"You don't know?" Sero spun in glee as Solanji rolled her eyes. "Well, let me tell you."

"No time." Solanji laughed and clapped her hands over her ears. "Mav is calling me." And she rushed down the stairs.

Sero's gleeful chuckle followed her. "Liar!"

20

DEMAVRIAN – PURONIA, CITADEL

av shuffled the papers on his desk into a pile as Felather entered his chambers in the citadel and sat opposite him.

"Is it confirmed?"

Mav didn't bother to ask what Felather was referring to but only leaned back in his chair and rubbed his temple. There was only one topic at the top of everyone's mind: the massacre at the Crossroads. "Yes."

"Kaenera?"

"No one else who would perform such an atrocity. And don't forget, he left me a personal message."

"If it is supposed to be a warning, it's a bit heavy-handed. How are you feeling?"

Mav snorted. "Oji and I have been working on a way to shield against the soulless. I can't be incapacitated in the middle of a battle. Oji thinks he found a way to divert them until I'm able to pass them through the Gate. I expect Kaenera was hoping to overwhelm me. He doesn't care about anyone else as long as he gets his message across."

Felather leaned forward. "And what's that? That he still controls Eidolon?"

"And that he's not without power. No one in Eidolon will stand up to him after that."

"What are we going to do?

"We have to stop him before he kills or subjugates everyone in this country. We must find his stronghold in Eidolon, and then I will deal with him for good. I need you to focus your time on finding where he is hiding. With the number of dybbuks he is rumoured to have, his garrison can't be small. He must be shielding it, as I've not heard or seen any mention of it."

Felather frowned. "I'll start straight away. I have time now, as your fledglings have gone to see Xabier. Are you sure it was wise to allow them to go unsupervised?"

"They'll be fine. Xabier will look after them."

"I was more concerned about what he might wheedle out of them."

"I'm hoping he will. It will be good for them to talk to someone independently. Give them a more balanced response to their questions. Xabier would not betray their confidences, and I'm hoping he might see Shandra as a possible project. She couldn't ask for a better teacher."

Felather hesitated and then said, "You think Shandra could be a custodian?"

"I would think it's obvious. Organising others is in her blood."

Felather wrinkled his nose. "She might have difficulty being accepted in such a role. A custodian knows everything about a household. They have to be trustworthy and able to keep secrets, even if they don't agree with them."

"She'll be fine. She'll have my provenance if that's what she wants to do. Let's see if the idea appeals first."

"Fine. By the way, I said I'd take them to see their first

sunrise tomorrow morning. They ought to see at least one before we go to Eidolon."

"Thank you. If their reaction to the sunset is anything to go by, they'll love it." Mav leaned back in his chair, tapping his quill on the pad, and then he gestured at the paperwork on his desk. "I need to complete this. The councillors are blocking every request for support I make, even after the massacre. You'd think they would want to make sure Kaenera was dealt with once and for all."

"I spoke to Golaran. He said he would support your claim for a division of guards. Send your request to him to second. It may help."

"I will. Thank you. At least one archangel has some common sense."

Felather inspected his hands for a moment and then took a deep breath before he looked at Mav. "Isn't it about time you dealt with Serenia?"

Mav stiffened, his gut roiling. Just the sound of her name made his heart rate spike. She had been like his mother for so many years, strict and unbending, but always there. Her betrayal had cut deep, and he wasn't sure he could face her.

She had tried to kill him, literally stabbed him in the back. She had killed his mother and many others. Death was too good for her. His shadows swirled around him in agitation, and opposite him, Felather flinched as his aura, no doubt, filled the room. He inhaled and dampened the effects of his presence.

"My apologies."

Felather waved his apology away. "I know it's hard, but once you deal with her, that's one more threat out of the way."

"I want her to suffer," Mav said, guilt at the thought filling him. "Killing her is too easy. Is that a terrible thing to say? The fact that she still has the power to affect me galls me."

"It is not terrible. She is a vile person. I would suggest the worst thing you could do to her is remove her soul and let her rage against her ending for a whole day."

Mav smiled as the twinge in his chest eased. "That would be an apt punishment and soothe my need for revenge." He rubbed his face. "Not a very good attitude for a god," he said with a wry twist of his lips.

"I think you're allowed one small act of revenge. Get it out of your system," Felather said with a grin.

Mav chuckled. His oathsworn knew how to manage him. He was thankful that he did. Re-energised, he pulled the papers in front of him and scrawled his request for troops. "Would you take this to Golaran for me? We can't do this alone; we need military support. I'll go and speak with Amaridin, and see if he can influence the council to be more reasonable."

Felather rose. "Don't put Serenia off for too long."

Mav grimaced and stood, glad their discussion was over. "I won't."

Leaving his study, Mav walked through the citadel corridors. Adriz was a reassuring presence behind his shoulder. When he considered it, he didn't actually need a bodyguard anymore, but it looked good. Angels and administrators alike veered out of his path, even though he wasn't hogging the hallway. Their eyes burned into his back as he passed.

"Are you being particularly menacing today?" he asked.

Adriz's snort vibrated through his mind. *"You are Deus. Not only have you regained some of your old confidence, but your aura is leaking out all over the place."* Adriz paused, and her voice in his mind was thoughtful. *"It is a powerful combination, a reminder of who you are, and what they did to you. They are afraid. As they should be."*

"I keep forgetting to suppress it. You think it's like my father's?"

"Yes, but it's stronger than Averdeus', more focused. It's part of you. Don't suppress it," Adriz said quickly as he tried to dampen his aura.

"I don't want to terrify everyone."

"You won't. They'll get used to it. If a person is fearful, then they have a guilty conscience, and we want to know what they have done."

"It doesn't need to be overwhelming, though."

Adriz shrugged. *"They need the reminder. I wouldn't worry too much about it. You are Deus. It comes with the job."*

Mav exhaled and turned into his brother's wing of the citadel. Two citadel guards bracketed the double doors that led into Amaridin's apartment. They stiffened to attention, slamming the butts of their pikes on the floor—a warning and a threat combined, even though they recognised him.

The guard on the left opened the door and gestured for him to enter.

Mav nodded his thanks and walked into Amaridin's rooms. Golden sunlight streamed in through the open windows, and a slight breeze caressed the gauzy curtains into a gentle dance. It was a sharp contrast to Mav's more shadowy chambers. He truly did walk a different path than his brother.

Amaridin was not alone; his partner, Valerian, rose to greet Mav. Valerian glowed, the sunlight a soft halo around him; he was a child of the sun for sure.

"Demavrian! You are very welcome." Valerian drew him into a hug and stiffened. "You have come into your own, my dear," he whispered in Mav's ear as Mav inhaled the citrus scent that clung to him.

"It seems so," Mav murmured as Valerian released him. "You remember Adriz?"

"Of course. Welcome." Valerian patted Amaridin's arm as his partner joined him, and then he returned to his seat.

Amaridin, in turn, hugged Mav and gestured to a chair. "Mav, please join us. We were expecting you before now."

"Claiming the Oblivion Gate took more of my time than expected. There are many things concealed within its halls, and I need to make it safe for my oathsworn."

Adriz took up position behind Mav's chair as a servant entered with a tray of refreshments. They waited for it to be placed on a side table, and Amaridin waved them away, rising to pour the bannoe himself. He handed Mav a cup and then Adriz, who smiled her thanks.

Valerian leaned forward, his face alight with interest. "Tell us about the Oblivion Gate. How did you manage to wake it? The citadel is still dormant, and we cannot wake her from her slumber."

"He woke as I walked his halls. I'm not sure I did anything specific. Maybe it was the change in Gate Keeper that made him more aware, or maybe my intentions woke him. He had been isolated and alone for centuries. Kaenera deliberately bound him, whereas I offered a full partnership." Mav frowned in thought. "Removing the chains and offering him freedom may have been the catalyst, though I had help. Oji loves Kiara and is eager to meet my fledglings and oathsworn. We are his family, and I think that is the stronger bond."

Valerian sat back with a smile and accepted a cup from Amaridin. "Only you would think to move in a whole family. Your takeover bid was assured from the start."

"But how do we do the same? The citadel should be awake and more involved. She resists our attempts to wake her," Amaridin said as he sat.

"The citadel must be happy in its current state," Mav said. "It has a family. Its halls buzz with life and purpose. You need to offer it something it doesn't have."

Amaridin exhaled. "Like what?"

"I don't know. A challenge? New experiences? Why don't you give the citadel a new purpose? Barring soulless from its walls is not particularly fulfilling. Maybe it would wake for something more meaningful, like helping to return souls to the soulless."

"Maybe," Amaridin said, his brow wrinkling as he thought. "Though that would mean many soulless would be able to enter to Puronia. I'm not sure we could cope with the influx."

"They would have the *choice* to visit," Mav said. "I think you'll find that they may choose not to. And their families in Angelicus may choose to join them in Eidolon as they are reconnected and we improve conditions."

"It will balance itself out naturally," Valerian said.

"Yes, though it will take centuries. We have to match souls to bodies, and even then, we only have one SoulBreather. Solanji can only return so many souls at a time, and she has other responsibilities by my side."

Amaridin exhaled as he slowly nodded, his gaze distant. "A worthy cause," he murmured. His gaze focused on Mav. "Speaking of Solanji, she asked for the painting of you and Athenia."

"She told me. She wants it for our library. I think I ought to advise Julius it is being moved. He might be upset."

"We can ask him to join us," Valerian offered.

"I think we have some things we need to address privately first," Mav said. "But thank you for suggesting it. I've requested support from the Host. Golaran offered to support my request in the Assembly. Depending on how that conversation goes, I was going to ask Julius to join me in Eidolon. Kaenera has not given up on reclaiming the Oblivion Gate, nor his intention to kill me, and I don't have any protection except Adriz and Ryvalin. No matter how formidable they are, we need help against Kaenera's ranks of dybbuks."

Amaridin nodded. "That may be for the best. Julius has lost his way, and he needs a new direction. Helping you may ease some of his anger and grief. The citadel will only ever remind him of Athenia."

Mav grimaced. "I'm not sure I'm any less of a reminder."

"True," Valerian said, "but you stayed with Athenia in her last moments. Julius knows you loved her, and she was with her best friend when she died. That has to be more comforting than passing the steps on which she died every single day."

"What is the feeling in the ranks? Would Julius' men resist being seconded to Eidolon?" Adriz asked.

Amaridin tilted his head. "I think that is more a question for Julius. I have no issue with him taking his division. We have sufficient guards. The issue with Eidolon is that it is unknown, mysterious."

"A place of shadows where the unwanted lurk," Valerian added with an apologetic smile. "Which is totally our fault because that is what we've been saying for centuries. We need to update our narrative."

"Which will take time," Mav said.

"We have to start somewhere."

Mav exhaled. It was daunting, just the thought of trying to unravel a lifetime of doctrine. "Kaenera's threat is not just against me. I am his immediate focus, but I think his ultimate goal is to eradicate all of us and rule both Angelicus and Eidolon." He shrugged. "Or destroy it all."

Amaridin stiffened. "Is that even a possibility?"

"Yes," Mav said bluntly. "Has father not mentioned the Aeora sigils?"

"Not a word," Amaridin replied, a look of curiosity on his face. "What are they?"

Mav cursed under his breath. "Our father has some serious avoidance issues."

Amaridin laughed. "Why do you think he flits off to his hideaways all the time, leaving us holding the bag?"

"Father confiscated the Aeora sigils from an imploding planet and hid them so no one could find them."

"He should have left them to implode with the planet," Adriz said.

"Yes, he should have, but he didn't." A sullen ache throbbed in Mav's temple. "The sigils can be used to destroy the citadel or the Oblivion Gate, a god, or a whole world."

"Why would anyone create such a terrible thing?" Valerian stiffened in his seat.

"Does Kaenera have them?" Amaridin asked, fear widening his eyes.

The room dimmed as the curtains swirled, blocking the sun, and Mav shivered. "Not yet. But he wants them."

"Where are they?" Valerian asked.

Mav hesitated and then said, "I believe Kaenera stashed them in the Oblivion Gate and now wants them back. Father is checking whether they are missing, but I believe I have them."

"You can have as many citadel guards as you want," Amaridin said, and Mav laughed, a short, hard bark that hurt his throat. He took a sip of his cold bannoe.

"No, I'm serious," Amaridin said. "If they are as destructive as you say, then we cannot let Kaenera get his hands on those sigils."

"I know."

"Go and speak to Julius now. You need to get his men transferred as soon as possible. Tell him you have my full support. If he baulks or the Assembly argues, send them to me."

"I will. In the meantime, you need to see if the citadel has any ideas on how to destroy the sigils without annihilating all of us. The best way to keep them out of Kaenera's hands is to get rid of them."

"A righteous purpose to wake a sluggish sentience," Valerian said.

"Go and speak to Julius." Amaridin made a shooing motion. "Go on. Stop wasting time. We'll work on the citadel."

Mav rose. "Alright. I'm going!" He hugged his brother and then Valerian.

Valerian gripped his arms and held his eyes. "Take care of yourself, Demavrian. If you need anything at all, you ask. Hear me? You don't hesitate, you ask."

"Thank you," Mav replied, squeezing Valerian's arms in return. Then he left, with Adriz close behind him.

"That was intense," she said as they walked down the corridor.

"Indeed. Valerian grasped the nuances of the situation. Without me holding the Gate, there is no one who can stop Kaenera."

"So, we get to defend the whole world, then?"

"Looks like it."

They fell silent as they traversed the citadel. Mav's brooding expression was as much a deterrent as his aura, which swept before him.

"I know I said you shouldn't dampen your aura, but on this occasion, maybe you should," Adriz said. *"You are like an Angel of Death sweeping in to defeat your foes. Maybe not the impression you want to give Julius and his men?"*

Mav relaxed, trying to ease the tension in his neck and shoulders.

"I need them to know I mean business."

"I think they'll know."

Mav chuckled and shielded his thoughts.

"Whoa! How did you do that?"

"Do what?"

"It was like you…umm…I don't know. That brooding intensity just disappeared."

"I shielded."

"You can explain that later."

"If I must."

Mav stopped at the entrance to the garrison, which housed the Heavenly Host. A stout woman stood behind the counter, the badges on her sleeve denoting her rank as a sergeant. She looked up from the ledger she had been writing in as Mav paused in front of her.

"I am looking for Captain Julius Teravin."

"Who's asking?" The woman inspected him and curled her lip.

Mav raised an eyebrow, and Adriz snapped, "Deus Demavrian."

The woman stiffened.

"I've changed my mind. Hit her with the aura," Adriz murmured.

Mav stifled a laugh. "Where can I find him?"

"Should be in his office. Second floor, room 210. Stairs are to the right."

"Thank you," Mav said and followed her pointing finger. He climbed the stairs, followed by Adriz, who was muttering under breath about bone-headed soldiers. Arriving outside the door, Mav knocked and waited.

There was no response.

"Maybe he's not in?" Adriz said, peering up and down the corridor.

Mav tried the door, and it opened easily, but the room was deserted.

She moved to a neighbouring office and banged on the door.

"Come in!" a voice yelled.

Adriz opened the door. "Apologies for the interruption, but I'm trying to find Captain Julius Teravin."

"So's everyone else," the grey-haired man snorted.

"What do you mean?"

"His office times are his own. He turns up when he feels like it, which is not at all. He'll be losing his unit if he's not careful. Extenuating circumstances only cover so much."

Mav spoke from behind Adriz. "That is unlike the Julius I remember."

The man lurched to his feet. "General, ah…I mean, um, Deus Demavrian."

"If Julius is not here, where is he usually to be found?"

"I'd prefer not to say, sir."

"I cannot help him if I cannot find him," Mav said gently.

The man fought with his conscience for a moment and then exhaled. "Ever since you upset the apple cart, sir, he's been drowning his sorrows in the Cross Keys."

Mav frowned. "Not the Minstrel's Rest?"

"No, sir. A bit too close to home, if you know what I mean."

"I see."

The man grimaced.

"And you think he'll be there now?"

Glancing at the timepiece, the man nodded. "It'll have just opened."

"Thank you for your help," Mav said and, turning on his heel, strode down the corridor. Adriz hurried to catch up with him.

"That's in the seedier part of town, isn't it?"

"Afraid so."

Adriz looked down at her uniform. "We'll be a bit obvious, won't we?"

"If anyone wants to start any trouble, I'll be more than happy to accommodate them. And that includes Julius," Mav replied grimly. "But Julius will have to wait. I want Ryvalin to accompany me. She will be his commanding officer. She needs to know what she is dealing with."

21

BAILEY – CITADEL

Bailey closed his book and grinned at Kerris, sprawled over the desk in mock exhaustion. "For an apprentice scribe, you sure do hate bookwork."

"Pointless bookwork," Kerris clarified. "I don't mind it if it's for a purpose."

"It *is* for a purpose. We need to understand the basics before we can attempt the more difficult stuff."

Kerris raised his eyebrow. "Since when have you been the voice of reason?"

"He's always been the voice of reason; you just never listen to him," Muntra said as he stretched, cracking his joints.

"Do you fancy exploring the citadel?" Shandra asked, heading off an argument. "I haven't seen much yet other than Mav's chambers, our rooms, and here." She gestured at the brightly lit room. "We have a full turn before our next lesson."

"Do you think we could go and visit the Assembly Hall?" Bailey asked wistfully. "I heard it is magnificent."

"Isn't that where they held the Apologia?" Kerris said,

sitting up. "Everyone agrees that Felather was amazing. One of the other fledglings said that he cut right through the evidence against Mav."

"Of course he did. Felather is one of the best scribes in the citadel. I wouldn't want anyone else defending me," Shandra said, stacking her books in a pile and rising. "Come on. Let's make the most of our break."

They hurried down the corridors, keeping their eyes downcast and avoiding angels and administrators alike. None of them wanted to catch the attention of an angel and be sent on some errand.

Shandra pushed open a tall door, and Bailey's thoughts dribbled to a halt as he stared at the cavernous room. The ceiling was framed with thick beams. Two enormous chandeliers hung in the space above. White marble gleamed underfoot and covered the walls.

A long, wide aisle led to the opposite end of the room where there was a dais, on top of which sat three backless golden thrones with purple cushions on the seats. They were ornate, beautiful, and obviously made for angels.

On either side of the nave, wooden seating rose in ranked tiers, enough to hold the whole Assembly. A soft swish caught Bailey's attention, and he drifted down the aisle, searching for the source.

To the left of the dais, an intricate mechanism hung on the wall. A gleaming silver ball rolled down a channel and through a tube and dropped into a collecting jar at the bottom. Cogs whirred, pulling at linked chains, and the large pointer clicked a notch further around the dial. It was a timepiece, counting the turns throughout the day.

Bailey gaped at it. Who could have designed such a complex mechanism?

"Wow!" Kerris said from beside him. "Kiara would love that."

Bailey nodded. "She would," he breathed.

"Do you think one of these thrones is Mav's?" Muntra asked.

"Once, maybe. But now he rules Eidolon," Bailey replied

"Mav needs a throne room," Shandra said. "I'll make sure he gets one."

Muntra laughed. "He needs to secure the Gate first. Don't get ahead of yourself."

"He will. You know he will. And then we will all go and live with him there."

"Of course we will," Bailey said. "Kiara's waiting for us, too, don't forget."

"What do you think would happen if I sat on one of those thrones?" Kerris asked.

Shandra snorted a laugh. "You probably wouldn't be able to sit down again for a week."

"We are not looking for any more trouble," Bailey said. "Mav has enough to deal with."

Another ball swished through the channels and tubes until it clinked into the collecting jar. The long hand clicked another notch.

"Then I suppose we'd better go." Shandra peered around her. "Isn't it funny how places like this always seem…I don't know, different!" she finished, gesturing at the cavernous ceiling.

"Special," Bailey murmured, letting the rarefied atmosphere seep into him. It was soothing, even welcoming, and he snapped his eyes open in shock as he recognised the awareness residing in the hall. The citadel had welcomed him.

"If we hurry, we'll have time to grab a bannoe from the dining hall," Shandra suggested as she ushered the boys into the corridor and shut the door behind them.

"What are you fledglings doing here?" asked a thin-faced angel, dressed in pale blue robes.

"Saying hello to the citadel," Bailey replied in a dreamy voice.

"Bailey, snap out of it," Kerris whispered, digging him in the ribs.

"Nothing, sir. We were just going to the dining hall. We have ten minutes before our next lesson begins," Muntra said.

"Then stop loitering in places you shouldn't be and return to your lessons." The angel stalked off, and the fledglings hurried off, glad they hadn't been caught in the Assembly Hall.

"Bailey, wait!"

Bailey looked down the corridor to see Solanji hurrying towards them. She wore the golden robes of an archangel. He'd never really considered it before, but he supposed she was one, if not an Archdeus, seeing as how she was heartsworn to Mav.

"Hi, Solanji," the fledglings chorused.

"I have some amazing news for you, but let's go somewhere more private." Solanji opened the door to the Assembly Hall and peered in. "This will do." She ushered them back into the hall. "Take a pew," she said, gesturing at the nearest bench.

She grinned at Bailey. "I found your soul."

Bailey's stomach jolted. "You what?" A spurt of panic made him feel light-headed. He didn't need his soul; Mav had given him one.

Shandra exclaimed in delight and squeezed his shoulder.

"While I was searching for Brennan's soul, I found yours, too."

"I don't want it," Bailey said. He really didn't. He didn't

need it. "I have a shadow soul. Mav gave me my soul. That is enough."

"You can have both. It won't replace your shadow soul. Mav has two souls; Ellaria had Mav's soulmist. It is all entwined as one within him."

Bailey swallowed. "It is?"

Solanji nodded and leaned forward to rub his arm. "You will feel better with it. It's yours. A part of you."

"What about Muntra or Kerris and Shandra?"

"I will search for theirs as well. When I find them, I will return theirs as well."

Bailey searched her face, looking for reassurance. "I don't want to lose my shadowsoul. That belongs to me now."

"You won't. I promise. Mav's shadowsoul is his dominant soul. Like you, he has chosen his shadows. They are an integral part of him."

"I'll only accept it on condition it doesn't take away my shadowsoul."

Solanji smiled and released the soulmist. It shot across the short distance and entered Bailey.

He clasped his chest. "Oh," he said. An odd feeling spread through his body and down to his extremities. A tingle shimmered through him, and everything seemed to tighten and come into focus. It was as if there had been a film over his eyes, and now it was gone. His surroundings were crisper, brighter, clearer.

A soft beat thumped in the air and vibrated through Bailey's bones. "What was that?" he asked.

"What was what?" Kerris asked, glancing around him.

"That is the citadel's heartbeat," Solanji said. "All angels can hear it."

"I'm not an angel."

"Oh?" Solanji asked with a small smile.

"What does it feel like?" Kerris asked. "You do look different."

"I don't want to look different."

"He means you look sharper, more complete," Shandra reassured him, squeezing his arm. "You look just the same, Bailey."

"You're sure?"

"Positive."

Bailey exhaled in relief. He did feel better. Complete. As if he had known all along there had been something missing, not realising it was his missing soul. He didn't remember having a soul until Mav had given him one.

"Your shadowsoul is sparkling with soulmist," Solanji said with a smile. "It is very pretty."

"But what does it feel like?" Kerris asked again.

"Odd," Bailey replied. "But I feel whole. I think I've known that something wasn't quite right, but I didn't realise that it was because my soulmist was missing." He smiled, feeling lighter and happier than he had in a long time.

"That is good, then," Shandra said a little wistfully.

"I promise I will keep searching for your souls," Solanji said. She grinned at them. "I need to go and give Brennan his so he can go home. My mother will be so relieved to see him."

Bailey stood. "Then what are you still doing here? Go! You should have given Brennan his soul back first."

"I was here in the citadel, and I saw you. But I'm going now!" Solanji said, raising her hands against his insistence.

22

AMARIDIN – CITADEL

Amaridin relaxed on the sofa beside Valerian and exhaled. "If Demavrian has woken the Oblivion Gate, then we need to wake the citadel."

"I agree, though I'm not sure how he did it." Valerian shifted to pull Amaridin's head and shoulders into his lap, and Amaridin sighed as Valerian started carding his fingers through his hair.

"That is so nice," Amaridin murmured, closing his eyes.

"You are too tense; you need to learn how to relax. You are stressing over things that do not need worrying about."

"There is so much to do, and now that both my father and Demavrian have stepped down from the citadel, I feel overwhelmed."

"That's why you have me," Valerian said, continuing to soothe his lover. "We'll do it together."

"My father made it look so easy. Even Demavrian copes with all this change better than I do, and some of the stuff he is dealing with would destroy a lesser man."

"Your brother is formidable for a reason, Amaridin. He has always been the warrior. You are the diplomat."

"I'm not doing a very good job, then. The Assembly is in chaos. There are calls for reform. Many are questioning why the citadel failed them. Why *we* failed them. They conveniently forget that they were complicit in all that Serenia did. We need new archangels in place to help with the administration. They are even questioning why the SoulBreather is living in Eidolon and not in the citadel."

"We will deal with all of it together. First, let's see if we can wake the citadel."

"What if she doesn't want to help us?"

"She?" Valerian asked. "Why do you say she?"

Amaridin wrinkled his brow, and Valerian smoothed the lines from his face.

"I have the impression the citadel is female."

"Then lead the way, beloved. We could use a little female perspective in our decision-making."

Amaridin snorted. "After Serenia?"

"Serenia was a power-grabbing maniac. Not all women are like her. Take Athenia, for example, or Solanji. They are both intelligent women I would include in our administration, if we had one."

"True."

"Well then, let's see if we can find her." Valerian wriggled into a more comfortable position, jostling Amaridin, and then began threading his fingers through Amaridin's hair again.

Amaridin closed his eyes and reached for the connection Solanji had created between him, Valerian, and the citadel. He drifted, listening to Valerian's calm breathing, feeling the rise and fall of his stomach beneath him.

Valerian's presence beneath him faded as another took his place. *"About time,"* a sharp female voice said.

"For what?" Amaridin asked.

"That you came into your own. Averdeus is too flighty. Always looking for something else. I need someone here."

"You had Demavrian for many years."

"Sweet boy. Always too serious. Much like you. Now I do like your partner. He is yummy."

"Erm…"

The citadel laughed. *"Can't take a compliment? You chose well."*

"Can he hear you like I can?"

"Not yet. I wanted to speak to you first."

Amaridin breathed a little easier. *"Why were you dormant for so long?"*

"Ah, straight in with the hard questions. I don't really know. I wasn't always dormant. It might have been a defensive mechanism, a way to prevent anyone from subverting me."

"But the citadel was supposed to protect us."

"I did. You haven't been attacked, have you?"

"But the Assembly was subverted by Serenia. My actions were influenced by Kaenera. Athenia killed. Don't they count?"

"You have the abilities to protect yourself against such control. That you did not avail yourself of them is your failure, not mine. I regret not being able to assist Athenia. I should have called for help earlier, but I thought she could heal herself. I did not realise the extent of her injuries. Once Averdeus left, there was little I could do. Without his presence or the cornerstone, I could only sleep."

There was an extended silence as Amaridin digested her words. *"But you didn't wake when Demavrian returned."*

"I tried. But he was different. He couldn't reach me the way he used to."

"But I can?"

"Yes, Amaridin. You can. And if you wish it, you and your partner may bond fully with me, and we will see what we can do to set things straight. I will have more cognisance of things going on within my building. I will interfere as little or as much as you need me to. I think

some of your angels need a little discipline; they have become lax and inattentive.”

Amaridin chuckled. *“Now, that, I can’t wait to see.”*

“You have authority, Amaridin. You needn’t be afraid to use it. You are the Archdeus of the citadel. Once you become one with your partner, so will he be, and he will hear my voice.”

“He won’t hear you until we swear our oaths?” Amaridin asked, tensing in concern.

“No.”

“Then we should swear them now and forget the ceremony.”

“That is your choice. But he won’t hear me until he is Archdeus.”

“Solanji bound our soulmist together and into you. Why does that not make any difference?”

“He is not an Archdeus. There is one other thing, Amaridin. Once we bond, I will be fully aware. A part of you. What I see, you see. What you see, I see. We become one, and you will feel all those souls bursting at my seams. It is painful, and they need to be removed. Sooner rather than later. I feel like I am going to explode.”

“Painful, how?”

“Ask Demavrian. I think he was struggling to hold the soulless, and it affected his health. Just as holding the souls will affect you.”

Amaridin stiffened. *“Demavrian was suffering from severe migraines. If Valerian and I become heartsworn, will he be affected as well?”*

“Yes.”

“Then we need to get Solanji returning souls before we swear our oaths.”

“You would choose to wait and take the burden yourself?”

“Valerian has suffered enough already.”

“So be it. Open yourself to me, Amaridin. Let me show you who I am and who we will become.”

• • •

Amaridin shuddered in Valerian's arms, and Valerian tightened his embrace. He hadn't managed to contact the citadel, but Amaridin must have, as his shudders were increasing.

"Sweetheart?" he murmured, kissing Amaridin's temple. His partner's skin was damp and clammy, and he didn't respond.

Valerian sat up in alarm, slid out from under Amaridin, and laid him on the sofa. He rubbed Amaridin's cold hands between his own. No one had mentioned that connecting to the citadel would be dangerous or put Amaridin in harm's way. He would never have suggested it if there had been the slightest risk.

He twisted his lips. Nothing in this life was without risks.

Kneeling beside Amaridin, he pushed his damp hair off his face. Hovering over him, he inspected his face with concern. Then he bent and kissed him on the lips. "Love? Can you hear me?"

Lines of pain creased Amaridin's face. Valerian's chest tightened as he caressed his partner's cheek. Amaridin's face paled, and his lashes fluttered. Clasping Amaridin's hand, Valerian kissed his knuckles and waited.

Amaridin opened his eyes. His pupils were blown wide, leaving the thinnest rim of blue, and his brow creased as he shuddered. Lurching up, he dashed for the bathroom and vomited down the toilet.

Valerian followed. He grabbed a towel and wiped Amaridin's face, which was chalk white, his lips grey. "What happened?" Valerian asked.

Amaridin waved a hand and vomited again.

"I'll call a healer," Valerian said, but Amaridin caught his hand.

"No, not yet," he managed to utter before heaving again.

"But you're ill. You need help."

"Headache."

Valerian sat back on his heels and stared at his partner. A headache had caused this?

"Light, too bright."

Valerian left him to close all the curtains. "A migraine? Like Mav suffered?" he asked when he returned.

"Mmm."

"Let's clean you up and get you to bed. The healers will treat it." He guided Amaridin to the bedchamber and helped him lie on the bed. Sitting beside him, he gently massaged Amaridin's temples.

"Bonding with the citadel caused this? You have bonded, haven't you?"

"Too many souls. Need to return them."

"That, we agree on," Valerian said. "Why haven't I bonded as well? I thought we were going to do it together?"

"We will," Amaridin said, clasping his hand. "We will do everything together, always."

"Tell me what I need to do."

"We'll talk tomorrow. Could you get me that pain relief? I don't think I can open my eyes." Amaridin moaned. "How did Mav put up with this?"

Valerian frowned. Put up with what? Tomorrow, he and Amaridin were going to have a serious discussion about not sharing things. But for now, he would do whatever he could to ease his suffering.

23

DEMAVRIAN – OBLIVION GATE

The next morning, Mav was feeling restless. He hadn't trained in months. He wondered how Oji would feel about him running through the corridors. Maybe it would be better to join Adriz in the sparring ring with Muntra.

"My halls are your halls," Oji said. *"If you want to run in them, that is fine, though maybe we should warn the others that it is just for exercise and not an emergency. People don't usually run in the corridors by choice. They tend to glide."*

Mav laughed and transported himself to the Oblivion Gate. It really was time he moved into his rooms here.

"We could create a training area here," Oji suggested. "Then Adriz and Muntra can train here. Adriz was muttering about wanting a sparring arena. Maybe she could spar with you?"

"That is an excellent idea," Mav replied as he jogged down the hall. "Where should we put it?"

"Well, seeing as I need to add the barracks for the guards you are planning, I would prefer to leave the rest of the ground floor for public use, for when we have visitors.

"Your private rooms and the bedchambers are on the second level. The library takes up much of the third floor and rises through all levels, so I was thinking maybe the fourth floor? If you run up the stairs, that should be a good workout?"

Mav grinned at the happiness pervading Oji's voice. His once-empty halls were filling up. He veered off towards the staircase and began jogging up the stairs. His breath became more laboured. He needed the exercise.

"Let me show you where I think it should be," Oji said as Mav arrived on the fourth floor, panting heavily. He stopped on the landing and bent over, clasping his knees as he tried to catch his breath.

"You are out of shape," Adriz said from behind him.

"I know," Mav replied as he straightened and grinned at her. She wore tightfitting black trousers and a shirt that was moulded to her trim body, revealing her muscles as she moved. She had come ready to train. "Which is why Oji and I are planning a training arena."

"So I am informed." A door swung open in front of them, and Adriz peered inside. "Oh, my. Oji! You don't do things by half, do you?" She entered the room and Mav followed.

The training area was huge. A rack of weapons and training implements filled one wall, and a large, matted section took up half the room. Ropes hung from the ceiling, along with a row of punching bags, and one of the walls had some sort of climbing challenge. A sand-filled arena with tiered seating at one end took up the other half of the room.

"It's perfect," Adriz breathed, walking further into the room. "Wait until Ryvalin sees it."

"There are showers and a changing area off to your left, through the door," Oji said.

"You've thought of everything," Mav said as he inspected the weapons rack.

Their voices echoed in the large space, and Mav shivered at the anticipation hovering in the air.

"You said we would have a full complement of guards," Oji said. "They will need to train as well, won't they?"

"Definitely, though once we decide where we want to locate ourselves, some of the facilities can be outside."

"Maybe," Oji said. "If they are outside, they would not be under my control."

"We'll figure something out when we need to. For now, this is exactly what I need." Mav grinned at Adriz. "Ready to try it out?"

Adriz grinned back at him. "You bet. Choose your weapon."

Mav jumped up and down and stretched out his legs. "A bit of hand-to-hand wouldn't go amiss."

Adriz nodded as she joined him in performing a series of stretching exercises. "Good choice. Let's see what you've got." She charged forward.

Mav blocked her strike, responding instinctively as she jabbed and dodged. Adriz was a powerful woman. He knew she was going to work him over thoroughly, and he grinned as he counterattacked.

His oathsworn was an old sparring partner, and even after fifty years apart, they moved seamlessly, testing each other's reflexes, their limits, and finding their match.

A turn later, sitting in his study, Mav groaned as he stretched out aching muscles. At the time, sparring with Adriz had felt amazing. Now, he regretted their enthusiasm. He was supposed to go and see Xabier, but his limbs felt like lead.

He would need to use that training facility every day to get his muscles back in shape.

Adriz was indefatigable and had left to drag Muntra back into the citadel training ring. Bailey, Kerris, and Shandra were in lessons. An apprehensive Solanji had gone to see her brother, Brennan, hoping she could return his soul. She had also taken Mav's message to Ryvalin, asking the dragonair to return to the citadel.

With everyone safely occupied, Mav headed for Xabier's rooms, escorted by Felather. He had a favour to ask.

An awareness accompanied him wherever he went. Oji observed everything with an eager interest, and at the same time, he sensed every inch of the Oblivion Gate and everything within it, including those pesky shadows. It was quite distracting.

A constant yearning tugged at Mav's gut, a need to return to the Oblivion Gate and explore. To learn every nook and cranny, to make it his. To make it a part of him. Lingering in the citadel was an irritation, a reminder of what he'd lost and what he should be gaining. He wanted to spend time with Oji, along with a whole list of other obligations he needed to fulfil. He wished one of his abilities was to slow down time.

A lurking shadow at the back of his mind was the need to deal with Serenia. He would have to pass her through the Gate, and he was uncertain how bad it was going to be. Sometimes, it felt like it was more a punishment for him than for her.

"I will help you," Oji whispered in his mind. *"We will work together."*

Mav clung to the promise. *"Thank you,"* he whispered back.

His fledglings would settle in time, and once he'd

arranged a mentor for Shandra, he could return to the Gate. Thus, here he was, visiting Xabier.

Felather hovered behind his shoulder, an anxious shadow. "Are you sure Xabier will be up to it?"

"I think he will jump at the opportunity; at least, I hope he will."

"But why?"

Mav chuckled. "Why not? I bet he misses the satisfaction of a well-organised event. He's used to being in the centre of the action. I imagine life feels flat now."

Felather laughed. "I would have thought he'd be glad of a rest."

"Sometimes," Mav said softly, "a lack of purpose can be as detrimental to your health as overwork." He knocked on the door of Xabier's chambers.

The door opened, and the attendant gestured for Mav to enter.

Mav found Xabier seated in his chair, a book in hand. He shut the book and placed it on the table next to him.

"Demavrian. Somehow, I am not surprised."

Mav grinned. "Somehow, I'm not surprised you're not surprised."

Xabier chuckled and then coughed. "We'll leave it there."

"Agreed. You're still unwell? I thought the healer had seen you."

Xabier waved his hand. "He did. It's much better. And I have you to thank for that." He peered at Mav from under his bushy eyebrows. "Whatever you did lifted a weight off my chest, and I thank you for it."

"I'm glad I could help," Mav replied.

"Please sit, and you, too, Felather. You hover over me and make me feel like I've forgotten something."

Felather grinned and sat. "You never forget anything."

Xabier wheezed out a laugh, and Mav frowned.

He sent his senses questing and inspected Xabier, trying to find the underlying issue. His heart sank as he found it. That was something he couldn't fix.

He met Xabier's eyes and sensed that Xabier knew.

"I believe you have a job for me," Xabier said with a small smile.

"If you feel up to it," Mav replied.

Xabier shrugged. "The young lady is worth it. Shandra has ambition."

"That, she has," Mav said.

"Then we are in agreement." Xabier raised his hand. "I'll expect her at second chime every afternoon."

Mav nodded, his gaze never leaving Xabier's face. "I thank you on her behalf. She isn't aware of the honour you bestow on her."

"As it should be," Xabier said with a small nod.

Mav smiled. "When you feel up to it, I would love to show you the Oblivion Gate."

After a slight hesitation, Xabier inclined his head. "I would be honoured."

It was at that moment that Mav knew it would never happen. And Xabier knew it, too.

Felather frowned, glancing between the two men as if sensing the undercurrent but not understanding what was happening.

"Shandra has the organisational skills. She needs help with scale and managing people. She's coped on her own for too long, and now she needs to learn to manage a team and delegate."

Xabier nodded. "We can start there and see how far we get."

"I will be spending much of my time at the Gate. Felather will be here if you need to contact me. My fledglings need to achieve journeyman, or woman, status before they can join me."

"Ah," Xabier said, his eyes twinkling. "A challenge, I see."

"We'll see how long it takes them."

"Somehow, I think they will surprise you. They strike me as very determined."

"Of that, I have no doubt."

Xabier coughed again.

Mav sighed. "Xabier…" he began, but Xabier held up his hand.

"Don't. You're making an old man very happy. Let me inspire your young lady. You won't regret it."

"I know I won't. Thank you, Xabier. But I must insist you don't overdo it. If you need to rest, you should rest."

"Your fledgling will be doing all the work. I will rest while I observe her efforts. Now, off with you. I'm sure you have much to do."

Arriving back at his citadel chambers, Mav found Adriz waiting for him. He collapsed into his chair and waved for Felather to sit. "So, that's all of the fledglings sorted. Working towards their journeyman or woman status will keep them busy and out of trouble while I secure the Gate."

Adriz nodded as she sat opposite him. "In theory, though, I am sure they would rather be with you in Eidolon."

"Not yet." Mav scowled. "They have much to learn before they join me, and I need you to help me in Eidolon."

"We shouldn't leave them here unprotected."

"Once I know the Oblivion Gate is safe, we can take them with us. But you're right. Until then, how about if I recall Ryvalin and Xylvin? They can keep an eye on them."

"I think they're probably fed up with babysitting duty."

Mav raised an eyebrow. "Are you offering?"

Adriz rocked back and bit her lip. "Ryvalin doesn't know the fledglings as well as I do. And I'm only just getting Muntra into a routine." She grimaced. "We have a lot of work to do. Everything is new and daunting. But they need to be with you, Mav. They trust you; they'll open up to you. You need to speak to the fledglings before you go. Especially Bailey. He is really fragile, and suppressing what they went through is not good for any of them."

"I know. There isn't enough time in the day to do everything. But I will stay and speak to them before they go to bed. That's why I'm prioritising the Gate. Once I know it's safe, we can all move in together."

"Well, I'll stay with you until Ryvalin joins you in Eidolon. Felather can be on Fledgling duty." She paused as Felather snorted under his breath. "And then, once Ryvalin arrives, she can help you secure everything in Eidolon." Adriz frowned, her eyes distant. "We'll need a way to travel back and forth between Eidolon and Puronia, though. I need to work with Muntra every day, and you can't keep transporting me. However it is you're doing it, it must tire you." She leaned forward. "Don't you overdo it, either, Mav. I know you are a Deus, but you must have limits."

Mav ran a hand through his hair. "I'd create a portal, but I've only just claimed the Gate. Our bond is tenuous, and he is uncertain. We need to work out how to support each other and establish some house rules before I start making holes in his defences. I don't want any surprises."

"You speak as though the Gate is a person," Felather said.

"He is. He is a separate person with thoughts and feelings, and he makes mistakes just like us. The citadel is dormant compared to him."

"But how is he so self-aware? Can you trust him? After all these years, he must have been influenced by Kaenera."

"As far as I can tell, we are fully bonded. I have his memories; his knowledge, in here"—Mav tapped his temple—"and I can see no sign of subterfuge. He appears independent of Kaenera, but that's what I need to confirm. I don't want to move in the family and lead them into a trap. Kaenera could wipe us all out in one go. And then there are the 'others'."

Adriz tensed. "Others?"

"Yes, Kiara mentioned seeing shadows as well. There are some other beings in the halls. I haven't met them yet, nor do I know their purpose."

"Mav, I'm not liking this at all. Are you sure the halls are safe?" Adriz said.

"You can come back with me tonight and see for yourself."

"I will, but in the meantime, maybe your father knows more about the Gate? He was pushing you to claim it."

"Excellent point. I will make time to speak with him after I've dealt with the fledglings." He glanced at the timepiece on the mantle. "They should be back soon for dinner."

"Well, I'll leave you to contact Ryvalin." Adriz rose. "I'll see you at dinner."

Mav exhaled. "I wish I could transport Xylvin here, but she's too big."

Felather laughed. "I'd love to see her face if you did."

"The trouble is, I don't know how to tell them how to get to the Gate. Maybe I'll try when I'm there. She might be able to pick up my position."

"If in doubt, head south. You said you were by the sea, didn't you?"

"But which sea?"

Felather stared at him. "There's only one large expanse of water, isn't there?"

Mav shrugged. "No idea. I've never seen the sea in Eidolon before."

"But wouldn't it be the same sea as in Angelicus? That's to the south."

"I suppose that would be logical, though I'm not sure how much logic there is in a magical building appearing out of thin air. I'm told that the previous Gate Keeper kept the gate ephemeral. It didn't have a permanent location."

"Ah," Felather said, and then he squinted at him. "In that case, can't you decide where you want it to be?"

Mav grimaced. "Maybe. I don't know."

"I think you need to find out. I'm not visiting until I know it's not going to disappear on me."

"Coward," Mav muttered, and they were interrupted before Felather could reply as the fledglings tumbled into the room, all eager to tell Mav about their day.

24

SOLANJI – EIDOLON

When Solanji and Ellaria arrived to visit her brother, the yard outside the safehouse was quiet and empty. It was still early, but the kids were usually all up and out as soon as the sky lightened. Peering up at the grey clouds, Solanji wondered if Mav would improve the weather or leave it as it was.

Ryvalin strolled out of the barn, steam rising from the mug in her hand, a small black vemlow trailing after her. It frolicked around Ryvalin's legs, its tail wagging. Solanji hadn't seen one so close; they were wild beasts, hunting in the forests.

Ryvalin was casually dressed in a thick woollen top and trousers. Solanji had never seen her out of her uniform before. She looked a lot younger and not so tough, even with her grey hair cut short.

"You're early," Ryvalin noted in the quiet voice people use before the day has really started. The vemlow sat by her feet and began chewing the end of her boot.

"Find a new friend?"

"One of the kids rescued it. Its mother had been killed,

so we've been raising it by hand. It follows whoever feeds it. My turn today."

"I found Brennan's soul."

Ryvalin's eyebrows rose, and then she grinned. "Well, good news at last."

"Where's Xylvin?"

"Morning sweep. Not that she's seen anything since we've been here. Everyone's kept their heads down. I'll be glad to move on."

"Well, you'll be happy to know that Mav wants you at the Oblivion Gate. He needs help securing it. There was an attack, and there are still some unsecure areas. Only, he's not sure how to get you there, so he suggests you go back to the citadel first, and he'll try to guide you from there."

Ryvalin scowled. "Why didn't he call us sooner? He shouldn't be on his own."

"He's not. He's got Adriz, Felather, and Kiara, and the Gate itself." Though, as Solanji said it, she realised how little support Mav actually had in his battle against Kaenera. "Maybe you could suggest who should be seconded from the Heavenly Host."

"Julius should be helping him; he could bring his unit. He owes Mav that much."

"Excellent idea. Make sure you recommend him." Solanji had forgotten about Julius. He was an old friend of Mav's; they had grown up together, trained together, and yet he had believed Mav had killed Athenia, Julius' partner. Solanji thought there was probably still some work to do to repair that friendship, but his help at the Gate would get them on the right path.

"I will." Ryvalin stared off into the distance, and Solanji knew she was communing with her dragon.

"Xylvin's on her way back. I'll pack, and we'll be off. Mrs Bridges will be glad to see the back of us."

"The kids will miss you."

"They'll miss Xylvin, you mean."

Solanji laughed and rubbed Ellaria's eye ridge as she leaned against her. "I think you would be surprised if you asked them. I'd better go find Brennan."

She left Ellaria to occupy herself with peering out across the bracken, and headed towards the house. The door opened as she approached, and her brother came running out. He looked a lot healthier. His gaunt appearance and lingering air of ill health had finally been replaced with that of a sturdy, energetic child more interested in what life had to offer.

"Solanji! I saw Ellaria and knew you had to be here."

Solanji opened her arms wide, and Brennan ran into them. She hugged him tight, relieved once more that he'd had the good fortune to stumble upon Mav's fledglings when he had. She wasn't sure he would have survived on his own.

"I have wonderful news. I found your soul! You can go home."

"Oh," Brennan said, stepping back as he dropped his gaze and scuffed his shoe in the dirt.

"What's the matter? I thought you'd be pleased."

Brennan flushed. "I am. But it seems so unfair when everyone else doesn't have a soul."

"One day, they might; it doesn't mean you shouldn't take yours. Whether I can find everyone else's souls or whether Mav finds a way to give them shadow souls, we won't stop trying. But it will take time."

Brennan squirmed. "I know I need to go and see Ma, but I don't think I can just go home, not now that I've seen all this." He waved his hand around, encompassing all of Eidolon, she supposed. "I want to help."

"Oh, Brennan." Solanji hugged him. "You are young yet. You have plenty of time. Go home. Spend time with Ma and

Georgi. Enjoy being who you were supposed to be. You'll be able to come and visit Mav and me."

Squaring his shoulders, Brennan inhaled. "You promise?"

"Of course. But you know how sad Ma is without you."

Brennan nodded. "How do we do it?"

"It's easy." Solanji laughed. "Your soul knows where it belongs. Let's go sit with Ellaria." She led him over to the golden dragon, still peering into the gloom.

Solanji stroked her neck. *"What do you see?"*

"A juicy buck."

"If you want to go and hunt, you can. Let me just return Brennan's soul, first."

"I'll ask Xylvin. Then I think I might go grab it. She won't be happy if I'm hunting on her lands without her permission."

"It's not Xylvin's land."

"Yes, it is."

"I don't understand." Solanji frowned in confusion.

"It's her territory. She flies over it."

"Does that mean Puronia is hers as well?"

"It was. But I think she'll stay wherever Mav is, and that is here in Eidolon."

Ellaria leapt into the air.

"I thought she was going to help?" Brennan asked, watching the dragon fly away.

"She's hungry."

"Oh."

Solanji found a wooden stump to sit on, and Bren sat at her feet.

"Will it hurt?" Brennan whispered.

"No, it's a part of you. If anything, you'll feel better. Removing a soul is probably more…not painful but disorienting. Returning it is more of a sensation than a pain."

Solanji patted his shoulder and selected his soul from the

swirl of golden soulmist she was carrying. She squinted, trying to see where she should return it to, but there wasn't an obvious empty space. She exhaled, and the soulmist swirled in the air between them. Then Bren sucked it in; the soulmist instinctively seemed to know where it belonged.

He shuddered and straightened, and a smile slowly spread over his face. There was a subtle difference to his appearance: a sharpening of his posture, a glint in his eyes. It wouldn't have been noticeable if she hadn't been watching so closely.

"Alright?" Solanji asked.

"Oh, yes," Brennan breathed. "It's…I don't know how to explain it. It's like I was wrong before and now I feel right." He suddenly frowned. "You have to give back as many souls as you can, Solanji. It isn't right taking them away."

"I know," Solanji replied, gripping his arm. "I will return all that I can."

"Good."

"In that case, do you want to collect your belongings, and we'll go home?"

"I only have a few clothes. I don't need them. The kids here need them more than me. I'll just say goodbye." He peered into the sky. "Will Xylvin be back before we go? I'd like to say goodbye to her as well."

"I'll ask Ryvalin while you go say your goodbyes."

Bren nodded and hurried off.

"Ellaria, do you know how far away Xylvin is?"

"Not far. I'll be finished before she gets here."

"It's not that. Bren wants to say goodbye."

"I'll tell her."

"Thank you."

It wasn't until Solanji started walking back towards the house that she remembered she could have spoken to Xylvin herself. They were all oathsworn to Mav, so they could all speak to each other telepathically. With Mav and Ellaria, it was instinctive, with the others, she tended to forget.

"Try harder," Ellaria said, and Solanji laughed.

"I thought you were hunting."

"I hunted. Now I eat." Ellaria sounded very content. *"Xylvin comes."*

Solanji paused on the veranda and watched Xylvin land in the courtyard. Even in the dull light, her scales rippled with colour, a beautiful shimmer of iridescent reds, blues, greens, and everything in between. Her huge, wedged head swung towards Solanji, and her muti-faceted eyes winked at her.

"You returned Bren's soul? That bodes well for others," Xylvin said, her deep voice a warming caress in Solanji's mind.

"Yes. It was easy, as if the soul wanted *to return and knew where to go."*

"Makes sense. What is this about Mav being attacked? Why weren't we told?"

"You were here."

Doesn't mean we stay here."

Solanji twisted her lips, accepting the rebuke. Felather had said much the same. *"Well, Mav needs you now at the Oblivion Gate. Only he's not sure how to give you directions. The Gate is not always seated on the land. It tends to disappear. When it's ephemeral, I'm not sure it has a location."*

"Of course it does. Just not in Eidolon."

"Umm, okay. Where else would it be?"

"Wherever it wants to be."

Solanji's head began to ache. *"Can you find it?"*

"Not if it doesn't want to be found."

Solanji rubbed her temples. *"Mav and Oji want you to find them. Would that mean you could?"*

"I expect so."

"Please do. Otherwise, Mav said go back to the citadel, and he'll

try to guide you from there. In the meantime, I'm taking Brennan home to Bruatra. He wanted to say goodbye to you before we went."

If dragons could smile, then that's what Xylvin did, even if there were a lot of pointed teeth. Her tail thumped all five fronds in turn like fingers tapping a table. *"Sweet boy,"* she said.

"He likes you, too, and here he is."

Solanji turned to greet her brother as he tumbled down the steps and ran towards Xylvin. She was surprised when Bren didn't stop but ran right up and hugged Xylvin's snout as she lowered it. Solanji walked back down the steps.

"I'm gonna miss you, Xylvin," Brennan said.

"And I'll miss you, young Brennan. But it is time for you to go and live with your mother."

"I know, but I'll still miss you. Will I see you again?"

"I am sure of it."

"Good," Brennan said as he released her.

"Will you miss me just as much?" Ryvalin asked dryly as she reached them, her carryall slung over her shoulder.

Brennan grinned. "Of course. You two go together." And to Solanji's even greater surprise, he rushed over and hugged Ryvalin so hard she had to drop her bag.

Ryvalin hugged him back and dropped a kiss on his tousled hair. "Be good for your mother."

"I'll try."

Ryvalin laughed as she released him. "That's all we can ask. We've been recalled, so we're going home, too."

"That's good. I think Mrs Bridges will be happy to hear that. If you're not going to be here, I don't mind leaving so much."

"Thought it might help," Ryvalin said as she picked up her bag.

Ellaria landed beside Solanji. She looked delicate and fragile against Xylvin's larger bulk. The dragons bumped noses and then seemed to ignore each other, though Solanji was sure they were in deep discussion about Mav and what had happened at the Gate.

"Time to go," Solanji said, and Ellaria wrapped herself around Solanji as she held her hand out to Bren. "I'll see you at the Gate," she said to Xylvin and Ryvalin.

Ryvalin nodded and turned to climb up on Xylvin's back. Xylvin bent her foreleg, and Ryvalin scrambled up.

Bren grabbed Solanji's hand, and they shimmered out of sight as Ellaria transported them to Bruatra.

Bren staggered when they appeared on the grassy headland overlooking the picturesque fishing village.

"It's so bright!" he said as he shielded his eyes against the glare of the morning sun and squinted at his home.

The village was nestled in the lea of the headland, and the bay curved into a pebbly beach stretching off into the distance. A slow-moving river split the beach, and the two sides were connected by a low stone bridge wide enough for a cart. Small boats and piles of nets were scattered on the beach. Behind them, white-painted, single-storey buildings crawled their way inland, hemming in the river.

Solanji gripped Bren to steady him and inhaled the warm, salty air. The sea gleamed, a constant ripple of silvery blue deepening to a darker blue on the horizon. As she raised her face to the sun, her shoulders relaxed, and the warmth made her smile.

"I'll go for a swim," Ellaria murmured and leapt back into the air.

"It looks just the same!" Bren exclaimed as he gazed around him. He scurried down the worn path, sniffing the air as he led the way to their home. Solanji followed more slowly. It was Bren who had changed, not Bruatra. Solanji suddenly worried that he wouldn't be able to settle back into the slow way of life after his recent experiences.

Rushing from one side of the road to the other, he inspected everything: from the pile of boulders forming the beacon where they lit the fires to guide boats back in bad weather to the newly created steps that made it easier to descend the steep headland.

As they reached the bottom, the stench of fish permeated the air, and Solanji wrinkled her nose.

Bren leapt into the air. "Now I know I'm home!" he cried as he ran down the road towards their home.

Solanji followed, deliberately slowing, giving Bren time to get home and overwhelm their mother. She should have sent a message warning her they were coming, but it was too late now. She smiled as shrieks drifted on the balmy air; Bren had found his mother.

Their home was a small dwelling of four rooms: two bedrooms, a living space, and a kitchen. A lean-to had been extended off the back, which had once been where Solanji slept. The boys had shared the other bedroom. Now Georgi and Bren each had a room.

Flower borders ran down either side of the path leading to the house, a splash of colour against the whitewashed walls.

Their mother was still hugging Bren when Solanji arrived. She exclaimed over how much he had grown as she checked her son over, pulled him back into a hug, and then inspected his face again.

"I'm fine, Ma," Bren said with a laugh, but Solanji knew it would be a while before her mother believed it.

"I've been so worried," their mother said. "Georgi even stayed home for a week, but I told him he had to get back to sea. What would we live on otherwise?"

Solanji bit her lip to stop herself from retorting that she had sent money.

"You must be hungry," her mother said as she patted

Bren's shoulder. "I bet they never fed you in that place. Sit down, and I'll get you your favourite cookies."

"Hi, Ma," Solanji said as she entered the kitchen.

"Solanji. Is Demavrian with you?" Her mother peered over Solanji's shoulder. Once she had gotten over the shock of who Mav actually was, she had become quite smitten.

"He couldn't come with me this time. Ellaria brought us here."

Her mother stiffened. "You'll not bring that thing in with you."

"Thing? Ellaria is not a thing, Ma. She is my dragon."

"Ellaria is gorgeous!" Bren said. "And I met another dragon in Eidolon called Xylvin. She is three times as big as Ellaria, but she is just as amazing."

Their mother shuddered. "Unnatural," she whispered under her breath.

"It is not unnatural," Solanji said, unable to keep the bite from her voice. "They are perfectly natural and a blessing to us all."

"They are my friends," Brennan said.

"Yes, dear. You'll soon get over it. Now that you're home, we can get back to normal."

Solanji hadn't realised how narrow-minded her mother was. Watching Brennan stiffen, she knew he wouldn't stay here. His original plan to join Georgi on the boats had been blown to smithereens as his experiences had broadened his mind.

As her mother fluttered around the kitchen, planning the evening meal, a celebration for Brennan's return, Solanji walked back out of the house. She didn't think she would be staying. Her family was in Eidolon facing untold danger, and she wanted to be with them. Her life had been changed by her experiences as well.

"Now I understand why you left," Bren said from behind her. "I never did before. I thought this life was perfect."

"It is when it's all you know," Solanji replied.

"But now I know there is more to life."

"Yes," Solanji said with a sigh.

Bren gazed out over the sparkling sea. "It's funny. I thought I couldn't wait to leave Eidolon. But now that I'm here, I miss it."

"It has a way of growing on you," Solanji agreed.

"I don't think a life on the boats is really for me anymore."

Solanji wasn't surprised. "Ma will be upset."

"She'll get used to it. I'll stay here for a while, but not forever. I want to join you in Eidolon. I want to help. I want to be a fledgling like Bailey and Muntra."

"That is between you and Demavrian."

"Don't leave me here forever, Solanji. Please. Give me a chance."

Solanji exhaled and nodded. "Once we've got Eidolon stable, you'll get your chance to speak to Demavrian. But you stay out of trouble and make do here until then. Promise me?"

"I promise."

Solanji wrapped an arm around his shoulders and kissed his cheek. "In that case, brother of mine, make the most of your holiday because, when you join us in Eidolon, there is a lot of work to be done."

Brennan's smile was reward enough.

25

SHANDRA – CITADEL

After suffering through a second day of lessons with the other fledglings, Shandra decided learning about the ancient history of Puronia was not for her. She had better things to do with her time than listen to a lecturer droning on about a subject she had no interest in.

Once they were released for lunch, she went to hunt down Mav. Fortunately, she met him as he was on his way back to his office.

"Can I speak to you?"

Mav waved her through the door. "Of course. How are you finding life in the citadel?"

"I want to go with you to the Gate and see Kiara."

"Enjoying it that much, are you?"

Shandra twisted her lips. "I know you want me to learn all this stuff I'm never going to use, but I'd prefer to learn on the job. You need a housekeeper, a custodian, if you will, and I mean to fill that position. Let me go with you to the Oblivion Gate so I can learn its layout and what is needed.

"I ran a house for twenty or more children. I think I can run your home for you. If you still want me to be trained, they'll have to come to me." Shandra glared at Mav as he sank into his chair.

His lips twitched as she continued to glare at him, and she struggled not to smile. He leaned forward and steepled his fingers as he considered her. "You've never been to Puronia. Don't you want to enjoy its amenities before you turn your back on them?"

"Mav. You need a custodian. Oji needs someone to organise him. I need to be busy. I can't stand this waiting around."

"Very well. I would love for you to be my custodian, but your on-the-job training will be here in the citadel with Xabier. He cannot travel to the Oblivion Gate, as much as he would like to. And don't you suggest it; he is not fit enough to keep travelling back and forth. So, if you join me at the Gate, you will return here for lessons with him. Agreed?"

Shandra grinned at him as a flush of warmth spreading through her. Mav had already been preparing the way for her. She rushed around the desk and hugged him tight. "Yes, of course. I would love to study with Xabier, but my morning would be better spent putting his lessons into practice at the Gate."

Mav exhaled. "I have to warn you, though, not all is settled at the gate. There are some residents who may not be very welcoming, so you will have a guard with you at all times until I find out who they are."

"Maybe I can help flush them out."

"I haven't had the time to find them. Oji doesn't know who they are, so he is watching for them."

Shandra frowned. "How can he not know who is within him?"

"Oji has not been fully conscious. Kaenera never completely bonded with him."

Shandra chuckled. "And you have, of course. You don't do half-measures." She inspected him. "It looks good on you. You look much better, not so weary."

"Indeed, you know me so well. This is not for general consumption. I would prefer to keep it quiet, but not only have I fully bonded with him, but he is now completely cognizant as to what is going on. We can both see and experience what the other sees and feels. He is his own person." Mav pursed his lips. "Shandra, I need you to be the one with the common sense. He is a bit excitable at the moment, everything being so new."

Shandra grinned as Mav rolled his eyes and said, "You are!"

"Are you talking to him right now?"

"Yes. You know what? Why don't I just take you to the Gate and introduce you? He is not going to shut up until I do."

Happiness filled Shandra, and she laughed. She offered Mav her hand, and he rose as he clasped it.

"Hold on a moment." Mav released her hand, rounded his desk and opened his door. "Adriz, would you come with us to the Gate?"

Adriz raised an eyebrow. "Of course," she murmured and followed Mav into his chambers. "Where are you going to ground the Gate?"

"In the bay by the sea. I think that is a natural site, and we won't disturb anyone else there."

Adriz nodded. "What about Kaenera? He knows that location, doesn't he?"

"Even if he does, Oji assures me he won't get in. We'll be safe enough."

Offering each of them a hand, Mav gave Shandra a small smile of reassurance.

Shandra hung on tight as her surroundings blurred and

then shuddered to a stop, and she staggered. Mav steadied her as she couldn't help but gaze up at the high-vaulted ceilings. She rotated, staring at gleaming walls, the chandeliers with glass lights suspending from them, the sconces holding torches—but the flames were green! It was all so unexpected.

She gasped as she saw Mav. He looked so young, with his glorious wings extended and their shadowy feathers gilded in an exquisite green sheen and glinting with silver sparkles.

"Welcome to the Oblivion Gate," Mav said with a soft smile, which lit his face with an inner glow.

"It's beautiful," she whispered. She wanted to say *he* was beautiful, but she managed to keep the words behind her teeth.

"Thank you," said a deep resonating voice.

"Oji?" she squeaked.

"Yes, Shandra. It is such a pleasure to meet you. I've never had a custodian before."

Shandra laughed. "I've never *been* a custodian before, but I am sure that between us, we will figure it out."

"That, we will. I have much to show you."

"We have one turn, Oji, and then I have to return to the citadel," Mav said. "I have work I need to complete."

"Can't you finish it here? I furnished your study. You'll love it."

Mav sighed, and Oji began his argument.

"Adriz can accompany Shandra. I will protect you, and Adriz will know where you are. No one can get in, so you are perfectly safe. You can bring your work here. Please?"

Mav gave in. "I will work here, but only for the afternoon. Adriz, would you escort Shandra on her tour?"

"Only if you don't leave your study."

"Deal," Mav said immediately, and Shandra couldn't help but laugh again. Everything felt so…right.

"What should I see first?" Shandra asked, lifting her face to the ceiling.

"My dear custodian, let me show you the ballroom," Oji said, his voice filled with excitement.

Mav groaned and led the way down the hall. Shandra rotated, admiring the beautiful space while Mav climbed the stairs and disappeared into the depths of the Gate.

Shandra gazed after him and then, with great anticipation, asked, "Where is Kiara?"

"Here," a breathless voice replied as Kiara manifested beside her.

Shandra caught her breath. Shock froze her for a moment before tears gathered in her eyes as she inspected her friend. Kiara was the same but so different. On a sob, Shandra opened her arms, and Kiara slammed into her.

"I thought we'd lost you," Shandra sobbed.

"If it hadn't been for Mav, you would have," Kiara replied, her voice muffled against Shandra's chest.

"How is this possible?"

Kiara shrugged. "No idea. But when Mav is here, I'm solid. It's like he grounds me. When he's not here, I'm more wraith-like." Kiara stepped back. out of Shandra's embrace, though she clung to her hand, and Shandra tightened her grip. "Well, I am a Gate Wraith."

"Are you alright remaining here? I mean, you're not staying here because you think you have to?"

"Shandra, don't be daft. Of course I love being here. Have you seen Oji's mechanics? They are to die for!"

Shandra laughed and rolled her eyes. "Not yet. But I would think it's the perfect job for you."

Kiara tilted her head. "Are you really going to move in with Mav? All of you?"

"Yes. I am here to stay. The others have to achieve their journeyman status, and then they'll be here like a shot."

"What's that?"

"It's when you pass your tests proving you have the knowledge and expertise to specialise." Adriz's voice came from behind them. "At that point, you can choose to swear your oath to your sponsoring angel if you so desire."

Shandra's stomach dropped, and she turned towards Adriz, fear consuming her. "Does that mean I can't swear my oath to Mav?"

Adriz patted her on her shoulder. "You're one of Mav's fledglings. He'll find a way, if that's what you want."

"What about me?" Kiara asked.

Adriz snorted. "You are his Gate Wraith. I'd say you are a done deal."

Kiara beamed at her and spun in the air with happiness as she pumped her fist. "Yes!"

Scowling, Shandra grabbed Kiara's arm. "In that case, I want a complete tour so I know what I need to ask Xabier about." She paused. "In fact, he'll be asking *me*, so I need to know everything."

Kiara grinned. "Then you're in the right place. Oji? Let the tour commence!"

"You are currently in the ballroom, but if you walk behind the staircase, you will find the door that leads to the kitchens." Oji's deep, warm voice came from the walls, surrounding Shandra, and she relaxed as he directed her where to go.

Kiara flitted on ahead, and Adriz followed close behind.

"Oji?"

"Yes, Shandra."

"Do you mind having us all traipsing through your halls?"

"I am honoured that you want to live with me. My halls were meant for people. What is the point of them existing if they aren't used?"

"I know. But you are used to being alone. We fledglings can be noisy. I don't want to disturb your peace."

Shandra heard the smile in his voice as he spoke. "I have had aeons of peace. A little bit of liveliness won't go amiss."

Shandra twisted her lips. "You may regret saying that."

Oji laughed. "No, I won't. I know what Mav is planning, and I find myself in agreement. Whatever you bring to his plan will only enhance it."

Catching her breath, Shandra halted on the stairs. "Really?"

Oji's voice was soft as he said, "Shandra, I see into your heart, and I see only love for others. All that you bring to my halls will be welcomed."

Tears gathered in her eyes as she mounted the rest of the stairs. "I will make you the best Oblivion Gate ever."

"I know you will. Let me show you all that I am and all that I could be."

26

DEMAVRIAN – CITADEL

Mav was beginning to feel stretched. Bouncing from the citadel to the Oblivion Gate and back again was exhausting. It was time to transfer his family to the Gate and leave Amaridin to run the citadel. The Gate would be his new base. Relief coursed through him as he made the decision.

Xylvin's presence pinged in his mind like a warm caress, and Mav relaxed as Ryvalin entered his chambers in the citadel. She looked rested and refreshed, though she scowled at him as she sat in the chair opposite.

"Took you long enough to recall us," she grumbled. "I've forgotten what the citadel looks like. Xylvin has already claimed her fountain and scared off all the guards."

Mav grinned at her. "You needed a break. There is much that will keep you busy now that I have claimed the Gate."

Ryvalin raised an eyebrow. "I'm glad to hear it. Do you want Xylvin and I to go to the Oblivion Gate? I can't defend what I don't know."

"We will, but first, I need you to help me collect our Host. Julius has been assigned to me, but he's wallowing in self-pity. You're going to have to drag him out of the bottle and keep him occupied."

"As long as we get his division, I'll manage him."

"You'll have six cohorts, a whole division. The Oblivion Gate, Oji, is adding on barracks as we speak. Once we have Julius onboard, we'll go to the Gate, and you can start acquainting yourself." Mav stared at Ryvalin for a moment. "I'm sure Kaenera is organising his army somewhere in Eidolon. We must find out where it is located. We need to be ready for an assault and planning our own."

"Xylvin searched much of the northeast and found nothing. She can start searching further south while I learn the strengths and weaknesses of the Gate."

"Sounds good. First, though, we need to go into Puronia and reclaim Julius." Mav's mouth tightened. "I had hoped he could influence Lynen to support us, but I have a feeling that is a lost cause."

The Cross Keys tavern was even seedier than Mav remembered. The building had a general air of dilapidation. The windows were crazed, and the timbers sagged, giving it an appearance of leaning to one side. He was surprised it was still standing.

The front door was wedged open, and an awful smell pervaded the air, a combination of the foul and baser scents found in the dregs of a city.

Ryvalin wrinkled her nose. "He chooses to drink here? What's he trying to do, poison himself?"

"Yes. I expect that's exactly what he is trying to do," Mav replied. Squaring his shoulders, he entered the tavern and tried to breathe shallowly.

Disgust rippled through him as his boots stuck to the floor. It was alleviated a bit as Ryvalin muttered colourful curses under her breath behind him. The taproom was larger inside than it first seemed. It had a bar at one end, and a single table with benches ran down the centre of the room. Shadowy alcoves lined either side of the long bench, housing smaller tables.

A few of the alcoves were occupied, but the main table was empty.

Ryvalin went up to the bar and ordered two mugs of ale while Mav inspected the occupants of the alcoves. He peered closer as he saw a dishevelled Julius slumped over the table, gripping a mug.

As he neared Julius' alcove, another man rose from the neighbouring booth, his hand on the hilt of his sword. "Who are you, and what do you want?"

Mav stopped. "You can stand down, soldier; I mean him no harm." The man was a member of the Heavenly Host. Though out of uniform, his posture gave him away. The fluid way he moved meant he knew what he was doing, and he had probably run interference for Julius many times. His blond hair was cut short, his face clean-shaven, and he conveyed a no-nonsense attitude.

"How long has he been like this?" Mav gestured at Julius.

"Who's asking?"

Mav moved into the dim lamplight and allowed some of his aura to leak, and the soldier gasped and stepped back.

Ryvalin came up beside Mav and offered him a mug. "Here you go, but I don't recommend you drink it."

Mav glanced at her. "Why did you buy it, then?"

"I thought we were blending in with the locals."

"I think that is a lost cause," the soldier said and then clapped a hand over his mouth.

Mav laughed. "What's your name, soldier?"

"Sergeant Kaz Gurida, sir. First cohort."

"And how long have you been keeping Captain Teravin out of trouble?"

"Since he found out Archangel Serenia killed Archangel Athenia and realised he had falsely accused and hounded you for over five decades, sir."

"I see. You are in his division?"

"Yes, sir. We've been keeping the men in training and covering for each other while we keep an eye on the captain."

"Well, I think this has gone on long enough. You and your division are about to be seconded to me at the Oblivion Gate in Eidolon. What do you think your men will think of that?"

"That it would be an honour to serve you, sir."

"He's good," Ryvalin said, sniffing her ale and then placing it on the table behind her.

"And what will they really think about serving in Eidolon?" Mav asked.

Gurida grinned. "They'll be relieved to be doing something worthwhile, sir. And every single one of them will be honoured to serve, if only to atone for chasing you, on occasion, through Eidolon."

Mav's eyebrows rose. "So, most have already served time in Eidolon? That is unexpected but much preferred." Mav glanced down at Julius. "How long has he been drinking today?"

"About three turns. They open early for him. They like his money."

"I think it's time we sobered him up so I can have a chat with him."

Gurida rocked back. "He'll wake up swinging, sir. He forgets where he is."

"In that case, we'll wake him up at the Gate. If you

would help me, Sergeant, it's time to get your captain back in the game."

"It would be a pleasure, sir."

"I like him," Ryvalin said as she watched Mav and Gurida haul Julius out of the alcove.

Julius hung limply between them for a moment, and then he groaned and began to struggle. Mav transported all of them to the training arena in the Oblivion Gate and dropped Julius in the sand.

Ryvalin dragged a gaping Gurida over to the benches, saying, "Mouth shut, Gurida, or you'll catch flies in it," while Mav scowled down at Julius.

"Yes, ma'am," Gurida said, snapping his mouth shut.

Ryvalin pushed him onto a bench. "Best we let them slug it out. I'm Captain Ryvalin, by the way, Demavrian's captain of the host. Julius is lucky to have you."

"That you are, my friend," Mav said as he crouched beside Julius. "Very lucky." He shook Julius' shoulder. "Julius. Wake up."

"Do you need anything, Demavrian?" Oji asked, his voice echoing around the arena.

Mav rose. "Only that you keep everyone else out of here for now." He walked over to the shower area and filled a bucket with water. Returning, he dumped it over Julius' head. Julius swore and swung his fist. He rolled over when he only met empty air.

Ryvalin raised her voice. "Oji, I'd like you to meet Sergeant Gurida. He and Julius are coming to live here with us. Julius is that lout over there who is rather inebriated." She gestured to the spluttering man. "Gurida, meet Oji, the Oblivion Gate."

Gurida stared around him, not sure where to look, and Ryvalin laughed.

"Welcome, Sergeant Gurida. Why is Julius inebriated?" Oji asked.

"Because he chose to drink pisswater in a shithole," Mav said as Julius managed to rise up on all fours and sway, his head hanging down.

"Fuck you," Julius mumbled, and he peered up at Mav as he leaned back on his heels. "Where am I?"

Mav winced at the sight of Julius' haggard face. The man had lost weight, and it did not look good on him. The usually elegant captain looked very much worse for wear.

"Welcome to the Oblivion Gate."

Julius stiffened and then wiped his hands down his clothes. "Why am I covered in sand?" He tried to flick the grit off his fingers.

"Because you were so drunk that you fell over," Mav said.

"I'm not drunk."

Mav raised his voice. "Sergeant, is your captain inebriated on duty?"

"Afraid so, sir," Gurida replied.

Julius peered towards the benches. "Gurida? What is going on? Where are we?"

"Deus Demavrian found you in the Cross Keys, sir, and brought us to the Oblivion Gate. They have an amazing training facility, sir. I can't wait to get our men working in here."

Julius rubbed his face and then spat out sand.

"Why would we be training in here?"

"Because the Eleventh Division has been seconded to Deus Demavrian, sir."

"Maybe you should have a shower?" Mav suggested. "It might clear your head." He transported Julius under the shower, fully clothed, and held him there just by using the power of his mind.

Julius yelped as the icy water pounded him. "Mav! You bastard. I'll get you for this!" Julius struggled against Mav's hold until he suddenly gave up and went limp. He hung in Mav's grip, letting the water pour over him. Mav switched the water off, gently lowered him to the ground, and dropped a towel on him.

Julius buried his face in the towel, and when his shoulders began to shake, Ryvalin rose. "Let me show you around the Oblivion Gate," she said as she escorted Gurida out of the arena.

27

DEMAVRIAN – OBLIVION GATE

Grabbing another towel, Mav walked over and began to rub Julius' hair. When Julius pushed him away, he sat on a stool in the shower area. "What's going on, Julius? Why are you trying to destroy yourself, your reputation, and your career?"

Julius' laugh was harsh as he lifted his face out of the towel. His face was drawn, his eyes bloodshot and full of self-loathing. His shoulders drooped. "What reputation? The idiot who dragged the wrong man back to the citadel and forced him through Apologia?"

"You were fed misinformation; it wasn't your fault."

"You were my friend. I should have known better."

"You were grieving. Such a loss as you experienced it was bound to affect your judgement."

Julius ducked his face back into the towel and then took a deeper breath. "Have you got any water to drink?"

Mav transported a jug and glass from the kitchen, ignoring Cook's protests, and placed them beside Julius. Picking up the jug, Julius drained it. Mav walked over to the sink and refilled it. Julius drank half of it again before putting it down. He wiped his mouth, and Mav offered him another glass filled with clear liquid.

Julius eyed it.

"For the headache," Mav said, and Julius took it.

"How did you find me?" Julius asked.

"Man in the office next to yours. You haven't been particularly discreet."

Julius exhaled.

"Talk to me," Mav said.

Rubbing a hand over his face, Julius said, "What does it matter?"

"You're my friend, and you're hurting. Athenia wouldn't want you to be suffering like this."

"She's gone, Mav, and she won't be coming back. That's what hurts. She should be here with us for eternity. Nothing you can say or do will change that." The bitterness in Julius' voice sliced deep, reopening partly healed wounds that Mav still carried.

"I know. I'm sorry I couldn't save her."

Julius stiffened. "If it's not my fault, it certainly isn't yours. You did what you could. You comforted her in her last moments, and I knocked you out for it. You should hate me."

"I may have for a while, but I was just as messed up as you were. I don't hate you, and I don't blame you for anything that happened."

"Why not? You should."

"Because the blame lies with Serenia and Kaenera, and I want to make them pay. Will you help me?"

Julius tensed, his jaw working as he stared at Mav. "You want *my* help?"

"Yes. I need you and your men to help me protect the Oblivion Gate. Kaenera wants it back, and he'll kill me to get it."

"Do I get a choice?"

"Do you want one? Amaridin said I could take as many of his men as I needed. I chose you."

"You did?" Julius blinked and then rubbed his temple as if he could wipe away his confusion.

"Yes. Now, come on. Let's find you some dry clothes, and I'll introduce you to Oji."

"Oji?"

"Oji. The Oblivion Gate."

"I'm glad you are feeling better, Captain Teravin," Oji said, his voice echoing in the arena. "Sergeant Gurida has been a little overwhelmed by his tour. He can be found in the kitchen with Cook."

Mav laughed. "Cook allowed a stranger in his kitchen?"

"Apparently, he is firmly ensconced in the kitchen, which is where Ryvalin and Gurida found him. I'm not sure how it happened, but they are swapping recipes. I think it will be a while before they are finished."

"Very well. Julius needs to change, and then we'll meet him there."

Julius wrung out his shirt and sighed. "You sure you want me dripping through your halls?"

"Don't worry. I'll transport us and you can have a nice, hot shower. My clothes should fit you, and then maybe Cook can give you something to eat before you return to the citadel."

"I thought you said I was seconded here? Shouldn't I stay here?"

"You need to get your men, but there's some stuff we need to talk about first."

"Ah, we come to the crux of the matter."

"We'll talk about it in a moment." Mav helped Julius to his feet and transported them to his bedchamber.

Julius staggered and peered around.

"Shower's in there," Mav said. "Go get cleaned up."

"You've got to stop shifting me about. It's not doing my stomach any good."

"You'll be fine once you've eaten."

Julius grunted and disappeared into the bathing room. Mav stacked a change of clothes on his bed and left him to it. He sat at his desk and pondered on how much to tell Julius.

"You should tell him everything," Oji said. *"He and his men will be risking their lives for us. He, at least, should know why."*

"Agreed. Has Shandra decided where she's going to house them?"

"She was asking about numbers."

"A division is six cohorts; that's one hundred and twenty men."

Oji was silent for a moment. *"I don't think she was expecting that many,"* he said eventually.

"Do we not have space?"

"I'll add a wing just for them; it's the support staff we need to consider."

"They are used to looking after themselves."

"They still need to be fed, and have clean linen, beds, and laundry."

"Ah, the supply chain."

"What about the supply chain?" Julius asked as he came out of Mav's bedchamber and sat in the chair opposite Mav.

"We don't have one," Mav replied, inspecting the resurrected captain. Julius looked a bit better. His blond hair was swept back off his face, but his eyes were red-rimmed and dull. His face was pale and haggard and Mav's clothes hung off him.

"That could be a problem."

"A huge problem that you and Ryvalin will need to fix. Oji is adding a wing for your barracks, but you need to work with him and my custodian, Shandra, on the rest."

"A wing? The Gate can just expand?"

"Yes, I can add or remove as needed," Oji said, and Julius flinched.

"Is Oji everywhere?" Julius asked peering around.

"Oji *is* the Gate. Of course he is all around us. We are bonded. What I see, he sees, and vice versa. We are one."

Julius stared at Mav. "And how does that feel?"

"It feels right, as if I have been missing something for many years, and now, I've found it."

Julius nodded. "And Kaenera wants it back."

"Yes. He's tried and failed once. He won't wait much longer to try again."

Looking away, Julius asked with some difficulty. "After everything that happened, why would you give me a second chance?"

"Because you are my friend, and I don't want Serenia's actions to take you away from me as well."

Julius stiffened and rapidly blinked. "So I report to Ryvalin?" he asked gruffly.

"She is my captain."

"Of course. Just checking."

"The Oblivion Gate is a sentient building. He is awake and actively engaged with everyone. He has oversight of everything that happens within our halls," Mav said.

"And you woke him up."

"Yes. We are a partnership."

"And all your oathsworn are here. What about your fledglings?"

"Shandra is my custodian, Kerris is a journeyman scribe, and Kiara is my Gate Wraith, responsible for maintaining the halls. Bailey and Muntra are still at the citadel but will be joining us here soon."

Julius nodded. "Gate Wraith?" he asked, wrinkling his brow at the unfamiliar term.

"There are wraiths within these halls. Those who are soulless and have died but chose not to pass through the Gate."

"Like dybbuks?"

"No, dybbuks are those who died and were bound to Kaenera, prevented from crossing. He controls them, and they have no free will. Once Kaenera releases them, they will cease to exist, but the wraiths are bound to the Gate and will remain here until *they* choose to pass through the Gate. Until now, the Gate was dormant, so they were unable to pass on. Some have passed; others remain. We are just clearing out the undesirables."

"I didn't realise there was a difference," Julius said, raising his eyebrows. "So there are some who are not to be trusted?"

"I think I have removed those with ill intent, though until I meet them all I can't be sure. Oji can watch them while they are in the Gate, but once they go elsewhere, we lose track of them."

"That is concerning."

"Just one of many concerning items."

"Will I meet these wraiths?"

"Those who choose to stay, I expect so."

Julius nodded, staring at Mav a little blearily. "What else?"

Mav grinned. Julius was absorbing the information but not necessarily understanding. No doubt, he would have lots of questions once he'd digested everything. His hangover was probably numbing his reactions. "Kaenera wants the Gate back, and he wants to kill me."

"Why does he have such a fixation on you? He's been planning your downfall for centuries."

"I really don't know. I think he's been jealous of everything my father had and arbitrarily decided I was his." Mav shrugged. "It makes no sense, but there it is."

Julius frowned and leaned forward. "There's something else, isn't there? You are Deus. You have the Gate. You should be able to handle Kaenera. He's weakened since you defeated him."

"He is not to be underestimated. I have been Deus for a fraction of the time he has. He knows how everything works; I am just learning. And there is something in the Gate he is desperate to retrieve. Something that could destroy us all."

Julius hissed his breath out. "What?"

"They're called the Aeora sigils. I'm trying to find a way to destroy them, without annihilating all of us, but it's slow progress. In the meantime, we have to ensure Kaenera doesn't reclaim the Gate."

"He won't," Julius vowed. "We'll protect you and your family."

"You don't know how happy that makes me. I've missed you."

"I'm so sorry, Mav. I swear I won't betray you again."

"That is finished and done with. We have a new challenge to face, and I'm glad you're by my side. There is one more thing I need to tell you. I don't want to cause you further distress…and I debated about telling you, but…full disclosure…"

Mav inhaled and exhaled to try and control his racing heart. He didn't know how Julius would react, and he was unsure if he should say anything, but he pulled out the red vendetta stone from his shirt.

"You know I told you this vendetta stone was for Athenia?"

Julius nodded, his breath catching.

"Solanji believes I still have this stone because Athenia's

soul is still in the citadel, waiting to pass on, and I agree with her."

Julius lurched to his feet. "What?" His face paled as he gaped at Mav, and Mav cringed at what must be going through his friend's mind.

"I'm sorry, Julius. She hasn't passed on because there was no one *to* pass her on with my father missing. Solanji is searching for her."

Julius paced back and forth. "Are you sure? No, it's not possible." He clutched at his hair. "Do you think she'll find her?"

"It's very likely."

Unable to keep still, Julius continued to pace.

"I'm sorry," Mav said, and Julius came to a halt. Mav rose and came around his desk.

"Don't be." Julius stared at him for a long moment, his eyes wild and glazed. And then he swallowed and closed his eyes. "If Solanji can help Athenia rest, then I'll be forever in her debt."

Mav gripped his shoulder. "Solanji wants the painting of me and Athenia here in our library. I hope you don't mind if it is relocated."

"It's your painting." Julius ran his hands through his hair. "You can do what you like with it. It will be nice to see her here, though."

"Right. That's everything I have for you. Let's get some food." Mav rose.

Julius raised his hand, halting Mav. "She's really still in the citadel? Will I...will I be able to speak to her?"

"I don't know, Julius. But we'll try."

"Alright. Let's get some food." Julius rubbed his temples. "Then, I suppose I need to speak with Ryvalin and figure out where she wants to deploy us."

Mav led Julius down the main staircase, and Julius halted

when he saw Xylvin curled around her fountain. "It's so good to see you, Xylvin."

Xylvin lifted her head. *"Welcome to the crazy house, Julius."*

Julius laughed, the first free-sounding laugh Mav had heard from him. "Just like the old times, then."

"Mav, are we staying here for a while? I want to go for a swim," Xylvin asked.

"Yes. We'll certainly stay here overnight."

The tall doors to the main entrance swung open, and cool, misty air flowed in.

"Where are we?" Julius asked.

"To the south of Eidolon. Near the sea." Mav pivoted as a flicker caught his eye.

"What is it?" Julius murmured.

"I thought I saw someone."

"It was a wraith," Oji murmured.

"I don't like not knowing who these wraiths are."

"Agreed."

"Can I eat them?" Xylvin asked, and Mav laughed.

"Food first," Mav said, leading the way to the kitchen as Xylvin walked out of the building, intent on going for her swim. The tall doors swung shut behind her.

Gurida lurched to his feet and saluted as they entered the kitchen. Ryvalin gave them a lazy wave.

Julius flapped his hand. "Sit down, Gurida. You just scraped me off the floor. I think you're allowed to relax."

"Cook here has a mean broth, ideal for hangovers. I mean, dealing with headaches," Gurida said. "He used to make it in a restaurant in Puronia."

Mav raised an eyebrow as the grumpy wraith scowled at Julius and pushed a bowl towards him. "Drink that. It'll do you wonders." It seemed that Shandra had approved the cook and was still here to make them dinner. Gurida had already wheedled more information out of the cook than

Mav had—not that Mav had had much time to spend with the wraiths.

Julius sat beside Gurida. "So, what do you make of the Oblivion Gate?" he asked as he picked up the bowl with both hands and sipped. He inhaled the warming aroma of spices and vegetables. "Mmm. Tastes delicious."

Gurida grinned. "The Oblivion Gate is amazing. I can't wait to be billeted here."

"Julius has agreed that your division will be seconded to the Gate for the foreseeable future," Mav said. He glanced at Ryvalin. "You have your division, Ryvalin. So, I suggest you work with Julius on the supply-chain issues, and get them settled in."

Ryvalin scowled at him. "Really? You expect us to solve that overnight?"

"The barracks will be ready tomorrow," Oji said. "Shandra has advised me on what is needed."

"What's this I hear of over one hundred men staying here?" Cook asked. "How am I supposed to feed all of them?"

"We'll get you some help," Mav promised.

"What sort of help?"

"Whatever you want. You tell us."

"You need some assistants to do the vegetables and peel the potatoes." Gurida said. "We'll have at least three shifts, if not more. This place is enormous. And there will be off-duty men, so meals will be needed at all times of the day and night. It's endless food prep, and our men have huge appetites."

"I'll need more stoves," the cook said.

"Work with Oji and Shandra on logistics," Mav said.

"You should eat." The cook thumped a bowl in front of Mav.

Mav grinned and picked up a spoon.

28

KAENERA – DOVETON, EIDOLON

The large estate in Doveton was Kaenera's favourite property. A stone-built, square dwelling surrounded by outhouses, stables, and barracks. Far to the east, beyond the sight of snooping angels, Kaenera had built his garrison. Here, he collected and trained his army of dybbuks, spies, and slaves.

His guards bracketed the tall double doors, and opened them at a wave of his hand to allow those who had failed him to be brought before him.

Seated in the long hall, surrounded by empty seats and silver-plated dishes piled high with exotic fruits and bread, Kaenera scowled at the dybbuk kneeling on the stone floor. The man was shaking so much that his armour rattled, and Kaenera hissed his breath out in annoyance. It wasn't that cold.

"Stand," Kaenera said, snapping his fingers.

The man stood, his head bent. His straggly brown hair covered his face, and he cowered behind the greasy strands with his eyes glued to the ground.

"Are you trying to tell me no one came back from the Oblivion Gate?"

"Yes, sir," the man mumbled, flicking his gaze up and latching onto Kaenera's fingers. His armour began rattling again.

Kaenera slowly stripped the skin off a grape. The man watched Kaenera's thin, bony fingers as he deskinned the fruit. Once Kaenera finished, he popped it in his mouth, and as his teeth shut with a click, the man flinched. Kaenera smiled.

"You lie."

"S-sir. The b-building appeared out of thin air as you s-said it would." The man twisted the cap in his hands. "But we couldn't get in."

"Why not?"

"None of the commands worked. The doors wouldn't open. The Gate didn't respond." The man took a step back as Kaenera's fingers stilled. "It weren't my fault."

"How did you get in, then?" Kaenera paused. "You *did* get in?"

"Steraf used your inhibitor. He managed to block communications between the Gate and its…its keeper." The man's voice faltered to a stop as Kaenera growled. He waved his cap in front of him. "Y-you said there was a new—"

"That usurper is not the keeper." Kaenera clenched his jaw, aware of his body stiffening at the idea that Demavrian would call himself the Gate Keeper. It was laughable. It was intolerable. His jaw cracked. It was insufferable.

"But there was a golden dragon who intervened."

Kaenera stilled. "A dragon? In the Gate?"

"Yes, sir. She broke Steraf's neck and killed the others."

A dragon? Kaenera smiled. *The SoulBreather was in the Gate.* "What about Ana? She hasn't reported in."

"I don't know. No one came back out before the building disappeared."

"Wait! What? The building disappeared?" The echo of the chair scraping across the stone flags had the man scuttling backwards as Kaenera lurched to his feet and lunged for him. Kaenera grabbed the man by the throat and squeezed, his claws biting into the man's grimy skin and drawing blood. "Why didn't you say that first?"

"I-I'm sorry, sir. Please, don't kill me."

"I can't track the Gate while it's ephemeral, only when it's solid. I told you to anchor it."

"I'm sorry, sir. There was nothing to anchor."

Kaenera shook him, and the man flailed in his grip. "You failed me," he growled, sparks flying off his fingers. "Why do you always fail me?" He paused, glaring at the dybbuk, and then he squeezed harder, and the man's eyes bulged as he struggled to free himself.

Raising his head, Kaenera smiled as the councillor he had summoned arrived in a flash of light. Bones snapped beneath Kaenera's grip and the dybbuk disintegrated. Brushing the dust off his fingers, Kaenera returned to his seat.

"Gineray," he said as he inspected his nails. He extended his claws and frowned at the grime coating them. Cleaning his nails with the point of his dagger, he waited for the councillor to approach.

"You can't keep dragging me here without warning. People will get suspicious," Gineray said as he rearranged the chairs, moving one in front of the desk before sitting in it. "What is so important?"

Raising an eyebrow, Kaenera rotated his knife between his fingers as he observed Gineray for a moment, waiting for the portly man to realise his mistake. The silence lengthened, and Gineray ran a finger around his collar. A sheen of sweat gleamed on his forehead, and he dipped his head.

"My apologies, my lord. I meant no disrespect, but these summonses are inconvenient. I have already sent you my report. I have nothing more to add."

Kaenera gripped the hilt of his dagger and pointed it at Gineray. The man straightened as he watched Kaenera wave the blade back and forth as if deciding where to plant it. "You do my bidding. You do it where and when I tell you."

"Yes, m'lord."

"What news from the citadel?"

"I've already sent my report."

Kaenera leaned forward and jabbed the dagger point down into the wood of his desk. "You are not indispensable. Serenia still lives. I could use her instead of you."

Gineray cleared his throat. "Amaridin and Valerian are insufferable, always in each other's arms. Where you find one, you'll find the other. The rumour is they've both bonded with the citadel, though I'm having difficulty getting anyone to confirm it. Demavrian would've had to release it for them to bond, but he is silent as well."

"Demavrian is at the Gate. He claimed it."

Gineray raised an eyebrow. "Well, there's your confirmation, then. Demavrian couldn't claim the Gate if he still had the citadel." He paused and licked his pale lips. "Have you thought about how you are going to draw Demavrian out?"

"Why would I need to draw him out?"

"You said the Oblivion Gate would be unassailable if Demavrian claimed it. I imagine we will have trouble getting in now…" Gineray twirled his fingers, and Kaenera hissed his breath out.

"His fledglings," Gineray said quickly. "Demavrian has fledglings at the citadel, and his oathsworn. He can't protect them all of the time. They are all points of weakness. Leverage."

Kaenera hated to admit it, but Gineray had a point. "Find out where the fledglings are. Find me the most vulnerable one." He scowled at the councillor. "What about Averdeus?"

"Very upset with you and Serenia."

Kaenera snorted. "That woman failed me. Make sure you don't."

"Your suggestion that she might yet be of use is a good one, my lord. She still has a soul; as far as I know, they haven't removed it yet. She could move around Puronia freely, whereas I need to remain inconspicuous. You know she'd do anything for you."

"Except deliver Demavrian as she was supposed to."

Gineray waved his hand. "At least she knows all the vagaries of the citadel. We…I mean, *you* need another way in. Maybe you could use her to infiltrate the heart of the citadel?"

Kaenera pursed his lips as a shaft of anger flashed through him at his own stupidity. He had to get the sigils before Demavrian realised what they were. "She's too well known."

"Hooded, they won't realise it's her. She has the confidence to pull it off. If you save her before she loses her soul, she'll be forever in your debt."

"And if they do discover her, she'll be no loss."

"My thoughts exactly, m'lord."

"And then it will all be mine."

"And I will rule the citadel on your behalf." Gineray smirked as he inspected his fingers. "What about the Gate? Have you considered how you are going to retrieve that weapon you spoke of?"

"We don't know that Ana failed. If she does not report in, then, as you say, I will need leverage."

"What about the wraiths? Are there any left we can use?"

"I won't know until the Gate reappears," Kaenera said, hating to admit there was one more thing he didn't control. "Demavrian will have to ground it. As soon as it does, I'll send in more dybbuks."

"I thought you still had a connection?"

"It's not a connection as such, more an awareness of when it is about to appear. But I can't watch for it continuously. I have other more important things I need to do."

"I'd have thought reclaiming the Gate was your priority. You need to nullify Demavrian."

Kaenera stiffened. "You forget yourself, Gineray. Do I have to remind you that your pitiful life is mine? I could still reft it away from you and replace you with another." Kaenera curled his fingers, and his claws glinted in the candle light.

"But then you'd lose your influence in the citadel, and you'd have to start again. As I said in my report, I have worked hard to get my people ready. Within a few weeks, I will have them positioned inside the citadel and poised to act."

"If you want to control the citadel, then a few weeks is not good enough. You will get them in position immediately. Do not fail me. I expect to hear of your success within two days."

Satisfaction flashed through Kaenera as he watched the man pale.

Rising, Gineray gripped the back of his chair so hard his knuckles cracked. He bowed. "Yes, m'lord. I won't fail you," he said and disappeared as Kaenera transported him back to Purnonia.

29

KIARA – OBLIVION GATE

Kiara left Shandra to her tour of the Oblivion Gate and returned to the area that she was calling the engine room. It was where all the levers and pulleys that controlled the gate were located. As she worked, she was aware of a visitor hovering in the shadows. Brushing the rust off one of the huge chain links which connected the pulleys, she blew the rust flakes away and continued cleaning. The wraith drifted closer, clutching a broom.

"Why do you make such a mess everywhere?" the wraith asked.

"To give you a job," Kiara said without looking up.

"I don't need your help for that."

"No? There doesn't seem to be much else for you to do. And if you've nothing to do here, then you'll…" Kiara waved her brush. "Be elsewhere."

"I prefer to be here."

"Me too."

"How do you know the Gate Keeper?"

"I knew him before I died."

The wraith was quiet for a moment before he said, "Can I help?"

"I thought you'd never ask." Kaira looked up and grinned at him. The form of a young boy rippled. She threw him another wire brush. "Oji has so many chains and rods and links, and they are all rusted. It'll take forever to clean them all."

The boy discarded his broom with a clatter and started brushing another large chain. "Who's Oji? he asked.

"That's what we call the Oblivion Gate. Oji for short."

"You speak to the Oblivion Gate?" the boy asked in wonder.

"Of course. The Gate Keeper woke him. I can introduce you to him if you like. My name's Kiara. What's yours?"

"Liam."

"Nice to meet you, Liam." Kiara raised her voice. "Hey, Oji, you got a minute?"

"For you, Kiara, you may have as many minutes as you need," Oji replied.

Liam stiffened and dropped his brush. He scrabbled on the floor for it and then hugged it to his chest.

Kiara laughed. "I'd like you to meet Liam. He is going to help keep your mechanisms clean and greased."

"Liam. It is a pleasure to meet you. Thank you for helping Kiara keep my mechanics functional. They have been long neglected."

"H-hello," Liam stuttered.

"How many wraiths are there in the halls?" Kiara asked him. "Will we get any more help?".

"I'm not sure. Not all of them speak to me. Wenson's been here the longest. You'll find him in the library. He won't stoop to do any cleaning; he thinks he's too good for that. He organises the library, keeps the books in the right places. Then there's Cook; he comes and goes because there's been no one to cook for. Laurel and Jessica do a bit of cleaning. Clarence used to organise everyone, except Wenson, who never listens to anyone, but I haven't seen Clarence around lately. There are a few others, but they've faded recently."

Kiara tilted her head and nodded thoughtfully. "If anyone wants to pass through the Gate, Mav will take them. They just need to ask."

"Mav?"

"You know, Mav, the Gate Keeper. I'm his Gate Wraith."

"You're more solid than any wraith I've seen."

Kiara shrugged. "That's Mav. He grounds me here so I don't fade and go elsewhere." She wrinkled her nose. "Though I am new, so that may have something to do with it."

Liam shook his head. "Wraiths are never solid. Would the Gate Keeper ground me? I don't like going elsewhere."

"You'd have to ask him."

"Do you like Mav?"

"Oh, yes. He's really nice."

"Nicer than…nicer than the other Gate Keeper?"

"If you mean Kaenera, then there is no contest. Mav is by far the better Gate Keeper."

"He won't make us do things we don't want to?"

Kiara stopped working and observed Liam. "Like what?"

"Umm, he sent some wraiths to Angelicus…but they never came back." Liam stared down at his hands for a moment and exhaled. "My brother was one of them."

Kiara leaned forward and squeezed his arm. "I am so sorry."

"Not your fault. The Gate Keeper wouldn't allow anyone to pass through the Gate without earning the right. No one ever seemed to earn the right, no matter what they did."

"Mav isn't like that. He'll let you go through the Gate if

you want to. And I'm sure he'll let you stay here as long as you help protect the Gate."

Liam nodded thoughtfully and then went back to brushing the chain.

"Could you pass the message on to the other wraiths?" Kiara asked.

"Might be better if you tell them," Liam replied. "They won't believe me."

"I'd be happy to. Could you call them all together in the library? We can have a wraith convention! I'd be happy to answer any questions, maybe introduce the Gate Keeper."

"I can ask, but you'd be better off speaking to Wenson. The others'll listen to him."

"Oji? Could you ask Mav to join me in the library? He needs to meet the wraiths lurking in your corridors."

"*I'd* like to meet the wraiths lurking in my corridors," Oji replied.

"You can come, too," Kiara said with a laugh as she saw Liam's horrified expression. She wiped her hands on a rag and then tucked it back in her pocket. "Come on. You can introduce us to Wenson."

"Umm, he might not be there."

"If he's as precious about his library as you said, then he'll be there."

"I didn't say that."

Kiara patted his shoulder. "Don't worry. I won't say anything."

By the time they reached the library, Liam was hanging back, wringing his hands in a parody of a sinner about to be sentenced.

"Stop worrying," Kiara whispered. "Mav is really nice."

"It's not Mav I'm worried about," Liam whispered back.

Kiara grinned and opened the door. The library looked much as she remembered from her first visit with Mav to the

OblivionGate. Wooden shelves filled with books stood in regimented lines. Comfortable chairs were grouped in the centre, and a gate-leg table stood against the wall. Low side tables flanked the chairs.

Kiara inhaled the musty aroma of paper and dust. "I can smell the dust. He doesn't like to clean, does he?"

"My library is clean at all times," a stern voice said from the depths of the bookcases.

"You kept the armchairs," Kiara said as she walked further into the room.

"Of course. You have to sit somewhere."

"My name is Kiara. Are you Wenson?"

"Who else would I be?" Wenson replied as he walked out from the book stacks, an irritable scowl on his face. He was whip-thin and held himself very erect. Grey, bushy eyebrows bunched up over deep-set eyes as he glared at them. His skin was wrinkled and lined, and he wore a permanent frown. An archaic-looking suit with pointed collars and an intricately tied neckerchief added to the impression that he wasn't only old; he was ancient.

"I don't know. But seeing as we've never formally met, I didn't like to assume."

Wenson peered at her and then straightened. "I don't know you."

"No, I am Kiara. The Gate Wraith."

"You are not the Gate Wraith."

"Yes, I am. The Gate Keeper proclaimed me as such. You gave me the book of maps when I arrived. And you gave the Gate Keeper a book of poems."

"Which he has not returned."

"He's probably still reading it. He is really busy."

"I *am* busy," Mav said as he entered the library, "but I have read it, and here I am returning it. I wanted to thank you, librarian, for such an enlightening recommendation."

Wenson snorted under his breath. "Books should stay in the library."

"Ah. I will remember that in future."

"This is Wenson," Kiara said.

"It is a pleasure to meet you, Wenson." Mav cocked his head and observed the little man. "You seem familiar."

"I can assure you, we have never met before," Wenson said, crossing his arms across his chest.

"Maybe not, then. Kiara, Oji informs me there are some more wraiths I need to meet?"

Kiara smiled at Wenson. "Could you call the other wraiths to join us? We'd like to speak to them altogether."

Wenson scowled. "I do not want that rabble in here."

"Just for this one meeting? It will be easier to introduce the Gate Keeper to them all at once."

Muttering under his breath, Wenson disappeared back into the stacks.

Kiara glanced at Liam. "Does that mean he agreed to call them?"

Liam shrugged. "No idea."

"Oh, well. Mav, this is Liam. He's going to help me in the engine room."

"Liam, it's a pleasure to meet you," Mav said. "Oji will bless you for looking after his workings."

"Umm. Nice to meet you too," Liam replied.

Kiara nudged him in the ribs. "Ask him."

Mav grinned at Liam and moved to one of the armchairs. As he sat, a glass of basinthe appeared on the table beside him, and another book sat next to it.

"What did you want to ask?" Mav asked as he picked up the book and read the spine. He flipped it open and glanced down at the contents.

"Umm. Can you ground me like you do Kiara?"

"He doesn't like the elsewhere; he wants to stay here," Kiara added.

Mav observed Liam for a moment, and Liam rippled as he waited. "What is the elsewhere?"

Liam shrugged. "If we are not here, then we are there. It's like a…a limbo. We wait there until we are needed here again." He frowned. "It's like losing a bit of yourself every time, as there are no memories, only a gap where I should have been. I'm not explaining it very well." Liam dropped his gaze and rubbed his palms on his trousers.

"I expect it is not something that was meant to be explained," Mav said. "It just is."

Liam nodded, still gazing at the floor.

"How did you become a wraith?" Mav asked.

Kiara winced at the expression of anguish that flitted across Liam's face, and she leaned forward to rub his shoulder.

"My brother, Adam, had this great plan to make us rich," Liam said to the floor. "He thought he was unbeatable at games of chance." His form rippled. "He was accused of cheating, and I got dragged down with him."

"And was he cheating?"

Liam shrugged. "Probably. No one is unbeatable. He wasn't very good at subterfuge. We were soul-stripped and sold into slavery. Got passed around the mines for a few years and ended up in Doveton."

"Doveton?"

"It's a large estate well to the east of Jinnel, deep in the shadows of Eidolon." Liam paused and lifted his face. He met Mav's eyes. "It's hidden from normal sight."

"Then how did you see it?"

"I didn't at first. Just thought it was a training camp. There were lots of soldiers and weapons. Troops going back and forth. I was seen as weak and ended up in the kitchens, washing pots all the time. My brother joined the training program.

"After a couple of months, he started to go on missions. He was quite proud." Liam twisted his lips. "We were working for an archangel, or so he said. By then, I wasn't sure what I believed. He said we were earning our souls back. And then he began to go on sorties into Puronia."

"Do you know who you were working for?"

"Not then."

"But you do now?"

Liam exhaled and gritted his teeth. "I never knew who the archangel was. Only briefly saw a pretty angel once. Blond hair, blue eyes. One day, Adam's troop returned, but they had failed their objective."

"What was their objective?"

He faded before solidifying again, and Kiara gripped his arm as if she could ground him.

"I don't know. Adam said they were infiltrating, but they were discovered or something. His whole troop were executed. Made an example of. Only they didn't die; they became mindless puppets controlled by Kaenera. He wouldn't let them pass through the Gate because they'd failed him."

"How did you end up here?"

Kiara shivered at the care with which Mav asked the question. A soft caress surrounded the words, and Liam's form rippled again.

"It was a few years later," Liam said, his gaze dropping to the floor again. "I tried to stay out of trouble. Didn't want to draw attention to myself. That was a quick way to an endless death. But I saw Adam again. He was a walking skeleton, looked really bad. I tried to speak to him, but he didn't know me. He attacked me. He didn't know what he was doing, and he ran me through. My own brother killed me.

"I found myself wandering these halls, one of the many soulless lost and unable to move on." He twisted his lips. "The only good part was that Kaenera didn't have the chance to turn me into a dybbuk. If he ever came to the Gate, which was rare, I went into the elsewhere. I knew he wouldn't pass me on; he'd just find a way to use me."

"Would you like to pass on?" Mav asked. "Go through the Gate?"

Kiara tightened her grip on Liam's arm.

"I-I want to be useful for once, to make a difference, to help Kiara look after the Gate. I'm good at cleaning things."

Mav rose and crossed the room. He clasped Liam's shoulder and Liam gasped as he solidified. Tears glistened in his eyes and he lifted his chin, meeting Mav's gaze.

"Do you swear you'll do the Oblivion Gate and its occupants no harm?"

"This is my home. Of course I won't."

"Swear it," Mav said.

Liam straightened. "I swear I'll protect the Oblivion Gate and its occupants with my life."

"That wasn't what I asked, but it is perfectly acceptable. Welcome to the Oblivion Gate, Liam. We're glad to have you as part of the family." Mav held his hand out, and as Liam shook it, his form sharpened as if he had suddenly come into focus. He appeared as a young man in his early twenties with ginger hair, green eyes, and a swathe of freckles across his cheeks and nose.

"I also need you to tell my captain, Ryvalin, whatever you can remember about Doveton," Mav said.

Of course, though, I'm not sure how it will help."

"Information is key and can make a difference."

"Welcome, Liam," Oji said. "I am very happy to have another helper to look after my mechanics."

Liam stared at his hands and then patted his body, and a huge grin spread across his face. "Thank you."

"Wenson, is anyone else joining us?" Mav asked.

"Jessica. If you're coming in, then come in. Don't loiter in the corridor," Wenson's annoyed voice came from the other side of the room, and Kiara realised the wraith was watching Liam closely. His expression was unguarded for a moment, and Kiara could have sworn he was surprised. She moved to stand beside Mav and slipped her hand in his. He squeezed her hand, and she relaxed.

A nearly transparent wraith stepped over the threshold and hesitated.

"Hi Jessica. Is Laurel with you?" Liam asked.

Jessica shook her head. "She doesn't want to stay," she whispered.

"Do you want to stay?" Mav asked. "If you and Laurel wish to pass through the Gate, I can take you there now."

Jessica glanced at Liam and then away.

"I can leave?" a soft voice asked from the doorway.

"Of course," Mav replied. "You are welcome to stay with us, but if it's time, then I will guide you through the Gate."

"What nonsense," Wenson muttered and stomped back into the shadows.

"Is there anyone else that wants to leave? We can go to the gate now," Mav said.

"You'd let us pass on?" Laurel was nearly in tears.

"Don't cry. Mav will take you through the gate, and you can rest," Kiara said.

"What's all the bother about?" a grumpy voice asked. Cecil, the cook, briefly appeared before flickering out of sight.

"Hey, Cook. Do you want to go or stay?" Liam asked.

"Go? Go where? I've too much to do." Cecil solidified for

a moment. "I have meals to prepare," he said and disappeared.

Liam shrugged. "I guess that means he's staying. I've only ever known him as Cook. He used to cook the meals in the kitchen. But there's been no reason to cook anything for ages."

"We've already met," Mav said, "and Cecil has reclaimed the kitchen." He walked towards Laurel and held out his hand. "Let me take you to the Gate."

Laurel grasped his hand. Her form shivered, and then she said, "Thank you."

Mav tucked her hand in his arm and escorted her out the door. He halted on the threshold, turned back, and asked, "Jessica? Do you wish to join us?"

Kiara nudged Liam.

"What?" he whispered.

"Do you want Jessica to stay?" Kiara whispered back.

All eyes swivelled to Liam, and he blushed. "Umm. Well…of course, if she wants to."

Wenson stomped towards him. "There's no 'of course' about it. Master Demavrian doesn't have all day. Answer the question, you dolt."

Kiara glanced at Wenson in surprise. His voice had an unexpected note of respect in it. He was watching Mav, though he was tapping his foot as he waited for Liam's response.

Liam flushed a deeper red, all the way to the tips of his ears. "Umm, err."

"They are all idiots," Wenson muttered. "I don't know what she sees in you."

Jessica blushed in turn.

Mav smiled. "There is no time limit on the offer. You two can discuss it, and then you can let me know." He patted Laurel's hand. "Let me show you the rose gate."

Kiara watched as they left the library, a lump in her throat. That anyone would choose to walk through the Gate when there was so much opportunity to exist saddened her. Yes, she was dead, but Mav had given her a second chance at some sort of life, and the Oblivion Gate and all his complexities were a dream come true for her.

She flicked a glance at Jessica and then glared at Liam. "Don't mess her around," she growled and followed Mav out of the door.

30

VALERIAN – CITADEL

Valerian made sure all the curtains were tightly shut before he prepared to wake Amaridin. He was determined to find out what had happened the day before, but the healer's draught had knocked Amaridin out, and the healer had advised that he sleep it off.

It was time for a serious discussion. He wanted to know why Amaridin had collapsed, and his partner was going to tell him. He had his suspicions that the silly man was trying to protect him, taking on the burden of the citadel on his own, and that was not how their partnership worked.

Placing a mug of bannoe on the bedside table, Valerian climbed onto the bed behind Amaridin and rubbed his back in soothing circles designed to massage his partner into submission. Amaridin didn't have a chance.

Valerian worked his way down his lover's back, and Amaridin groaned as he stirred.

"Morning, my love."

"Morning."

"How are you feeling? Headache gone?"

"Unfortunately not."

"Was the citadel that unhappy with you?"

"No. She said it was all the souls she was holding. Much like the soulless Mav was carrying. We need to offload them as soon as we can. The citadel isn't supposed to hold that many." Amaridin's voice was soft and dreamy, soothed by Valerian's massage.

"We can give Solanji more help. All the SoulSingers could be assigned to cataloguing, and we can send scribes to help organise the information," Valerian said, keeping his voice soft. "And you bonded alright with the citadel? And you were right? She is female?"

"Yes."

"And when will I bond with her?"

Amaridin stiffened under his touch, and Valerian kept massaging.

"There's no point in us both suffering."

Ah, and there it was. Amaridin *was* trying to protect him.

"Don't you think that is my decision to make?"

Amaridin shifted around so he faced Valerian. "Darling, you've suffered enough."

Valerian snorted. "I don't remember being frozen in time. I was comatose. I lost years with you, yes, but I wasn't in pain. If I bond, will it lessen your pain? Between us, we can manage the burden so neither of us is incapacitated."

Amaridin hesitated, and then his gaze unfocussed for a moment.

Valerian smiled. "I bet the citadel is agreeing with me."

Amaridin huffed. "She says there is no guarantee, that we could both suffer the same pain but also that your logic is sound and a burden shared should alleviate some of it."

Valerian kissed him, soft and gentle at first and then more demanding until Amaridin responded, submitting to his touch. He broke off the kiss and ran his hand down Amaridin's stomach, sliding under his nightshirt. "What do I need to do to bond to the citadel?" he asked and then kissed Amaridin again, his fingers stroking and teasing.

Amaridin groaned into his mouth and shivered.

"What do I need to do?" Valerian whispered again as he climbed on top of Amaridin and ground himself against him.

"Become archdeus," Amaridin gasped. "We need to exchange our oaths."

Valerian stopped moving in surprise. "And you would choose not to?"

Amaridin whimpered, and Valerian began moving again.

"Offload some souls first," Amaridin said, thrusting upwards.

Oh, no. Valerian was not having that. He was not going to stand by and allow Amaridin to suffer when the one thing they both desired most would relieve some of his pain.

"You are my heart, my love, my life. I swear I'll be by your side forever, loving you, protecting you, desiring you," he said, and then he kissed Amaridin. Their kiss deepened, and he tugged at Amaridin's shirt, eager to feel heated skin against him.

Amaridin shuddered beneath him, his hands busy with Valerian's pants. "What about the ceremony?" he gasped out.

"We can still have the ceremony. No one will know unless we tell them."

"I swear my heart is yours, now and forever, just as it has always been." Amaridin's breath caught, and then he continued, "I will love, honour, and protect you until my dying day."

"Good," Valerian whispered as their vows locked into place. As he went to kiss Amaridin, he stiffened as another presence flooded through him and the citadel's awareness consumed him.

"An interesting time to decide to bond, my dearest Archdeus, but I am not complaining," the citadel purred in Valerian's ear, and he flushed as Amaridin took over the love-making and desire swept through his body like a rising tide.

His breath caught, and he, in turn, groaned as Amaridin's kisses fluttered against his throat, the softest touch, and yet he shuddered with need. "Amaridin," he pleaded as his lover coaxed him to his peak. The citadel laughed in Valerian's head as he shouted and came all over Amaridin, who soon joined him. Amaridin had neatly turned the tables on his new husband.

"That's a first," Amaridin said after he caught his breath.

"What is?" Valerian mumbled, still coming down from his high.

"I didn't realise the citadel would be such a voyeur."

"I'm not," the citadel said, *"but you didn't give me much choice. And I must say, that was a first for me, too. Welcome, Valerian. I am honoured that you are so determined to be bonded with me."*

"We come as a pair," Valerian said, rubbing his temple against the persistent ache throbbing in his head. "I hope you will help me curb Amaridin's tendency to melodrama."

"The pain *has* eased to a dull throb," Amaridin said.

"Which is more manageable than being incapacitated by migraines. Don't try to be such a hero again," Valerian said with a mock scowl.

"Well," Amaridin said as he rolled over to kiss Valerian, "if it means you'll wake me up like that every morning, I'd say it was worth it."

Valerian laughed and kissed him back.

"Congratulations on becoming heartsworn," the citadel said. *"One thing you may have overlooked, Valerian, is that both Averdeus and Demavrian will know there is a new Archdeus."*

Valerian lifted his head. "They will?"

"Of course. How could they not?"

Valerian looked up at his husband, but he couldn't stop the smile spreading over his face as he said, "Oops."

Amaridin chuckled. "My father is going to be most upset with us. All his hard work, and the ceremony is redundant."

31

SOLANJI – OBLIVION GATE

Solanji breathed a sigh of relief as she and Ellaria appeared in her newly appointed study in the Oblivion Gate. Like Mav had said, it felt like coming home, a warm embrace welcoming you inside. It made sense to relocate to the Gate. There was plenty of space for them all, and they couldn't expect the Host to move in if they were not in residence. The question was, what to do with the fledglings?

"How do you know how to find the Gate? Did you tell Xylvin where it is?" Solanji asked as she hurried out of the study and strode down the hall, intent on finding Mav.

"Of course I did. She's already here."

"She is?"

Ellaria snorted. *"You think a dragon couldn't find the Gate?"*

"Mav doesn't know where it is."

"He would if he stopped long enough to think about it."

"And is that likely?"

"You have a point."

Solanji had to admit that it was comforting that the Gate

at least had a location. *"And did you warn Oji that an enormous dragon was arriving?"*

"I may have forgotten that bit."

Solanji quickened her pace. The ballroom was the only space large enough to house Xylvin, so she headed there. She heard voices long before she saw Xylvin's iridescent scales.

"It's a dragon." Oji's voice surrounded them, higher pitched than usual.

"I told you," Mav said patiently. "Xylvin and Ryvalin are my oathsworn. They wouldn't have been able to enter, otherwise."

"But it's a dragon."

"You've broken Oji," Kiara said with a soft chuckle. Her smile widened as she saw Solanji. "Hi Solanji."

Solanji grinned back at her. "Hello."

"Oji, do you think you can allocate enough space for an eyrie for Xylvin when she is here?" Mav asked. "I'm sorry, Xylvin. I wasn't expecting you to find us so quickly. How *did* you find us?"

"Demavrian. Use your brain. I'm sure you have one," Xylvin said. *"We are oathsworn, and now you are Deus, you shine brightly, so I know where you are. I used you as the beacon. And even if I couldn't see you, I knew where Ryvalin was, and she was with you."*

"Even when we are ephemeral and the Gate is not situated anywhere?" Mav asked in surprise.

"Of course. Why would that make a difference? You still exist."

Solanji winced as she realised Xylvin was broadcasting to everyone and not just the oathsworn. Solanji wormed her way into Mav's arms and sighed as she rested her cheek against his chest. She smiled as his arm tightened around her and lifted her face for the kiss she knew was coming.

"Dragon logic," Mav said under his breath. "I'm glad you are home. Was Brennan alright?"

"He's fine. We'll talk about him later." No matter how busy Mav was, he always asked about her concerns. "What's the problem here?"

"Oji has never seen a dragon in the flesh before," Kiara said. "He's still trying to process it."

"He's met Ellaria."

"Ellaria is part of you," Oji said. "Xylvin is…Xylvin."

Xylvin whipped her tail back and forth.

"And she is magnificent," Oji continued.

"Thank you," Xylvin said.

Ryvalin rolled her eyes. "Oh, God. Another worshipper. Her head will get even bigger."

Solanji laughed. "Well, she can't stay in the ballroom."

"I don't see why not. We're not using it right now," Mav replied.

"I need a fountain," Xylvin said. *"I like the spray."*

A simple stone fountain appeared in the middle of the ballroom, and Xylvin sighed as she curled around it, her wedged head pointing towards the large double doors at the end, which had grown big enough for her to pass through.

"Don't even think it," Mav murmured.

Solanji stifled a laugh. The notion of an overlarge vemlow guarding their door had flitted through her mind.

"Kiara, would you be so kind as to show Ryvalin a bedchamber and then guide her to my study?" Mav asked.

"Of course," Kiara said, wiping her grease-covered hands on a cloth she pulled from her pocket.

Solanji eyed her. "You know, you don't have to cover yourself in grease as well."

Kiara shrugged. Her eyes were bright as she gave Solanji a cheeky grin. "A perk of the job."

"I'm sure there are other perks."

"Nah. This one's the best."

"Well, don't get it on anything else."

"I won't." Kiara grinned at Ryvalin. "I'm Mav's Gate Wraith. I look after Oji's mechanisms."

"I remember you," Ryvalin said. "I'm glad you've made the Gate your home. You'll have to show me what you are working on,"

"I'll give you the tour later," Kiara promised and led Ryvalin down the corridor.

As Solanji watched them go, Kiara was already explaining Oji's gate mechanics to her. "I think it's good that Ryvalin and Xylvin are here."

Mav nodded, his gaze following Kiara. "I think you are right, for more reasons than we initially thought. Anyway." He twined his fingers in Solanji's, and she gladly clasped his back as he tugged her towards the stairs. "You can tell me about Bren."

Solanji bumped into Mav's side as he suddenly halted, exhaling in a whoosh as if someone had hit in him in the stomach. "Mav? What's wrong?" Solanji patted his chest and then cupped his face.

"My father is going to be so miffed," he said with a low laugh as he hugged Solanji close. "Valerian just became Archdeus. They must have sworn their oaths to each other."

Solanji relaxed. "Oh, that's nice. I thought for a moment..." She bit the words off. No need to share her fears.

"You should," Ellaria murmured. *"He needs to know what you are worrying about."*

"It's nonsense."

"Then stop worrying about it."

Solanji rolled her eyes and, sliding her hand into Mav's, accompanied him back to their chambers.

32

DEMAVRIAN – OBLIVION GATE

"Mav?" Oji said later that afternoon, interrupting Mav's concentration as he sat at his desk in the Oblivion Gate and read the report Ryvalin had compiled for him. Liam had remembered a lot more about Doveton than he'd realised, and Ryvalin and Xylvin were off searching for its location.

Ryvalin had delegated to Julius the relocation of his men to the Oblivion Gate. Oji was working on the west barracks, and Mav would have to start transporting the Host into the Gate as soon as it was complete. He needed soldiers to plan an assault on Doveton. Until he knew the number of dybbuks Kaenera had, he couldn't plan properly. He needed information.

As Solanji uncurled from the chair in the corner where she had been reading a book, Mav looked up and said, "Yes?" She placed a marker in the page and put it down.

"I've been thinking about the wraiths. The only one I have any memories of is Wenson, so I have spoken to him. He gave me a list of the wraiths he is aware of within the

Gate. We have accounted for them all. The rest, you cleared out."

Mav frowned. "How is it Wenson knows about the wraiths and you don't?"

"I think maybe Wenson has always been a part of me. He keeps to his domain, but he is aware of what is going on. As he is a wraith, I think he is more attuned to them."

"You trust Wenson?"

"Implicitly."

Mav's eyebrows rose. "Then there is no more to be said."

A comfortable silence fell again as he returned to his reports and Solanji to her book.

When Averdeus contacted him, Mav felt a moment of disquiet. He had a premonition that his father hadn't found the sigils where he'd left them, which meant the box in the Oblivion Gate *was* the Aeora sigils.

He exhaled, calming his fluttering pulse. He'd let his father confirm it first, before he started panicking. If it were true, then the upside was that at least Mav could keep the box safe in the Gate and away from any nefarious person intending to use them to kill a lot of people.

"I can take you to the sigils if now is a good time," Mav offered. *"Oji has no issue with you visiting if you are able to join me here."*

Mav felt Oji's interest sharpen as he spoke the words.

In answer, Averdeus appeared in Mav's new study. Dark shadows curved under his father's strained eyes, and his shoulders drooped in unaccustomed dejection. Mav rose and walked around his desk. Gripping his father's arms, he said, "Let's confirm that I have the sigils first before you start casting blame on yourself."

Averdeus shook his head. "As terrible as it sounds, I need for that box to be the sigils. Otherwise, I don't know where they are, and that would be even worse."

Mav grimaced. "I'm not sure that I want the sigils in my Gate."

"As long as you are the Gate Keeper, there is no safer place."

"Father, I would like to introduce you to Oji, the Oblivion Gate."

"It's a pleasure to meet you," Oji said, his voice resonating with excitement.

Averdeus' dark expression lightened for a moment. "Oji. Thank you for allowing me entry to your home. I look forward to many discussions in the future. Unfortunately, right now, we have a bit of an emergency that we need to resolve." His gaze fell on Solanji as she rose. "My dear, I didn't realise you were here. How lovely to see you, though I could wish it were under better circumstances." He hugged her close before releasing her.

"You want to see the sigils," Oji said.

Averdeus gave a grim laugh. "I do, and I don't. I don't know which one is worse!"

"Oji, make sure no one is following us," Mav said. He glanced at his father. "I'd prefer that no one but us has the burden of knowing where they are."

"It's your house," his father replied, though his attention was obviously elsewhere.

"I'll go and speak with Shandra," Solanji said with a smile and slipped out of the room.

"Well, let's check what we have stored here, then." Mav led the way through the corridors and down the stairs to the chamber where they had locked the box of sigils.

"There's no one around. You are clear to proceed," Oji murmured as he revealed the concealed door, and Mav pushed it open and led the way to the sub-basement.

The cast-iron box sat in the corner, still wrapped in the mesh cover Ana had used. Mav walked over and unwrapped it, revealing the sullen red glow as the weird objects moved around inside the box. They undulated as if they were not solid, but each was a distinct shape, like a curved rune or symbol.

When his father deflated and gripped his hair in his hands, Mav knew he was now the custodian of one of the most destructive weapons in the universe. He covered the box again, hiding the sullen glow.

"How did Kaenera ever find them?" his father whispered.

"I have no idea," Mav said. "I didn't even know they existed."

His chest ached at the sight of his father's expression, a look of such complete, abject failure. Mav pulled his father into a heartfelt embrace. "It is not your fault."

"If not mine, then whose?" his father replied, clutching him tight, before releasing him to stalk back and forth across the room.

"Whoever betrayed your trust. Who else knew about the sigils?"

"No one. I told no one."

"You must have. Kaenera couldn't have found them otherwise."

Averdeus wrenched himself out of Mav's arms and stalked away. His voice was sharp, edged with anguish when he finally spoke. "I told no one. Not even your mother."

"They've been hidden for that long? Why have they only been discovered now?"

Averdeus paced. "I don't know."

"What about Amaridin? Could he have known?"

"I never told him."

"A cherub, then. Could they have seen the memory from somewhere?"

Averdeus stilled and then shrugged. "I don't know. It's

possible, I suppose. But they wouldn't have known what the sigils were."

"Kaenera knew about them; otherwise, he would never have found them."

"But how?"

"There must be some mention of them in a record," Mav said. "You need to check the citadel library. I'll check the Oblivion Gate's. Somewhere, there is a reference to the sigils."

Averdeus closed his eyes. "I wish I'd never got involved."

"You were trying to protect humanity. Imagine if those sigils had been in anyone else's hands."

"I suppose."

"At least we still have them," Mav said.

"True."

Mav didn't think his father could get any more dejected. "Let's go back to my study," he suggested and led the way, taking care to lock the door, and Oji disguised the passageway so that there was no doorway.

Once they were seated in Mav's study, with a glass in hand, Mav asked, "What can you tell me about the Gate? How long was it in Kaenera's hands?"

"Since I took on the citadel. There is always a balance between light and darkness. Kaenera always tried to tilt that balance a little further. I suppose I should have known that if I had something, he would want it." Averdeus fell silent, staring into his glass, and Mav winced.

Kaenera had wanted Mav's mother, Averdeus' wife, and Archangel Serenia had murdered her instead. At the root of all their troubles lay the same two people. Mav wondered if Kaenera had some overarching plan that had been running for centuries. He would not be surprised. Kaenera had out-thought and out-planned all of them so far.

But while Kaenera was executing his plan, Mav hadn't

even known there was a plot they should have been defending themselves against.

"Why haven't you told Amaridin and Valerian what we are facing?" Mav asked.

"I didn't want to say anything until I knew for sure."

Mav inwardly groaned. His father's need for secrecy was part of the problem. Mav had only known half of the picture. He'd had no chance of forestalling any of Kaenera's actions. "I assume they're heartsworn now that Valerian is Archdeus. Don't you think you should tell them about the sigils?"

"They were supposed to wait," Averdeus growled. He threw his hands in the air. "Why does no one listen to me?"

Mav shrugged. "They were trying to claim the citadel. Maybe that had something to do with it."

"The ceremony was only a couple of weeks away."

"And I'm sure it can still take place. Speak to them, Father. Now, is there anything else I should know? I can't prepare to defend the Gate if I don't know what I'm facing."

"Demavrian, you are the Gate Keeper. The Keeper of Shadows. You are a god. You defeated Kaenera and stole most of his powers, though not all. You are the only person who *can* defend the Gate."

"What powers have I stolen?"

Averdeus sighed. "You should really discover those as you need them. If there is no need, then the abilities lie dormant."

"Father," Mav growled.

"Alright." Averdeus threw up his hands. "Unlimited ability to transport people and things. Mind reading, persuasion, suggestion, healing, shielding, blocking, grounding."

"I don't know what any of that means," Mav said with a growing apprehension.

"You're not supposed to. Just because you can do something, it doesn't mean you should. You can read a person's mind if they are not shielded. That is not always as glamorous as it sounds. Some people's thoughts are disgusting."

Mav laughed.

"You can shield your own mind, prevent others with the ability from reading your thoughts or intentions. You can also block suggestion or persuasion so no one can control your actions." Averdeus glared at Mav. "Though your aptitude in that area is naturally high. I've never been able to see through your shield. That's what made you so frustrating. Your brother is an open book."

Mav winced. "It was not deliberate. I had no idea I had a shield."

Averdeus waved his son's apology away. "It is fortunate that you did. Neither Serenia nor Kaenera could ever penetrate it, either, nor could they plant suggestions. Amaridin was not so fortunate."

"But you never warned us about any of these skills."

"I thought I had time. And when your mother died…" Averdeus rubbed his face. "I lost focus. Lost track of time. Forgot about my responsibilities."

"It's understandable."

"But unforgivable. I made you and your brother vulnerable, when you should have been indestructible."

"Then make sure we are armed to win this fight. Don't leave us ignorant."

Averdeus nodded. "I won't make the same mistake twice. I will tell Amaridin about the citadel and how he can leverage it. But you, Demavrian, you are a Deus, my equal and far superior to Kaenera." Averdeus began pacing, his blue eyes hard. "We must strike while he is weakened. We need to plan his downfall once and for all. I'll not have that miscreant take anything else that is mine. It is time he paid for his sins."

"I still have a dybbuk under lock and key," Mav said. "Her name is Ana. There is no future for her here; her existence is only at Kaenera's whim. I'm actually surprised Kaenera hasn't snuffed her out yet."

"Kaenera cannot penetrate my walls," Oji said.

"Ah, that's good to know. I was going to pass her through the Gate, but she is one of Kaenera's tools. Did you want to speak to her before I pass her on?"

Averdeus narrowed his eyes as he thought for a moment. "Yes, let me see if she has any knowledge of his plans. Unlikely, but worth a try."

"What can you tell me about the Oblivion Gate?" Mav asked.

Averdeus smiled. "The Oblivion Gate, my son, amplifies your power by a factor of two. You double your strength, and Kaenera is left with a pittance. But don't underestimate him. He has had centuries to hone his skill. That counts for something."

"I don't feel any different," Mav said dubiously. "In fact, I would say the soulless weigh me down more than anything else."

"Strength is fluid. Power is inherent. You'll discover more as you use it. As I said, as you access your power, it will grow. Until you need it, it simmers, waiting." His father grimaced. "Though your presence is already naturally strong."

"My presence?"

"Your Deus aura. You leak it all the time, which is why I think you will be much stronger than Kaenera."

"How do I control it?"

"You can dampen it by shielding. Extend your barrier to encase your aura as well."

"I don't even know how I'm creating the shield in the first place."

His father nodded. "It's a natural skill for you. Some

people struggle all their lives to control a shield. Think about how you protect your thoughts, the defensive barrier you wrap around your mind."

Ah, Mav thought—the defensive barrier he had dropped without realising it to allow Oji entry. He found the tensile shield easily and extended the invisible protection outwards, pushing the sense of safety to encase himself.

"There you go," Averdeus said with a small smile. "I can't sense your aura at all now."

Mav ran his fingers through his hair. "What do I do with the sigils?"

"Keep them concealed in the Gate for now. I'll search for a new hiding place. If we could find a way to destroy them, that would be preferable."

Mav shuddered. "Is that even feasible?"

"I don't know," his father admitted. "In the meantime, I'll consider what to do with them. You need to deal with Serenia and consolidate your control of the Oblivion Gate. It will be your only defence against Kaenera."

Mav tensed as Oji snorted in his head. *"Your father has no idea what you have done. Partnership is much stronger than force. You are far more powerful than he realises."*

"Which doesn't help if I don't know how to use it," Mav replied.

"I know a few tricks that may be useful."

"I look forward to learning them."

Mav placed his glass on the table beside him. "Let's go and visit Ana before you leave. See if there is anything you can find out from her."

Averdeus rose. "Kaenera was never a very good sharer. I don't hold out much hope, but we would be foolish not to try."

33

DEMAVRIAN – OBLIVION GATE

Mav led his father through the corridors to the cell block Oji had created at the back of the Gate. The entrance was an innocuous doorway leading off an empty corridor. Stone steps led down, much like they did to the sub-basement, and Mav suddenly wondered how close they were to each other.

"Not at all," Oji reassured him. *"The sub-basement is a completely different level. It's much deeper."*

"It didn't seem that deep."

"I can collapse the dimensions so you can reach a place quicker or expand as needed if you want someone to get lost." Mav heard the amusement in Oji's voice and wondered whom he had deliberately led astray and what other secrets he had hidden. He supposed he would learn them all in time.

Arriving at the cell, Oji opened the door, and Mav entered, glancing around the small space.

Ana immediately rose, tugging at the chain connecting her to the wall. "You can't keep me here like this. I have rights."

"Which you forfeited when you tried to kill me."

"I was defending myself."

"Which you wouldn't have needed to do if you hadn't broken into the Gate intent on stealing something that wasn't yours."

"Those sigils are not yours, either."

"They are certainly not Kaenera's, as he stole them from Averdeus to begin with."

Ana snorted under her breath. "He probably stole them as well."

"I didn't, actually," Averdeus said as he entered the cell and stood beside Demavrian. His aura rolled through the room, and Ana flinched away from him. "What I want to know is how Kaenera found the sigils in the first place."

Ana shrugged. "How should I know?"

"Funnily enough, I think you do," Averdeus replied. "I can see it in your eyes, the knowledge of how he tricked me, and you are eager to tell me."

"No, I'm not."

"But you are. You can't wait to tell me. In fact, you are wondering why you are resisting. Such a silly thing to do. It doesn't matter now. Kaenera will never know."

Ana sank down on the hard cot behind her and stared at Averdeus as she slowly nodded. "It was years ago. If Kaenera had never lost the Gate, you would never have known they were missing until it was too late."

Mav realised he was watching his father use persuasion and suggestion simultaneously. His father had persuaded Ana to tell him by suggesting that it no longer mattered if he knew and by adding subtle pressure for her to tell him. He absently twisted his signet ring on his finger, listened, and learned with interest.

"How did Kaenera first hear of them?

Ana wrinkled her nose. "I believe Archangel Serenia told him. She had found a reference in an old history book to a powerful artifact that was salvaged from a mining planet. The refugees from the planet formed a coalition, offering a reward to anyone who found it, so Serenia started looking."

"Why did Serenia think the artifact was here in Angelicus?"

Ana shrugged. "I'm not sure she did, but the reward was huge, and as far as she could tell, it had never been claimed. Once she told Kaenera, he wouldn't consider anything else. That was when he began abducting people, searching their memories, or using them as leverage to influence key officials." Ana gestured at Averdeus. "He said taking the sigils and hiding them was something you would do for the greater good."

"Kaenera started abducting people years before I left Angelicus?" Mav asked, somewhat incredulously.

Ana ignored him, so Averdeus repeated the question.

"When his holding cells became too full, he used to kill the older ones off. A lot of the time, their families had lost their influence, and they were no longer useful. It had been so long, so no one noticed.

Averdeus' face paled. "I couldn't have missed that happening within the citadel."

"Oh, we didn't start using the citadel until it fell silent and you and Demavrian went missing. After that, it was simple."

"How?" Averdeus' question had a slight edge to it, but Ana didn't notice.

"Kaenera is very good at planting suggestions. Most people, including Archdeus Amaridin, looked the other way."

"You really need to teach both him and Valerian how to shield," Mav said through gritted teeth. The fact that this woman thought such behaviour was acceptable, even expected, appalled Mav. If he hadn't returned to the citadel when he had, Valerian and many others could have been summarily killed, and no one would have known. Nausea swept through him at the thought, and Averdeus gripped his arm.

"Contain your reaction. Strong emotions can affect a persuasion. You must remain neutral and calm at all times. You can fall apart after we've finished."

It was impossible to remain calm, but Mav did pull his shield tighter around himself. His shadows cinched tight, offering comfort. His distress eased, and he concentrated on his breathing.

"And who was it that knew about the sigils and their location?" Averdeus asked.

"It was a cherub. Used to be one of your advisors." Ana frowned in thought. "Dera. No Dora, something like that."

"Vora," Averdeus said.

"Yes," Ana smiled happily. "That was it. Vora."

"And what happened to Vora?"

"Oh, Kaenera pumped him dry, and then we killed him."

This time, it was Mav who had to hold his father back. His father trembled in his arms as he grappled with the knowledge that one of his oldest friends had probably been tortured and then murdered and this woman didn't give a damn.

"Let's take a break," Mav suggested. "We can return tomorrow."

"No, let's finish this, and then you can pass her through the Gate. She has no remorse for any of her actions. None whatsoever."

"She may not have had a choice."

"Then she at least should be horrified by what she's done, but she's not. If Kaenera manages to retrieve her, she will continue to do his bidding without question."

"Very well. What else do you need to know?" Mav asked.

Averdeus inhaled deeply and exhaled. Then he asked. "When did Kaenera find the sigils?"

"Just after your wife died. You were distracted. Kaenera is good at distractions."

"That long ago?" Averdeus' breath hitched.

"Kaenera is good at concealment as well," Ana said proudly.

Mav's stomach dropped, and he thought he might vomit. Had his mother's death, her murder, transpired because Kaenera needed a *distraction*? For no other reason than to incapacitate Averdeus and his sons? Mav couldn't voice his suspicion—his father was already consumed by guilt for not protecting her—but it was a thought he couldn't shake off.

Any reluctance he had felt in passing Ana through the Gate vanished.

"You can transport her there now. I'll open the rose gate for you." Oji was just as shocked as he was.

"I think you have everything you need to know," Mav said, gentling his voice at his father's dazed expression.

"I...I think I'll return to the citadel," Averdeus said eventually.

"Do you want me to come with you?" Mav asked.

"No." Averdeus' voice strengthened. "You must keep the sigils safe and deal with *her*. I need to warn Amaridin and Valerian."

"If you are sure?"

Averdeus took a shaky breath. "Yes."

Mav wasn't convinced, and he watched his father with concern. "Oji will show you the way upstairs while I deal with Ana."

Averdeus gripped his arm. "I am so sorry, Demavrian. I never meant for any of this to fall on your shoulders."

"I know, Father. I'll protect the Gate and all it contains.

You warn Amaridin and Valerian to remain alert and teach them how to shield."

Mav watched his father stumble out of the cell, off to do his bidding without protest—a sign of how shocked he was. Mav turned back to Ana, who was still sitting quietly on the cot.

"Oji, release her chains and open the rose gate. We are en route."

Mav gripped Ana's arm as the cuffs around her wrists fell to the ground. He transported her to the rose gate and walked her through the open trellis without stopping.

"Any last words?" Mav asked.

Ana stared at him and then her fingers as they began to disintegrate. "I'm sorry," she whispered. Her eyes widened with sudden fear, and she opened her mouth to say more, but her body winnowed away to dust, and she was no more.

Mav waited until she had completely dissipated. Then he returned to corridor and silently watched the rose-strewn gate while it faded from view as Oji concealed the entrance.

34

KIARA – OBLIVION GATE

Kiara scrubbed away at the rusted cogs; it seemed a never-ending job. Liam was high above her, humming as he worked on loosening the loops of linkages. Becoming aware of a shadow hovering in the doorway, Kiara looked up and saw Jessica staring up at Liam, clutching her mop so tightly that her knuckles gleamed solidly against the wood.

"Hey, Jessica. You here to see Liam? Come on in."

Liam dropped his wire brush, narrowly missing Kiara, and descended fast, blushing bright red and full of profuse apologies.

"Liam, calm down," Kiara whispered.

Swallowing so hard that his Adam's apple bobbed, Liam wiped his hands on his trousers and approached Jessica. "Hi," he said, his voice squeaking, and he cleared his throat.

Kiara shook her head. He was so adorably awkward. Picking up the pot of grease, she began slathering the cogs with it. She didn't intend to listen in on their conversation, but Liam didn't know how to speak quietly, and Jessica's voice carried.

"We have to tell them," Jessica said, her whisper floating across the room.

"No, we can't," Liam replied. "It's nothing to do with us, and we have no proof."

"But we know, so they need to know."

"They might accuse us. What do we do then?"

"If the Gate Keeper knows, he can protect you," Kiara said, appearing behind them, her hands on her hips. "What's going on?"

Liam grimaced at Jess and threw his hands in the air. "We not sure, but we think there might be a gap in Oji's defences."

"Where?" Oji asked immediately, his voice echoing around them.

"We don't know exactly, but we were…" Liam flushed bright red again.

Kiara laughed. "Get on with it, Liam. We know you are seeing Jessica. It's no secret, so stop behaving as if it is."

Jessica gasped and covered her face with her hands. "You know?"

"It's sweet. I'm happy for you both. Now, what's this about a hole in our defences?"

"We think it's how the dybbuks got in. One of the other wraiths used it to get in and out. We caught him once, and he made up a stupid excuse that couldn't have been true."

"Where is it?" Oji asked.

Jessica squared her shoulders and lifted her chin. "It's down past the kitchen. Off one of the disused corridors, only now that there are more people in the building, I think it should be sealed."

"You are correct, young lady," Oji said. "It should be sealed. But I cannot see any exits or breaches in my walls in that area. Can you show us?"

"Of course." Jessica set off immediately.

Kiara followed with Liam. "Why didn't you want to tell anyone?" she asked him.

"I didn't want to get us into trouble. We like it here."

"But it's in your interest to keep everyone safe. If Kaenera found a way inside…" Kiara's voice faltered to a stop. "We could all lose our home."

"But we didn't know for sure. We never went down there. Clarence threatened to send us through the gate if we did."

"I don't know a Clarence," Kiara said. "Is he still here?"

"We haven't seen him since Demavrian took over the Gate. Jessica said he's probably gone, swept away by those shadows that cleaned out the halls when the dybbuks attacked, so his threats mean nothing." Liam's shoulders drooped. "But I was worried we'd be punished for not saying something earlier. I don't want to die like my brother."

Kiara rubbed his shoulder. "Mav would never treat anyone like that. You never need to be afraid of speaking up if something concerns you or if you see something that you don't think is right, no matter who is doing it."

Liam exhaled. "I feel stupid now."

"You are not stupid. It takes time to learn that not all people are evil like Kaenera and Clarence. Mav knows it will take time to earn your trust."

"You are very wise, young Kiara," Oji whispered in her mind, and Kiara smiled.

Jessica had sped up, eager to show Oji what she had found. When she reached the kitchen entrance, she hurried on past, down to the end of the corridor. She took a couple of turns and then stopped in front of a grey-painted wall. She pushed at a mid-point in the wall, and a door swung open, revealing a flight of stairs.

Kiara frowned. "How did you know there was a door there? I couldn't see it."

"I saw Clarence come out of it."

"There is no door," Oji said, his voice uncertain. "That is a solid wall."

"No, it isn't," Kiara said. "Jessica just stepped through it, and there is a flight of stairs on the other side going down."

"Let me just call Adriz," Oji said. "I want to check if she can see it, because you are all wraiths. Wait a moment for her to join us."

Kiara shut the door on Jessica, leaving her on the other side, and then waited.

When Adriz arrived, she was accompanied by Ryvalin, which meant Xylvin would be in the entrance hall, listening in.

"What's up?" Adriz asked.

"Can you see a door in this wall?" Oji asked.

Ryvalin ran her hands over the smooth plaster. "Can't feel anything," she said and began tapping. "Sounds solid enough." She pushed at the wall, but nothing happened. "Nope, can't see any door. Adriz?"

Adriz repeated her actions and then shook her head. "Seems solid to me."

Kiara pushed the midpoint of the wall, and the door swung open, and Jessica waved at her from the other side.

"Still can't see any door," Adriz said, and Kiara stepped through it.

"Whoa! Kiara just vanished into a wall," Ryvalin said, running her hands over the section where she had disappeared.

"It's a doorway," Kiara said as she stepped back out, and Ryvalin skittered backwards, holding her chest.

"That is not what it looks like to us, and it is still solid," Adriz said, rapping her knuckles against the open doorway that she couldn't see. The wall still sounded solid.

"What is behind this invisible door?" Adriz asked.

"Jessica says she thinks there's an exit that one of Kaenera's dybbuks, Clarence, used to use."

"A doorway only for dybbuks or wraiths? That is concerning." Adriz peered more closely at the wall.

"It doesn't appear as a doorway to me," Oji said, worry now clear in his voice.

"We need to check what Mav can see. Is this a suggestion or an illusion? Or is this truly a space that only wraiths can see?"

"You call Mav," Kiara said. "We'll see where the stairs go." She stepped through the doorway again.

Ryvalin shuddered. "That is not natural, and there goes another!" she said as Liam rushed through the door with a "Hey, wait for me."

"We needed one of them to stay here so we could show Mav where it is," Adriz said with a huff.

"I can still bespeak Kiara," Oji said. "She said she'll come back when Mav arrives. The stairs end in another corridor that leads to an empty room. They are searching for an exit."

"And in theory," Ryvalin said, "the door is still open, as they didn't shut it. I think." She scowled at the wall. "Would an illusion be this solid?"

"Doubt it," Mav said from behind her, and Ryvalin swore as she startled.

She swung round and glared at him. "Are you trying to give me a heart attack? What with ghosts walking through walls and now you appearing out of nowhere!"

"My apologies. I came as soon as I could. Oji said it was urgent," Mav said with an apologetic smile.

"Can you see a doorway behind Ryvalin?" Adriz asked.

"Yes, I can," Mav said and stepped through the wall.

"Dammit," Ryvalin said. She bounced off the wall when she tried to follow Mav. "This doesn't make any sense. If

Mav can pass through, why can't we? And why can't Oji see it?"

"No idea," Adriz said. The wall shimmered under her fingers and disappeared, leaving the open doorway. Adriz stretched her arm and wiggled her fingers through the gap. "What did Mav do?"

"I broke Kaenera's seal on the exit and went through the door," Mav replied, as he climbed the stairs, followed by the wraiths, and scowled at the doorway. "It must have severed the rest of his persuasions. The question is, are there any other hidden exits like this?"

"I will check if any new doors that have appeared," Oji said. "And I will seal this one so no one can use it."

"At least that explains how Ana got in," Mav said. "I never thought to ask her."

"That was a persuasion?" Ryvalin asked. "It looked and felt so real. How are we supposed to know the difference?"

"I don't know," Mav replied. "Ana was rather proud of the fact that Kaenera was good at illusions. I should have paid more attention."

"What else did Ana say Kaenera was good at?" Adriz asked.

Mav stared at the door as he tried to remember. "According to Ana, he is very good at planting suggestions and distractions. We'll need to work on your mind shields."

"We should have been doing that already!" Adriz exclaimed.

"Well, we'll start after we've checked the Gate for any more hidden exits. Let's hope breaking one persuasion broke them all."

"You really think we are going to rely on hope?" Adriz asked.

"No, I suppose not. Oji, do a sweep and see if you can

find any more areas that may have appeared that you weren't aware of before."

"Yes, Mav."

"Let's keep finding this door quiet. We might be able to use it to set a trap now that we know about it. I don't think there are any other wraiths we haven't met, but if they are trying to contact Kaenera, they may try and use it. I suggest the rest of you pair up with a wraith and take a level each. Check every surface and make sure you can both confirm it is solid. Kiara and I will take the ground floor and the kitchens."

35

DEMAVRIAN – OBLIVION GATE

The next morning, Mav was up early. Kissing Solanji on the cheek, he left her sleeping. Ellaria would take her to the citadel after first meal to continue her work with Sero and the SoulSingers.

Their search the previous day had not revealed any further concealed doors or passages in the Gate, which was a relief and one less thing to worry about. He had enough to concern him with all the issues already identified. A pile of reports sat on his desk, awaiting his attention, from preparations to transport Julius' division into the Gate to various plans for an assault on Kaenera's stronghold, if they could find it.

Oji had built one of the barracks and was working on the second. As soon as Mav completed the transfer, they could start training the men. It was time to deal with Kaenera before he did any more damage.

A soulless brushed past Mav's awareness, leaving behind the shadowy weight he would need to release in due course.

Oji's diversion shield was working, and he no longer had to take a soulless immediately. He could choose the time when he would allow each soulless to pass through him. At that time, he saw a brief flicker of their life and received what he had once called a tile, for lack of a better word, but it wasn't really. It was a small parcel of shadowy matter for him to carry and a glint of silver to sparkle within his feathers. The weight of the matter was growing. He was learning more about the passage of the soulless, that he could give them a choice. The matter he could pass on through the Gate; the sparkles seemed here to stay.

That first frantic scouring by the Gate had been his desperate need to relieve the pressure. The flood of soulless after the massacre had forced him to find a way to cope with processing them, which was to go to the rose gate, recognise the person passing through his hands, and then allow them the choice of staying within the Gate or being released into oblivion.

His shadows swirled around him. There was another silver glint in the strands, and he had the urge to flare his wings where he knew the sparkle would nestle among his shadowy feathers, a flash of light amongst the darkness. He was about to stand and do so when Felather's voice interrupted his concentration.

"Mav?"

He answered absently. *"Yes?"*

"Kerris wants to speak to you. He's had an idea that might help with…you know, things."

"Things? What things?" Mav asked, lifting his head and abandoning his work with relief as he leaned back in his chair.

"You'll have to ask him; he won't tell me."

Another good reason to make his fledglings oathsworn. They would be able to contact him directly if they needed to. He concentrated a moment, and then Kerris staggered as he appeared in Mav's office.

"A-a little warning might be helpful."

Mav raised his eyebrow. "You contacted me. What else did you expect when you demanded to see me?"

"I was expecting you to appear in the citadel."

"I've got too much to do to flit about. What did you want to discuss?"

Kerris fidgeted under Mav's expectant gaze. "Umm. Well…" He rubbed the back of his neck. "Well, I thought it might help Solanji if we did a census in Eidolon. You know, where we list everyone who lives in each village."

"I know what a census is," Mav murmured, frowning in thought.

"If we can list families by village, with all their details, wouldn't that help Solanji match souls more easily?"

"Yes, I'm sure it would. But that is an enormous job."

"You could send out multiple groups. Once the people know you intend to return their souls, I bet they would be willing to cooperate."

"That is an excellent idea."

"And…"

"And?"

"I thought we could set up some safehouses for the orphans. Just because you ousted Kaenera, it doesn't mean every kid has a place to stay." Kerris squirmed under Mav's gaze. "I want to help. I hate being confined at the citadel. I'm not one for book learning, though I'll learn whatever you want me to, but I can do that whilst helping others as well."

Mav leaned back in his chair, suddenly overwhelmed by the rush of gratification. No, it was love he felt for this child who consistently thought of others before himself. Why he had thought any of his fledglings would wait for him to tell them what to do was beyond him, and he exhaled a long sigh.

Kerris stilled, his expression fearful.

Mav lurched to his feet. He never wanted any of his fledglings to fear him. He rounded his desk and pulled Kerris into a hug. "You are amazing, do you know that? A census is a fantastic idea, and you will be the ideal candidate to smooth the way for those less trusting. I should have thought about safehouses. Of course, you were not the only children struggling."

"You've been a bit busy," Kerris offered, hugging Mav back.

"No excuse. I lost sight of what we were trying to achieve."

"I think Kaenera is enough to distract you. We don't want to lose you, either, Mav."

"Which is why you should be here in Eidolon. You are quite right. And the others. I can create a portal to allow Shandra, Muntra, and Bailey to travel back and forth as needed. But I need you all here."

Mav released Kerris and looked up. "Oji?"

"Yes, Demavrian?" Oji replied, his voice echoing around the room.

Kerris stiffened as he glanced around him.

"I want to introduce you to Kerris, one of my fledglings. He will be living here with us, along with Shandra."

"Kerris! I am very happy to meet you," Oji said, his voice rising.

Mav grinned. "He gets quite excited when more of the family move in."

Kerris flushed. "Thank you. I'm glad to meet you, too."

"Kerris is a scribe and a trainee healer. He will lead our census project. I think this is something Solanji and Felather can help you with." Mav inspected Kerris. "Do you think you could plan out what is needed? How you see it working? Discuss it with Solanji and Felather.

"I recommend you start the census at the safehouse,

somewhere we know, and see if there's anything else you need and then work your way south, back to us. I expect you to be home in the evenings, though. That will keep you busy for the foreseeable future. Make sure you track where you see a need for a safehouse, and we'll set one up."

"Really?"

"Yes. In fact, Felather can go with you to help you get organised. Sero can keep an eye on Bailey, and Adriz has Muntra under her wing, so we should be good."

"What about Shandra?"

Mav chuckled. "She has claimed the Gate, and Oji has fallen for her charms. They are busy making an inventory of supplies and whatnot."

"She is very methodical," Oji murmured, and Kerris grinned at the uncertain tone in his voice.

"Bossy, you mean. May I see her before I go?" Kerris asked.

"Of course," Mav said. "I need to recall Felather, so go find her and Kiara, and I'll speak to you later. Oji will show you where to go,"

Kerris hugged him and dashed off, leaving Mav to shake his head at the energy his fledglings had.

Searching a moment for the connection to his oathsworn, he found Felather and was relieved at how easy it was to contact each of them. *"Felather?"*

"Yes?"

"Would you mind joining me at the Gate?"

"Of course. What do you need?" Felather appeared, brushing down his sleeves as he sauntered over to a chair.

"Kerris and Shandra are here, both demanding a job, in place of lessons."

Felather chuckled. "Are you really surprised? They have been surviving on their own for years."

"True. Well, Shandra is determined to take over Oji. Not sure if he's pleased or not."

"Very pleased," Oji said, and Felather laughed.

"And Kerris has come up with a brilliant suggestion that you need to help him implement. He has suggested we do a census of Eidolon."

Felather's eyes widened, and his jaw dropped. "Oh, what a clever boy."

"Yes. But it's a huge job, and you need to help him figure out the best way to ensure we find everyone. Create a plan, identify the optimum number of teams, and brief them all, Solanji can support you."

"Of course," Felather replied, leaning forward. From his intense expression, his brain was already calculating options.

"Kerris also reminded me that we need to set up safehouses for the orphans who have nowhere to call home. I've been sidetracked by Kaenera and the Gate, but there is still much that needs to be done for the people of Eidolon."

Felather waved his hand. "Understandable. A death threat should not be ignored."

"True, but many of these children are vulnerable and under a similar threat."

"Would Amaridin provide resources to help us, do you think?" Felather asked. "Until you can find the right people in Eidolon?"

"I'll ask him. Don't see why he wouldn't. I think the fledglings are going to be based here, and they'll travel to the citadel when needed. Adriz can keep Muntra training. I'm hoping Sero will end up here eventually. Solanji is working on him. Bailey should stay at the citadel until Sero is happy for him to come here."

Felather chuckled. "Got it all planned out, haven't you?"

"No," Mav replied, his voice a low groan. "I haven't. What I have planned is driven by my fledglings. I think I need to make them journeymen and offer them the choice to become oathsworn. I can protect them better, and they're the ones with all the ideas."

"Then do it. You know they are yours, and they wouldn't hesitate."

"I wanted to give them more time to enjoy Puronia."

"They can visit the city later. They are not interested now, except for maybe the Emporium."

Mav laughed. "Aren't we all?" Feeling much lighter, he grinned at Felather. "Very well. You've got a couple of turns. Why don't you hunt down Adriz? Kerris and Shandra will be fine under Oji's eye."

Felather leapt to his feet. "You're sure?"

"Positive." Mav waved him away. "Go find Adriz. Oji will show you the way."

Felather didn't need to be told twice.

Mav was staring out the window when he felt Ellaria arrive with his heartsworn. Their dragon was managing them again.

"I'm not," Ellaria said. *"But it's rare when you have managed to occupy all your oathsworn. I thought you both needed a little time togeth-er."* She preened, her golden scales glinting in the emerald light from the lamps.

Solanji chuckled. "When Ellaria mentioned you weren't busy, I thought we could make better use of your time. We haven't had much time on our own. Sero was not impressed when I cut our session short. He'll be saying I'm not giving my job the attention it needs."

"You'll have to tell him that your heartsworn had a prior claim," Mav said as he rose from his seat and met Solanji in the middle of the room. She lifted her face and their lips touched, and all the tension flowed out of his body.

Her body moulded against his, and her warmth drove away the heaviness that had been creeping through his limbs as each soul passed through him, leaving behind evidence of their passage.

As he relaxed, he flared his wings, curving them around her protectively.

"I've missed you," Solanji whispered against his lips, and she reached up to caress the feathery strands.

Mav shivered, sensitive to her light touch. "A day seems like a year," he replied, entwining his fingers in hers as he reluctantly released her lips and led them towards their chambers.

"Someone's been busy," Solanji said as she inspected the rooms. They looked very similar to Mav's chambers in the citadel. Tall bookshelves full of leather-bound books, large paintings of Puronia and the citadel on the walls, and thick rugs on the floor softened the austere room.

"Oji wants us to feel like we are at home. If there's anything you want to change, feel free. He's lifted the images of my rooms from me, but they were not your choice."

Solanji snorted. "You saw my room. There is nothing I would bring from there."

"But there may be something you've always wanted."

"Can't think of anything I want right now except you."

"In that case," Mav said as he pulled her back into his arms. Gently clasping her neck, he kissed her.

He groaned as she slipped her hands around his back, tugging him closer and pulling his shirt out of his trousers. She ran her palms up under his shirt, smoothing his skin. Heat followed her fingertips as her tongue quested deeper, and she pressed tighter against his body. Wherever her fingers explored, fire followed.

He tugged at her clothes, ignoring the sound of ripping fabric. Buttons pinged as Solanji ripped open his shirt, belts thudded to the floor, and material was discarded wherever it fell as they strove to find each other's skin.

Mav smoothed his fingers over Solanji's neck. His lips followed them, dropping soft kisses across her throat. "You are so beautiful," he murmured as Solanji pushed his trousers down and freed his straining erection.

The cool air on his skin brought him back to his senses for a moment, but Solanji was ahead of him. When her firm hands grasped him, he lost all threads of thought as she pushed him down on the bed and climbed on top of him.

"You've been working too hard," she said, smoothing her fingers over his skin. "I need to be taking better care of you."

"I am well looked after," Mav gasped, struggling to form the words as she stroked him.

"A burden shared is half the weight."

"Yes," Mav agreed, trying not to buck his hips as her slick heat slowly engulfed him. His breath hissed out as he pushed up to meet her. "I've missed you…"

"I know," Solanji murmured, capturing his mouth again as she undulated against him. He relished the heat of her skin, silky soft against his. Mav's thoughts scattered as she took him deep, firmly taking charge, filling his mind with her and only her. She made love to him, long and slow, driving him to mindless ecstasy, joining him as he keened his release until he collapsed beneath her, sated and exhausted.

Mav drifted in the moment, aware of Solanji's tight embrace as she held him for a little longer, trying to stave off reality and all the worries that would crowd back as soon as he regained his senses.

He took a deeper breath, and Solanji's embrace tightened. She clenched down on him, trying to keep him still, but he knew the moment had passed as he kissed her soft skin. He rolled them over and smiled down at her. "I have missed you not being here."

"I have missed not being here with you."

"Then maybe it's time we took up residence permanently."

"That sounds like an excellent idea to me."

"Good. Decision made."

Solanji smiled up at him, her black eyes gleaming. She ran a gentle finger down his cheek, and he shivered. "See. Decision-making is easier when we are together."

"A burden shared," he agreed, and her smile widened.

"You listened."

"I always listen to you, my heart."

She reached up to kiss him, and he was enveloped in her love as if it were a physical blanket. He relaxed into it, drawing it deep and treasuring it in his core.

Solanji sighed, nuzzling his shoulder. "I love you so much."

"As I love you, but we have to get cleaned up and send Kerris and Felather on their way." He eased off her and pulled her into his arms as he tugged the covers over them.

"Where are they going?" Solanji asked as she snuggled close and kissed his throat.

"Kerris has suggested we perform a census, which will make it easier for the SoulSingers to match bodies and souls and so make your life a lot easier."

"What a great idea."

"It is. I suggested you and Felather should support him. And Shandra has decided she needs no more lessons and has taken Oji in hand. I should have known my fledglings would use their initiative."

"They wouldn't be yours if they didn't."

"True. I think I'm going to offer Shandra and Kerris the option to become my oathsworn."

"About time."

Mav chuckled. "I wanted…I don't know. I hoped they could enjoy their childhood for a bit first."

"Mav, they lost their childhood a long time ago. Shandra is what, seventeen? They've grown up quickly. For them, it's better to move forward."

"I suppose so."

Solanji kissed him. "You know so, love. They are already showing you what they can do. Holding them back will only cause more harm. They are ready. All of them."

"I am so lucky to have you."

"I know."

Mav gave a shout of laughter and rolled off her. Sitting up, he untangled himself from the sheet and swung his legs over the side of the bed. "I'll start the shower," he said as he rose and walked across the room to the bathing room.

Solanji flopped back on the bed. "I don't want to move," she complained, tugging the blanket around her as she watched him.

Mav gave her a sultry grin. "I'll wash your back," he offered, "and other parts as well."

Solanji threw the covers aside and chased him into the bathing room.

36

DEMAVRIAN – OBLIVION GATE

The shared first meal at the Oblivion Gate early the next morning was a taste of what family life could be like, and Mav loved every moment of it. Oji did as well, as there was a soft hum of contentment in the back of Mav's mind.

They were gradually finding uses for all the rooms in the Gate. This room, off the same corridor as Mav and Solanji's suite on the second floor, had been designated the dining room. Mav thought it might be too far from the kitchen, but he'd let Shandra figure that out.

A table long enough to cater for his family took up most of the space, with chairs set all around it. The table was covered with a white cloth and set with cutlery and crockery at each place.

His oathsworn were content, and his fledglings, soon to be oathsworn, were full of joy, the happiest he had seen them. This was the first time in recent memory that he had all his oathsworn together. It was interesting to see how they had chosen to sit, oathsworn interspersed with his fledglings, each taking one under their wing, as he had.

Kiara had manifested at the table and was trying to eat whatever her friends placed on her plate. That was not necessarily going so well, but that was maybe more because of their shrieks of laughter than what she actually managed to push into her mouth.

The cook appeared with another plate of warm bread and slices of crispy meat. He set it on the table and asked Shandra, "How many for dinner tonight?"

"Thank you." Shandra smiled at the cook. "We'll be eight for dinner tonight. Could you prepare it for seventh turn this evening, here in the dining room. I'll come down to the kitchen and discuss menus with you after we finish here."

The wraith straightened, solidifying for a moment. "Very well," he said. "And when do the soldiers arrive?"

"I'll begin transferring them today," Mav said.

The wraith nodded. "I'll be ready," he said and then he disappeared.

"A man of few words," Mav said.

"He's happy in his work," Shandra said.

"We need to invite Bailey and Muntra to join us. They should be here, too," Mav said, staring at the space where the cook had been.

"Yes," Kerris said. "Why don't you bring them here now?"

"An even better plan."

"Maybe ask them first?" Solanji suggested. "Invite them to join us tomorrow. Bailey doesn't do well with surprises at the moment."

Mav nodded slowly. "True."

"I'll speak to them," Adriz said as she rose from her seat. "I should go, or Muntra will wear himself out by the time I get there."

Ryvalin rose as well. "I need to go as well. Final prep to receive the troops."

"Before you both go, there's something I want you to witness." Mav stood and walked around to Kiara's seat. Placing his hands on her shoulders, he said, "Kiara. It would be my honour if you chose to become one of my oathsworn."

Kiara launched herself at him. Hugging him tight, she gasped, "I thought you'd never ask."

Mav laughed and hugged her back. "You are my Gate Wraith. Who else would I ask?"

"That's why," she mumbled into his neck, her warm tears trickling beneath his collar. "I'm a wraith."

"You are so much more than a wraith, my dear. I have to warn you, though, that I have no idea how being my oathsworn will manifest in you. Typically, you would be immortal and able to communicate with me telepathically. We'll have to see how it develops."

"As long as you're mine, I don't care," Kiara said, snuffling into Mav's shirt.

"I'll take that as a yes." Mav released her and turned to Shandra. "Shandra, my dear."

"Yes!" Shandra shouted as she leapt to her feet.

Mav laughed. "I would be honoured to have you as my oathsworn and custodian." He swept her into his arms.

"Yes, yes, yes," Shandra chanted.

He turned to Kerris, and the lad grinned at him, his dark eyes gleaming with unshed tears.

"Kerris." Mav's voice choked as he met Kerris' gaze. "I would be so very honoured if you chose to be my oathsworn."

"There is no one else I would ever consider," Kerris replied as he walked around the table and into Mav's arms.

Mav kissed the top of his head as his vision blurred.

"You are killing me," Adriz said as she wiped a tear away.

Mav cleared his throat. "Adriz, Felather, Ryvalin, Xylvin, Solanji. Do you acknowledge Kiara, Shandra, and Kerris as my oathsworn and beloved members of our family?"

Xylvin's roar rattled the crockery, and Ryvalin grinned. "That would be an emphatic yes."

"You bet!" Adriz replied, tugging Shandra to her side. "Welcome to the crazy house."

Felather pumped his fist in the air and tugged Kerris out of Mav's arms and into his. "Help at last. We're so glad to have you, brother."

"Kiara, my darling," Solanji whispered as she pulled the girl close. "Welcome to the family."

"What about me?" Oji's voice reverberated all around them. "I want to be part of your family."

Mav wiped his cheeks and grinned. Why not? "Oblivion Gate, Oji. You are our home, and we are already bonded, but if you want to be oathsworn to my oathsworn, then, as someone very dear to me once told me, a burden shared is much lighter, and I would be honoured to welcome you into our family."

"Yes!" Oji hissed, and Mav could just see him dancing a jig in celebration. "Consider yourselves all claimed!"

"Then we should celebrate!" Mav said, and a small glass of mountain wine appeared in each person's hand. He raised his glass. "I know it's early, but celebrations require mountain wine. To family!"

"To family!" his oathsworn all chanted.

Once everyone had calmed down and congratulated each other, Mav raised his hands for quiet. "There is one more thing I wanted to discuss." He smiled around the room. "Our family grows, and hopefully, Muntra and Bailey will join us soon. Once we are complete and all is safe, we will perform the ceremony. It is a public acknowledgement of our personal promises. But although you are my oathsworn, this does not negate your lessons." He paused as his oathsworn's cheers turned to groans.

"Therefore, you need to be able to travel back and forth between the citadel and the Gate. Oji and I have created a portal in the chamber off the main entrance hall." His lips quirked at the renaming of the ballroom, but Xylvin had claimed the space.

Shandra was determined to have a ball at the Gate; therefore, they still needed a ballroom, and Oji was considering the best location for it.

"The portal will be closed by default. We are trying to secure the Gate, not create weaknesses in our defences. So, you must apply to either Oji or me to open the portal for you to use it. Adriz, Felather, or Ryvalin must accompany you. I do not want you travelling to the citadel nor venturing into Puronia alone. You will have to ask us to open the portal for each trip."

His oathsworn dutifully nodded.

"You will be transported to my rooms in the citadel. When you want to return, you call me, and I'll open the portal.

"Oh, and for clarity, permission will only be granted to oathsworn. Maybe once we've dealt with Kaenera, we can ease up on the restrictions, but for now, we must concentrate on being safe. If you need to bring anyone else with you, contact me, and if justified, I will transport them. Understand?"

"Yes, Mav," they all chanted.

Mav grinned. "Excellent. Then, have a wonderful day, everyone."

Adriz departed for the citadel, giving them a wave and a grin as she went off to use the brand-new portal. Felather and Kerris huddled over a sheet of paper, making final plans on how to conduct their census.

Ryvalin rolled her eyes at them. "Mav, let me know when you're ready to transport the first cohort."

"Give me half a turn, and I'll be ready," Mav replied.

And then Ryvalin and Kiara vanished into the depths of the Oblivion Gate with similar expressions of anticipation on their faces.

Mav glanced around the room and smiled. He just needed to persuade Muntra and Bailey to join them, and his family would be complete.

"This is a wonderful thing," Oji murmured. *"I can feel their happiness. It is soaking into my walls."*

"I am glad. And Oji, I never meant to leave you out. Without you, this family wouldn't be complete."

"Yes, it would, but I would be the one who would suffer without you all."

"Then let's make ourselves as secure as possible and protect this treasure we have within us."

"Agreed. I have been speaking to Wenson in the library."

"And what does Wenson have to say?"

"He is very knowledgeable. I think he is more than a librarian, but I do not remember what. I don't know why I have memory lapses. Do you think Kaenera damaged me?"

"I don't know. It is possible. But Oji, we'll work our way through everything together. You are no longer alone."

"No, I have a family."

Mav placed his cup on the table and leaned back in his chair. He was loath to leave the room. The buzz of conversation and ideas was warming. Both Shandra and Kerris were animated, full of ideas and solutions to problems he hadn't even thought of. He had to stop thinking of them as children. They had shed their childhood in Eidolon and were young men and women eager to embrace their new roles and perfectly capable of doing so. Once they had completed their training, Mav knew they would all be formidable.

"I'm going to the citadel this morning," he said. "Does anyone want to come with me?"

Kerris shook his head.

"I don't need to go until this afternoon," Shandra said. "My lesson with Master Xabier isn't until two."

"I can take her if you're not back by then," Solanji offered. "I can spend the afternoon with Sero."

"Very well. Then I had better go and see if Julius and his men are ready to join us." Mav rose and bent to kiss Solanji farewell.

"Ah, there is one thing I want to bring here," Solanji said, cupping his face and dropping a soft kiss on his lips. "I asked Amaridin for one of the paintings in the citadel, and he agreed. Could you transport the painting of you and Athenia from the library? I want the youthful general and his best friend here in our library. Athenia should be with us."

Mav's breath caught, and then he slowly nodded. "I spoke to Julius about it and he agreed. I believe that is one of the few paintings of Athenia in the citadel, but as he is relocating here, he'll still be able to see it."

"Thank you." Solanji kissed him again. "Go and meet Ryvalin. I'll see you for dinner."

37

MUNTRA – CITADEL

Muntra hovered over Bailey as he sat at the table in the citadel library with books spread out in a semi-circle in front of him. He knew he was being overbearing, but he couldn't help it; he needed to reassure himself that Bailey was alright.

The memory of the attack on Bailey in Eidolon haunted him. Being trapped inside that compound, too large to get his bulk through the hole he had cut in the chain-link fence for them to escape, was a nightmare on repeat. No matter how he struggled to get through that fence, he just couldn't fit. All the while, Bailey screamed as he was attacked, and then there was the awful moment when his screams were choked off as he was strangled. It tortured his dreams, though it was the silence that was the worst. The silence meant he had failed.

Muntra hated the distance that had crept between them, the hesitant withdrawal whenever he touched Bailey. And now that Bailey had his soul back, it was one more thing between them.

Bailey reached for his quill, and without thought, Muntra

hurried to get it for him. Bailey hissed his breath out. "Muntra, I am quite capable of picking up a quill."

"I just want to help."

"I know, and you do. Only, why don't you pick a book to read? There's plenty to choose from."

"I don't want to read."

"Yes, you do. Go find one on military strategy or something."

"I want to stay with you." Muntra couldn't keep the whine out of his voice, and inwardly, he cringed.

"You are being pathetic, Muntra."

Muntra jerked in surprise at the sharp voice that came from behind them. He spun and gaped at Adriz, who stood in the doorway, scowling at him.

"No more moping about. You are supposed to be training every day. Bailey needs to study so he can join us at the Gate. In half a turn, I expect to see you in the training ground. Don't make me come and get you." Adriz stomped away.

Despair forced Muntra's shoulders into a slump. What would happen to Bailey if he left him? "Will you be alright?" he asked, knowing it was the wrong question as Bailey's beautiful face scrunched up in annoyance.

"I'll see you later?" he added hurriedly. Uncertainty tugged his voice up at the end, and Bailey leapt to his feet.

"You silly oaf! I just need a little time to myself." He mock-scowled at his books. "I have no doubt I'll still be here when you're finished." He hugged Muntra, and Muntra was so relieved that he hugged him back, inhaling the sweet scent that was Bailey. At least that hadn't changed.

"Will you still be here?" Muntra asked, unable to keep the fear out of his voice.

"Of course I will." Bailey shrugged an elegant shoulder. "Where else am I going to go?"

Muntra gently cupped Bailey's face in his hands. "You could go wherever you wanted to," he whispered, "and I would go with you."

The sweetest smile spread over Bailey's face, and he leaned forward and kissed Muntra's cheek. Muntra dropped his hands to slide them around Bailey's slender waist, but Bailey stepped back out of the embrace, and Muntra let him go.

"And I would be glad of your company," Bailey said and glanced at the timepiece on the shelf. "You shouldn't keep Adriz waiting."

"Bailey."

"I'll still be here. I promise."

Muntra bit off his reply. Scanning Bailey's face, he memorised every precious curve, every new line of strain that marred his perfect skin, the vivid blue eyes that no longer seemed so innocent or joyful. After one last stroke of his soft cheek, Muntra nodded and left. The unsaid "Are you sure?" hung in the air behind him.

Adriz was waiting for him in the corridor, and he inwardly cringed. Had she heard them? His cheeks heated at the thought, and he stared at his feet.

"Ready?" Adriz asked, her voice softer than he'd expected.

Muntra nodded.

Adriz led the way through the brightly lit corridors, past sedate, red-robed administrators and grey-robed fledglings rushing about on errands. Muntra silently followed until they reached the central staircase and descended.

Conflicting emotions swirled in Muntra's chest. He wasn't sure if he was more excited at the thought of sparring with Adriz or distraught that he might be losing Bailey. Nausea rose, and he swallowed fast, blinking away sudden tears. He was pathetic. He couldn't do anything right.

Adriz led him out of a side entrance, around the building, and into the circular training area. Four citadel guards were sparring, their movements quick and precise. The rhythm of the strikes was somehow soothing.

His feet sank into the soft sand as he followed Adriz across the arena.

Adriz waved her hand. "I could use the portal every day, but I think I'll stay here. You need to get into a routine and stick to it. You'll never improve if you don't practice."

Muntra was stuck on the mention of a portal.

"Portal?" he asked.

"Yes. Mav created a portal from the gate to his rooms in the citadel. We just step through, and we'll arrive in his study. Wouldn't want to appear here and find someone swinging their sword at us, would we?" Adriz grinned at him. "For now, you need me or Felather to escort you through it, but once everything settles and we know it's secure, as his oathsworn, you'll be able to use it on your own."

That was Muntra's dream, to be deemed worthy of becoming one of Mav's oathsworn. To truly be family. Adriz and Felather, as well as Ryvalin, were Mav's staunchest supporters. Muntra wanted to be like them so that Bailey would be proud of him and would believe in him.

Muntra listened to Adriz's instructions and then moved through the training exercise, but he knew his actions were mechanical, not as smooth and fluid as they should have been.

He stiffened as Adriz shouted at him. "Relax, Muntra! Feel your body, your muscles, how they work to give you strength. Again."

Muntra began the exercise again, but it was no use; he couldn't relax. He was wound up like a spring, with frustration tightening his body. Adriz kept him working, over and over, until his muscles burned and anger flooded his veins.

Adriz suddenly thrust a wooden stick in front of him, and he tripped over it, landing flat on his face in the sand. He heard the snickers of the guards training on the side of the arena and gritted his teeth.

"Stop! You are not listening! It's not about being angry; it's about being focused. Why are you here, Muntra? Is it because you want to be the best you can be? To serve and to honour Demavrian? Or is it just for revenge? Because revenge is fleeting and won't heal the pain. Killing for revenge won't undo whatever happened in Eidolon. It will sour and twist you until you no longer recognise yourself. Is that why you are here?"

"Yes," Muntra hissed. "No! I don't know."

"Well, which one is it?"

Muntra lurched to his feet, fury coursing through him. "I said I don't know! I failed him. I failed to protect him because I wasn't strong enough." He launched himself at Adriz. "I wasn't tough enough. Is that what you want to hear?"

Adriz grabbed him, holding him tight as he struggled to escape. A sudden panic ripped through him; he couldn't get free. He wasn't strong enough. Anguish stabbed at him like a knife in his side.

"Bailey wanted to die because of me. Because I let him down." Muntra suddenly keened, a high-pitched wail he couldn't prevent, and he slumped against her in despair. "I failed him!"

He gasped in shock as Adriz drove him to the ground, pinning him beneath her. Staring up at her, he struggled to gain his breath as his chest constricted. Tears blurred his vision and ran unheeded down his cheeks. "He's not the same," he whispered. "He doesn't want me because I couldn't save him." He tried to cover his face with his hands, but Adriz had him pinned, and he couldn't move. He was such a failure. "I couldn't stop them hurting him."

Strong arms embraced him and hauled him up until he was sitting, and he hid his face in her shoulder. Heat flushed through him, and he slumped. He was an embarrassment. Adriz could push him about with ease. He wished he had her strength, her confidence.

"There are some battles you can't win," Adriz murmured, "no matter how good you are. It doesn't mean you are weak or a failure. It doesn't mean others believe you failed them." She rocked him in her arms. "*You* didn't attack Bailey. *You* didn't cause his injuries."

"I couldn't prevent them, either," Muntra muttered.

"Bailey chose to defend that child. He knew he couldn't win that fight, but he stood up for what he believed was right. You need to respect his choice. That's why you love him. You love his fierce loyalty, his gentle nature.

"Don't let some imagined failure eat you alive. You did not fail him. You have to accept that you did what you could and there was nothing you could do to stop them. Bailey made his choices. You were outnumbered and overpowered, but you still live. You have been offered the chance to try and prevent it from happening again. Don't waste it, Muntra."

"What if I can't protect him?" he mumbled into her shoulder, unable to lift his face and meet her eyes. She would judge him a failure, just as everyone else did.

"It's not your responsibility to protect him. But you should work your hardest to know what to do if you are attacked again. Everyone makes mistakes. It's what you learn from them that's important, so the next time, you succeed. You have to learn that people make choices that are out of your control. You have to respect those decisions and do what you can to keep them safe anyway."

Muntra exhaled. Did she really mean that? He had a feeling she was talking about Mav. The amount of times Mav had been abducted, tortured, and injured while in Eidolon was horrifying. None of that had been Adriz's fault. Muntra's eyes widened as the new concept took root. Adriz was confident, respected, and competent. The guards across the arena wouldn't dare to challenge her. No one blamed her for Mav's injuries.

"Muntra, you have the ability to be an extraordinary cherubim; don't waste it. Be the best that you can be so you can help Mav and Bailey with all the work they need to do. This is just the beginning if you want it to be."

Muntra tensed. To be useful. To be worthy of Mav. To become his oathsworn. If he could do that for himself, if he could forgive and respect himself, then maybe Bailey would too.

"Now, are you ready to try again?" Adriz asked.

Muntra rose to his feet, grim determination in every line of his body. He would do this. For himself, for Mav, and especially for Bailey.

38

BAILEY – CITADEL

As Muntra left the library, Bailey exhaled in relief. He could finally breathe. As much as he loved Muntra, his constant attention was suffocating. Unable to sit at the table any longer, he rose and walked around the library, peering at the paintings on the wall until he reached one that stretched from floor to ceiling.

Bailey stared at the oil painting of Mav and a woman called Athenia. Archdeus General Demavrian, son of Averdeus, the god of their world. The painting was of him and the SoulBreather, Archangel Athenia.

She looked angelic, so beautiful and innocent, and someone had killed her.

Her hand reached for Mav in belief rather than a benediction. Athenia knew Mav would fulfil his destiny; you could see it in her expression. Mav looked so young—the youthful general, as he'd heard Solanji call him. Bailey wished that he could do something good, that he, too, could be seen as clearly as the artist had this couple.

And yet they had both been cut down, their lives irrevocably changed. Mav was older, more world weary, even if he was now a god, and Athenia was dead.

Bailey idly wondered what memories rested within the painting, but he hesitated to touch it. Sero had warned him to be careful. Without the ability to block the worst memories, which was something he just couldn't figure out how to do, he could be overwhelmed and sucked into the horrors that were inevitably woven in with the happier ones. And the older the item, the longer the history and the more likely that he could get stuck in the memories, unable to release himself.

He shuddered. He had enough bad memories already; he didn't need any more. Slipping on the pair of white gloves Sero had given him, he moved towards the stack of books labelled "Cherubs". He was supposed to read up on their history and their etiquette so that when he did finally speak with a cherub other than Sero, he wouldn't offend them.

Idly, he perused the titles, wondering if he'd offended Sero without realising it. He sighed. Probably, knowing his luck. Sero had been very kind to him, however, so kind, that Bailey was sure he would never mention it if he had.

Tears prickled, blurring his vision, and he wiped them away. Why was everyone so nice to him? He didn't deserve it. Was he so weak that everyone thought he needed protecting all the time?

Choosing a book at random, he sat in one of the curtained alcoves. He drew the curtain shut, glad to be hidden for a while. No expectations, only peace and quiet. The book was titled *Unseen Powers of the Cherub*. Bailey frowned and opened it. Running a finger down the contents page, he tensed as the list of possible powers extended into the weird and terrifying. *Personification?* What was that?

He flipped through the pages until he reached the chapter and began reading.

· · ·

Personification may only be performed with the subject's permission. Severe consequences will be imposed on any cherub who flaunts this rule.

Personification is a level eight skill and rarely manifests before the third century.

Bailey gulped. Third century? Was he going to live that long? Did he *want* to live that long? Certainly not without Muntra by his side. The thought made him pause. He needed to speak to Muntra. They were both sending confusing signals and frustrating each other. The problem was that, although he felt safe when he was with Muntra, was that the right reason to be with him? And yet, the thought of not having Muntra beside him was like a physical pain in his chest.

Sudden tears filled his eyes again, and he angrily wiped them away. He had to stop weeping at the slightest provocation. No wonder everyone thought him weak and fragile when he wasn't.

Taking a deep breath, he went back to the book.

Personification is the skill of controlling other people's actions and desires. The cherub enters the subject and emulates them. The most typical scenario is when the subject has been incapacitated and needs assistance or the subject refuses to obey Angelic law. Personification of a subject may be granted when Angelic law is broken.

Cherubs who manifest this skill must be proficient in GROUNDING and SHIELDING. Lack of either of these skills may result in the cherub being trapped within the subject, a situation not desired by either party.

Bailey scoffed. Too right. Talk about stating the obvious. But why would anyone want to enter another person in the first place? That was creepy. He made a note to read the chapters on grounding and shielding. Sero had been eloquent on the need for shielding, but he hadn't mentioned grounding. Was shielding the same as blocking?

He flipped back to the contents and saw a chapter on blocking. He guessed not, so he turned to the section on blocking and began reading.

Blocking is a level-one skill, and all cherubs manifest this ability.

Blocking is a basic requirement for cherubs to maintain their sanity. Without the ability to block unwanted memories, a cherub can be over-whelmed by the sheer volume of memories, emotions, and sensations, such that they are reduced to a catatonic state. Once catatonic, it is very rare for a cherub to return to their former state.

Bailey swallowed. Sero hadn't told him that!

"That was because I didn't want to frighten you, silly," Sero said from above him.

"Is mind-reading another skill I haven't got as well?" Bailey asked somewhat bitterly.

"For some, though, it's not mind-reading as such; it's more like interpretation. But in this case, it was pretty obvious what you were thinking. You broadcast your emotions very loudly, which is why you need to learn to shield."

"I think blocking is more important."

"That, too."

"What skills do *you* have, Sero?"

"That would be telling," Sero said with a grin. "But for every skill you demonstrate, I'll tell you one of my non-basic skills."

Bailey picked up the book and waggled it at Sero. "There is a list as long as my arm in here of skills and abilities. How many skills does a cherub usually manifest?"

"We're getting to the interesting questions at last," Sero said as he perched on the edge of the table. "There are four basic skills that all cherubs gain, then usually one, maybe two of the higher-level abilities. Those are typically between levels two and five. The higher skills are rare and have mainly died out. Probably because they are so dangerous and the cherub dies of it eventually."

"That's reassuring," Bailey said.

Sero chuckled. "Every beautiful thing has its darker side. Doesn't mean it's bad. It's learning to balance them that is important."

"And how do you learn that?"

"Practice, experience. You can't beat experience for learning."

"You can if it kills you."

"Basic skills won't kill you. And it will be centuries before the upper skills show up. Plenty of time to get proficient before the difficult stuff turns up."

"How old is the oldest cherub?"

"We don't tend to count years; it can get a bit frightening. We count centuries. The oldest is twelve. In your first century, we just call you newbies."

"So, that's why you always look so young?"

"He's finally using his brain!"

Bailey snorted under his breath.

"I see you are reading about blocking, typically the first skill to manifest. It's a self-preservation skill, which is why every cherub learns it quickly. Except you, of course. I can see you are going to go about all of this backwards just to try me."

Bailey flicked him a grin. "It doesn't make sense. Look." He bent over the page and began reading aloud.

A cherub may select which memories to accept by blocking those that are undesirable. As the memory rises, skim the surface and pull the memory towards you or push it away. As the cherub grows more proficient, it becomes second nature to skim through a batch of memories without absorbing them.

"Push and pull what?"

"Let's try one. Take your glove off. Don't touch anything but me. I am going to give you my memory of my first meal this morning. As the memory forms, note its texture, how it feels. What emotion does it evoke in you? You are sensing what this memory contains without actually entering it. Just skim the surface. Don't dive into it."

Bailey pulled his glove off and held out his hand.

Sero leaned forward and touched Bailey's palm with his fingertips.

Bailey recoiled as the memory swirled in his mind, soft and warm, unthreatening.

"See how smooth and slippery the memory is? It could slide straight off you and you'd not notice."

"But how do I tell what it is without entering it? Ugh, you licked out the jam pot again."

"You were not supposed to look into it! Try again."

"I've seen it now; I can't unsee it."

"That's the point. If you can't block, you'll keep these memories forever, and some will haunt you no matter how hard you try to forget them."

"Your breakfast will haunt me, for sure."

"Be serious, or I'll give you a memory of my shower this morning."

"Really?"

Sero clipped him around the ear.

"Ouch!"

"Behave, or I'll tell Muntra."

"Spoilsport."

39

DEMAVRIAN – OBLIVION GATE

The after-first-meal glow carried Mav all the way back to his study. His oathsworn's joy had been infectious, and they were all buoyed by a sense of commitment and purpose. He didn't want to lose the warm feeling that cocooned him with more talk about Kaenera and his threats, but dealing with Serenia was long overdue, and he couldn't put it off any longer.

First, he would transport the cohorts to the Gate—anything to delay having to see Serenia again. A tap on the door preceded Ryvalin entering his study. Mav smiled. "Are you ready to receive the first units?"

"Yes, we decided the training arena would act as the receiving area. Julius is with the first cohort in the citadel parade ground. You can pick them up from there, or however you do it." Ryvalin twirled her fingers and grinned at him. "The barracks are prepared for the first three cohorts, but we thought it would be easier for you to transfer them a unit at a time."

"Preferable I only lose ten men instead of the whole cohort?" Mav asked with a grin.

Ryvalin glared at him. "Don't lose any of them. We need them all! It's easier for Shandra and Oji to manage a unit at a time. Just transfer the two units. Once we've sorted them, Julius will prepare the second cohort in two turns and the third two turns after that. I'll meet them in the training arena."

Ryvalin left. Mav exhaled and reached for the citadel. He searched through the corridors and then went outside the building to the parade ground. Julius stood at the head of two columns of men. They all had sacks at their feet and their weapons sheathed.

He appeared beside Julius, and the guards swayed, though most managed to contain their gasps of dismay.

"Ready?" Mav asked.

"Unit one!" Julius shouted. "Prepare to transport!"

The men grabbed their sacks and stiffened. "Be back in a minute," Mav said, and he and the unit disappeared.

They reappeared in the Oblivion Gate training arena as planned. Ryvalin strode forward as the guards stared around with wide eyes, their heads tipping back to see the high ceilings. "Take a seat on the benches. We'll move out once Deus Demavrian has transported the second unit."

The men shuffled to the side of the room and collapsed unceremoniously on the bench. Mav grinned at their dazed expressions, and he took Ryvalin's order as the cue to return to the citadel. Moments later, the second unit arrived.

Exclamations filled the arena, and the guards twisted to see their surroundings.

"Welcome to the Oblivion Gate," Mav said. Ryvalin is my captain of the Host. Captain Teravin and the Eleventh Division now report to her. The Oblivion Gate is your base, though you may be posted throughout Eidolon. Find your barracks and settle in. Once the rest of your colleagues arrive, we'll tell you more."

Mav left Ryvalin to organise them and returned to his study. Tension eased in his shoulders at the knowledge that they would soon have the means to defend Eidolon. Once the division was settled, one of Julius' units would be stationed at the escarpment at all times in place of the checkpoint. The units might rotate, but they would have a presence, and it was their job to support the people as needed. He had left those instructions fairly loose. It was difficult to tell what they would face, but whatever happened, they were there to ensure the Eidolon people were protected.

It was the first step in the shift of balance from fear of the Gate Keeper, to acceptance of a benevolent god. He had to start somewhere. He would be leaning on Solanji's soul-breathing ability, but she had no qualms about allowing him to exploit her. As she said, it was the quickest way to make an impact, to show the people he meant what he said.

The next project was the orphanages, but for that, he needed to wait on Kerris to recommend the best locations or, hopefully, for people to register a need. The offices he was setting up were not only to reclaim a souls but to ask for help or advise areas that were struggling.

Mav hoped the innate goodness of people would prevail over avarice or greed and they would try and help each other. For that, he would have to wait and see, though he knew it was unlikely to be the case.

Exhaling, he squared his shoulders. His next job was to deliver Serenia's fate. He couldn't put it off any longer, no matter how much he wanted to. He glanced at the timepiece and contacted Adriz.

"Adriz? Are you finished with Muntra?"

"Mav? We're almost done."

"Meet me in the cell block in a turn. It's time to deal with Serenia.

"Of course. I'll see you there."

After a turn of completing more paperwork, Mav transported himself to the cell block beneath the citadel. Adriz was waiting for him.

Serenia had been incarcerated in the securest section, her cell warded by Averdeus. As they walked down the dim corridor lined by thick stone walls that muffled all sound, Mav tried to remember Serenia as she had been when he was a child, but the memory was faded and elusive. He took a deep breath and descended the stone steps, leading down under the citadel building.

"Mav, don't forget," Adriz murmured as she followed him down the never-ending stairs. "She is a liar and traitor. No matter what she says, she is trying to twist the truth and save herself."

"I know, but she was like a mother to me for many years. I still can't believe that she betrayed us all."

"She would have handed you over to Kaenera to achieve her goals. Remember what she is capable of."

Mav exhaled. He knew who Serenia was, it just saddened him that most of his childhood had been a lie and she had been the perpetrator, even to the extent of killing his mother to take her place. And she had succeeded. That, he would never forgive.

Mav steeled himself as another soulless passed through him. He didn't understand why some hurt more than others. He dreaded to think how Serenia would feel. He was sure she would make her passing as painful as possible.

When they finally reached the bottom of the stairs, the tunnel led to a small open chamber with another door on the other side. A middle-aged woman waited beside a burly guard in full armour—the SoulSinger he had requested.

She inclined her head when she met Mav's gaze. "My name is Nehna. Just call when you need me," she said in a low and melodious voice.

"Thank you," Mav murmured as the citadel guard

unbolted the cell. He clenched his hands into fists and relaxed them in an effort to release the tension running through his body. His chest ached. He never wanted to see this woman again. Mav entered with Adriz close behind his shoulder, a comforting presence.

Within the cell, behind a wall of bars, Serenia sat at the table, her hands clasped in front of her. The cell was empty except for a basic cot by the wall and a bucket in the corner. It was a far cry from the opulent rooms she'd had in the citadel.

Mav still couldn't accept that she had thrown away her life of leading the citadel, the highest position possible, for the chance of becoming…what? Kaenera's wife? Did she really believe Kaenera would share his power? She couldn't be so stupid.

Serenia leaned back in her chair and observed him, her lips twisting into a sneer. "Finally," she said. "I thought you were too afraid to make a decision."

Mav raised an eyebrow and inspected her. She wore a drab tunic and trousers, and her blonde hair was tied back off her face, which was denuded of all artificial colouring. And yet, even though she looked drained, she was still a dominating presence. Lines creased her face, and Mav was surprised to see how old she looked. He stiffened his resolve. This was the last time he would need to face her.

"Letting yourself go?" he asked as he stood in front of the bars.

Serenia waved an elegant hand. "Not much point bothering in here."

"True," Mav agreed.

"Aren't you coming in? After all, I've been like a mother to you for centuries. Don't I get a kiss in greeting?" Serenia gestured at the chair opposite her, and Adriz tensed.

Mav drew in a slow, steadying breath. That she would

remind him of his mother's death when her life hung in the balance. This was her punishment, not his. "You were never my mother. You didn't have the aptitude for it." Mav ignored her sharp intake of breath and continued. "I'm here to execute your sentence."

"Oh? But there is so much I could tell you about Kaenera. I thought you would have come before now."

"I doubt much of what you say would be true," Mav replied. "No, I came to tell you that it's time to pay for your crimes."

Serenia laughed. "You would not waste such a valuable source of information."

"Nothing you have to say would be of value."

"Really? Are you sure about that?"

"Completely."

"Not even a hint about a certain box concealed in the Oblivion Gate that Kaenera would be desperate to retrieve?"

Mav's heart stuttered. Did she know about the sigils, or was she just testing him? "No."

"Not even if it might mean the destruction of your world?"

"You've already attempted that, Serenia. If you or Kaenera had the means, you would have attacked."

"Ah, but Kaenera hesitated. The idiot." Her smile was pure vitriol. "But if he gets hold of that chest, and I'm sure he will, he will finally succeed in destroying you all. He knows the Gate better than you ever will, and then, bye-bye." She waved her fingers at him.

"If he destroys our world, then he'll have nothing left to rule over."

"I never said he was sane."

"And yet you sided with him and betrayed your family. You were prepared to destroy us all."

"I could have managed him if you hadn't interfered. The citadel would have been mine."

"Angelicus is more than the citadel. That was your error, Serenia, believing you could own something that would outlive us all."

"It was mine, and you stole it," Serenia hissed.

Mav took a step forward. "This world will flourish without you. Such a shame you won't be here to see it."

Serenia lurched to her feet. "Don't be an idiot, Demavrian. You need my help to stop him."

"I will never again accept your help for anything," Mav stated. "You killed my mother and attempted to kill me. You will pass through the Oblivion Gate and never return." Mav turned to the door. "Nehna," he called.

Nehna entered the cell, glanced at Serenia and then stared at the floor and curled her fingers in front of her.

"Don't you dare!" Serenia screeched. "You don't know what you're doing! I know things. About Kaenera and the Gate. I know the secret passages, the wraiths who support him."

"There is nothing you could say that is of interest to me," Mav replied, folding his arms over his chest.

"Clarence will get Kaenera back in the Gate. You'll see!"

"No, he won't."

"I know where you can find Kaenera."

"Well?"

"His main garrison is in Doveton, an estate deep in Eidolon."

"That tells me nothing. Where is it located? How many men does he have?"

"He hides it so no one knows exactly where it is, but it is east of the Crossroads. He has been building his army of dybbuks for years. He has thousands of them."

"Details, Serenia. I need numbers."

Serenia lurched for the bars, her knuckles whitening at the strength of her grip. Her voice dropped to a whisper. "Promise me you'll let me live. Please, Demavrian, I beg you. Don't take my soul. I'll tell you everything I know."

"Which is not much so far. I doubt Kaenera told you anything. You don't know enough to redeem your soul. Your time is up, Serenia." Mav nodded at Nina.

"Noo!" Serenia screeched as she thrust her arm through the bars, wildly trying to grab Mav, even though he had stepped out of reach. "Kaenera has spies everywhere, even in the citadel. You can't trust anyone. I'll point them out to you."

"Too little, too late," Mav said. "You betrayed us, gave up your position, and for what? What did Kaenera promise you?"

The SoulSinger tensed as she drew Serenia's soul away.

Serenia gaped at him, her face paling to a shocking white. "You wouldn't understand."

"No, I don't think I would. You have one day, Serenia. Make the most of every second, because they will be your last."

"You're making a big mistake." Serenia stiffened in shock. Her hand went to her chest as her furious expression drained from her face. She staggered back and slumped down onto the chair, her breath hissing out as she huddled in on herself.

Nehna quietly left.

"You bastard," Serenia whispered. "You'll regret this. I know what the Aeora sigils can do. And what Kaenera intends. You can't kill me. I have information you need!"

Mav turned to leave. He stopped at the door and looked back at her. "No, you don't." He sighed. "See you soon," he said and walked away.

"You don't even have the guts to kill me yourself?"

Serenia screamed after him. Her voice was cut off as the guard slammed the door shut and bolted it.

Mav exhaled and continued walking. Behind him, the clanking of the bolt sealing the cell was like a final death knell. He tried to control the tremor that threatened to overtake his body, a precursor to the exhaustion that swept through him, along with the grief he had tried so hard to ignore. No matter what he'd said, Serenia had been the mainstay of his childhood. He had trusted her, looked up to her. Tears pricked his eyes, and he blinked rapidly as he climbed the steps.

Adriz walked silently behind his shoulder as he returned to the parade ground and concentrated on transferring the next cohort to the Gate.

He was relieved when he was finally able to relax for a turn in his study in the Gate. The peace and quiet soothed his strained nerves.

40

KAENERA – CITADEL

Gritting his teeth, Kaenera slipped through the citadel corridors, blending with sparse shadows where he could find them. It was annoying that the citadel had so few, but he'd make do. After all, a little persuasion for the guards to look the other way didn't take much effort. He grimaced. It hadn't used to.

Since losing the Oblivion Gate, everything took more effort. When he got his hands on Demavrian, he would string out his death, make him suffer, make him beg for the agony to end. Make him watch his oathsworn die one by one as he pulled out their entrails with a silver hook that he had been sharpening for that exact purpose. He could smell the luxurious tang of warm blood as it splashed on the stone flagstones. *If* he could get them out of the Oblivion Gate.

Two of Demavrian's fledglings were at the citadel, but they were closely guarded. No, he needed to catch them out in the city when they were exposed.

Clarence had gone silent on him. That wraith had been his last hope of getting into the Oblivion Gate. No doubt, the insufferable man had got himself caught. No matter.

There were others he could use. Serenia, for one. She owed him for messing up all his plans.

He would use her as his courier. She could move around in Puronia more easily than he could. Then he would get rid of her, too.

Silently, he descended the stairs. He didn't like venturing so deep into the citadel, but he had no choice. None of his dybbuks had the intelligence or skills needed to slip past the guards.

He whispered another instruction, and the guard at the door moved away and stared down the corridor. Kaenera cursed under his breath as he sensed a ward. Averdeus had added another layer of security. No wonder he hadn't been able to find Serenia and transport her out.

He checked his timepiece and waited, whispering suggestions to keep the guard occupied. If Averdeus were on this plane, which was most probable, he would know Kaenera was tampering with his wards.

The sound of running feet thudded overhead, followed by shouts and swords clashing. A slow-building roar echoed down the corridors, and Kaenera smiled. Gineray's men had stormed the main gate and gained entry rather easily by the sound of it. The citadel guards were lazy.

Kaenera concentrated on dismantling the ward, and the air shimmered. He positioned his own protective shields, and sweat trickled down his brow as the air cleared. The lock clicked open. He steadied himself, gritting his teeth, as a wave of nausea flowed through him.

Shaking the feeling off, he opened the door and entered Serenia's cell. For a moment, he didn't think she was in there. No one moved on the other side of the bars. He unlocked the gate with a flick of his fingers. Was she asleep? "Serenia?" He walked over to the cot and shook her shoulder. "Wake up. We need to get out of here."

Serenia was slow to respond. Was she drugged?

"Serenia?"

The woman sat up and stared at him blankly. Her blonde hair straggled around her drawn face, and an air of despondency hung over her as if she'd given up. He held her shoulders, observed her glazed eyes, and swore under his breath. He didn't have time for this. They had taken her soul and left her to die? A spurt of admiration for Demavrian sped through him. He hadn't thought he'd have the guts to execute the sentence.

If Kaenera didn't need her help, he, too, would have abandoned her. The sound of many feet pounding down the stairs reminded him he was in a precarious position. That ward failing must have alerted someone. He tightened his grip on Serenia and transported them out of the citadel and into a nearby warehouse.

Kaenera released her and staggered, his vision greying. Damn Demavrian. He would wreak havoc on him; that was a promise. Straightening, he inspected the men waiting beside a wagon. They were all watching him as if he were a predator and they were the prey. As it should be.

"Get her in the wagon. We need to leave Puronia immediately," he snapped and began changing his clothes for the homespun woollen jacket and trousers of a well-to-do merchant. The material was harsh against his skin, but he didn't have the strength to transport them all to his compound in Eidolon. The disguise was a necessary evil. He'd used it before, and no doubt, he would use it again. It worked, and it didn't drain him.

Not knowing when they had taken Serenia's soul, he didn't know how long she could remain in Puronia. After all his efforts, he wasn't going to lose her because time had caught up with her. It would be one more barb he could throw at Demavrian. But this meant leaving immediately and not having the luxury of time to mislead as he had originally planned. But Serenia was almost catatonic. It would take a few days for her to recover some of her senses.

At least she would be manageable, and he could more easily plant his suggestions. She wouldn't even know. That would be a good use of their journey down the escarpment. However, it did mean she wouldn't be much use in Puronia.

His mind spun as he recalibrated his plans, substituting beguiled people where necessary. The citadel guards he had suborned, he left to their own devices. They had their orders; they knew what to do.

Observing Serenia, he knew he would have to build up her ego again. Her arrogance was what had made her so successful. Her utter belief in her right to behave the way she did overrode anyone else's protests. That was what he needed. He would send her into battle with all the bravado he could instil.

Once he had recovered his strength.

41

KERRIS – OBLIVION GATE

Kerris was quietly excited as he packed his saddle bag for his extended trip. He and Felather would be away for two days to begin with. Mav had recommended they test their processes and see what kind of reception they got before committing to a longer period.

That made sense to Kerris. He was a little nervous about being out in Eidolon on his own, so Felather's company was reassuring. The unit of guards they were to meet at the base of the escarpment was a reminder that Eidolon was not necessarily safe just yet.

Although Felather might laugh and joke, there was an underlying strength about the man; he was someone you could depend on. Kerris supposed Mav wouldn't have chosen him as an oathsworn otherwise.

Kerris only hoped he could live up to the high standard Felather had set. He blew his breath out as he buckled the strap over his bag, hoping he could live up to the high standard Felather had set. The census was his idea. Here was his chance to prove he could help Mav and Solanji, and the people of Eidolon.

Kerris had a map of Eidolon in his satchel with his parchment and ink, but he knew the map was not correct. Part of his other job was to list all the villages that were missing. Mav expected him to identify all the people living in his gloomy realm.

It was a project that would take years to complete. Kerris knew many more people were hidden in the shadows; there had been no reason for them to show themselves before now.

Kerris slung his satchel over his head, adjusted it across his body, and then hauled his bag to Oji's main entrance. Felather had brought round two of the calopes and one of the mules that now resided in the stables. They were already saddled, and Felather was tying bags of supplies onto the mule. He looked up as Kerris joined him, his expression serious.

"Cook obviously thinks we'll starve," Felather said, smoothing his hand over the mule's rump as he stepped back.

"That's a good thing, isn't it? I'd rather not go hungry."

"We're being spoilt. We'll forget how to trap our dinner." Felather's eyes brightened. "Just think, miles of countryside for us to explore. There'll be countless opportunities to catch our dinner."

"I'd rather spend my time mapping out the land and finding all the people."

"That's *your* job. I'm just here to make sure you get to do it. This is your project."

Kerris swallowed. A sudden fear that he wasn't good enough flashed through him. "I thought that was what the guards were for? To guard us so we can perform the census."

"They will protect us, protect our camp. But we'll need to convince them to be less scary as we enter the villages. Otherwise, the villagers will all hide. Soldiers don't have such a good reputation in Eidolon."

"Maybe we can disguise them as assistants when we arrive in the villages."

There you go," Felather said with a strained smile. "You're already coming up with solutions."

Kerris frowned at him. "What's the matter?"

Ferris scrubbed his face. "Kaenera managed to sneak into the citadel yesterday and absconded with Serenia. Mav is furious."

"Why does Kaenera need Serenia?"

"We don't know. But it's for nothing good, I'm sure." He twisted around. "Where is Mav? He promised to transport us to the base of the escarpment. Once we collect our guards, we can begin."

"I'm here," Mav said as he descended the steps. "You got everything you need?"

"More than enough," Felather said.

"Good. Stay alert. Kaenera is planning something, and we don't know what."

"Should we delay going?" Felather suggested.

"No!" Kerris said and cringed at the harsh edge to his voice. He didn't want any delays. It was time for him to contribute. "If we allow Kaenera to dictate our every move, we'll never start anything."

"He's right," Mav agreed.

"But we need to understand why Kaenera wanted Serenia," Felather protested, and Kerris had the impression this wasn't the first time Felather had argued this.

Mav's lips tightened, but he shook his head. "Ryvalin and Julius are here. We will work on it. I bet Kaenera's plans will have had a setback when he realises Serenia doesn't have a soul. You just need to be sensible and take precautions. Sergeant Gurida and his men will meet you at the escarpment. They should be on their way down as we speak, so you shouldn't have to wait for them for too long."

"Very well. We'll contact you in two days," Felather said.

"You'll report in every night," Mav warned. "And you'll call me immediately if there is an issue of any sort."

Felather rolled his eyes. "Alright, Grandpa."

Mav ignored him and pulled Kerris into an embrace. "This is a good thing you are doing."

Kerris hugged him back and, gathering his confidence, went to stand by his calope. His surroundings shimmered, his stomach lurched, and then an open field and heavy grey skies surrounded him. They had been deposited well back from the road leading to the escarpment, No doubt, Mav had wanted to avoid unwanted collisions.

Kerris scrunched his nose as he looked up. It was raining, a fine, misty rain that seemed quite innocent but, in time, would soak you through to the bone. He pulled his coat tighter around himself and tried not to shiver.

The scent of soggy dirt and vegetation permeated the air, and Kerris inhaled deeply. It hadn't taken him long to get used to the warm embrace of sunshiny Puronia, nor the dry, slightly stale aroma of the Oblivion Gate, but it was nice to smell the real Eidolon again.

Felather chopped at the long grass surrounding him with his sword and, once he'd made a gap, led his calope along it. The mule trailed after him, taking a swipe at the seed heads as she passed on the way to the road.

"Let the adventure begin!" Felather said and elegantly swung up onto his calope.

Unable to ignore Felather's enthusiasm, Kerris mounted his calope and followed.

Two turns later, they were waiting at the base of the escarpment when Felather tensed as he recognised the guards leading their horses off the narrow trail that looped its way down the ridge face. They passed the checkpoint without issue, and Felather waved at the officer as he searched the area.

"Ah, Sergeant Gurida, I believe. I am Felather, and this is Kerris. You've come to join us on our travels?" Felather asked as the soldiers approached them.

"So it seems," Gurida replied with a grin. "Captain Teravin suggested we accompany you."

None of the guards looked particularly happy, and Kerris wondered if they weren't pleased to be assigned to him.

"Let's get off the road, and we can do the introductions," Felather said.

"We can set up camp off one of these trails," Gurida said, pointing at the worn paths leading into the gorse bushes. "There are quite a few homesteads tucked away around here. I suggest we start with them; let's see what kind of reception we get before we try any of the larger villages."

Felather smiled grimly. "Familiar with this area, are you, Gurida?"

"Some."

Kerris wondered why a guard of the Heavenly Host would know Eidolon.

They camped that first night under a copse of trees. The air was damp, the night chilly, and large raindrops dropped on their tents with loud plops. They huddled around the small campfire and hugged their mugs of bannoe as they exchanged names and discussed the census.

Gurida introduced them. The woman was Vinial, and the men Danbers, Sindley, and Winters.

Kerris was relieved when the guards showed a little more interest, and the woman, in her early twenties, offered to help with the mapping and notations. She wasn't as tall as the men, but she was sturdily built, if lean. Her blonde hair was tied back off her face and twisted into a knot at the base of her neck.

"Vinial was going to be a scribe but found her calling in the Host instead," Gurida said.

Felather raised an eyebrow. "So, you swapped safe, warm libraries for damp campfires?"

Vinial flushed when one of the other guards snickered, but her eyes were hard as she glared at him. "I wanted to see some of the world before I resorted to just reading about it."

"Noble quest," Felather said with a nod.

"Danbers, first watch," Gurida snapped, and Kerris watched as the guard stiffened, flicking a glare at Vinial and then Kerris before rising.

"Yes, sir."

Gurida ignored him and turned to Kerris. "So, what are we actually collecting from these people?"

"Mav's wife, Solanji, is working with the SoulSingers and the cherubs to identify the souls trapped in the citadel. We need to collect the details of the people without soulmist, and then we have to match them up so that Solanji can return their souls. So, things like name, age, description, location, how they lost their soul, and where they first ended up in Eidolon. Anything that will help us identify them."

Vinial whistled, her blue eyes widening. "That will take forever."

Kerris nodded. "We want to create a repeatable process so we can send out multiple teams to collect the information, but we need to understand what works first."

"The SoulBreather will be kept busy," Gurida said.

"Hopefully," Kerris said with a twist of his lips.

"Wouldn't it be easier to have one central location and have all the people come to you?" Vinial asked. "The chance to get their souls back would be incentive enough to make people register."

Kerris was much struck by the suggestion. "Maybe for larger villages," he said, gazing into the fire. He followed the thought through. "We could use the meeting hall and send a runner to round everyone up. Would be quicker."

"Well, we'll start tomorrow," Felather said, emptying the dregs of his bannoe on the grass. "Time for bed."

The next morning, the guards broke camp with practised ease, and they were riding down the trail by the time the greying sky lightened. It was still raining.

Kerris glanced up at the clouds. "It will be nice when Mav does something about the weather."

Felather chuckled. "I think you'll have to wait a while. It's not that high on his priority list."

"Shame."

Once they had been travelling for a turn, Vinial moved up beside Kerris, and Felather fell back to ride next to Gurida.

"Kerris, I had some more ideas about making sure people come to be registered."

"Oh?"

"Yes. We need to tap into the things they normally do."

"Like what?"

"Market day."

"What about it?"

"We could nail posters up or distribute flyers in the square, and then hold a registration event the following market day. It should increase traffic for the merchants as well."

Kerris frowned at her. "That would mean we need a timetable."

Felather exchanged glances with Gurida. "I think Vinial needs to be seconded to Kerris as his assistant."

Gurida grimaced. "Or a future registration team leader."

They fell silent as they rode into a well-kept homestead. Before they had a chance to dismount, the door opened, and a dark-haired man came out and stood on the porch. "You lost?" he shouted.

Felather grinned at Kerris and then gestured at the man. "There's your first customer."

Kerris dismounted and took a few steps forward. "Hello. My name is Kerris, and I am performing a census in Eidolon."

"Yer doin' a what?" the man asked, eyeing him suspiciously.

That was the first time of many that Kerris explained what a census was and why he was doing it.

The man watched him for a moment and then laughed. "Yer expect me to believe yer'll give our souls back?"

Kerris pointed at the guards. "These are guards of the Heavenly Host. They would not be here if I didn't mean what I say."

"And 'ow much will it cost?"

"Nothing. It will cost you nothing."

"Yer expect us to believe that? There's always a cost." The man moved to shut the door.

"No, please. Deus Demavrian is the new Gate Keeper, and he intends to return as many souls as he can. His heartsworn is a SoulBreather, but she can't return the souls if she doesn't know who they belong to."

The man hesitated. "A SoulBreather, yer say?"

"Yes. And if we can match the souls to their host, then she *will* return them, but we need your help to do that."

After glancing over Kerris' companions and then up at the falling rain, the man exhaled and muttered to himself, "What difference does it make?" Then, to Kerris, he said.

"Yer'd better come in, then. No point in getting wetter. Yer men can use the barn."

"Vinial, accompany Kerris and Felather," Gurida said. "We'll be in the barn if you need us."

"Yes, sir." Vinial dismounted and handed her reins to one of the other guards. Easing the sword at her waist, she followed Kerris and Felather up the steps.

Inside the house, the air was much warmer and smelt of freshly baked bread. The man indicated the table. "Have a seat. I'm Teo, and this is my wife, Aida."

"It's a pleasure to meet you, sir," Kerris said as he tugged parchment and ink out of his bag. He laid the parchment on the table and unscrewed the lid of the ink pot. "I'm Kerris, and this is Felather and Vinial."

Vinial nodded and took up guard beside Kerris.

"Is it just yourselves, or do you have any hands to help you?" Felather asked. "We'd like to register everyone, if possible."

"Just one hand out in the fields. He'll be in once he's fed the animals."

Kerris started asking his questions, carefully filling in each column on the parchment with his neat handwriting.

"Are there any other homesteads nearby?" Felather asked. "The map doesn't show them."

Teo laughed. "No one's ever cared 'afore. There are a few homesteads and some huts near Sturzefield."

Felather moved around to the other side of the table and unrolled the map. "Could you show me where? We need to visit them all today."

Kerris watched Felather mark all the locations Teo pointed out. A warmth spread through his chest as one tiny portion of the map was populated. Felather wrote the names Teo gave him next to each homestead. The details of the people in the hamlet, they would have to investigate themselves.

It was like a treasure trail. Each place they visited would reveal more of the people hidden in the country. The map would become more accurate, and Eidolon would be richer for it.

When the farmhand entered the house, he arrived with a blast of cold wind, which ruffled Kerris' parchment, forcing him to hold it down.

Kerris repeated his reason for being there, and once again, it took some explaining for the farmhand to believe him. Kerris wasn't convinced that the farmhand believed him, but he filled in the blanks that Teo hadn't been able to provide.

Biting his lip, Kerris carefully rolled up his parchment and returned it to his bag. It had taken turns just to get the details of three people. This was going to take much longer than he had thought. His grand idea of handing Solanji a list of all the people in Eidolon had been ridiculous.

"Will we really get our souls back?" Aida asked as she hovered behind Teo.

"If we can find your soul at the citadel, then yes, but we can't guarantee it," Kerris replied.

"And we could go back to Angelicus if we wanted?" the farmhand asked.

"If you wanted to," Kerris said.

Teo hugged his wife. "Our home is here now. Been here twenty years. Don't see no point going back now."

"You could visit just to see Puronia," Vinial said, her voice soft. "Doesn't mean you can't come home again."

Teo shuddered. "I'd be a nervous wreck, worrying about not leavin' Puronia in time."

"But there wouldn't be a time limit," Kerris pointed out. "You could stay as long as you liked."

"That's not something you just forget," Aida said. "I don't think I'd want to take the risk."

Kerris nodded slowly. He had believed Mav when he'd said he had a shadowsoul. These people did not have the same level of trust. Even if Solanji returned their souls, few would test it by returning to Anglelicus—at least, not until proof percolated through the country that you could survive more than one day.

This was the first of many such discussions around dimly lit kitchen tables over the next two days. Each visit took much longer than Kerris had expected, but the questions and the cynicism were all very similar.

By the time they arrived at the village of Swyre, nestled under the willow trees near the riverbank, Kerris was eager to try a new method. The day was well advanced, and he wanted to register as many people as he could before dark. It would be trial and error until they found what worked, but he was making notes in his journal so he would remember the results.

He glanced at the fast-moving river as it whipped past them, tumbling its way downstream over submerged rocks, some of which were marked by a froth of white foam as the water swirled onwards. It was a very pretty location, and Kerris looked forward to a bit of fish-spotting when they stopped for the day. The water was so clear that he was sure they would see some.

Vinial persuaded Kerris to set up at a table in the run down inn and brought the villagers to him. He drank copious amounts of bannoe to appease the inn keeper and captured the details of every person the host brought to him.

Later that afternoon, as they strolled towards their camp, Kerris tucked the parchment into his bag. A strong gust of wind suddenly buffeted them and whipped the paper away. A strangled cry left his throat as he lunged for it and missed. After all of Vinial's hard work, he couldn't lose it. He chased after it as the wind lifted it in the air, and it rose and dipped amongst the flurry of leaves that joined it.

"Kerris, wait!" Vinial's voice was lost in the stiffening breeze.

With his eyes glued to the fluttering parchment, Kerris ran down the road, and he leapt into the air, trying to grab it. He missed it again and ground his teeth. The parchment finally snagged on a fallen tree, and he gazed at it as he caught his breath.

The tree had partially fallen into the river and extended over the rushing water. The parchment, of course, was caught on one of the upper branches. It fluttered, and Kerris' stomach twisted. Either the wind would snatch it away again or it would be ruined in the river.

Dropping his bag on the ground, he crawled out along the thin, if sturdy, trunk and stretched to grab the parchment. He had it in his fingers when a sickening crunch sounded below him, and he pitched headfirst into the water as the trunk gave way beneath him.

His first thought was that the parchment was ruined even after all his efforts, and when he inhaled a mouthful of water and choked, the second was that he was going to drown. He forced himself up, kicking hard, and his foot connected with a rock. The shock as the pain vibrated through his leg made him inhale more water, and he submerged again.

The rushing water filled his ears, an echoing mass of noise and confusion. He choked again, panicking as he tried to orient himself. But the river was stronger than it looked, and he tumbled downstream, glancing off slippery boulders that slid under his fingers, giving him no purchase.

He broached the surface, frantically gasping for breath. He couldn't see anything. His vision was blurred, his chest heaving, and he slammed into another rock. His head hit it so hard that the world went dark.

———

"Kerris!" Vinial screamed as she ran after him. "Mind the river!"

"Leave it, Kerris!" Felather yelled, and he rode past in a flurry of thudding hooves and flapping leather as his coat streamed behind him. God, the boy was fast. How had he reached the river so quickly?

Felather's heart jumped into his mouth as he saw Kerris crawling along a log, but before he could draw breath, the boy was in the water and sucked out of view. The piece of parchment fluttered as the wind tugged it, and then it spun up into the air, dropped into the water, and floated after him.

Felather cursed as he kicked his calope faster, but the river was swift, and Kerris was soon swept away. Reaching the bend in the river and catching sight of the boy's body snagged against a rock, Felather leapt off the back of his calope, struggled out of his coat and boots, and then rushed down the bank and dived straight into the turbulent river.

Felather shuddered at the shock of the cold water, and he coughed and spluttered as the turbulent current splashed in his face while he struggled to reach Kerris. Just as he stretched out an arm to grab him, the river tugged Kerris' body loose and swept him downstream. Felather ploughed after him, trying to swim with the current. A boulder struck his knee, and he was dragged under the water for a moment. He rose to the surface, kicking and spluttering, and narrowly avoided another rock.

The water swirled and pushed Kerris back towards him, and he grabbed the boy, skinning his knuckles on another rock. Hugging him close, he tried to see a break in the river bank, but they were being swept downriver too swiftly. Bashed against another rock by the strength of the current, pain glanced through Felather's shoulder, and he inhaled a mouthful of water. His grip slipped on Kerris, and his fingers spasmed, gripping Kerris' body tighter.

When Felather caught sight of another tree dangling out over the water, he kicked hard for the bank, ignoring his aching muscles and heavy limbs. They had to get out of the river.

Branches bent and snapped, their sharp edges slicing Felather's face and hands as he desperately tried to grab anything that would hold their weight. Foaming water flowed past them, tugging at his clothes, tugging at Kerris. Felather's shoulders burned as he tightened his grip on a sturdier branch. Burdened by Kerris' limp body, he struggled to hold on.

Felather cried out in relief as the end of a rope dropped into the water beside him. As it swept into his body, he released the branch and grabbed the rope, wrapping it around his wrist.

The rope burned his skin as he was tugged towards the bank, and then many hands reached down to grab him and his burden. Kerris was dragged out of his arms, and once Felather had been hauled out of the water, he heaved for breath, his muscles trembling, his body shaking.

Lurching to his feet, he pushed past their rescuers and dropped beside Kerris. Vinial was pumping Kerris' chest, but the boy lay still and unmoving. Felather searched for a pulse but couldn't find one, and an even colder chill spread through him.

When Vinial paused her pumping, Felather breathed into Kerris mouth, sending a tendril of his healing power into Kerris' lungs. He repeated the action and then let Vinial resume her chest compressions. He breathed for Kerris again and encouraged his heart to beat. He watched in relief as Kerris' chest rose and fell on its own. Placing a hand on the ground, he steadied himself as the boy coughed and then vomited up a lot of water.

A horrible bruise discoloured Kerris' temple where he must have collided with a rock, and as Felather searched his body for other injuries, he realised the boy had been well battered by the river.

He pushed another tendril of healing into Kerris, and the boy groaned and then vomited again, expelling more water. Someone wrapped a blanket around Felather's shoulders, and the warmth eased a little of the chill. Water dripped from his hair and clothes, and he couldn't stop shaking.

Vinial glanced at Felather. "Are you hurt? That was dangerous, diving into such a turbulent river. You could have hit a submerged rock."

"I'm fine," Felather replied. "Just cold. He was face down in the water. I couldn't leave him to drown."

Gurida gripped his shoulder, and Felather winced. Gurida frowned. "I thought you said you weren't injured."

"Bruises. Scratches. Nothing serious." Watching Kerris breathe on his own, Felather exhaled in relief, raised a trembling hand to push his wet hair out of his eyes, and called Mav.

Kerris regained consciousness and groaned. His chest ached, and it hurt to breathe. He tensed as he realised he felt soft linen under his fingertips.

"Welcome back to the land of the living," Mav said.

Rolling his head on the pillow, Kerris stared at him in

confusion. Mav was seated in a chair beside his bed. "Where am I?" He patted the sheets.

"In our brand-new healerie, though I wasn't expecting it to be used so quickly."

Kerris squirmed and tugged the sheet tighter around him. He was back in the Oblivion Gate?

"Felather called me," Mav said as he loosened Kerris' fingers from the material and held his hand between his own. Mav's hands were warm and safe. "What I want to know is why *you* didn't call me for help?"

Heat burned Kerris' face and down his neck. "It was all so fast, and I thought I'd be able to grab something."

"Even while you were drowning? Felather dived in after you." Mav's grip tightened on his hand. "He could have died as well."

"I'm sorry," Kerris whispered, trying to shrink into the bed. He was such a failure. He hadn't even managed two days of his census, and he had lost his records and nearly killed Felather.

"It's Felather you need to apologise to, not me," Mav said, interrupting Kerris' thoughts. "If he hadn't risked his life, you wouldn't be here. Just because we have longer lives, it doesn't mean we can't die. I don't want you taking such dangerous risks for a piece of parchment."

"I'm sorry I lost the records."

Mav exhaled. "The records are not important. They can be rewritten; the people can be interviewed again. *You* are irreplaceable." Mav leaned over and hugged him tight. "Don't scare me like that again," he murmured in Kerris' ear. When Mav released him, tears pooled in Kerris' eyes and overflowed.

Mav wiped them away as he cupped Kerris' face and kissed him on the forehead.

"I'm so sorry," Kerris said again.

"Next time, you write it straight in the ledger," Mav said. "It's much heavier and won't blow away."

"Next time?" Kerris looked up in surprise.

Mav sat back in his chair and smiled. "Rest for a few days. Dry out," he said as his eyes twinkled, "and you can resume your census."

Kerris flushed again. "You'll let me go back?"

"As long as you promise to be more careful."

Kerris nodded vigorously as warmth bloomed in his chest. "I promise."

"Gurida and his unit will question the hamlet again and replace what you lost. Felather collated what you found so far and gave the list to Solanji." Mav grinned. "I think returning a soul would be proof of your good intentions. Word will soon spread, and your job should get easier."

Kerris knew Mav was right. Returning a soul would break down so many barriers.

Mav rose and squeezed his arm. "Rest for now. Solanji will find one of the souls and you can plan from there." He twisted his lips. "I believe Shandra and Kiara wish to have a few words with you."

His stomach sinking, Kerris hauled the sheets over his head and ignored Mav's unsympathetic laughter.

42

FELATHER – OBLIVION GATE

F elather pushed his bedchamber door open and wasn't surprised to find Adriz lounging on the comfortable sofa that faced the fireplace. A roaring fire filled the grate; its yellow-green flames flared high, and emitting a delicious heat that still didn't quite alleviate the chill that pervaded his bones.

He had almost lost Kerris, and the memory of the boy's pale face and limp body still haunted him. He couldn't shift the image. Drifting over to the fire, he dropped his damp coat on the floor and toed off his boots.

Adriz placed her glass on the table and rose. "Your bath is ready. It's nice and hot. Come on. I've been waiting for you."

Felather numbly followed her into the bathing room. The sight of the steaming water unlocked some rigidity inside him, and he shuddered. He struggled to unfasten his sodden clothes, and Adriz tutted, pushed his trembling fingers away, and did it for him. She methodically stripped off his clothes, and he let her.

Gently, she tugged him towards the bath. Kissing his

shoulder, she simply said, "Get in," and he did. The water was divine, a warm blanket enveloping him, and he closed his eyes, ignoring the tears streaming down his cheeks. He wasn't sure why he was crying.

Strong hands smoothed his skin and massaged his tense shoulders, avoiding the fading bruises marking his body. Soft lips kissed his back, his neck, and his nose, and he slowly relaxed, sinking deeper into the water. "My sweet Felather," Adriz murmured. "Always saving everyone else."

He rolled his head towards her and opened his eyes. To his surprise, her expression was one of the most tender he had ever seen. He wasn't surprised she knew what had happened. He had never made the mistake of underestimating her, and he never would. Adriz was highly intelligent women, with ways and means to find out things which surpassed him, and he was supposed to be the sneaky one. She leaned over and kissed him on the lips, her fingers still swirling over his skin. The kiss was gentle, sensuous, undemanding, but fulfilling. He sighed as she pulled away.

"I think you are the most amazing person I know," Adriz said. "Do you realise that? So selfless, so committed, so prepared to risk all for others. All-or-nothing Felather, that's what I should call you. Here." She handed him a slender wine glass filled with a pale gold liquid. "Why don't we drink to you?"

"It wasn't just me."

"If you hadn't held him up out of the water, the others would never have been able to grab him, and he would have drowned even faster."

"He still nearly died." Felather shuddered and then took a sip. The mountain wine was sweet and warming, like soft honey on a fresh pastry. He exhaled, relaxing as the warmth trailed down his gullet and into his stomach.

"But you were able to save him," Adriz replied, "so there is nothing to beat yourself up about."

"Where did you get this wine? It's divine."

"Suitable for a god's palette, huh?"

Felather raised an eyebrow and grinned. The chill within him was rapidly dissipating. "You didn't."

Adriz shrugged. "Mav can't drink it all, and I'm not letting Sero grab it. Why shouldn't we have at least one bottle to ourselves?"

Felather took another sip and concentrated on enjoying the flavour of this amazing nectar that rarely saw the light of day. "I dread to think how much these bottles cost."

"Stop balancing the books. That's not your job anymore. Mav has a custodian now."

"The next generation."

"Nice, isn't it? We might have a chance to relax and enjoy life a bit."

"What a novel thought."

"We just need to get the kids through the terrible teens."

Felather choked on his drink. "Don't make me laugh while I'm luxuriating in this ambrosia."

Adriz gave him a sultry smile. "You'll be luxuriating in more than that in a moment. It's time to think about more than just enjoying a luscious drink; think about the pleasure that's about to follow it."

Heat rose across Felather's face as he blushed. He couldn't help it. The way she was looking at him burned right through his body as if he were the wick in the candle and she were the flame.

Chuckling, Adriz took his glass. "I think you've warmed up enough. Time to get up."

He groaned as his flush extended up his body, but he let her pull him out of the water and wrap him in a soft, fluffy towel. He was touched that she had made such careful preparations to seduce him. It was easy to forget that beneath her tough exterior was the most loving and sensitive woman you could ever wish to meet.

All thoughts flew out of his head except for the anticipation of what Adriz intended to do with him. He didn't care that she was the dominant one in the relationship; he just cared that she loved him. She was so sweet and considerate, careful to ensure he enjoyed their lovemaking. Whatever she wanted him to do was fine by him; he loved all of it.

When they reached the bedroom, his body aflame with desire just from the way she cast such a possessive glance over him, he dropped his towel and let her look. She circled him, trailing her fingers across his skin, leaving a scorching trail that dipped to the part of his body that was definitely interested.

She dragged a fingernail up his jutting length, and he nearly died from sheer lust. Pushing him back onto the bed, Adriz climbed on top of him, still fully clothed, and he shuddered beneath her. There was something erotic about being seduced by someone who hadn't removed a stitch of their own clothing.

Seduction was definitely what Adriz had on her mind, and he melted beneath her. If her intention had been to drag his thoughts away from that river, then she had succeeded with that first sultry glance she had teased him with.

The fire had died down, and there was a chill in the air when Felather carefully extricated himself from Adriz's embrace. He scuttled to the bathing room, a smile still plastered on his face, and relieved himself. After washing his hands, he rushed back to the bed and Adriz. He wormed his way back into her arms.

"You're cold," she murmured.

"Warm me up, then," Felather replied, kissing her neck. Working his way up to her ear, he sucked on her ear lobe. He chuckled as she shivered and then rolled him over so he was beneath her.

Smiling up into her gleaming brown eyes, he slid his fingers up and down her smooth skin and waited with great anticipation to be devoured.

43

SOLANJI – OBLIVION GATE

Ellaria snuffled at the flames in the fireplace in Solanji and Mav's rooms in the Oblivion Gate. As she breathed, the flames flared brighter, and her scales reflected the light in bright flashes against the walls.

Solanji rubbed Mav's back and forced him to sit down. She placed a glass in his hand and sat next to him, her own glass in her hand.

"Kerris will be fine," she said.

"I know, but we could have lost Kerris *and* Felather."

Solanji cupped his cheek and leaned forward to kiss him. "But we didn't. And from what I overheard from his conversation with Shandra and Kiara, Kerris won't be making such a stupid mistake again."

Mav chuckled and finally relaxed, taking a sip of his drink.

"We've made some progress, cataloguing the souls, but we've hardly touched the surface. There are so many." Solanji paused to take a sip of her own drink. The smooth, aromatic blend of the basinthe made her smile. She had never drunk it until she'd met Mav, and now it was her favourite drink. "I'll return to the citadel tomorrow and compare the lists, but I don't think there will be a match. So, I'll have to investigate further."

"What about your search for Athenia?"

"Nothing yet. Do you have any ideas where she might have hidden? Any special places? Sero checked with the other cherubs, but no one has come across any memories of her. Wherever she went, she hasn't come back out."

"She would have been traumatised. It would have been somewhere safe. But do you still think her soul would exist all these years later? Don't souls degrade over time?"

"According to the SoulSingers, they do unless they are sustained by the citadel or a SoulBreather. She was a SoulBreather, and she was inside the citadel, so we have a good chance that her soul is still intact." She poked him in the side. "Ideas of where she could be?"

Mav shrugged and rubbed his face. "I don't know. Her rooms? Julius' rooms?"

"Sero already checked her old chambers, and she wasn't there. I don't know about Julius' rooms." Solanji glanced at Ellaria. Her silly dragon was almost in the fireplace.

"Ellaria, you're blocking all the heat."

"No, I'm not," Ellaria grumbled, but she did move back from the fire.

"What about you, Ellaria?" Solanji asked, watching the dragon intently. "Any ideas? You were her familiar, after all."

Ellaria flexed her feet as she tamped down the rug before curling up and tucking her wings flat against her back. *"No idea."*

Solanji scowled at her. "You are not very helpful."

"What about the library?" Mav asked. "Have you found any more of her books? I'm sure there would be more than one."

Now, there was an interesting idea. "I haven't looked."

"Maybe you should." Mav stretched and placed his glass on the side table. "But that's for tomorrow." He rose, pulling Solanji to her feet. She slipped her arms around him and lifted her face for a kiss.

One of the many things she loved about this man was how affectionate he was. He never stinted anyone and was always ready to hug or squeeze a reassuring arm. She was determined he would receive as much affection as he doled out, especially from her.

Their kiss lingered and deepened. Gods, she loved this man. Grasping his hand, she tugged him towards the bedchamber. He followed willingly.

"Goodnight, Ellaria. Enjoy the fire," Mav said as he closed the door behind him.

Solanji laughed as Ellaria grumbled in her head. But she wasn't interested in Ellaria's complaints; she was more interested in helping Mav out of his clothes.

The next morning, Solanji awoke, enjoying the heat at her back, the warm body that embraced her, the soft breath on the back of her neck. She was wrapped in Mav, and she never wanted to move.

She sighed as he kissed her neck and tightened his embrace.

"Good morning," he murmured.

"Is it?" she asked, turning so she faced him. She kissed him slowly and sensually, trying to demonstrate how much she loved him. If anything happened to him…Her stomach dropped at the thought, and she clutched him tighter, tucking her head in his neck.

"What's the matter?" he asked and lifted her chin so he could see her face.

Easy tears pooled in her eyes.

"Hey, what's this? What's upset you?"

"Kaenera wants to kill you."

"That's not a new threat." Mav hugged her tight.

"I know. But…I think it's everything. Nearly losing Kerris, the massacre, all your plans. It brought it home how dangerous our life is, how depraved Kaenera is." Her fingers spasmed on his arm. "I don't want to lose you."

"You won't," he promised. "We have centuries to enjoy together. Maybe add to our family. You're more likely to get fed up with me."

"Never!" Solanji couldn't help her fierce response. This man could never be boring. He didn't know the meaning of the word.

"In that case"—Mav paused to kiss her, and Solanji relaxed in his embrace—"the day advances. Join me for a shower and something to eat before you depart?"

"Always," she replied, kissing his neck and inhaling his comforting scent.

Mav's chuckle had her looking up and meeting his heated amber gaze. The love she saw in his expression warmed her soul. His shadows caressed her and wrapped around her, keeping her safe. "We can't stay in bed, no matter how much we want to."

"Why not? You're a Deus. You can do what you want."

"You are such a temptress, leading me astray," he said, kissing her chin, her neck, and her shoulder. She shivered under his touch. "But we both have busy days and much to do." He pulled away, and she groaned. "But," he said as he swung his legs out of bed, and she trailed her fingertips across his back, "I will meet you back here tonight for a repeat performance."

"Don't be late," Solanji replied, smiling back at him.

"I won't be," he promised, and she rolled onto her

stomach to watch him walk into the bathing room. His naked body was a sight she would never get bored of.

Exhaling deeply, she untangled herself from the sheets and followed him into the bathing room. A shower with Mav would be an amazing start to the day.

After a quiet first meal, Ellaria transported Solanji to Mav's chambers in the citadel. The rooms were silent and still, dimly lit, with the curtains still drawn against the brilliant sunlight. She traced her fingers over Mav's desk and noticed the dust. Without Mav or his oathsworn here, no one would be allowed in the rooms to clean. It was time they moved everything to the Gate.

"Can you sense if Athenia is here?" she asked Ellaria. It would be silly not to check Mav's chambers, after all. Mav and Athenia had been close friends.

"No, I don't sense her at all," Ellaria replied.

Solanji wasn't surprised. "Let's go to the library before Sero finds us." Solanji knew that Sero would have her cataloguing souls as soon as he realised she had arrived.

"Why don't we ask Sero to help us search? He'll be the first to know if Athenia is in the vicinity."

Solanji switched to silent speech as they left Mav's rooms, and she walked down the corridor with Ellaria gliding above her. *"It's not fair to ask him to absorb so many memories. You know he won't be able to forget them."*

"A terrible thing that would be, indeed. Years of adolescent tricks as fledglings grow into angels."

"Not all are so innocent, and you know it."

"True. Do you really think Athenia will be in the library? Wouldn't she have shown herself before now?"

"I have no idea."

"Would she be a wraith like Kiara?"

Solanji came to a halt in the middle of the corridor. *"You know, I never considered that. I suppose it is possible."*

"You're blocking the way. Start walking or move to the side," Ellaria said, preening as the various fledglings and administrators gazed at her in admiration as they passed beneath her.

"Stop showing off," Solanji replied, but she did start walking again.

Arriving at the library, Solanji pushed open the heavy door and, after waiting for Ellaria to fly inside, pushed it closed again.

The librarian came rushing towards her. "No animals allowed in the library! You must take it away immediately."

"Animal? It?" Ellaria repeated, rearing back and flaring her wings, making the man even more agitated.

"Make yourself invisible, Ellaria," Solanji said as she tried to placate the little man. "My familiar won't damage anything. We are searching for lost souls."

"There are no lost souls here. Out." The librarian made shooing motions.

Ellaria faded from view.

"Where did it go?"

"She left. She doesn't stay where she's not wanted."

"I doubt you're going to find anything in here today. Athenia wouldn't come out with that person yapping so much," Ellaria said with a snort.

Solanji sighed. *"You're probably right."*

"The painting has gone. They must have relocated it to the Gate."

"It has? Mav never said it had been delivered."

"Maybe check with Shandra.

"Good idea. I'll search for Athenia's books and then go and join the SoulSingers. You can meet me there if you want."

"Back to work, then, cataloguing souls," Ellaria said with a distinct lack of enthusiasm.

"I have Kerris' list to check. I want to go with him when he returns to that village."

Ellaria perked up. *"A worthy cause; let's catalogue, then."*

After a turn of fruitless searching, Solanji left the library. Working with the SoulSingers was much more rewarding than with irascible angels. At least they understood the world of souls.

44

KIARA – OBLIVION GATE

Kiara watched from the shadows beneath the stairs as another cohort of the Heavenly Host arrived in the Oblivion Gate's entry hall. Xylvin had vacated her fountain and was out sweeping the area because Mav had grounded the Gate to onload the Host.

Kiara wasn't sure how she felt about so many strangers arriving at the Gate. She supposed she would get used to it, but it felt a little like an invasion, even if they were supposed to be their protectors.

Shandra had been possessed. There wasn't another word she could think of to describe her frenzied behaviour as she tried to organise the barracks. A whole new wing extended off the east side of the building. The east barracks. Oji had then built out a west barracks as well, along with stables, a room for a blacksmith or weapons master, and a lot of storage space.

It felt more like a castle preparing for war. She exhaled. But then, she supposed they were. Kaenera would destroy them all to get what he wanted.

The guards marched off to the west garrison. They must

be one of the fourth to sixth cohorts. There were three cohorts in each garrison. Soon, they would be allocated throughout the Gate, and it would become more like the citadel every day.

What would these guards make of the wraiths? She hadn't crossed paths with any of them yet, but she knew it would happen soon. As they settled, they would begin to explore.

"Kiara?" Shandra's voice echoed through the Gate, and Kiara manifested next to her. Shandra hissed her breath out and held her chest. "Don't do that! If I wasn't so angry with Kerris, I'd yell at you, but I don't have the energy."

Kiara hugged her. "Sorry. I'll come and yell at Kerris with you again."

"I can't believe he was so stupid. He could have died."

"But he didn't, Shandra. I'm sure he feels guilty enough for worrying us."

Shandra laughed bitterly. "I'm still not going to let him off lightly. I've got to yell at someone, or I might explode. We already lost you. We're not losing anyone else!"

As tears welled in Shandra's eyes, Kiara grasped her shoulders. "But you haven't lost me. I'm still here."

"But you're not you."

"Yes, I am. Shandra, you have to accept me as a wraith. I am still the same person, just a little transparent on occasion. In fact, I love it here. I've never been happier."

"Truly?" Shandra asked, searching Kiara's face.

"Truly," Kiara replied. "I am oathsworn to Mav. My family live with me. I get to look after the Oblivion Gate. What is there not to like?"

Shandra slowly smiled. "Only you would be happy being dead."

"But I am, so don't think I'm not."

"I love you, Kiara."

"I love you just as much." Kiara hugged her again. "Was there anything specific you wanted?"

"I just wanted to warn you that the Host will be arriving all day. Mav wants to get the transfer completed. There will be patrols on all the floors, and the Host will have access to the training arena and the library."

Kiara frowned. "They'll be everywhere?"

"Mav wants them to know the layout of the Gate, and he said that until Kaenera is defeated, he's not taking any risks with our safety."

"Well, I hope Oji keeps the Gate hidden. I wouldn't want anyone passing through accidentally."

Shandra laughed. "Don't worry. Oji is on high alert. There are bound to be some teething problems as we settle in so many new people."

"Well, rather you than me. I think I'll stay in the engine room." Kiara began to fade as Shandra chuckled.

"I'll see you for dinner," Shandra called as Kiara popped out of view and appeared in the engine room.

Liam hovered halfway up the Gate, lubricating the pulleys and freeing the chains. He hummed under his breath as he worked, and the chains rattled as he tugged them back and forth.

"Hey, Liam," Kiara said as she rummaged in the toolbox for a wire brush and a screwdriver. She had noticed a rusted plate at the side of the Gate and wanted to see what was behind it. First, she needed to brush off all the encrusted rust.

As Kiara scrubbed at the rust, she cursed Kaenera for allowing Oji's mechanisms to become so neglected.

"That tickles," Oji murmured in her ear. *"What are you doing?"*

Kiara laughed. *"Cleaning. Everything needs de-rusting. You are seized up."*

"I know, and you are both doing a great job, but that *tickles."*

Kiara leaned back and scowled at the metal plate. *"It's a cover of some sort."*

Oji was silent for a moment. *"I think it's a control panel."*

"For what?"

"Manual overrides to open the Gate."

"I doubt any of it works, but we'll see once I get inside."

"I'll leave you to it."

Kiara went back to work, though she knew Oji was watching, even if he was also busy elsewhere. Something as important as manual overrides would not be left to her. Inspecting the screws, Kiara slopped a bit of grease on them and rubbed it in. Then she slotted the screwdriver in and tried to turn it. It wouldn't budge.

She released the pressure and tried again. She didn't want to sheer the shank off.

Voices echoed down the corridor, and Kiara looked up as a couple of guards wandered into the hall. One of the men gave a low whistle as he peered up at the imposing gate.

"I thought you were going to hide the corridor that leads into here," Kiara said.

"Why?" Oji asked.

"You wouldn't want anyone going through the Gate accidentally."

"Well, they wouldn't be coming back, so that would teach them to be so stupid."

A burst of laughter escaped Kiara, and the guards spotted her. Their footsteps echoed as they approached, and Kiara stood, stretching her aching back.

"May I help you?" she asked.

"Is this the actual Oblivion Gate?" the shorter man asked. He was stockily built, whereas the other man was taller and thinner.

"Yes," Kiara replied. It was the simple answer.

"And you maintain it? I bet the mechanisms are killer," the taller man said.

"They are, and yes, I am the Gate Wraith."

The guards froze and stared at her. "You're a wraith? They actually exist?"

"Well, I'm here, and you can see me, so I must exist."

"My apologies." The taller man elbowed his companion. "We didn't mean to be rude. It's just all of this"—he waved his hand—"takes some getting used to."

"I'm not offended." Kiara grinned at him. He had a nice face, round and smooth. She thought he was quite young, maybe late teens, a couple of years older than her.

"My name is Savant, and this is Horrie," the shorter man said, extending his hand.

Kiara eyed it. Although she was solid when Mav was around, and her oath to Mav had made her feel more present, she hadn't tried to touch any of the humans now populating the building.

Savant flushed, his skin turning red all the way to the tips of his ears, and Horrie chuckled as Savant dropped his hand. "Sorry. I didn't think."

Kiara blushed in turn. "No, it's alright. I'm not sure if I could touch you. We can but try." She wiped her hand on a rag and extended it to Savant. "I'm Kiara."

Savant gripped it, and she squeaked in surprise when he held onto her. "Kiara, it's a pleasure to meet you."

"Hi. I'm Liam," Liam called from above them.

Savant swore and stepped back, releasing Kiara's hand.

"Sorry! I'm a wraith, too," Liam said with a laugh, not sorry at all.

"There are quite a few wraiths in the building," Kiara said with a grin. "If you're billeted here, I expect you'll meet them all."

"This place is so strange," Savant said under his breath.

"Just because it's different, it doesn't make it bad," Kiara snapped.

"I didn't mean…" Savant stuttered to a halt.

"If you'll excuse us, we have work to do." Kiara turned her back on the men, and returned to the plate.

"Give the screw a couple of bangs first," Savant said from immediately behind her. "It will loosen the rust locking it in place."

Kiara lurched to her feet, and Savant backed away, holding his hands in the air.

"Sorry, but it looks rusted solid."

Kiara silently handed him the screwdriver and gestured him forward. Savant grinned at her and knelt by the panel. He gave each of the screws a couple of hard raps, slapped some grease on them, and rubbed it in with a cloth he tugged out of his pocket. He slotted the screwdriver in and gently twisted it back and forth. "Do you have a pair of pliers?"

Kiara rummaged in the toolbox, came out with a pair, and she handed them to him. Savant used the pliers to grip the screw head and give it a deft twist. "Stubborn," he murmured under his breath. Then he slapped on more grease and repositioned the pliers. He gave it another twist and lurched back as the screw came free.

Kiara peered at the panel. "Well, that's one." She grinned at Savant. "Thank you for your help."

Savant handed her the pliers. "My pleasure." He wiped his hands on his cloth, smearing more grease over his skin.

Kiara handed him a cleaner rag.

"Savant, we need to report in," Horrie said from the other side of the room. "Don't get covered in grease on the first day."

Savant shrugged and looked up to where Liam was still working. "It's an amazing piece of mechanics."

"That, it is," Kiara agreed.

"I'll see you around," Savant said as he strolled back to Horrie.

"I expect so," Kiara said with a smile and went back to work. Maybe having the guards around wouldn't be so bad after all. She started humming as she worked.

45

SOLANJI – CITADEL

When Solanji arrived at the SoulSingers' office, two middle-aged women, Nina and Riona, and a man, Seran, sat at a table in the sun-filled room. Large ledgers lay open before them, covering the table. The air was warm, the room bright, and Solanji relaxed into the balmy atmosphere.

"Good morning," Solanji said as she sat next to the man.

Nina looked up and smiled. "Solanji. We have made progress cataloguing the first two rooms." She gestured at the long list of names and details written in the ledger before her. "And Archdeus Amaridin has promised us more scribes to help. They should be here tomorrow."

"Excellent. Here is the initial list from the homesteads near the Crossroads for cross-reference. We need to find a match so we can demonstrate that we mean what we say."

Nina took the paper and scanned it. "Seran, you have the As. Do you have an Aida, forty-four years old, originated from Feraxo?"

The man flicked back through the pages of his ledger. There was silence for a while as they checked the ledgers, but they had a limited number of names catalogued. Seran shook his head. "No, we don't have her listed."

Solanji ran her eye down the list. "There are quite a few Ts. I'll see if I can find, Trina, a seamstress from Drelia, or Teo, a scribe from Puronia. Oh, look at this. There's a Rednian who seems to be only six years old. So young. What could a child that young have done to deserve soulstripping?"

Nina grimaced. "I'm sorry, Solanji. We didn't question it. It was bad enough having to remove the soul without looking too deeply into the person's life. It was like we were executing them. In a way, I suppose we were." She looked down at the table, clasping her hands tight.

"At least you are giving them back now," Solanji murmured.

"But it is so slow."

"Then ask Amaridin for some scribes to assist us as well. You could spend more of your time with the soulmist and dictate what you find to the scribes. You are wasting time doing both parts of the job."

"An excellent idea," Nina said. "I'll go and speak to Archdeus Amaridin now."

Solanji leaned back in her chair and watched the SoulSinger leave. It *was* a slow process and frustrating for all of them. She would do what she could to help until they matched some souls. Extending her awareness, she followed the brilliant cord that bound her and Ellaria to the citadel. She suddenly craved a similar bond with the Oblivion Gate so she could be even closer to Mav. She wanted to share his burden. It didn't seem right that he had to carry it alone. Amaridin had help. Why couldn't Mav have help, too?

Concentrate, she chided herself and imagined the soulmist archives, as they were calling them.

Sunlight painted the walls yellow, and as she floated down the corridor, she was aware of a heavier sensation, as if someone were now focused and paying attention to the area.

"Hello?" she said, a little breathlessly.

"Hello, SoulBreather," a light, feminine voice said.

Solanji drifted to a stop. Could this be the citadel? *"My name is Solanji. What's yours?"*

"I think you know. You are bound to one who knows my brother."

"I think you are the citadel, but I don't know your name."

A light laugh tinkled with merriment. *"Don't be silly. We don't have names. We're buildings."*

"Oji has a name," Solanji pointed out. *"You should tell Amaridin what you want your name to be."*

"I could choose my name? Yes, why shouldn't I? Where are you going?"

"You've been asleep for many years, and over that time, a lot of souls have been collected. We are trying to return them."

"The souls in this wing? I would appreciate it if you would take them away. They hurt."

"They are hurting you?"

"Yes. They are not supposed to be here. They belong somewhere else."

"Until we find where they are supposed to be, they need to stay here."

"Not for much longer. There are too many. I can't hold them all in. My seams will split, and once they leak out, they will be lost for good."

Solanji's heart sank. *"Please, Cee. Hold on for a little longer. We'll work as fast as possible."*

"Cee. I like that. I might use it. I'll tell Amaridin he needs to work faster."

The presence disappeared, and Solanji exhaled. Could the Oblivion Gate hold some of the souls for the citadel? It was a question she would have to ask Oji.

Solanji resumed walking all the way to the end of the corridor and found the door labelled "T". Taking a deep breath, she pushed the door open. Soulmist swirled around her, and she pushed it away from her face. *"I'm looking for Teo or Trina."*

Names bombarded her. Every name she could think of beginning with T, except for the ones she was looking for. *"Trina, originally from Drelia? Or Teo from Puronia?"*

A swirl of agitated soulmist appeared before her, and Solanji extended her soul fingers. Images of a young woman, Trina, flowed through her, along with a sense of concern. The soulmist swirled away, and Solanji hurried after it.

Solanji blindly followed, blocking the soulmist that desperately tried to latch onto her. There had to be a better way of doing this. The souls were getting more desperate, and she was being emotionally battered.

In the corner lay a tangle of soulmist clumped on the floor. Solanji gaped at the mess. What had happened? Carefully, she began untangling the muddle. A lighter patch of soulmist was a young child. Solanji had a feeling that the darker soulmist had tried to somehow comfort the little one and had become entangled.

It was Teo. His memories of Aida and their life in Puronia spooled through her, and her fingers shook as she parted the soulmist. Trillin was the child. What was Trillin doing with Teo?

Gently, Solanji spooled Teo, Trina, and Trillin's soulmist within her.

Ellaria transported them back to the Oblivion Gate, and Solanji paused in her chambers to ask Kerris where he was.

"I'm in the library. Doing Mav's research for him."

Solanji grinned at the tinge of boredom in his voice.

"Where is Mav?"

"He is here with me."

Solanji hurried through the corridors and, arriving at the library, pushed open the door. The oil painting of Mav and Athenia filled the far wall. It was the first thing Solanji saw when she entered, and it brought a smile to her face. The library was the perfect home for it. She was so glad Oji had convinced Wenson to move the shelving and free up the wall.

Kerris sat at the long table situated before it. Piles of books formed a barrier around him. He lifted his head as she approached and tossed his book aside. Mav sat in an armchair next to him, his head deep in a heavy tome. He put his book down as Solanji entered.

"Now, you treat those books with better care, young Kerris," Wenson said as he suddenly appeared beside him. "I've already had words with Master Demavrian. I don't expect to have to tell you, too."

"Sorry," Kerris said, and he picked the book up and placed it neatly on the pile.

"Better," Wenson said and stomped off.

Solanji grinned. "I have some good news for you. I've found two souls we can return."

Kerris leapt to his feet. "You did? Whose?"

"A man called Teo from one of the first homesteads you visited and a woman called Trina from the village of Swyrc."

"Thank goodness. I can't wait to return them and show them we meant what we said."

"We need to find out where your team is. I'll accompany you instead of Felather this time. But you know, Kerris, you need more teams out there performing your census. You should be the one coordinating and collating all the reports and liaising with the SoulSingers. You don't have time to be gallivanting all over the countryside."

"I know, but I want to do the job for a few weeks so I can

understand what works best. And if I do the job myself, I'll know how to train others."

Solanji patted his shoulder. "Let me know when you're ready to return. Until then, I'll continue working with the SoulSingers and see if I can match more souls."

"Mav, would you transport us to Swyre tomorrow? And can you ask Sergeant Gurida to meet us there?"

"I suppose I could," Mav replied, closing his book and lifting his face so Solanji could kiss him before she left.

Kerris went back to his books, turned a page, and then stiffened. "Wait a minute. Mav, look at this. Is this a picture of the sigils? They look weird."

Mav leaned over, aware of Wenson hovering over his shoulder. "It is. Which book is that?"

"*An Encyclopaedia of Ruthlian Legends.*"

Mav frowned. "Ruthlian? Never heard of it."

Wenson tutted. "That's because it doesn't exist anymore."

"What happened to it?" Kerris asked, his eyes glued to the page.

"Poof!" Wenson said, flicking his fingers wide in the air in front of him.

"Poof?" Mav repeated.

"Big explosion, half the planet lost. Eventually, the whole thing imploded. Nothing left."

"Do they know what caused the explosion?"

"It was a mining world. They dug up something they shouldn't have."

"But if it was destroyed how do people know what they dug up?" Kerris asked, raising his eyes from the page.

"Because they shipped some of it off the planet before it could be restricted."

"The Aeora sigils?"

"Yes."

Kerris' eyes widened. "They are powerful enough to destroy a whole planet?"

Wenson silently nodded.

"Why would Kaenera want to use them here?" Kerris' voice squeaked on the last word.

"I sometimes wonder if he thinks he can control them," Mav said, "so they only destroy what he wants them to. No matter what, he can't be allowed to find them."

"Can't we destroy them?" Kerris whispered.

"Unless we can find out how from these books, we are stuck with them," Mav said grimly.

That evening, as Mav's oathsworn gathered for dinner, Kerris was full of plans to return to his census. "According to Sergeant Gurida's last report, they are working their way south along the river." Kerris winced at the reminder but carried on, hoping Mav wouldn't comment. "Solanji can collect the reports and take them to the SoulSingers."

"You'll come home with Solanji in the evening," Mav said. "It will be too damp for you to camp out overnight. Your lungs still need time to recover."

"I'm fine."

"The healer said two weeks. You're lucky I'm letting you go back now as it is."

"Why can't I heal myself?"

Felather laughed and grinned at Adriz. "You don't know how many times I've said the same thing. If I have the ability to heal, why does it not work on me?"

"I can vouch for that," Adriz said with a huge sigh, though her eyes twinkled as she said it.

"Well, you can imagine how I felt when I could heal

myself but no one else," Mav said. "That was even worse. I always felt so helpless."

Kerris screwed his face up. "I suppose I would prefer to help others," he agreed.

"I'll tell Cook to pack you a hot lunch," Shandra said. "That should help keep the chill away."

Kerris rolled his eyes but concentrated on eating his dinner instead of responding.

The conversation moved to Eidolon in general. Ryvalin reported that Xylvin was continuing her sweeps but there was no sign of any mobilisation by Kaenera. His silence was concerning, even more so now that he had Serenia, but they had their hands full with the census, searching for information about the sigils, and assimilating Julius' men into the Gate.

The next morning, Solanji rose and dressed in her golden robes. She was getting quite used to them and the respect the other angels showed her as she passed them in the citadel corridors. After a hasty first meal with Mav, she was eager to return to work.

"I am working with the SoulSingers again today. You'll find me at the citadel if you need me."

"All day?"

"I'll be back by lunchtime. Kerris wants to go to Swyre, remember?" She met his molten gaze and smiled at the promise it contained. "I expect your shadows to be ready and waiting for me tonight," she said as Ellaria appeared and whisked her away.

46

SHANDRA – CITADEL

Later that same morning, Shandra accosted Felather as he left the Oblivion Gate's library, no doubt taking a break from the research he had taken over from Kerris. She followed him as he walked down the brightly lit corridor. Jessica had been working hard. Shandra could clearly see her reflection in the highly polished floor.

"Felather, would you escort me back to the citadel? I want to surprise Bailey when he comes home. He comfort bakes, and we don't have any ingredients for him to use. I don't like to ask Cook; he has enough on his hands feeding everyone."

"Are you sure Cook will allow Bailey into his kitchen? You know how busy he is catering for a full Host."

"Kiara promised to sweet talk him for us. She knows as well as I do how much Bailey needs this."

"Write a list, and we can order the supplies for you," Felather suggested.

"It would be better if I choose what I want. It's easier when you can see the options in front of you, and anyway, I want to speak to Xabier as well."

"In that case, it would be my pleasure. When do you want to go?"

Shandra smiled at him with genuine pleasure. Felather was so lovely, so supportive. "Whenever suits you is good, though the sooner we go, the sooner we return."

"I am at your disposal. I need to collect some books for Mav from the citadel library, anyway."

"Have you made much progress?"

Felather sighed and scrubbed his face. "Some. The sigils are not native to the Gate, so Oji has no knowledge of them, only that they are dangerous and Kaenera wants them."

"And Wenson has no suggestions?"

"He has been assisting us, but he stomped off muttering under his breath about ingrates lolling about in his library, so I'm not holding out much hope."

Shandra chuckled. "You know he doesn't mean it. I bet he would be able to find what Mav needs. He just has to ask for it."

"Why don't you tell him, then?" Felather tapped his temple. "You can tell him just as easily as I can."

Shandra blushed. "I keep forgetting. It doesn't feel real, being oathsworn to Mav."

"We'll have a full ceremony. That will cement it for you. We can initiate everyone together and make it a party. You could arrange your first ball and invite Amaridin and Valerian."

"Oh, what an excellent idea. I'll tell Mav."

She wrinkled her nose as she concentrated.

"You don't need to try so hard," Felather said with a chuckle as she screwed up her face.

Ignoring Felather's chuckle, she reached out to Mav. *"Mav?"*

Mav's surprised voice filled her mind, and she relaxed. *"Yes, Shandra?"*

"I'm not disturbing you, am I?"

"Not at all. How can I help you?" Warmth replaced his surprise, and Shandra smiled. She was speaking to someone using her mind! It didn't seem real.

"I just wanted to remind you to ask Wenson to have a look at what he has in his library. If you make him think it's his *library, he's sure to be more helpful and not so grumpy. I bet he has a restricted section. I read once that all good libraries do."*

Mav's chuckle filled her head. *"That is very political of you."*

"It doesn't hurt to make him feel useful."

"True. I'll couch my request carefully."

"Oh, and by the way, I am going to arrange a ball for our oath-swearing ceremony as soon as we know it's safe."

"That sounds like an excellent idea. Oji is excited at the plan, though I think you'll have to work up to it with Cook. He was complaining about there being too much to do as it is."

"I'll find him some help."

"Do you think he'll let anyone else in his kitchen?"

"I'm sure he will. Kiara's working on him. Could you open the portal for Felather and me to go to the citadel? We are going to get Bailey's ingredients before I have my lesson with Xabier."

"Of course. Have fun, my dear."

"See you later. Love you, Mav."

"Love you, too, Shandra."

Shandra grinned and shoved Felather's shoulder as he burst out laughing. "Stop it."

"You know we should practice," Felather said silently. *"It will soon be second nature."*

Shandra shivered. Felather's voice was lighter than Mav's and tinged with amusement. *"What you can practice is leading me to the portal."*

"Your wish is my command," Felather said with a flourish, and linking arms, he tugged her down the hallway.

Kerris impatiently waited for Solanji's return to the Oblivion Gate. Mav had said he would transfer them to Swyre as soon as she arrived. He was so restless that Wenson had kicked him out of the library and left him to pace the entrance hall.

The empty hall echoed without Xylvin's bulk filling the space. The tinkle of water from the fountain soothed Kerris for a moment, and then he resumed pacing unable to keep still.

He wondered where Xylvin was. She had been flying sweeps over the surrounding area, making sure Kaenera wasn't about to ambush them. With all the people now housed in the Gate, Mav kept it seated near the sea, to the south of Eidolon.

Relief flooded him as he heard Solanji's voice and she came skipping down the main staircase. "Are you ready, Kerris?" she asked with a bright grin. She had changed out of the robes she had worn to go to the citadel that morning and into her favourite leather trousers and jacket.

Everyone, including Mav, preferred grey or black clothes when they were at the Gate.

"Ready when you are," Kerris sang out in reply.

Kerris staggered as Mav deposited him and Solanji near the village of Swyre. He inhaled the damp air of Eidolon, and his chest felt tight. He hated to admit that the healers were right about how long it would take for him to fully recover.

Gurida and his team had already set up camp outside the village and stood waiting for them.

"Who did you find?" Vinial asked, her eyes bright with interest.

"Trina, the seamstress who lived in the third cottage near the green."

"Let's go make her famous, then. The first person in Eidolon to get their soulmist returned."

A thrill sped through Kerris. They *were* making history.

Solanji tapped his arm. "It's not that big of a spectacle, so don't build it up too much. Remember what happened with Bailey. The change was subtle."

"But it was noticeable when it occurred, though I agree, you'd never know now."

"And most of the time, it will be a private moment without an audience."

"You're taking all the fun out of this," Kerris complained.

They arrived at the cottage, and Kerris knocked on the door. While he waited, some of the neighbours came out to see what was happening, and the news began to spread.

A young woman, maybe in her early twenties, opened the door. A man about the same age hovered behind her.

"Trina? My name is Kerris. A few days ago, we came here to take a census."

"I remember," Trina replied.

"Well, I am very pleased to tell you we found your soul and we're here to return it to you."

"What, all eight of you?" she asked, a little flustered.

"No, it only takes me," Solanji said as she stepped forward, holding out her hand. "My name is Solanji, and I am a SoulBreather."

An audible gasp passed through their audience.

"Oh!" Trina took a step back, but her husband pushed her out the door.

"How do we know you're tellin' the truth?"

"Well, I'm certainly not here to *take* her soul, so I'm not sure what else you think I might be doing."

The man spluttered, but Trina slapped his shoulder. "Give over, Lenny. It's my soul, and I want it back."

Solanji smiled. "Very well, then."

As before, the soulmist was eager to return to its host. Once Solanji released it, the soulmist shot into Trina, and she yelped as she clasped her chest. Her eyes widened, and her jaw dropped. An expression of pure exultation passed over her face. After a moment, her mouth snapped shut, and she stared greedily around her.

"Oh, everything is so much clearer!" she exclaimed. Her whole posture became more defined, and for a few heart-beats, she seemed to be more present. Then everything settled, and she looked as she had before. Now, though, she had an enormous smile on her face, and her eyes were bright and clear.

"I want my name on yer list!" a man yelled, shoving his way through the crowd. Others started clamouring for the same.

Gurida stepped forward. "You are all welcome to be listed. Let us get ready, and we'll get the ledger set up and record anyone who didn't register last time we were here."

"When will we get our souls back?" a woman asked.

"Once we have your details," Kerris replied, "we'll match them to the souls in the citadel. There are thousands of souls we need to work through. It may take a little time." He followed Gurida over to where they were setting up the book.

There was some pushing and shoving, but eventually, everyone lined up in an orderly fashion.

Solanji shouted. Kerris spun, and he gasped when he realised he'd left her on her own with Trina, unguarded. And now, two men were trying to drag her away.

A knife flashed in Solanji's hand as she twisted out of the grip of one man and thrust hard into his unprotected stom-ach. The man squealed as she wrenched the blade out, ready to strike again, but before Kerris could call Mav for help, a golden dragon appeared in the air and dove at the men attacking Solanji.

Everything stopped. Kerris watched with his heart in his mouth as Ellaria hovered, her golden scales gleaming in the weak sunlight. Kerris frowned and looked up at the sky. The sun was penetrating the clouds.

He shivered.

The two men cowered back from Ellaria, the one on the ground clasping his stomach as he tried to wriggle further away. Ellaria pounced on the man who was still standing, and he screamed.

Trina backed away, gaping at the sight of a dragon mauling a man.

Ellaria lifted her head and glared at her audience of watchers. Then she swung her head towards Solanji. Solanji glared back at her, and Ellaria bared her blood-drenched teeth and snarled before reluctantly releasing the man she had pinned to the floor.

"Be warned," Solanji said, anger flashing in her eyes. "We are not unprotected, nor are we stupid. Who knows these men?"

Ellaria hovered beside the men, a low growl in her throat, a warning that if they moved, they wouldn't get far. She flipped her wings back as Gurida instructed his guards to restrain them.

"They're not from around 'ere," Lenny said, scowling down at them. He glanced at the soldiers nervously. "They ain't nothing to do with us."

"You'll still give us our souls back, won't you?" an older woman asked.

Kerris watched as Solanji lifted her chin and re-sheathed her knife. "If you encourage behaviour like that"—she gestured at the injured men—"then you will *never* get your souls back." Solanji turned back to the cowering villagers.

"We were collecting names. Kerris, if you would." She waved him forward and stalked towards Gurida.

The crowd stared wide-eyed at Solanji and the golden dragon, then at Kerris and back again at the dragon.

Kerris swallowed, trying to calm his galloping heart, and then he joined Vinial beside the table where the ledger had been set up. He unscrewed the ink pot lid and dipped his quill.

Clearing his throat, he said. "We need as many details as possible so we can identify your soul. Who's first?"

Gurida's men dragged the attackers out of sight, and Gurida moved to stand next to Solanji. She flashed him a brief smile before resting her hand on Ellaria's head. Hesitantly, the people shuffled back into line.

"Who do you think they are?' Solanji asked in an undertone.

"Opportunists, I expect. We won't know until we interrogate them." Gurida glanced around the village and sighed. "Eidolon has been lawless for years. Kaenera encouraged it. I expect most of our time here will be spent enforcing Deus Demavrian's rule. He may not want to be seen as a ruler, but he'll need to be firm to begin with if he wants these people to truly be free."

"He's going to be furious when he hears about this."

"No doubt. I'll have some explaining to do. We shouldn't have let our guard down. It's my fault. I should have known better."

Solanji sighed. "Eidolon is deceptive in so many ways. It seems unassuming, but around every misty corner, there is always a surprise."

47

———

DEMAVRIAN – EIDOLON

Mav stood on the ledge looking out over the mountain range in Northern Elothia and exhaled his anger. It would only clutter his mind as he dealt with those who would dare to attack his heartsworn.

When he had received Gurida's report, he had first reassured himself that Solanji and Kerris were fine. Then he had transported Gurida and the two captives to the dungeon in Kyrill's castle, though he had left Gurida to drag the two men through the corridors and into the torture chamber where he had suffered for so long. He had debated taking his prisoners back to the Gate, but he didn't want these men sullying his home. Instead, he had chosen Kyrill's old torture chamber, which might have been a mistake. He shivered as old memories rose.

"Mav? What are you doing?" Oji asked, his voice full of concern.

"Finding out what I need to know."

"Torture isn't the way."

"It is for Kaenera. Why shouldn't it be for me?"

"Don't do this, Demavrian."

Ignoring Oji, Mav turned away from the majestic mountains and scowled. Both men were soulless and in their right minds. His shadows had removed any suggestions back in Swyre. Whatever they chose to do would be their own decision. Dark red blood pooled on the stone beneath them, much like his had. He didn't care. They had attacked his heartsworn, been prepared to harm her, to turn her over to Kaenera.

Pride fluttered in his chest at the way Solanji had fought. He had forgotten her skill with a blade.

He stood over them, his wings extended, blocking the dim light, and his shadows writhed around him. The men froze, and he saw their Adam's apples bob as they swallowed. They were afraid of him. Good. He let more of his aura leak, and the man with the stomach wound moaned, his eyes fluttering in terror.

"Who are you, and how did you meet Kaenera?" Mav asked.

"I'm dying," cried the man Solanji had stabbed. "I need a healer."

"There are no healers here. If you want a healer, you will tell me what you know. And if you know nothing, then there is no point in me wasting my time here."

"I don't know nothing," the other man said, glaring at Mav. Blood streaked his face and neck from Ellaria's teeth and claws. His clothes were shredded, revealing more weeping wounds.

"Nothing? Then why did you attack my wife?"

The men stilled and exchanged glances.

"Kaenera won't save you. He's already written you off. You are dispensable to him. I'm sure he has more where you came from. Who are you?"

They stared at him with similar mutinous expressions on their faces.

Mav stepped back to the open ledge and breathed in the cold night air. A slither of terror crept through him at the aroma of damp stone and the metallic tang of blood. He stiffened, blocking the memories it evoked. It had been a mistake to return here. More shadows leaked, swirling around him, desperate to reassure him. Mav sent his shadows questing, planting suggestions that they wanted to tell him everything.

"What do you want to know?" the man with the stab wound asked. He shuddered, squeezing his stomach.

"Everything. Start with your name, where you are from, and how you ended up working for Kaenera, and keep going."

"My name is Vern. I was once a scribe in Puronia. Got done for stealing. My employer refused to pay my full wage, so I took it myself. Stupid, really, but I was so angry that I wasn't thinking straight. Ended up soulless and abandoned somewhere out east. Must have been ten years ago now."

He paused, sweat dripping down his face. Mav extended a tendril of shadow, and the man relaxed. "Bummed about for a bit. Couldn't find good work; no one here has any money. It's a vicious circle. I was starving, near death, when I heard someone was willing to pay in food." He shrugged. "That was Kaenera. Once he got his claws in you, you were there for life." Vern twisted his lips. "Or until death, more like," he said to himself.

"Where is Kaenera based?"

"He has locations all over the place. Many in Eidolon. Some in Angelicus."

"And you know them all?"

The man nodded, and Mav sent another tendril of his healing power into the knife wound. If he were a scribe, he would be used to reading maps and documents. "How do you know them all?"

"I saw his map. He can't remember them all like he used to. He has to write stuff down. I heard that woman, Serenia, laughing at him."

"You tell me where every single one is, and I'll get you a healer." Mav moved his gaze to the other man. "Who are you, and what do you know?"

The man exhaled and grimaced. "My name's Fosert. Kaenera's got a mole in your Gate."

Mav's stomach dropped. "Who?" The only people new to the Gate were Julius' men. It must be one of them unless there was another wraith he didn't know about. Why hadn't he checked them before letting them waltz straight through his defences?

"I dunno his name, but I'd recognise him if I saw him. If I show him to you, then you've got to let me go."

Mav inspected him. "If I let you go, you'll run back to Kaenera and tell him what's happened."

"He'd kill me if I told him we failed. I wouldn't go back, I swear."

"Where would you go?"

"Dunno." The man exhaled and stared at his feet. "There ain't anywhere *to* go."

Mav gritted his teeth against the sympathy trying to edge through his guard. These people had tried to hurt his heartsworn. "Where is Kaenera's closest camp?"

"There's a camp east of Doveton," Vern said. "Most of his recruits are there or at the camp in the south."

"How far east is Doveton?"

Vern shrugged and then winced. "About fifty leagues or so east of the Crossroads."

"That would take days to reach. Does Kaenera move you around?"

Fosert shook his head. "He used to, but not anymore. It were that woman who sent us. She wanted the SoulBreather."

Ice cold chills ran down Mav's back and he shivered. Just the thought of Serenia getting her claws into Solanji was frightening. He should have known Serenia would retaliate.

"Ellaria?"

"Yes, Mav?"

"Keep an eye on Solanji. Warn her Serenia was behind the plan to snatch her."

"You should have dealt with that woman more permanently."

"I know."

"That bitch is an impatient one," Fosert said. "Kills too easily."

Mav debated for a moment, silently agreeing with Fosert. For someone supposedly so weakened, Kaenera was doing a good job of making him look a fool. He held Fosert's gaze. "You show me the man who is a mole and lead my host to Doveton, and I'll free you." He moved his gaze to the other man. "You mark all the locations of Kaenera's camps and tell me who is camped there or what it's used for, and I'll get you to a healer."

"How do we know we can trust you?" Fosert asked.

"You don't. That's a risk you'll have to take. Once I've confirmed that what you are telling me is the truth, I'll release you."

"And if it isn't?"

Mav let his shadows darken his features and blur his edges. "You'd better choose wisely."

The men paled.

Mav transported them to the healerie in the Oblivion Gate and assigned a guard to watch over both of them.

"You had no intention of torturing them," Oji said.

"I'm hurt that you thought I would."

Oji was silent for a moment. *"You were so dark. All I could see were shadows. I was worried."*

"Let's see if we can rehabilitate these two. There's good inside them somewhere. We just need to find it."

Oji chuckled. *"I knew it. You have no intention of letting them go."*

Mav exhaled. *"Keep an eye on them. I don't want them trying to sneak out. Let's hope they don't see kindness as another form of shackles. I lifted the image of the man Fosert said was the mole out of his mind. See if you can find him, but don't alert him. We need to discuss with Ryvalin if there is any way we can use him before we expose him. Make sure he doesn't go near the healerie."*

Mav went to his study to collect a map, paper, and ink for Vern. As soon as the healers had Vern stable, he could write down all he knew. He wondered if the men would realise he had allowed them to be healed *before* they gave him the information. He hoped they would appreciate the trust he had extended to them. If they didn't, then he'd know Kaenera had truly corrupted them beyond repair, and he would know who he was dealing with.

"Mav? Where are you? You're late." Solanji's voice filled his head, and he realised he was supposed to be in the citadel for his brother's rehearsal dinner.

"Sorry. Lost track of time," he muttered in reply.

"Well, hurry up. Your absence has been noted." Solanji's amusement soothed his irritation at the interruption.

He hurried to get changed.

48

SOLANJI – CITADEL

Solanji gazed around the beautiful room where the rehearsal dinner was being held. It was decorated in warm, golden tones with cream accents, and crystal glittered, from the chandeliers hanging from the vaulted ceiling to the glasses adorning the tables. Even though the room was large enough to cater for a hundred-plus guests, it was still cosy and inviting.

Solanji's gaze was drawn back up to the chandeliers suspended overhead and the candles flickering in their sconces. Such a waste of candles.

Amaridin and Valerian were positively glowing, radiant with their love for each other. Mav had told her they had already exchanged their vows, and she could see it shining in their eyes and in the way they constantly touched each other. Their happiness brought tears to her eyes, and she blinked them away, wishing Mav would arrive.

Mav was late, and Valerian's eyebrows rose in question as she approached him.

"He is on his way," she said in greeting as Valerian kissed her cheek.

"He'd better be," Valerian replied.

"Where is he?" Amaridin asked as he joined them. "He promised he would be here. We can't start without him."

"I'll call him again," Solanji said.

Amaridin nodded and greeted another guest. Servants in white uniforms drifted about the room, adjusting settings and polishing glasses.

Solanji exhaled and moved to a small alcove at the side of the room. Amaridin greeted his father as he entered the room, accompanied by a female archangel with long blonde hair, and Solanji turned her thoughts inwards, reaching for her bond with Mav.

"Mav? Where are you?"

There was no reply.

"Mav?"

Solanji's heart began to race. Had something happened to him? Had he been hurt in one of Kaenera's diversions? *"Ellaria, can you reach Mav? Can you check on him for me?"*

"Of course," Ellaria replied, her warm voice a soothing balm to Solanji's sudden panic.

Breathing deep, Solanji turned back to the room, and took a step towards Averdeus.

The room seemed to hold its breath for a moment, and then a wave of hot air blasted into her and threw her back into the alcove. She smashed into the wall, blinded by a brilliant flash and gasping for air. Following the silent blast, an enormous cacophony of protesting stone, splintering crystal, and twisting metal deafened her as the ceiling fell in, and the citadel screamed.

When Solanji regained her senses, she lay still, just trying to breathe; her jerking, gasping breaths couldn't seem to draw in enough air. Her desperate gasps echoed loudly, blocking out all other sounds.

It took some time for her to control her breathing.

She struggled to open her eyes, which seemed glued together. It was dark—not pitch black, but dark enough to not be able to see anything. She tried to move her arm and realised it was trapped, along with the rest of her body, under something heavy.

Her heart rate spiked, and she concentrated on breathing again. Slow and easy. She held her breath as a soft sifting of grit landed on her face, and she listened harder.

"Ellaria?"

Silence.

Until it wasn't.

The screams started, pure, unadulterated terror, piercing the muffling shroud that surrounded her, and with them came sensation.

The crackle of flames intruded, along with the acrid bite of smoke somewhere behind her. The stench of burnt flesh caught in the back of throat, and she coughed, her chest vibrating with the effort and waking a dull ache. When she tried to rub the ache away, she found she couldn't move her other arm, either. Dust and smoke swirled in the air, a lighter shadow in the darkness, and a heavy weight pressed down across her legs and body.

Grit bit into her palms as she tried to slide out from whatever was pinning her down. It wouldn't budge. Bemused, she peered around her. She couldn't recall where she was, nor what she had been doing.

A need to move surged through her, to help that poor person, screaming. Why was she screaming? Why didn't anyone help her? Solanji tried to push against the weight again, but pain flashed through her legs, and she panted, trying to control her sudden dizziness. Greyness filled her vision.

"Mav?" she whispered as the world went dark.

———

Ellaria appeared in the Oblivion Gate, hovering over Mav. *"Why aren't you answering Solanji?* she asked.

Mav looked up at her and frowned. *"I didn't hear her call."*

"You're late for the dinner. Amaridin is giving Solanji a hard time."

Mav winced. *"I was getting changed. I spoke to those men who attacked Solanji. It was definitely Kaenera."*

"Tell me later. You need to get to the citadel."

"Fine. I'm coming."

Adriz was waiting for him when he left his chamber. With a roll of his eyes, he said, "We're late," and transported them to his chambers in the citadel. They left his rooms and walked through the marble corridors towards the reception rooms his father had organised.

"What did Gurida have to say?" Adriz asked as they reached the antechamber doors. The set of intricately carved double doors was currently festooned with cream ribbons and scented blooms.

"It's what the men had to say that is more interesting. Apparently, we have a mole in the Gate. One of Julius' men."

Adriz hissed her breath out, but before Mav could continue, he spun as a flash of brilliant light blinded him. A huge explosion rocked the building, and he was thrown against the wall as the citadel screamed, a high, wailing shriek that made every angel cower. The ground trembled, and he blinked as bright orange flames shot up into the blue sky where, previously, there had been an ornate ceiling.

Thick black smoke rose and slowly cast a pall over the citadel like a shroud wrapped around a corpse.

Lurching to his feet, he flinched as Oji shouted in his head. *"The citadel is under attack!"*

"Solanji?" he threw the thought out as the citadel's terror ripped through him. Solanij was in those reception rooms, along with other members of his family.

There was no answer.

49

DEMAVRIAN – CITADEL

"Ryvalin, the citadel is under attack. Keep the Gate on high alert. Watch the mole."

"We're locked down tight," Ryvalin reassured him. *"We have the mole restrained just in case he has any ideas."*

As Mav reached for Solanji again, terror crawled up his chest, threatening to constrict his throat, to suffocate him. There was no response. His wife was in a battleground.

Cursing under his breath, he searched for Adriz. She was picking herself up, still gazing at the sky in horror. The ornate wooden doors hung drunkenly on their hinges. The ribbons were shredded, the flowers scattered, and the room beyond could only be described as carnage. They should have expected an attack on the citadel. Kaenera wouldn't have been able to resist such a juicy target. Mav's mouth tightened. After all, Kaenera had always been good at diversions. He had outdone himself this time, but what Kaenera really wanted was in the Gate. The thought that Kaenera was drawing Mav away from the Gate set off alarm bells.

"Father?" he called as he entered the room and faltered to a stop. The room was unrecognisable. In one corner, a raging

fire burned, and smoke continued to pour into the sky. The tables were gone, and in their place were piles of shattered marble and wooden beams. Here and there, an arm or a leg protruded from the rubble.

He began to clear the debris off the nearest body. *"Oji. Tell the citadel we need healers now!"* Mav snarled as Adriz helped him shift a beam. *"Oji? What is the citadel saying?"*

They carefully lifted a young woman out of the rubble and laid her to one side. Mav ran his senses over her. She was lucky, with only a concussion and bruising, as far as he could tell. He eased the swelling on her brain and left her for the healers. Then he returned to the search.

"She says there's a breach in the southwest corner. There are intruders. She's calling for help. There are many casualties."

"I can't hear her." But then, he wasn't connected to the citadel anymore, so he wouldn't. Citadel guards poured into the room. Grabbing the arm of the guard nearest him, Mav said, "There is a breach in the southwest corner. Pass the word. We have casualties here. Call the healers. Do what you can." He left the man to organise his men.

The corridors behind him were in utter chaos. No one knew what to do. An attack on the citadel was unheard of.

"Oji. You tell me immediately if anything seems off at the Gate."

"I will. I promise. Xylvin is airborne, and Ryvalin and Julius have all entry points guarded. They are all on high alert."

"Good. Thank them for me." Mav exhaled. How many spies did Kaenera have in the citadel? It would have been easy to find out when the rehearsal was to take place. It was surprising that Kaenera hadn't waited for the ceremony itself. More impact. Mav was glad he hadn't; the streets would have been crammed with spectators and people celebrating. The Heavenly Host would have had their hands full already.

"I can't find Solanji," Ellaria whimpered as she hovered above him.

Bodies lay everywhere, and healers rushed from one person to another, rapping out instructions to their assistants.

Mav stiffened as the sound of fighting penetrated the hall. The people nearest him froze, their skin paling.

"Concentrate on helping the injured," Mav snapped. "The Heavenly Host will protect you."

The healers numbly nodded and returned to their work. His stomach churning, Mav began to climb over the debris. *"Solanji? Father?"*

There was no response, only the clash of swords in the distance.

"Solanji?" he yelled.

What power had Kaenera discovered to cause so much damage? The destruction he could cause with the sigils was beyond comprehension.

Where was his father? Mav climbed off the debris and hurried through the corridors, circumventing the destroyed section of the building and heading towards the fighting. The Heavenly Host held a line, preventing the attackers from entering the citadel. Fury rushed through Mav's veins, he knew Kaenera wasn't here, just his lackeys, all primed and set off on to attack. Another diversion. How long had Kaenera been preparing for this?

Mav hesitated, his chest aching. A diversion? For what?

Gritting his teeth, Mav sent his aura across the battle-ground, adding a twist to cancel out any persuasion as it passed over the fighters. The attackers faltered as their minds cleared, the persuasion eddied away, and they came back to themselves. The Heavenly Host didn't hesitate; they surged forward, taking advantage of the hesitation, and they soon held the ground.

Councillor Gineray froze on the other side of the

carnage, his face pale, his expression horrified as his men died around him and he was left to face the Host alone. Gineray was a traitor? Mav gritted his teeth and held the man in place as the Host arrested him. He was lucky they didn't just run him through and be done with it, though, in retrospect, that may have been a mercy.

Mav grimly nodded at the officer and turned his attention to the exposed building behind them. The outer wall had been completely destroyed. Just as many guards were trying to move rubble.

"Do you know who was in here?" he asked as he reached the collapsed part of the building and stared at the room from the other side.

The guard stiffened as he recognised Mav. "Everyone at the rehearsal, sir."

Mav exhaled. "Including Averdeus, Amaridin, and Valerian?"

"Yes, sir. Also…" The guard hesitated. "Your wife arrived late, but she is under that, too." He gestured at the huge pile of stone, wooden beams, and other debris.

Mav's mouth went dry, and he found it hard to swallow. *"Ellaria, can you feel Solanji?"*

"No," Ellaria whimpered.

"Everyone, be quiet. Listen for anyone calling," Mav ordered as he sent his shadows searching, questing through any crack or hollow they could find. He concentrated on the sensations and the information his shadows shared. Nothing was left of the ballroom, just a pile of stone and wood.

A swirl of smoke caught in the back of his throat. "Someone put that fire out," he called, his attention still focussed on what his shadows were telling him.

One of the guards stiffened. "Someone is calling for help over here."

"Be careful as you move debris. We don't want to cause

any other areas to shift." Mav sent his shadows skimming, and he winced when they found Amaridin. His brother was crumpled beneath a slab of stone, his legs twisted at an impossible angle. Amaridin was unconscious, so it wasn't him calling.

"Get a stretcher ready," he said, and carefully wrapped his shadows around his brother, supporting shattered limbs. Once his shadows had confirmed that there was no one else near Amaridin, Mav transported his brother's body to the stretcher. The debris shifted a little, but nothing major, as it repositioned, filling in the space Amaridin had left.

Mav knelt beside him, gritting his teeth at his brother's injuries. Fortunately, none were life-threatening, so he sent him to the healerie and went back to searching. The guards began shifting stone from the area where they had heard the voice.

"Demavrian?"

Mav stiffened at the pain in his father's voice. *"Father? Where are you hurt?"*

"Tell them to stop moving the stone. There is a beam above us, and it is bowing each time they move something."

"Stop shifting debris. Everyone," Mav ordered. *"Who is with you, Father?"* Mav sent his shadows questing again.

"Valerian. He lives, but he is somewhat damaged."

"What about Solanji?"

"She was on the other side of the room. I don't know what happened to her."

"Solanji?" Mav sent his thoughts down their bond, but there was only silence in response. His shadows found the space where his father was trapped, and he gritted his teeth when he saw why he hadn't transported himself and the others out. Nausea swept through Mav at the sight of the stake pinning his father down, nearly cutting him in half. He was too weak to help the others.

"Get the stretchers ready," Mav growled as he wrapped Valerian in his shadows and sent a whisper of reassurance and healing through his broken body. Arm and ribs, he thought. Concussion, cuts, and contusions as well, no doubt. Gently, he deposited Valerian on the stretcher.

Another stretcher appeared next to Mav, and he wrapped his shadows around a servant, and an archangel, both with various broken bones. He slowly cleared the space, amazed his father had managed to protect so many. Finally, only Averdeus was left.

He shored up his father's protections that were holding the sagging beam above them. "Relax, Father. I have them," he whispered as he appeared next to Averdeus beneath the debris.

"It's too late for me," Averdeus said, weakly gripping Mav's arm. "I'm sorry."

"For what?"

"For not being indestructible."

"Don't you dare give up. We are not letting Kaenera win. There is no way he is getting away with this. I'll kill him ten times over for this." Mav hovered over his father as his shadows sought a way to release Averdeus without making his injuries worse.

"Sometimes, it is the unexpected that catches you out." Averdeus coughed, and dark blood trailed down his chin.

Mav tried to seal blood vessels, sinking his thoughts into his father's body, but Averdeus pushed him back out. *"Don't waste your strength on me. Find your wife. She needs you."*

"Father! Please." Agony seared through Mav, constricting his chest. He couldn't breathe.

"Let me go, son. There's nothing to be done." His father smiled. There was a gleam in his vivid blue eyes as he looked past Mav. "Malena…" He sighed, and then he stilled, the smile still curving his lips. His Deus aura faded away, leaving Mav desperately heaving for breath.

His father's chest was still under his palm. He was dead. Averdeus was dead.

No. It couldn't be possible.

Mav bent over him and keened, ignoring the groaning beam above him, the sifting grit sprinkling in his hair. He carefully rubbed the dust and grime off his father's face and kissed his cheek.

He inhaled as he grasped the wooden stake and tugged it out of his father's body. Wrapping his father in his shadows, he transported him to his chambers as the beam collapsed and a cloud of grit and dust rose into the air. Laying his father's body on his bed, he wrapped him in the sheets and left him there. Then he sealed the doors so no one could disturb him.

Disbelief warred with anguish. His father was gone, but it didn't seem real. Mav couldn't grieve now; he had to find Solanji. Stoking his anger at Kaenera, he let it burn his grief away and stiffen his spine. Dry-eyed, he returned to the site; they would discover Averdeus was dead soon enough.

Wearily, he sent his shadows searching again, this time into the other side of the room. The air was hazy with steam and smoke, and the damp tang of ash was on his tongue. Guards stepped back as he approached; no doubt, his aura had leaked along with his shadows. If his all-consuming fury had leaked into his expression, he wouldn't be surprised if everyone left at a run.

He was coated from head to foot in grime and blood. Concentrating on searching for Solanji, he blocked the numbing thoughts that his father was dead. That he would never perform the ceremony for Amaridin and Valerian. That he would not be at Mav's shoulder as he defeated Kaenera.

Vengeance burned in Mav's heart. He wouldn't just kill Kaenera, he would eviscerate him. He would make him feel every iota of pain Mav had suffered at his hands and then some. Killing was too good for him. Mav wanted him to suffer ever-lasting agony.

"Demavrian! I'm really sorry about your father, but you need to calm down," Oji said. *"Your emotions are making it difficult for me to maintain our position. We'll have to transition if you can't control your anger."*

"I'm sorry." Mav stiffened as he tried to clamp down on his tumultuous thoughts.

"We are one. I can feel you wherever we are. You will *deal with Kaenera, but you must remain calm until you've found Solanji. Then we'll tear him limb from limb for what he's done. We'll string him up by his entrails and let the crows eat him."*

Mav grimaced at Oji's bloodthirsty description. *"That is not helping."*

"Sorry! Forgot I was supposed to be calming you."

"Well, stay hidden. I can't leave here. I haven't found Solanji yet."

"You will. I know you will. We stand ready if you need us. The healerie is prepared. Ryvalin is offering to come and help you."

"No! She needs to guard you."

"Mav, you don't need to do this on your own." Oji's voice was soft and Mav's eyes stung as tears welled.

"I'm not on my own. I have you."

Shouts from the other side of the room heralded more bodies being dug out from the rubble. Mav rubbed his temple; the stabbing ache in his head was a result of over using his shadows. Gritting his teeth, he resumed his search for Solanji. His shadows questing, he helped to shift debris. His stomach clenched, as there was still no sign of Solanji.

Shandra's terrified voice tore into him, and he spun searching for her. *"Demavrian? Please help me!"*

"What's wrong?"

"Sero is hurt, and I don't know what to do!"

Mav glanced around the wreckage, hesitating in a moment of agonised indecision. *"Ellaria, keep searching!"* Then, his chest aching, he disappeared, taking Adriz with him.

50

BAILEY – PURONIA

Bailey fidgeted as he followed Sero down the winding road into the City of Puronia. The sun was high overhead and shone from a clear blue sky. He should have been feeling happy. His life was perfect. He was fed and clothed, surrounded by family and friends, and he knew they were all rooting for him to get his act together and join them at the Oblivion Gate.

An air of anticipation grew as the day of Amaridin and Valerian's heartswearing ceremony approached. Swags of cloth decorated the walls, bunting and flags crisscrossed the streets, and Bailey knew that many street parties were planned. The city was ready to celebrate with the Archdeus, as was the citadel.

A hum of excitement and busyness filled the air. Everyone had a job to do, and Averdeus was determined the day would be perfect.

And yet, Bailey felt like he was failing someone. Whether it be Muntra, Sero, or his friends, they all expected something of him, and he wasn't sure he could deliver.

A heavy weight sat in his stomach, and a brooding notion that something was wrong hovered in the back of his mind.

He wiped the sweat from his forehead and stared around them. "Where are we going, Sero?"

"I thought we could get a picnic for lunch from the bakery and sit by the river. Don't you just love feeding the birds?"

"I thought we were supposed to be practising blocking?" Bailey scowled. He had yet to block a memory. Mav wasn't prepared to let him in the Gate until he could block whatever horrible memories were going to bombard him as soon as he stepped through the door.

He didn't remember feeling horror the last time he was at the Gate. Only exhaustion.

"You've done enough practice. You know how to do it, but you're blocking yourself for some reason. It's time for a break. I want to feed the ducks."

"Fine," Bailey growled and followed Sero down the road. If Sero wanted to feed the ducks, then that was what they would be doing. He had never met such a stubborn cherub before. Not that he had met many. Sero kept the other cherubs away.

"Sero?"

"Yes?"

"Why won't you let me meet the other cherubs?"

Sero sighed and spun in the air. His golden curls and wings glinted in the sunlight. "Until you can block, it's not safe. Every cherub absorbs memories; it's as natural as breathing. But until you can block, if you touch one of them, you'll be hit by leakage. No matter how hard we try, we can't always hold them all in. They won't mean to flood you, but you won't know how to manage them."

"You don't leak."

"I am being very careful. But it's not only leakage. Your

memories are open to whoever touches you. You would flood them as well. You need to learn to shield your own memories."

Bailey came to a sudden stop. "What? Why didn't you tell me this before?"

"You have enough to deal with. I was trying to introduce things gradually."

"But…but does that mean you've seen all my memories?"

Sero's voice softened. "Yes. Just as I have seen Mav's."

"Mav's?"

"And though you may not believe me, his are worse than yours."

"They are?"

"Yes," Sero said with a sigh.

"Oh." Bailey wasn't sure why he was surprised. He hadn't thought of Mav's past. He was struggling with his own, Muntra's, and the others'.

"Mav can shield," he said in wonder. "He's never leaked memories when he's touched me."

"He is a Deus. Of course he can shield."

"Then how did you see his memories?"

"He was at a disadvantage, injured, hurting. I snuck through his guard."

"Why?"

"Because he needed help and he wouldn't ask for it." Sero turned to face down the road again. "Now, are we going to feed the ducks?"

"Yes." Bailey followed him. "Whereabouts is the bakery?"

"Around the next corner and over the bridge."

"And does the bakery do pastries as well?" Bailey asked with a grin as he rounded the corner. "Hey, there's Felather."

Felather stood outside a shop, his face raised to the sky as if he were either wishing for divine strength to help with something or just basking in the sunlight.

"He'd better not have bought up all the alvo buns," Sero growled as he fluttered towards the bridge.

Bailey hurried after him. He was about to call out a greeting when Felather spun. His sword appeared in his hand as if by magic, and he backed up as two men dressed in the citadel guard's uniforms rushed him.

Felather parried a strike, but he had no time to turn as two more guards rushed him from behind. One of them flicked his wrist, and Bailey heard the metal disk thud into Felather's back, even from the bridge, where he stood frozen in horror.

Felather staggered, and his cry caught in his throat as he landed on one knee. He forced himself upright again and charged the guards nearest the bakery, forcing them away from the alleyway that led to the shop entrance. Bailey's breath caught in his throat. Who was with Felather?

"Sero, we have to help him!" Bailey cried, starting to run over the bridge.

"Bailey, no!" Sero shouted, trying to grab his arm, but Bailey shook him off and continued running.

He didn't have a weapon! Bailey faltered, searching around him desperately. He grabbed a wooden bucket and an iron bar leaning against the wall.

Felather had cut one man down and hurt another, but he was weakening. Blood ran down the side of his face, and one arm hung limply. His back was drenched in blood. He swayed, and Bailey charged in front of him, swinging his bucket at the nearest guard's head. The bucket connected, catching the man completely by surprise, and he dropped to the ground.

"Bailey, no," Felather gasped.

"Bailey? He'll do just nicely," the guard growled and

swung the flat of his blade at Bailey's head. Felather managed to block the blow, though it spun him against the wall, and he moaned in pain.

More men rushed towards them.

Bailey swung his iron bar. The vibrations as it connected with a sword made his arm go numb. Pain exploded in the back of his head, and he stumbled, dropping to his knees. Darkness clouded his vision, and he collapsed to the ground.

As Felather's scream of anguish faded, Bailey lost consciousness.

"Get back, you traitors!" Sero yelled, firing his golden arrows at the men. They stuck true, and two of the men faltered to a stop, their eyes glazing over for a moment. Sero shot them both with a second arrow and snarled as soppy grins spread over their faces. They sagged to the ground, leaning against each other to hold themselves up.

Sero turned back towards Felather and Bailey, but then he tumbled through the air as something struck his shoulder. Pain blossomed in his chest, and he gasped for breath as he struggled to stay aloft.

"No," he whispered as men dragged Felather's and Bailey's bodies away. A trail of bright red blood smeared the golden stone, littered with a bucket, an iron bar, and Felather's sword.

A sharp sting slicing his throat bloomed into agony as it tore through one of his wings. Unable to remain airborne, Sero plummeted to the ground in a crumpled heap, but not before he saw both Felather and Bailey heaved over the back of a calope like sacks of grain and then disappear down a twisty alleyway.

Shandra rushed out of the bakery and dropped her

basket screaming, "Sero?" She fell to her knees beside him, her purchases tumbling over the flagstones. "Oh, my God, what happened? Who attacked you? Where's Felather?"

"Call Mav," Sero gasped through frothy bubbles. He was drowning in his own blood. "Citadel guards took..." He groaned.

Flashes of black streaked across his vision as Shandra tried to cradle him. Her horror and fear flooded him. He struggled to shield himself from her emotions, but his control was shattered.

"Oh, my God!" Shandra whispered as she held Sero. "Demavrian?" she screamed. "Help me!"

Shandra whimpered as she rocked Sero. Her hand clamped over the wound in his neck, which was spurting blood, and he choked.

Waves of her anguish and fear consumed him, and his breath stuttered. Fear for Felather and Bailey, anguish for the cherub dying in her arms, and *no one* would help her. Hissing filled his ears, and all he could taste was the cloying tang of blood. So much blood everywhere.

"I don't know what to do," Shandra moaned.

Sero's chest burned. The metal disk in his shoulder shifted as Shandra rocked him and warmth spread down his skin in a continuous flood.

"S-stop." Sero struggled to breathe as he tried to tell her what he'd seen.

Shandra stopped rocking. "What?"

"N-no move. Guards...attacked Felather."

Shandra peered around her, barely able to see through her tears. "Help me! Someone, help me!" she yelled, but those watching kept their distance. "Please," she whimpered. "Anyone!"

"Shandra?"

"Yes, Sero?" Shandra leaned over him.

"I-I need you to give this to Bailey."

Shandra's hand tightened on his. "You can give it to him yourself."

"No, please." Sero thrust his memories into Shandra, and she stiffened as she assimilated them.

Demavrian appeared beside her and dropped to his knees in the growing pool of blood on the cobblestones. Adriz took up a protective stance behind him.

"I've got you," Demavrian's hoarse voice cut through the noise and the clamour, and Sero hissed out his breath as cool grey nothingness soothed his anguish. Then horrific pain seared through his body as Demavrian tugged the piece of metal out of his shoulder and pressed down hard on the wound. His breath stuttered before he collapsed in Demavrian's arms.

"Felather injured...b-bad," Sero gasped out. "Took Bailey. Calopes. Down River Bank Alley."

"Adriz! They have Felather and Bailey. River Bank Alley!" he heard Demavrian shout.

"Got it!" Adriz yelled as she ran down the road.

Demavrian's voice faded in and out as he continued to list instructions. Other voices responded, sharp with fear.

"Shandra, you need to calm down; your emotions are battering Sero, and he can't handle it in his condition," Sero heard Mav say. "You must calm yourself. I know it's hard, but he can feel everything you are feeling."

Shandra gasped. "I'm so sorry." She stiffened beside him, and her emotions dimmed. Sero sighed in relief as she controlled her breathing and exhaled. Determination replaced fear, and she steadied.

Demavrian was still there. Sero struggled in his arms. No. Demavrian should be chasing after Felather and Bailey, not wasting time here with him.

"Demavrian?" Sero whispered.

"Don't worry, Sero. We've got you." Demavrian's voice soothed his fear, but his concern wasn't for himself but for somebody else. His fingers scrabbled against cloth, and strong hands grasped his.

"I-I…Demavrian?"

"Yes?"

"I would…have sworn your oath. I should have done it before now."

"I would be honoured to accept your oath at any time," Mav replied, still swamping him in waves of reassurance.

Sero exhaled, his awareness floating as if separate from his body. His voice slurred as he whispered, "Too late now."

Demavrian's voice was receding. "It's never too late, and I accept your oath."

"No, don't." If Mav accepted his oath and he died, Mav would feel the death so many times worse.

"You *are* family, Sero." A flood of warmth and love washed through him, but it was too late.

"I'm sorry, Mav." Darkness clouded his vision, and his fingers spasmed on Mav's hand. He was so cold. Tears pricked in Sero's eyes and trickled down his cheek. He'd never belonged anywhere before.

Soft lips kissed his forehead and gentle words caressed his ears. *"I'm here, Sero. I'll always hold you in my arms. Rest."* Warm tears dripped onto Sero's face. Demavrian was crying. For him.

Sero relaxed into Mav's embrace. Peace and rest. He closed his eyes and Mav's voice surrounded him, soothing and calm, welcoming him home.

A bright light resolved itself into Mav's brother, Amaridin. Robed in white, he glowed. His exquisite wings were extended, and his arms stretched wide in welcome. Demavrian lifted Sero and offered him to the new Deus, and Amaridin welcomed him into the light.

"Rest, Sero. You will be my heart forever," Demavrian whispered as he let him go.

Mav bent over Sero's body and desperately tried to control the pain constricting his chest, to stop the tears. He was still grappling with Sero's unexpected declaration and its subsequent loss. Tears fell as anguish tore through him, his oathsworn had passed, and he couldn't concentrate.

His world was falling apart, and he didn't know where to turn to first. He had left his wife buried somewhere in the citadel, his father was dead, and his oathsworn had been attacked, injured, abducted, and killed. He was numb. Overloaded with too many shocks, he mindlessly rocked Sero's body back and forth.

He raised his head and met Shandra's eyes. They, too, were brimming with tears, which scored a trail through the grime on her face as they fell. Shandra extended trembling fingers, stained red with Sero's blood. She knelt in a pool of it, as did Mav. Sero had lost so much, too much, and Mav hadn't been able to stem the flow. Burning hot fury scorched through him, and he stiffened as Shandra grasped his arm.

"I'm so sorry, Mav."

Mav stared at her, unable for a moment to produce any words that would make sense. He had to take her home, where she would be safe. Oji stirred behind his eyes, and as Mav inhaled, the world around him came back into focus. "You can't stay here," he whispered. "I have to get you safe. *Oji? I'm sending Sero and Shandra to the healerie.*"

"*Understood. We're ready.*" Oji replied.

Once Shandra and Sero disappeared, Mav rose and stared at his hands. Like Shandra's, they were coated in his oathsworn's blood. His chest aching, he clenched them into fists, and his shadows streamed out of him as he sent them questing. He ran down the road towards the alley Sero had mentioned. The ache in his chest intensified as he followed the blood trail. More of his oathsworn's blood. Brilliant red drops of his oathsworn's life splattered on the ground.

He entered the alleyway, a cut through the buildings wide enough for two people abreast or a laden calope. It wound between high walls and wooden fences which crowded him until he reached a junction with roads heading in all directions and the open doors of a hostelry opposite.

Adriz ran towards him. Her fear and worry bombarded him through their bond. She was too worried to block it. Ashen-faced, she grabbed his arm and stuttered, "There's no s-sign of them. I can't feel Felather. The men are searching the warehouses, but the blood trail stopped. They may have a cart." Her mouth stretched into a taut line. "How do we find where they went?" She spun, spreading her arms. "They could have gone anywhere!"

Mav tried to get his overloaded brain to work. "A cart would be slow. More likely, Kaenera has transported them somewhere. Although he is weak, he is not without some power." Mav stared off into the distance, searching for any hint of Felather. He cursed the fact that he hadn't asked Bailey to become his oathsworn. He couldn't sense either of them.

Mav rubbed his eyes. "I was expecting him to come after me, not my people."

Adriz gripped his shoulder. "Kaenera knows you value your people above yourself. He knows this will unbalance you more than a direct attack."

"If anyone else dies because of me…"

Adriz tensed. "Sero?" she asked.

Mav shook his head. "He didn't make it."

Adriz's face paled even more as tears filled her eyes. "Oh, Mav."

"Can you stay here and question anyone you can find? Someone at the bakery must have seen something. I need to get back to the citadel. I can't lose Solanji as well."

"Mav, you can't think like that. It will only cloud your thinking. For her sake, for Felather's sake, you must focus on finding them."

"And Bailey. He's been through so much already. He is so fragile. This will crush him."

"Stop it, Mav. He's stronger than you think. All your fledglings are. They keep surprising us. He climbed over the curtain wall as well, you know. That took some guts!"

Mav exhaled, and the tight band around his chest eased. "He did, didn't he?"

"Don't give up on them."

"Never." Adriz gripped Mav's arms and tugged him into a hug. "Go find your wife. I'll meet you in the citadel."

Mav transported himself back to the reception room, which still resembled a pile of rubble. It didn't look like the citadel guards had made much progress.

He examined the room. His father had said Solanji was on the other side of the room to from him, so he sent his shadows questing, gritting his teeth as fear and worry swept through him. Where was she? *"Solanji?"*

His shadows couldn't get through the stone, but Ellaria was hovering over an area that had been a corner of the room. Mav squinted through the dust-aden air. The motes glittered in the afternoon sunshine, but one area was dark with shadow. He clambered over the rubble and joined Ellaria.

"She's under that," Ellaria said, a snarl in her voice.

"And she's still alive," Mav replied, eagerly tossing fragments of marble aside, ignoring the bite of their sharp edges. *"Help me."*

Between them, they cleared a layer of rubble and

stopped to listen. *"Solanji?"* Was that a whimper? His shadows eked their way through narrow gaps, and he thought his heart might explode when they found her.

"Ellaria, can you fit in that gap? She's pinned beneath a wooden beam. Can you see if we can transport her out?"

Ellaria disappeared, and Mav continued tossing rocks aside. He found one end of the shattered beam and shuddered at the memory of his father impaled by the wood, but Solanji was pinned, not stabbed. She would be fine. She would. If he said it enough times, he might believe it.

"I have her," Ellaria said, and the pile of rubble beneath Mav shifted as she appeared on the other side of the room. He leapt into the air, wings flaring, and he hovered as the stone groaned and settled. Mav joined Ellaria, ignoring the gasps of the healers as he landed and folded his wings.

His senses quested, noting cracked ribs, internal bleeding, and broken bones. He concentrated on healing the worst. The healers could set bones, and he could help speed the healing afterwards. Solanji was alive; that was all that mattered. He gently caressed her cheek and then kissed her lips. *"Ellaria. Take her to the Gate. The healerie here is full."*

Ellaria disappeared with her burden, and Mav sagged as exhaustion swept through him. He couldn't think…Relief overwhelmed him, and tears trailed down his cheeks.

He stiffened as someone grabbed his shoulder. "Demavrian, can you tell if there is anyone else beneath this rubble?" Archangel Golaran asked. He was covered in dust and grime, and his expression was grim and foreboding.

Mav swayed and Golaran steadied him. His eyes widened as he inspected Mav, and all the blood staining his clothes. "Who?" he whispered.

Mav shook his head as a numbness spread through him. He couldn't speak the words. Instead, he cast his shadows over the room, searching for any signs of life. He found nothing.

"There's no-one alive."

"You should go and be with your wife, then. I've got this."

"Not until I know how Amaridin and Valerian are. We can't leave the citadel exposed."

"Check on them, and then you should go to the Gate. You've done enough."

"I've done nothing that makes any difference!" Mav launched to his feet. Blessed fire sparked through his veins, burning away the suffocating despair. Vengeance gave him strength, though he swayed again, and Golaran steadied him.

51

DEMAVRIAN – CITADEL

Mav sat in his father's study in the citadel and silently fumed. The unit of the Heavenly Host that Adriz had managed to suborn had searched the River Bank Alley area again and were questioning witnesses. With the attack on the citadel, Amaridin's captain of the guard, a cherubim called Ziriel, was not interested in helping him any further.

Kaenera kept beating them at every turn, and Mav was getting fed up with being on the back foot all the time. As a god, he should be able to protect his people.

His chest constricted, and he clenched his fists. That Kaenera had attacked his oathsworn and a cherub in broad daylight in the middle of Puronia horrified him. Both Felather and Bailey were injured; how badly he didn't know, but if it was anything like the injury Sero had received trying to help them, then the longer it took to find them, the worse it could be.

Oji and Ellaria were keeping him informed of Solanji's condition. For now, she was stable and as comfortable as she could be. They had sedated her as they'd reset bones and strapped ribs. She would sleep while her body healed. Shandra was keeping her company and wouldn't leave her side.

Mav looked up as Valerian limped into the room with a stick in one hand and his other arm in a sling. His beautiful face was pale and bruises lined the ridge of his left cheek, blackening his eye, which was almost swollen shut.

"Shouldn't you be with Amaridin?" Mav asked.

"Shouldn't you be with Solanji?" Valerian shot back before exhaling and gingerly sitting in a chair. "Sorry," he murmured. "I know there's no point. They have Amaridin drugged to the eyeballs. He wouldn't know if I was there. No doubt, Solanji is the same."

Mav sighed. "Shouldn't you be resting? You have your own injuries to contend with."

Valerian waved his hand. "We have too much to do. I can withstand a few aches and pains." He hesitated a moment. "Demavrian, I'm so sorry about Averdeus and Sero."

Mav nodded. The stabbing pain of loss had been muted by all the other worries bombarding him.

"Any word about Felather or Bailey?"

"No," Mav said. "I suppose I'll have to wait for Kaenera's demands."

"But they are your oathsworn. Can you not feel them?"

Mav shook his head. "Only Felather is oathsworn, and he is silent. Unconscious, maybe." Mav didn't like to even consider the alternative. Though, if Felather had died, he was sure he would have known, as he knew Sero was dead. After the brief flare of the bond being snuffed out, there was now just a gaping hole.

He leaned on his father's desk and dropped his head in his hands. So many of his oathsworn were injured and suffering, and there was little he could do until he found them. But no matter what he did, it would still take time.

Looking up, he met Valerian's sympathetic gaze. "I'm planning an attack on Kaenera's stronghold. Will you support me?"

Valerian nodded. "I'll speak to Ziriel. Kaenera will rue the day he underestimated the citadel. Ziriel is so mad that we could probably get her to agree to do anything at the moment."

"A couple of divisions of the Host would help. If we can wipe out his stronghold, he'll have no resources to wage war, and then it will be just him. And once I've killed Kaenera, all his suggestions and persuasions will die with him."

"Send Ryvalin to coordinate with Ziriel. I'll let her know I've authorised as much assistance as you need. Dealing with Kaenera has to be our priority. But Mav…" Valerian hesitated. "You look terrible; you should bathe and get some sleep."

"I'll sleep when Kaenera is dead and I have my oathsworn back," Mav growled. A flash of irritation consumed him, and his aura darkened.

Valerian swallowed and wilted under the wave of fury emanating from Mav.

Realising his shadows had leaked. Mav reined them in. "My apologies," he murmured.

"No, I understand. But even you need rest. You cannot beat Kaenera if you are exhausted."

Mav rose and strode to the window. He stared out over the moonlit garden. "I cannot sleep."

"I didn't say sleep, but at least rest. Conserve your energy."

Mav exhaled and then nodded at Valerian. He looked down at his bloodstained clothes and realised he should wash and change.

"You realise Amaridin has ascended to Deus now that my father is dead?"

Valerian stilled. "I hadn't thought."

"Amaridin will need to decide what to do with Averdeus. He took Sero and granted him eternal peace. He will need to do the same for our father."

"But Amaridin is unconscious."

Mav shrugged. "For now, I recommend you say nothing. We don't want Kaenera to discover my father is dead. Once Amaridin has recovered, he can make an announcement. I will return to the Gate and prepare for war while I wait for Kaenera's demands."

Valerian rose with a wince.

"I'll seal these rooms so no one but you, me, or Amaridin can enter," Mav said, staring at the door leading to his father's bedchamber. "Tell Amaridin he is with our mother." He faltered. "It may help."

Valerian rubbed his back. "Go home to your wife, Mav."

Mav slowly nodded. Leaving his father's study, he collected Adriz, who stood guard in the corridor. Her face was pale and strained, but she had refused to leave him. She had been insistent that Ryvalin was his captain of the guard and responsible for the security of the Gate, not her. Her place was behind Mav's shoulder. Mav acquiesced, knowing she needed to be occupied as much as he did.

"We're going to the Gate," he said and grasped her arm. She stiffened, and he pictured his study in the Gate.

Ryvalin lurched to her feet from her seat behind his desk as they appeared.

Mav relaxed as Oji's comforting presence embraced him, and his shadows undulated around him as his wings flared.

Home.

"Mav! Are you alright?"

Mav exhaled. "Not really. I need…" He trailed off, not sure what he needed. "I need the Host's report. Someone must have seen Felather and Bailey attacked.

Ryvalin gave him a sharp nod. "I have it here. I can give you the salient points. Xylvin is scouting for us. She believes she's found Doveton's exact location."

Mav stopped by the door to his chambers. "She has? That is good news." A vicious thrill sped through him. At last, some news he could do something with. "I'll just get cleaned up."

He shut the door behind him and leaned against it. The murmur of voices rose in the other room. Suddenly, he realised how large his family had become. Even with his losses, he had now gone from just four oathsworn to ten. How had that happened? There were more wraiths at the Gate whom he counted as part of their extended family, and he shouldn't forget the Oblivion Gate, Oji, himself. He had sworn himself into the family, not wanting to be left out.

The thought eased Mav's aching heart. His family were as desperate as he was to find their missing brethren. He wasn't alone in his suffering. Adriz was suffering just as much if not more. She and Felather had finally admitted their love for each other, and the blossoming of their shy relationship into a strong partnership had been a pleasure to watch. Only, Felather was now missing, badly injured, and in need of their help.

And Mav was back to his brooding thoughts.

He stripped of his grimy clothes and headed for the bathing room.

Feeling much better after a shower and a change of clothes, Mav leaned back in his chair and listened as Ryvalin reported what the Host had found. "One thing they discovered was that the back wheel looked a bit warped." Ryvalin tapped the report. "It won't last much longer. If they hit a hard patch or a rock, they'll lose it. One of the hands tried to tell him, but Kaenera wasn't interested."

"Thank you. That is good to know." Mav said. "So, we know Kaenera is disguised as a merchant in a brown wagon carrying textiles and they are at least a day ahead of us."

"Which means they would have reached the Crossroads and travelled on ages ago," Adriz said. "We won't know which way they went."

"There are enough workers at the Crossroads that someone may have seen them. I think the longer Kaenera has to hold the façade, the more tired he will get. But his attack on the citadel must have taken all his energy if he is not just transporting them away." Mav frowned in thought. "I think we need someone less conspicuous than Xylvin to trail them. Kerris, Muntra and one of the Host can track them from here. That will keep them occupied, and they won't be as noticeable as us. I don't want Kaenera to know we're following him. Felather and Bailey's safety is paramount."

"Do you think it is wise to send Muntra?" Adriz asked.

"If he wants to be a cherubim, then he needs to learn control. Isn't that what you've been trying to teach him? I'll instil in him that Bailey's safety is his responsibility and he's not to go rushing in but to send for reinforcements. I think he'll pay attention."

"I hope you're right."

Mav cocked an eyebrow at her. "Are you telling me you wouldn't?"

"Maybe. We don't know how bad Felather is."

"You wouldn't wait, knowing I am a thought away?"

Adriz flushed. "I don't know. It's Felather."

At least she was being honest. Mav rubbed her arm. "Sorry. That wasn't a fair question. I doubt I could wait if it was Solanji who had been abducted." He stared into the distance. "Maybe it isn't fair to ask Muntra to go."

Adriz exhaled. "Let's ask him what he thinks. He may surprise us."

"True."

"Mav?" Solanji's drowsy voice in Mav's mind interrupted them, and Mav stiffened.

"Solanji's awake," he said and disappeared.

He reappeared next to Solanji and gently clasped her hand, smiling as he saw Ellaria curled up by feet and Shandra dozing in the chair beside her. Loud snores drifted from the guarded beds at the other end of the room. The guard was alert and snapped to attention when Mav appeared.

Solanji smiled at Mav, though he was concerned to see lines of pain on her face.

"Sweetheart? How are you feeling?"

"I ache all over," Solanji replied with a groan. "How did I get here, and why are they here?" She tilted her head in the direction of the snores.

"The citadel healers were overwhelmed, and don't worry about them. I'm more worried about you." Mav pushed a tendril of his healing power into her, and she relaxed with a sigh.

She tightened her grip on his hand. *"What happened?"* she asked, switching to silent speech.

Mav sighed and perched on the edge of her bed. *"Kaenera attacked the citadel. He set off an explosion which destroyed the reception room. Amaridin and Valerian were also injured but they are recovering as you are. We lost twenty people."* He hesitated. *"Including my father."*

"Oh no, Mav. No! I am so sorry."

"There's more," Mav said.

Solanji stilled. *"More?"*

Mav stroked her hand. *"The attack was a diversion."*

Solanji reached for him and winced. Mav lay down beside her, carefully holding her close.

"A diversion for what?" Solanji prompted. Ellaria raised her head and watched them.

"Kaenera attacked my oathsworn. Felather and Bailey are missing… and…Sero is dead."

"Oh, my God, no. Not Sero too?" Tears trailed down Solanji's cheeks, and her grief resonated down their bond before she tried to control it so he wouldn't feel it.

"Don't suppress it, my love. I know you loved Sero as much as I did."

"Mav, why aren't you out hunting for them?"

"I am. But I don't want to put them in any more danger."

"Oh, Mav." Solanji raised her hand and, wincing, cupped his face. She drew his face closer and gently kissed him on the lips. *"My love, I am so sorry. You've had all this to deal with on your own, and me all banged up as well."*

"You are healing. I'll find Felather and Bailey, and Kaenera will pay for what he's done."

"Do I have to stay here?" Solanji closed her eyes. The strain was apparent on her face, and he kissed her cheek, pushing love and reassurance through their bond.

"As soon as the healers release you, I'll move you to our rooms."

"Please hurry them up. I'm not comfortable with my attackers in the same healerie as me."

"I am sorry, my love. We only have the one healerie, but I should have thought. Let me check with the healer, and I'll move you."

"It's more the fact the guard has remained extremely alert, even though both men are snoring their heads off."

Mav grinned down at her. "It's probably the best night's sleep they've had in years."

"Well, I'm glad someone is able to sleep," Solanji replied, and Mav chuckled at the tart edge to her voice.

The door opened and shut as Adriz entered the healerie, and the snoring stopped. Shandra sat up and stretched, her eyes heavy and shadowed, her face pale and strained. "Mav, if you're home, I'll go to bed." She kissed his cheek and then Solanji's. She hesitated and then said, *"Sero gave me his memories. He wanted me to give them to Bailey."*

"And you will," Mav said as he gave her a hug. *"You hold them for Bailey until he comes home."*

Shandra held his gaze, slowly nodded, and then said, "'Night, Adriz," and left the healerie.

Solanji watched Shandra leave and raised an eyebrow.

Mav rolled his neck, trying to ease the sudden tension. *"Shandra was with me when Sero died."*

"I'll speak to her tomorrow," Solanji said, her expression pinched, and then her gaze returned to the other patients. "Did you find out who they are, then?"

"Vern and Fosert. Two of Kaenera's minions, though they are no longer under his control and will be helping me instead."

"Where did they come from?" she asked.

"From Kaenera's camp." Mav scowled. "And in return for healing them, they are going to share everything they know with us." He sat up and glared at the two men. "Aren't you?"

Vern watched them, wide-eyed, and nodded. He looked much younger now that all the grime had been washed off him. Early-twenties maybe. Fosert was older and heavier built. He nodded as well.

Adriz approached the end of the bed and inspected Fosert. "I see you have recovered," she said.

"It's only like a golden dragon tried to eat me," Fosert

replied, though there was a ghost of a smile on his lips as he said it.

"There is an even larger dragon here at the Gate, so be warned," Mav said. "*She* will eat you once she finds out you tried to hurt Solanji."

Vern shrank back in his bed, and his guard's lips twitched.

Adriz moved to inspect Vern. "You're the scribe, aren't you? Before she does that, Vern, I need you to annotate this with what you know." Adriz offered him a folded map and a stick of charcoal. "I want to know the location of every camp Kaenera has ever set up."

Vern nodded and carefully eased himself upright. He opened the parchment, folded it to make the section more manageable, and began making notations.

"When did you last see Kaenera? And where was he?" Adriz asked.

Fosert frowned into the distance. "About five days ago?" He didn't sound too sure. "He turned up with that blonde-haired woman. Nasty piece of work, she is."

"Serenia?" Mav asked.

"Yeah. We didn't see her the first couple of days, but then she made her presence felt." Fosert rolled his eyes. "Very demanding."

"Where was that?"

Vern pointed to the furthest point on the section of the map he had on his lap. "Doveton. It's his main camp."

"Fosert here will tell you everything he can remember about the camp at Doveton," Mav said to Adriz. He raised an eyebrow and Fosert nodded. *"Get Liam to verify what he can,"* Mav added, and Adriz gave him a slight nod, her gaze never leaving Vern.

Fosert rubbed his arm. "The cuts were only superficial. It

seems your dragon was only playing with me. I'm fine. Most of the wounds have been dealt with."

"You were fortunate, then," Mav replied.

Fosert frowned, though he didn't say anything, just observed Mav.

The men's eyes widened when trays of food were brought in and they received the same fare as everyone else.

Solanji shuffled up her in bed as a tray was slid in front of her, and Mav stuffed another pillow behind her back.

"Eat your supper," Mav said. "I'll check if I can move you." He glanced down at her injuries. Her bones were mending; she just needed to rest and recuperate. He added another tendril of healing power to help her along and went to chat with the healers.

He soon returned. "I'll move you on condition you stay in bed and rest."

Solanji nodded, eager to leave.

"And you're honest about the level of pain you're in. Fel…" Mav bit the words off. "The healer will still keep an eye on you."

He smiled at her, and they both disappeared.

Ellaria growled at the men, making them rear back, and then she, too, disappeared.

Later that night, Mav paced his room as he searched for Felather. He couldn't sleep, not knowing. He wasn't sure Solanji slept, but she was holding to her word and stayed in bed. He extended his senses as far as he could reach and then even further. His aura rippled out from him, searching every street, house, nook, and cranny. He searched Angelicus, and people felt a moment of exhilaration as he passed over them, a moment of unexplained joy as a god's full presence washed through them and moved on. Mav knew Felather and Bailey were not there, which meant Kaenera had taken them to the depths of Eidolon. He just needed to confirm they weren't in Doveton so he could destroy it.

Mav slumped in his chair as exhaustion swept through him, the reward for his foolish sweep of a whole country. If his oathsworn knew how much energy he was using, they would eviscerate him. Instead, he would distract them, keep them too busy to watch him.

At least the remainder of his family were safe in the Gate. He had asked Muntra if he would like to be his oathsworn. It eased his mind that he could bespeak Muntra if needed, and it also reassured Muntra that he had a place, as promised, by Mav's side. The fact that he had delayed asking Bailey was now coming home to roost, and his reasons no longer seemed important.

Muntra was eager to help, and he had promised to put Bailey's and Felather's safety first if Mav trusted him to go and track Kaenera. Muntra had been so proud that both Mav and Adriz believed he would be able to control his emotions and make sensible decisions. In the morning, he would send two of his oathsworn back out into danger. But he had to accept that all his oathsworn were competent and he should use their strengths, not hide them out of sight.

Walking the halls of the Oblivion Gate, he sighed as he relaxed into Oji's comforting embrace. Even with the relief of Solanji's constant touch through their bond, Mav was too tense to sleep, so he walked, and he was unsurprised when he ended up in the training area. The lamps brightened as he entered, and he smiled when he saw the punching bag hanging in the centre of the training mat.

Stripping off his jacket and shirt, he grabbed some of the rags from a bucket next to the weapons rack and began binding his hands. He stood in front of the punching bag, trailing his fingers down its cool, smooth surface for a moment, and then he exploded into action.

Venting all his fear, his fury, his anguish, his helplessness out on the blameless bag, he flowed in a destructive rhythm. His muscles protested, but he drove himself onwards, determined to burn away all his tense energy, his sense of failure.

"Mav?" Oji's gentle voice penetrated his single-minded concentration, and he slowed, registering his body's exhaustion, his heaving chest as he gasped for breath. He swayed, lightheaded.

"Enough. You are hurting yourself, when it is Kaenera you should be punishing."

Mav grasped the bag and leaned his sweaty forehead against it, wincing as he saw the smear of blood. He had split his knuckles. Adriz would be furious. His body ached, and he was finally tired enough that, hopefully, he would sleep.

"Thank you," he murmured and began unwrapping his sore knuckles as he walked to the shower.

Kaenera would regret attacking his heartsworn. He would regret attacking his oathsworn and his family. If he were supposed to be an Angel of Death, the Keeper of the Shadows, then Kaenera would find out what that meant, up close and personal.

That was a promise Demavrian made to himself.

52

BAILEY – EIDOLON

Bailey groaned as he regained consciousness. His head hurt, a constant, thumping ache, and he swallowed as saliva flooded his mouth. He would not be sick! Grit bit into his hands as he rolled over onto his side and levered himself onto his knees. He swayed as pain spiked through his ribs. What had happened? Why did he hurt so much?

He lifted his head and squinted at his surroundings, and his heart nearly stopped at the sight of Felather sprawled on the ground in a pool of blood. Oh, no, no, no, no! Bailey crawled over to Felather and hesitated to touch him as he saw the metal disc protruding from his back and the dark stain surrounding it.

"Felather?" he whispered.

There was no response. Instead of trying to move the injured man, Bailey shuffled around in front of him. Felather's face was salt white, his eyes were closed, and his lips were grey. Blood had dried on his face and in his hair.

Hesitantly, Bailey reached out and touched his skin. Felather was ice cold. Biting his lip, Bailey checked for a pulse. Was he breathing? Relief flooded through him as he found a faint pulse, but it was very slow and thready.

Gritting his teeth, he leaned over and lifted Felather's jacket. It was snared by the circular blade embedded in his back. Carefully, he ripped the shirt beneath. He had never seen anything so horrific. The metal jutting out of Felather's body was just wrong, and the flesh was swollen and angry. The wound bled sluggishly, but at least it had slowed and wasn't pumping out blood anymore. Should he try and remove the blade? Just the thought was nauseating, but he'd do it if it would help Felather.

"Should I remove the blade, Felather?" he whispered. "Or leave it in? Will it make it worse if I try and remove it?"

Felather didn't respond.

Bailey didn't have anything to staunch the blood except his own clothes. He shivered, recognising the chill air, more reminiscent of Eidolon. He didn't think they were in Angelicus.

"You're not bleeding out, so I'll leave it. If I touch it, it'll start bleeding again. Let's make you more comfortable, shall we?"

Bailey straightened Felather's limbs and turned him more on his side so he wasn't straining his back. He shrugged out of his jacket and covered Felather's upper body with it.

A glance around the shadowy cell only revealed stone walls and iron bars across one end. The light came from the corridor on the other side of the iron bars, dim and grey. They were underground; Bailey was sure of it.

He rested his palm on the stone floor and pushed his mind against it. He waited, allowing memories to surface and slowly trickle through him. The stone remembered being hewn, the clash of metal on rock carving out the circular space. People flitted in and out, some locked in, a taste of their fear, fortunately ancient and fading. People retrieving stored goods, years of disuse.

He sighed as he saw the memory of Felather and him being dumped on the ground. Heedless of injuries, they had been kicked a couple of times for good measure. No wonder his body ached. The door had been locked, the keys had been clipped onto one of the men's belts, and they had disappeared down the corridor.

Rising, Bailey moved over to the gate and tugged at the iron bars. They rattled but held firm. "Hey! We need water. And bandages!"

There was no reply, and Bailey had the impression there was no one out there. His heart fluttered at the thought they had been abandoned, left to die, which was what would happen to Felather if they didn't get help soon.

His knees shook as relief swept through him at the echo of approaching footsteps. He hung to the bars and blinked away tears. One of the men, still dressed in a citadel guard's uniform, entered the chamber.

"You're no guard," Bailey growled.

The man leered at him. "What's a pretty boy like you know?"

"Felather needs help. Medicine, bandages, a healer," Bailey said, trying to ignore the way the man stared at him. The man's gaze made his skin crawl, and he shuddered.

"Well, that depends on your boss. If he don't pay up, there'll be no point in fixing him."

"If you don't keep us alive, you'll have nothing to trade," Bailey said tightening his grip on the bars. "At least give us some water and a blanket. It's freezing in here."

Memories seeped into him from the iron bars. They remembered being mined from a local mountain, a flash of rising rock against a dreary grey sky, being smelted in a scorching hot fire. Heat washed through him, a welcome reprieve from the cold.

"Please. Just some water." Bailey softened his voice and tried to look pitiful. He didn't have to try very hard.

The man rolled his eyes and stomped off, and he soon to returned with a clay jug. He twisted a key, lifted a flap, and pushed the jug between the metal bars. Bailey grabbed the jug with one hand and the man's wrist with the other.

"You think I'm pretty? Angelic? You have no idea how ugly I really am," Bailey whispered. "Open the door, or you'll regret it."

Grey, swirling mist greeted Bailey, no memories of a happy childhood or adult mistakes, only a miasma of hatred, blood, and death.

"Gerrof me!" The guard tried to pull his hand free.

Bailey dug deeper, searching for memories of their surroundings. Heavy grey sky, an unfamiliar landscape, a narrow, winding track leading to a pass through hilly peaks. Nothing notable, nothing he could use for directions. He gathered the man's emotions into a ball and pushed them back at him, forcing him to face his own depravity.

"I am an Angel of Death. I won't soothe your horrors," Bailey hissed. "I'll make them worse!"

The man screamed, his eyes bulging as he wrenched himself away from Bailey and ran out of the chamber. His screams echoed down the corridor and then, a distant door banging against a wall cut them off.

Bailey inhaled, hugging the jug to his chest. He concentrated on his breathing until the tremors wracking his body calmed.

The jug remembered standing on a table, being filled with cold water. The innocent memories confused Bailey for a moment.

His breath caught. What had he done? Was he truly

corrupted by all his experiences? He shivered as a chill raced down his spine.

If he were cold, Felather would be freezing. Relaxing his grip on the jug, he returned to sit beside Felather and lifted his head onto his lap. He wet a corner of his shirt and moistened Felather's dry lips. As Bailey brushed Felather's hair from his face, he cringed at the blood hardening his curls. Slowly stroking his scalp, Bailey detangled his hair, picking out clumps of dried blood.

He let Felather's memories flow through him without resisting. Images of Felather and Mav as children, mock fighting in a pretty garden full of colourful flowers. An older boy, who must have been Amaridin, criticising their moves and correcting their stance. Climbing trees, falling in rivers, paddling in the sea. Sweet, innocent childhood memories.

Bailey cleaned the blood off Felather's face. His skin was far too pale when he revealed it. A horrible, purpling bruise marred his temple, with an ugly, inflamed wound in the centre. At least it had stopped bleeding. Bailey left it well alone.

More memories. Felather's fear as he came into his healing powers. His distress when he failed to heal someone. Of not being there when he was needed. Mav's solid reassurance that Felather could never fail anyone and, if someone were to die, it was because it was their time, not because Felather had failed.

Bailey could hear the words as if he had been sitting beside them. He could feel Mav's love and belief in his friend. He understood Felather's steadfast love for Mav as he watched them grow together, support each other through every tragic loss, and face unimaginable challenges together.

He winced as he thought of his own challenges and how he had let them overwhelm him, to shape how he behaved.

He had allowed the actions of others to dictate how he felt, to stop him from living his life.

Muntra's anguished expression filled his mind. He would tell Muntra how much he loved him when he got out of there. His fear had caused so much suffering to the one person who had stood beside him no matter what.

Felather's memories continued to scroll past. Felather and Adriz becoming oathsworn to Mav. Standing behind Mav's shoulder in full ceremonial garb, so very proud. Mav's mother dying. Mav's pain and anguish. Felather's shy love for the brash and temperamental Adriz. Mav incarcerated in a cell, bruised and bloody, accused of murder. That had been the last glimpse Felather had had of him before Mav had disappeared for nearly fifty years. His joy at finding Mav. His fierce defence of his angel. And then Felather's constant fear that Mav would leave him again. For centuries, Felather had been oathsworn. Centuries. And not once had he wavered.

Bailey inhaled. "I'll protect your memories, Felather. Until you need reminding of them," he whispered. He wrapped his arms around the unconscious man, carefully hugging him tight, trying to share his meagre body heat.

Felather's memories soothed the self-disgust that filled Bailey, balancing out his terrifying actions and calming the anguish caused by knowing he was capable of inflicting such horror on others. That was not the behaviour of a cherub. There were always two sides to every ability; good and bad. It was up to him how he used them.

53

SERENIA – EIDOLON

Serenia huddled in a canvas chair and stared blankly at the grey sky. A grimy tent sheltered her from the icy wind, but it was still numbingly cold. Where was the sun, the golden light, the warmth on her skin? She shivered and pulled the shawl tighter around her shoulders and the blanket around her legs. The conditions were intolerable, but Kaenera didn't seem to notice.

They were camped in a deserted slave compound a few miles from the mine where Kaenera had dumped Felather and the boy. He didn't want to draw anyone's attention to the mine, so he'd left two guards to keep an eye on them and left.

Why did Kaenera's men have to snatch them? She needed the SoulBreather if she was going to get her soul back. Everything was so difficult, and she wanted to scream in frustration. The dybbuks were useless. Following complex orders was beyond them.

The two she had sent out hadn't returned. They had said the SoulBreather was returning souls to the people of Eidolon. What a waste that was, but if Demavrian was stupid enough to allow it, then she would take advantage.

Grinding her teeth, she huddled under her blanket and schemed.

She doubted Felather would survive, and the boy didn't look much stronger. She'd thought Felather was dead when she'd first seen him, but surprisingly, he'd still been breathing. It would be her job to check if they were still alive, tomorrow.

Kaenera was of two minds. Should he draw it out and make Demavrian suffer, or set up the trade and get the sigils as soon as possible? She hoped for the latter so they could upgrade their camp, and maybe, just maybe, she would have another shot at grabbing the SoulBreather.

With the SoulBreather, she could bargain for her soul, and then, she could return to Puronia.

What was the point of ruling everyone if you didn't get the rewards? Like comfort and adoration. Obedience and success. She scowled as she observed the busy camp. Instead, she got mud under foot, belligerence, and mindless slavery. Where was the fun in making a slave suffer if they knew no different? If they didn't remember what they had lost, then she couldn't hurt them.

Watching others suffer was the satisfying bit. Amaridin's anguish, Demavrian's pain. Much like Kaenera, she'd had everything in her palm, and she'd let it be snatched away.

Kaenera seemed even more removed than before. Now, he didn't even pretend to like or want her. He'd used her need for power, to be in control of everyone else, to manipulate her.

And now she was soulless. Her! She had thought she would be able to talk Demavrian around, persuade him that he needed her. Grinding her teeth, she admitted to herself that she had misjudged him. He was made of sterner stuff than Amaridin.

The sense of loss, that something wasn't quite right, was

a constant drag on her mind, confusing her. She couldn't shake the feeling off. It blunted her normally quick intelligence, causing her to stumble over words and to be a second too late with her questions.

What she had realised was that Kaenera was obsessed with killing Demavrian. His one thought was to steal the Aeora sigils so he could destroy Demavrian, the one person who had ever defeated him. Kaenera found even the word "defeat" intolerable. She would have taunted him with it, but he was teetering precariously on the edge, and she had no doubt he would kill her in an instant if she went too far.

Serenia also knew that he would use the sigils if he got them. The knowledge shocked her. Why destroy when you could rule? He would leave her with nothing, not even her life, if she weren't careful.

Instead, all she could do was torture the idiots who did his bidding. How he had found so many inane fools, she didn't know. Between them all, they didn't have a sensible thought in their heads.

But then, Kaenera didn't want anyone who would challenge his instructions. Blindly sending these mindless men out on jobs was a catastrophe just waiting to happen. If something went wrong, they wouldn't have a clue what to do. She was amazed that Kaenera had managed to achieve as much as he had.

She needed to remember that he was not powerless; he was just no longer all powerful. There was a difference, and it made him even more dangerous.

Running a finger over her chapped lips, she scowled at the ice-rimmed footprint preserved in the mud. If she could gather her wits enough, she would plan her own little coup. Maybe she could inherit the remainder of Kaenera's power, and she could become the thorn in Demavrian's side.

She stiffened as Kaenera's aura swept over her, and the

desire to please him consumed her. Gritting her teeth, she rose from her chair and waited with her head bent.

"Ah, there you are. I wondered where you'd got to." He paced around her. "I'm moving to a homestead nearby. They've got barns the men can work and sleep in. This mud is becoming untenable."

"Whose homestead is it?"

"Does it matter? It's mine now. And we're only a day from the Crossroads. Once you've checked on our guests tomorrow, you can join us there."

"Why do we need to be near the Crossroads? I thought your main camp was in Doveton?"

"It is, but it will be easier to move the dybbuks if I don't have to shift them so far. Demavrian will need to ground the Oblivion Gate when we meet, and that's when I'll strike."

"Are you sure—"

"Of course I'm sure.

Serenia flinched. He hadn't even let her finish her sentence. If anyone had ever interrupted her like that, she would have killed them on the spot.

"You will distract him for me." Kaenera's smile was cold and didn't reach his hard eyes. "I'm sure he'll be pleased to see you. Keep him occupied while I storm the back door. I bet he doesn't even know it exists."

"Of course," Serenia murmured, biting her lip trying to hold in the scream of frustration. What was she saying? Since when had she been this biddable? He was leaving her here, in this shithole, while he swanned off to some nice, warm house?

She remained with head bowed until his aura disappeared, and then she exhaled. Straightening, she snapped her fingers. "You, there. Get me some hot water. Now!"

At least with Kaenera gone, she could rule this roost for a day. She would make sure they were up early to check on their prisoners, and then she would be able to relax in the warmth of a house instead of these flimsy tents. The thought of a hot bath sustained her until her pot of steaming water arrived.

She eyed it and scowled but hurriedly washed before the water cooled.

54

MUNTRA – OBLIVION GATE

The next morning, after Mav grounded the Oblivion Gate, Muntra, Kerris, and Vinial waited for him at the bottom of the steps with their calopes and mules already loaded.

Not wasting any time, Mav hugged his oathsworn and then sent them on their way. He transported them to the ruins at the Crossroads, and Muntra hoped they would pick up Kaenera's trail soon enough. Much of the destruction had been cleared, and the skeleton of a new tavern was being built.

"We've all arrived together, and we'll report in tonight," Muntra said as he hauled himself onto his calope.

"Speak to you later. Be safe," Mav replied, his voice warm and comforting.

"According to Xylvin, they went east towards this Doveton place," Kerris said, scanning the report in his hand. "A wagon with a wonky back wheel, canvas painted brown, carrying textiles. Three people confirmed. Bailey is thought to be sedated, and Felather hidden under the material. According to Sero…" Kerris faltered and then, clearing his throat, he continued. "According to Sero, Felather was badly injured. A similar metal throwing disk was embedded in his shoulder, and he had defensive wounds. Bailey was knocked unconscious."

He looked at Muntra, his expression bleak. "We need to find the wagon and confirm whether they are holed up in this area or whether Kaenera transported them elsewhere. We have a day, maybe two, before Kaenera makes his demands. We need to find out as much as we can by then so Mav knows what he is dealing with."

"Then let's talk as we ride," Muntra said, urging his calope down the road. Vinial followed him, leaving Kerris to scramble into his saddle and tug the mule after him.

"Hey, wait for me!" Kerris trotted after them.

"A wagon is slow," Muntra said. "They'll only have gone a few leagues, if that. Are there any slave camps on your map?"

"Ryvalin marked them all. And the nearest marketplaces, and homesteads."

"Is it likely they would stop at a market and sell their goods?" Vinial asked.

"Unlikely," Muntra replied. "Unless they needed something." He shrugged. "Let's hope they had trouble with the wagon."

"Let's not," Kerris said. "Wouldn't that make him consider using other means of travel?"

"The next village is about a half day's ride," Vinial said. "We can see if anyone remembers the wagon passing through."

"It's been a couple of days," Kerris said a little dubiously.

"Do you think there are that many wagons on the road? They'll be remembered," Vinial said and urged her calope faster.

They arrived at the village by midday, and after a quick

discussion, Kerris remained with the animals since he looked the youngest.

Muntra strode into the tavern as if he didn't have a care in the world. Vinial accompanied him. She wore a brown homespun dress which reached her ankles, and a woollen shawl wrapped around her shoulders and pinned at the throat against the chill. Muntra's lips twitched as he glanced over at her. She looked uncomfortable to be out of uniform, and kept tugging the shawl as if it would slip off her shoulders.

After a quick inspection of the room, they chose a table near a group of merchants.

"I need at three yards of cotton, threads and some ribbons," Vinial said as she sat. She tapped her lip. "Or if there is a choice of colours, I could make some curtains for upstairs."

Muntra waved a hand and, when the serving girl arrived, ordered bannoe.

"Is there a textile merchant in the market?" Vinial asked, smiling up at the girl.

"Don't we wish there was!" the girl replied, rolling her eyes. "One passed through yesterday, but they wouldn't stop. No matter how much we tried to persuade them."

"Oh no. Did he have a selection? Do you know where they were headed? If it's local, maybe we catch them."

"Their wagon was piled high with material, but they said their kid was sick so they were going home."

"How disappointing."

"And for them, all that lost money," Muntra added. "Which way was home?"

The girl shrugged. "They took the Barlow Vale road towards Jinnel."

Muntra frowned. "That's a shame. We're headed in the other direction."

"Another time, maybe," the serving girl said and moved to the next table to clear the plates.

Muntra fidgeted as they waited for their bannoe. "We should just leave."

"It would be odd if we left without waiting for our order," Vinial said. "There could be watchers, so we need to act normally. Try and remember the map. Weren't there a couple of camps out past Barlow Vale?"

Muntra frowned as he tried to remember. *"Kerris? Can you check the map for any camps out towards Barlow Vale?"*

"Barlow Vale? That's further east isn't it?"

"Yes." Muntra grinned. Being able to mind speak with the others was amazing. He couldn't wait to speak to Bailey in the same way. His smile slipped. If only Bailey were oathsworn already.

The serving girl placed his bannoe on the table, and he grabbed the mug and gulped it down. The serving girl laughed. "You were thirsty. You want another?"

"No, that was perfect thank you." He offered her a coin in payment and impatiently waited for Vinial to sip her drink.

Vinial laughed at him over the brim of her mug, her eyes twinkling at him. But suddenly, she was finished, and she rose and led the way out.

Kerris showed them the map when they arrived. "There's two possibilities. The nearest camp is in the vale, by the river. The second one is an abandoned mine, but there a couple of homesteads and hamlets as well."

"Kaenera's used to holding prisoners in camps," Muntra said. "I bet he still thinks of them as his."

Vinial nodded. "I agree. Let's try the river first. We should get there by nightfall. And then we can try the other if needed."

Remounting, they set off. Their calopes splashed through

muddy puddles as the drizzle sifted down out of a heavy grey sky. Muntra pulled his coat tighter around him and grimaced up at the clouds as the soft rain pattered on his face like gentle kisses. His thoughts drifted to Bailey and how he was coping. At least he had Felather with him.

Turns passed, and the rain got heavier. They were all soaked by the time they reached the river crossing. They huddled under a tree, trying to keep their map dry as they determined which side of the river the camp was.

Kerris cursed under his breath as he folded the map away. "It will be dark soon. If we need to cross, we should do it while it's still light."

Muntra peered into the gloom. "You and Vinial cross. I'll search this side. If one of us finds it, we can call the other."

"We shouldn't split up," Vinial said.

"We don't have time. We maybe have another day before Kaenera's demands arrive. We need to know whether it's this camp or the other one today."

Kerris nodded and gripped Muntra's arm. "Don't do anything stupid. I'll contact you if we find them."

Muntra grasped his arm back. "As will I." He mounted and cantered along the river bank, eager to finally be nearing their destination.

Kerris stared at the river and sighed. Vinial buffeted his shoulder. "Come on. At least this time, you can't get any wetter than you already are. Keep a tight rein on your calope. Remember, they like the water."

They forded the river without incident, even though Kerris' calope wanted to lie down in the middle. Fortunately, the water only rose to their calopes' shins. They hurried down the track beside the river, following in the same direction as Muntra.

A turn later, Kerris was getting ready to give up. "Where

is it?" he grumbled and swiped his wet hair out of his eyes. Water trickled down his neck, and he shivered.

"I think we've either missed it or it's on the other side," Vinial replied, peering into the gloom. "The trees are thick around here. Maybe we should go back and see if we missed a turning."

"Kerris? I found the camp and it's deserted."

Stiffening, Kerris frowned at the river. *"You went in on your own?"*

"The camp is a disaster. Burnt out. There's nothing here."

"Alright. We'll meet you back at the ford and head for the mine." Kerris glanced at Vinial. Her brown hair was slick against her head, giving her a fragile appearance, though he knew hidden beneath her sodden clothes was a skilled soldier. "Muntra's found the camp. He says there's nothing there. We should head back to the ford."

Vinial turned her calope around and headed back the way they had come.

55

BAILEY – EIDOLON

Bailey startled awake as Felather groaned—a deep, pain-filled groan, that made Bailey wince. "I'm here with you, Felather," he said as he reached for the water jug. Felather would be thirsty, especially with the amount of blood he had lost. He wet the strip of cloth he had managed to tear off his shirt, soaked it in the liquid, and then dribbled the droplets into Felather's mouth. He repeated the action, desperate to get enough water in his mouth so he could swallow.

"That's right. It's just water," Bailey murmured, relieved when Felather's throat bobbed.

"Felather? Can you hear me? It's Bailey."

Felather's groan was quieter.

"We're in a cellar or somewhere underground. I think it's the next morning. I can see down the tunnels, but there's no light anywhere. Can you contact Mav? You need to let him know we're alive. He'll be worried."

Felather didn't respond, and Bailey rocked him. "Felather, you need to reach out to Mav. He doesn't know where we are." Tears dribbled down Bailey's cheeks as he realised Felather had slipped back into unconsciousness.

Gently, he lay the injured man on the floor and went back to the bars trapping them. He tugged the metal, but they didn't budge. Then he concentrated on listening for the memories, searching through them until he found the memory of the bars being installed. How deep did they go? Was there a weakness anywhere? Resting his forehead against the cold metal, he focused on what it was telling him. Faded images battered him, jostling for his attention, and he sternly told them to wait. The images halted in surprise and then scrolled past in a more orderly manner.

After a moment, he shuffled to the left side of the cell. He poked at the ground around the base where iron met rock and then tugged the bar. There was a slight movement. He picked at the rock. It was friable, and small flakes chipped off as he teased it away. He shredded his fingernails, but he continued working the rock loose around the bar.

After blowing the fragments away, he tugged on the bar. It moved, but nowhere near enough, so he continued picking at the rock. He needed a pickaxe or a dagger, something with a point, but there was nothing in the cell with them except the clay jug.

Staring at it, he knew the clay wouldn't be strong enough, even if he did break it. There was no point in wasting what little water they had.

He spun as Felather stirred and groaned again. Rushing back to his side, he held him still and said, "Don't move. You've got a blade in your back."

Felather mumbled something, but Bailey couldn't make out what he said. He wet the rag again and dribbled water into his mouth. Felather coughed feebly and inhaled. His breath rattled in his chest. He was too cold, but Bailey had nothing else to wrap him in.

"Wh-where are you?" Felather's voice was barely a whisper. "I c-can't find you."

"I'm right here, Felather. Can you call, Mav?" Bailey asked urgently.

"I keep looking, but I can't find you."

"Felather, can you hear me? You need to contact Demavrian."

"It's been so long." Felather sighed his breath out and fell silent again.

Bailey couldn't wake him.

Tucking his jacket tighter around Felather, Bailey went back to picking at the rock around the iron bar. A sudden thought had him scurrying back to Felather. Maybe Felather wore a belt. Would the buckle be of use? He patted Felather down, searching his clothes. He *was* wearing a belt! Bailey unbuckled it and carefully rolled Felather on his side, so he could tug the belt out from under him.

It took longer than he thought, but he was extra careful not to hurt Felather. He exhaled once he finally had the belt in his hands, and he stiffened as the belt's memory seeped into him. He clearly saw Felather sliding two pins into the seam of the leather.

It was too dark to see what he was doing, but he carefully felt the belt, his sore fingers searching for the slightest break in the seam. It took him three tries, feeling the full length of the belt, before he found it. It was so well concealed; it wasn't surprising the guards had missed it.

Easing the pins out of the belt, he sat holding them. Now what did he do? He had no idea how to pick a lock. He almost laughed out loud as one of the pins shared a memory of Felather using it to do just that.

"Memories are not that bad after all," he muttered to himself as he reached through the bars and pulled the lock towards him. "I can do this," he repeated as he re-ran the memory. The image showed Felather poking one of the pins into the bottom of the lock and holding it there. He then inserted the second pin, rocking it back and forth, listening intently. What was he listening for? A click, maybe?

How did a key open a lock? Keys had different shapes. Did they need to fit into different patterns? No, they must push parts of the lock into position and align them so they opened. That was what he needed to do: align the innards so they released the bar.

He reached through the bars and twisted the lock so he could see the keyhole. Wedging the lock against the bar, he pushed the first pin into the keyhole and held it in place. With his face pressed against the bar, he reached around, and inserted the second pin, and rummaged it about. Then he dropped the pin.

Cursing under his breath, he groped for the pin on the floor. His stomach clenched in sudden panic at the thought that the pin had bounced out of reach, but he exhaled as he found it. He trembled. He could have lost it.

His fingers were so cold that they were slippery, and it wasn't only the cold that made them shake. Baily took a moment to breathe on them to warm them up. He stuck them under his arm pits, and then, shivering, he started again.

Inserting the first pin, he wedged the lock against the bar to keep it still and reached through the bars with the second pin. More carefully, he inserted the second pin and wiggled it around.

Nothing happened. Slower, then. Feel the insides. He held the pin carefully between his fingers, allowing the tension of the pin to feel what was in the lock. He rocked it back and forth and met resistance. He eased the pin up and heard a click, so he pushed the first pin deeper into the mechanism and tried again.

His arms and shoulders ached, his knees were on fire, and he couldn't stop shivering by the time he heard the last click and the lock swung open. At first, he didn't realise he'd opened it. He was still trying to feel for the next pin, and then the lock slipped out of his numb fingers and fell to the ground.

Groaning, he rose to his feet. His body ached, and he was so stiff.

A dim grey light revealed the rough tunnel walls. Morning had arrived, and the guards would undoubtably arrive with it. He swung the door open and stumbled down the tunnel, desperate to see their surroundings. If he at least got a glimpse of the outside, he could tell Felather, who could share it with Mav.

When he shuffled out of the mine, bent over and shaking like an elderly man, he nearly burst into tears when he realised they weren't near a village at all. It was a deserted compound, and they were locked in the abandoned mine.

Spinning, he searched his surroundings, but he couldn't see anything notable from a landmark perspective. Trees crowded around the compound fences, concealing them from view. He looked back at the rock face the mine was carved into, but it was a sheer wall, and he couldn't see how far it went up.

No, this couldn't be all there was to see.

Felather was too injured to move and too heavy to drag, so he couldn't hide him anywhere. They couldn't leave, and he couldn't leave Felather alone. He dashed back into the tunnel. Blankets. Find some rugs. Anything.

He found a decaying pile of material in an alcove and grabbed it. Even as a buffer between Felather and the rock, it would be something. He also found a rusted pick axe leaning against the wall of another tunnel, and he grabbed that as well.

Loud voices on the morning air had him rushing back to his cell. He shut the door and clicked the lock shut. Hurriedly, his fingers clumsy in his haste, he pushed the pins back into the belt seam and wrapped it around his waist before buckling it in place.

The pick axe and the pile of rags, he pushed behind Felather, and then he lifted Felather's head into his lap and curled around him as much as possible.

Voices echoed down the tunnel. "See, told you they'd still be here. Nowhere for them to go."

"Is he still alive?" a woman asked.

Bailey shuddered at the cold edge to her voice. It was almost as if she were hoping Felather was dead. He glared at the woman as she stepped up to the bars. One of the guards held a lantern, shining a golden light over the cell.

The woman looked young. She had a smooth complexion, gleaming blonde hair, and vivid blue eyes. It wasn't fair that she was so beautiful yet so corrupted. She should have seemed out of place in this dreary dungeon, but the cruelty Bailey saw in her eyes and the arrogant curve of her lips said otherwise. This woman was exactly where she wanted to be, and she was enjoying his anguish.

"Felather is dying," Bailey said. "He needs a healer, blankets, water."

"I'm sure he'll hold on long enough. After all, he's been searching for his saviour for decades now. He's not going to leave us now."

"He's too cold."

"You'll keep him warm."

"What do you want with us?"

"Demavrian's dues are up, and it's time to pay. He thought he'd squirmed out of Apologia, but he was in error." The woman smiled, and Bailey shivered. "He will not escape this, and you two"—she pointed at him and then

Felather with an elegant finger—"will make him toe the line."

"It won't if Felather is dead."

The woman tutted. "Which is why you'll keep him alive." She turned to leave, and then glanced back at Bailey over her shoulder. "You only have to keep him alive until tomorrow; it will be all over then, and it won't matter anymore."

Bailey stared after her in horror until his body began to shake, and he folded over Felather to hide the tears streaming down his cheeks.

"Felather?" he whispered. "I don't know what to do."

56

DEMAVRIAN – OBLIVION GATE

The next morning, Mav shook with unadulterated fury as he read Kaenera's demands. His knuckles cracked as he gripped the scroll, which had been sealed with wax and bound with red tassels as if it were a formal declaration. Mav supposed it was in a way. It was a declaration of war.

Ryvalin carefully prised the scroll from his rigid fingers so she, Julius and Adriz could read it. Mav vibrated, his shadows searching for something to crush as she read aloud the words which were burned into his mind. Solanji rose from her seat and rubbed his shoulder as if that would calm him down.

He inhaled a steadying breath and wrapped an arm around her. "You shouldn't be up."

"You and Kerris have healed the worst. It's just aches and pains now."

"You promised to rest."

"And I will," she said, hugging him.

"Kaenera demands that Demavrian, in person and alone, bring the Aeora sigils to the Crossroads in Eidolon at midday today," Ryvalin read, her voice emotionless and clipped. "In exchange for the return of Scribe Felather and the fledgling, Demavrian will surrender himself and the sigils."

No one else was to accompany him.

Short, to the point, and impossible.

"He's not going," Adriz snarled.

Ryvalin flicked a glance at Adriz and then said, "There is nothing confirming they are unharmed."

"We know they're not!" Adriz spun so fast that she caught her swinging hand on the desk. She grunted as she clutched it to her chest and tried to calm herself.

There was absolutely no way Mav would give Kaenera the sigils. Mav should have insisted that his father relocate them. The fact that they were still stored in the Oblivion Gate was like a burning brand in his mind. He had the means to get his oathsworn back if he just handed over them over.

Adriz and Ryvalin stood over him, watching him closely. They knew perfectly well that if he chose to go on his own, they couldn't stop him. It was fortunate that he had a modicum of common sense left. He knew he couldn't do this on his own.

Solanji gripped his arm, grounding him in the moment. "Don't let Kaenera dictate the exchange. We have to control this somehow."

"He's not giving us any notice," Mav said. "He doesn't want us to be prepared."

"Solanji is right, though," Julius said. "We should be in control of the exchange point. We can at least plan ahead for what we know."

Adriz and Ryvalin exchanged worried glances. "You intend to meet Kaenera?"

"We must if we haven't found Felather and Bailey before

then," Mav said. "I will meet him. It's my only chance to face him, to find out where they are. According to Xylvin, there is no sign of Bailey and Felather in Doveton, so at the same time, Ryvalin, you will destroy his base. We need him off balance."

"How?" Adriz asked.

"By giving him what he wants," Oji said.

Mav slowly nodded. "And nothing more."

Adriz glared at Mav and threw her hands in the air. "And what does that entail, exactly?"

"It means that we need to execute what we have been planning. I will transfer Ryvalin and the Host to Doveton. You've been practising the pincer movement, the men are ready, and Kaenera doesn't have a clue. He won't be expecting it because he thinks he is in control and that I am only worried about my getting my oathsworn back.

"I will deal with Kaenera at the exchange. Once I kill him, all his dybbuks will die." Mav looked at Solanji, hating himself for asking her, but knowing she was his only choice. "Solanji, you and Ellaria must be ready to go and retrieve Felather and Bailey as soon as Kerris and Muntra find them. You and Ellaria should be able to manage any guards. After that you rest." He ignored her when she rolled her eyes at him.

Adriz snorted. "Muntra will tear them apart with his bare hands."

Mav hoped so. He shook off the murderous thought and concentrated on his plan. "You will transport them to the healerie here at the Gate. We will keep the third division here to defend the Gate. I need our guards positioned to cut off any attacks or distractions by Kaenera's dybbuks."

"I brought a map with me," Julius said as he flung it across Mav's desk, holding one end as it unrolled. "Oji, what is the best location for you to be, so you can appear as soon as we get Felather and Bailey back?"

"And that we can defend," Mav murmured. He weighted one end down with his inkstand and scanned the map.

"Wherever you think best," Oji murmured.

Ryvalin moved next to him. "No matter what he says, Kaenera won't come alone. And he can move people around just as you can."

"So, we need to set up defences around an area big enough for Oji to settle," Mav said, "and we need to restrict Kaenera's movements."

"Not asking for much, are we?" Adriz said as she joined him by the desk.

"You've got five minutes for suggestions. We can discuss the pros and cons and decide from there."

Silence fell as they examined the map.

Adriz exhaled. "It's got to be to the east of the Crossroads. We know that is the direction Muntra and Kerris are headed. They have sightings as far as here"—she tapped the map—"and there are two abandoned compounds for them to check in the vicinity. It has to be one of those."

Mav looked around the table, and everyone was nodding in agreement. "Very well. We will settle to the east. One cohort helps Oji to defend the back entrance, and the rest will be with me at the exchange.

"Let's begin the transfer to Doveton."

57

BAILEY – EIDOLON

Time passed, maybe a few turns, maybe a day, Bailey thought. It was difficult to tell by the slight changes in the dim light. He was cold and starving; they hadn't been given them any food or water. It was as if their captors didn't want them to survive.

Within his embrace, Felather was frigid and far too still. Lurching upright, Bailey pressed his shaking fingers to Felather's throat, but he couldn't find a pulse. His stomach churned as he realised Felather wasn't breathing.

He didn't know what to do. He wasn't a healer like Kerris, nor able to organise everything like Shandra so that life-or-death situations didn't occur, nor strong enough to have protected Felather like Muntra would have, nor as intelligent as the quick-witted Kiara.

He was just Bailey, the weak, hopeless failure. He drooped over Felather, consumed by despair. He had failed again.

A memory surfaced in his mind of Felather clasping his shoulder as they sat watching the sunrise. The scribe had said, "There is strength in the smallest belief, and you should always believe in yourself, Bailey, because Demavrian does. Demavrian sees what's in your heart, and he loves you for it. Don't ever forget that."

He *had* forgotten that. And Demavrian loved Felather. It was clear from all Felather's memories that however much they argued, they had a deep and abiding love for each other.

Bailey lay the injured man on the floor, propping him on his side using the mouldy material, and began massaging his chest. If he could just get Felather breathing again. He needed to get his heart pumping, his big, generous heart that loved all of them. They were not going to lose him.

Grim determination kept Bailey massaging Felather's chest. He shut his eyes and willed Felather's heart to start beating again. He was so focussed that he didn't notice when his awareness slipped under Felather's skin. When his fingers closed around a firm yet squishy substance, he almost squealed, and he opened his eyes to see his transparent hands plunged into Felather's chest. He was holding Felather's heart!

Emotions bombarded him, overwhelming him, all Felather's. He pushed them away. He couldn't concentrate with them clamouring at him. Cringing, he squeezed the organ. "Pump," he ordered. He winced at the stupid command, but the heart thumped in his hands.

"Again, thump, and keep thumping," he said as he squeezed the heart again. Each time he squeezed, the heart pulsed, so he kept squeezing, trying to regulate it to his own heartbeat.

He slipped further inside Felather, leaving his own body cold and still behind him.

"Felather? Tell me what else needs to be restarted? Breathe in and

out for me." There was no response, so Bailey breathed for him. The rise and fall of Felather's chest was the best thing Bailey had ever seen.

And then all of Felather's pain hit him, and his own heart stuttered as his whole body was consumed with agony. He spasmed, causing Felather's heart to stutter. Bailey inhaled a shaky breath and steadied himself, and with tears streaming down his cheeks, he pushed the pain away. He focused on breathing, deep and calm, and his fear eased as he watched Felather's chest expand in sync with his own.

Squeeze the heart, breathe in, *thump*, and out, *thump*. And repeat.

Was he blocking? Was this what Sero had meant? He hadn't blocked fast enough. This consuming torment and debilitating exhaustion would always be a memory that he and Felather shared. Forever. Assuming they lived forever. At least it no longer burned up his body. No wonder Felather was struggling to manage that much pain continuously. He was exhausted.

And Bailey realised that was why Felather's heart had stopped. Felather didn't have the strength to keep it beating. Well, Bailey would do it for him for as long as he needed him to.

Once he was in a rhythm, Bailey's mind drifted. He noted the tunnel out of the mine was dark; it must have taken all day for him to get Felather stable. The night seemed to drag on forever. Bailey was aware that his body was shuddering with the cold, but he no longer felt it. Time had no meaning; everything he had was focussed on keeping Felather alive.

Dim grey light stole down the corridor; morning had arrived, and Felather was still alive. What else did Felather need? To be rescued, Bailey's tired mind supplied, so Mav could help heal him. Mav! Could he reach Mav using Felather's oathsworn bond?

He hoped to have a bond with Mav one day. To be connected so deeply to someone he loved would be a gift to be treasured.

"Felather? I am so sorry that I can't ask your permission, but I need to try and reach Mav, and the only way I can think to do it is to use you."

Bailey sank deeper into Felather's awareness. He skimmed through the many thoughts, emotions, and beliefs, trying not to intrude until he came to Felather's…he didn't know what to call it, but it was a vast well of knowledge, all of Felather's experiences stored together, and Bailey was so tempted to dive in and explore, but then he reminded himself that it wasn't his to enjoy, it was Felather's.

A memory full of healing instruction jumped out at him. It was as if Felather had thrown it at him. And Bailey suddenly understood Felather's healing capability. Felather couldn't heal himself, but maybe *Bailey* could use the information to at least kickstart his healing.

Renewed hope had him skimming through the memories Felather had shared. There was something in here that Felather thought he could use, if only he could find it. *"Hang on Felather. Help is coming."*

"Bai…ley. Thank you." Felather's voice was faint, but he was aware and still here with Bailey. Even if he was hanging by a thread, he knew Bailey was trying to help. Hopefully, that would be enough for Felather to fight a little longer.

"You must stop. Dan…gerous."

For a moment, Bailey wanted to weep. He couldn't stop even if he wanted to, trapped as he was inside Felather, but he didn't want to, so he continued, squeezing Felather's heart and breathing for him. He knew Felather would understand.

Felather's exhaustion swept through him, instantly

followed by a wave of sheer agony which seized up Bailey's mind and threatened to lock up his limbs. Bailey scrambled to shore up his block, which he had allowed to slip. His own exhaustion was creeping up on him.

He glanced over at his body and winced. His skin was turning blue, his lips were colourless, and the shudders were getting stronger. His body was trying to keep him warm and failing. He suddenly wondered what would happen to him if his own body died. Would he be trapped inside Felather forever? Or would they both die?

Sero's warning about learning the basics slowly percolated in brain. He should have read the chapter on grounding! He should have read the whole book. Somehow, he had managed to manifest personification centuries before he was supposed to.

"When needs must," he muttered under his breath.

It was too late to worry about it now. A shout echoed down the tunnel, and Bailey ignored it. First, he needed to contact Mav. The sooner they were rescued, the sooner proper healers could help them.

Surely, Felather's connection to Mav would be obvious? He had expected some scintillating connection reaching out into the air; instead, eventually, he found a glowing core within Felather's heart, sheltered, nurtured, and hidden.

Exhaling, Bailey carefully cupped it in his hands and called, *"Mav?"*

Muntra knelt by the perimeter fence and watched the dybbuk standing in the main entrance stare out at the rain as he scratched himself. The guard was bored, which was in their favour. He snipped the links, memories of another rain-swept compound crowding him. He shivered and snipped more quickly. He pulled the chain-link fence apart and wriggled through.

Vinial strode into the yard, and the guard strode out. "Oy! This is private property."

"Oh, thank goodness. One of my wagon's wheels is stuck, and I can't lift it. Can you help me?" Vinial fluttered her eyelashes. "I'd make it worth your while." She patted her hip as she got nearer.

The dybbuk gawped at her. Before he could react, Vinial pounced, grabbing the man and slicing her dagger across his throat. The man collapsed with a gurgle, and Muntra dashed into the mine entrance as Kerris ran to join them.

The tunnel widened into a collecting area and split into three passages. Muntra pointed to the other tunnels, and gripping his sword, he took the left one. The passage curved, the rough walls jutting out in places, and ended in a small room with another door, which was separated by bars and locked with a padlock. The tang of damp stone was strong, and the air chilly.

"Bailey?" He hissed his breath out at the sight of a pale-faced Bailey hovering over Felather's limp body. *"Kerris? I found them. Call Solanji."*

A guard rose from the shadows, and Muntra instinctively blocked his strike, and moved within the man's reach. Pushing against his sword, the man gave away under his greater strength, and Muntra smoothly thrust his dagger into the man's gut and jabbed his knee into his groin. The man screamed, and Muntra wrenched his knife out and slit his throat.

Staring down at the man and then at his blood smeared blade, he shuddered. He had killed a man. He gritted his teeth and glanced at the pale faced Bailey, still frozen and unhearing. The man had deserved it for what they were doing to Bailey and Felather.

He patted down the man, searching for keys, and was unlocking the door when Kerris and Vinial arrived.

"Good job," Vinial said, and some of Muntra's guilt eased.

"That should not be possible," Kerris murmured as he peered through the bars at Bailey and Felather.

58

DEMAVRIAN – CROSSROADS, EIDOLON

That same dreary grey morning, Mav waited in the middle of the road at the junction of the Crossroads. Fear and anger licked down his veins, keeping him tense and alert. The shell of a new tavern stood forlornly on the north corner. The Crossroads were deserted.

Solanji and Shandra were camped in his study in the Oblivion Gate, waiting for word from Muntra and Kerris. Julius' division had claimed the right to defend the Gate, and Adriz was with the Host, poised to come to his defence as soon as he called her, or she got fed up with waiting.

The sky was heavy, and the air damp with promised rain, but Mav was sweating. He was shielding Julius' men from sight as they hovered, waiting for his command.

Serenia appeared opposite Mav and smiled.

"Where is Kaenera?" Mav asked, glaring at the elegant woman who was supposed to be dead and long forgotten. Her blonde hair was tucked into a neat bun, and she had found colourful silks to drape herself in, no doubt pretending she had never been deposed from office and still deserved respect.

"He'll be here. He just wanted to check something first."

"I want proof of life," Mav demanded through gritted teeth. "No proof, no box."

"You are such a sentimentalist. Allowing vulnerable children to influence your decisions," Serenia said as she slowly walked around Mav.

"Unlike you, Serenia? Did you never feel anything for any of us?"

"Emotions are so messy. They just confuse matters."

"And yet you believe Kaenera cares for you? Loves you? Enough that you'll do his dirty work for him?"

"He saved me when you were prepared to let me die."

"Do you really think there will be a world to live in if Kaenera gets the sigils? He will destroy us all."

Serenia shrugged. "He had them before and didn't use them."

"Then why does he want them now? No one should have them. They are an abomination."

"Kaenera is the rightful god of this land. Not you. He will control all. He wants the Gate back."

"It's not the Gate he wants. He just wants the power."

"Whatever." Serenia flicked her fingers as if dismissing Mav's argument.

"Where are Felather and Bailey? Are they still alive?"

A flicker of an image, a dark cell. Mav latched on to the impression. "Where are they?"

"I know what you are doing, and you won't find them."

"Oh? Why haven't you brought them with you? This is an exchange. Without them, there is no exchange."

An image of a compound flickered in his mind. A deserted compound.

"They are being held in one of the deserted compounds. I can't see where; it's too dark." Mav reported to his oathsworn, who were in Mav's study, huddled around the map of Eidolon.

"You haven't brought the box," Serenia said.

"But I am half of the bargain, so I am showing faith. You have offered nothing."

"Keep her talking," Solanji said. *"We'll go to the compound. We'll have to cross them off one by one unless you can narrow it down."*

"Are they alive?" Mav asked, stifling his worry at Solanji going into danger when she was barely healed. He stiffened at the image of Felather's still form in Bailey's arms. Serenia had seen them. "Where are they?"

"Demavrian, calm yourself," Kaenera's oily voice said from behind him, and Mav slowly turned to face him partially. He didn't trust Serenia at his back.

"I'm here alone. Where are Felather and Bailey?"

"Show me the sigils, and I'll show you your people," Kaenera replied.

Wenson appeared beside Mav with the box of Aeora sigils in his arms.

Kaenera stepped forward, his face brightening. Mav waved his hand, and Wenson disappeared again.

"You've seen the chest. Now show me Felather and Bailey."

"Bring him back," Kaenera growled.

"Not until you provide me proof of life."

"Mav?"

"Felather?" Mav's heart stuttered as he tried to reach his oathsworn, but he was so faint, barely present.

"It's Bailey. I don't know how long I can do this, but Felather's really bad. I-I think he's dying."

Mav's chest tightened. *"Where are you?*

"We're in a disused mine at one of the old compounds. It's deserted. There are a lot of a trees and the ridge faces west. The sun rises behind it, but I don't know anything more."

"I'm sending someone to find you. As soon as they do, they'll take you to a healer. You're too faint. I can't pinpoint you."

"Mav? I think I'm stuck."

"Stuck? What do you mean?"

"Inside Felather. I'm trying to keep him alive, but his heart keeps stopping."

Mav's blood ran cold, and he shivered. Then he poured all the reassurance and love he could into his connection to Bailey. *"Hold on, Bailey. We're coming."*

"Please hurry."

Mav focused back on his surroundings and Kaenera. "Show me that Felather and Bailey are still alive."

"Solanji? Bailey is in a mine at an abandoned compound. The ridge faces west. Trees conceal the compound."

"Understood," Solanji replied.

"I'll take you to them if you like?" Kaenera offered.

"Bring them here."

Kaenera inspected his fingernails. "But then you would have them, and I would not."

"That is the intent of an exchange."

Tutting, Kaenera shook his head. "You are stalling for some reason. What are you really doing, Demavrian?"

"I would have said you are the one stalling. I am here as demanded. I've shown you that I have the sigils. Why are you not showing me Felather and Bailey? Are they already dead?"

"No!" Kaenera raised his hand. "No," he said more calmly.

"Do you not have the power to transport them here? Give me the location, and I'll do it for you," Mav offered.

"It's more the fact that you didn't come alone," Kaenera said. He waved his hand and Mav's shield fell, revealing Julius and his men spread out around them.

Mav smiled. "But then, neither did you." He twisted his hand, and Kaenera's dybbuks were revealed. And they were stalemated again.

Kaenera growled under his breath, "Give me the box."

"I don't bow down to the demands of bullies."

"Then your oathsworn are lost."

"Did you really think I would give you the sigils without a fight?"

Kaenera snarled, showing his teeth, and he raised his hand as he extended claws from the ends of his bony fingers. "Not really."

His dybbuks charged, and Kaenera grabbed Serenia and disappeared. They reappeared behind the dybbuk lines, and Mav followed. Mav transported Adriz beside him, and she rushed forward.

Kaenera blasted her back and then wilted. Mav snarled and pushed a protective bubble around Adriz as she rose to her feet, sword at the ready. She charged at the dybbuks who had turned towards Mav.

Serenia's screech of laughter abruptly stopped as Mav froze her in place and he advanced on Kaenera. She struggled, but Mav's hold was like a vice. Kaenera ran towards his men, using them to shield him. Mav concentrated on Kaenera, trying to hold him in place like he had Serenia, but his grasp slipped off him. He manipulated one of his shadows into a hook and flicked it at Kaenera, and it caught, snagging on something. Mav peered after it, trying to discern whether Kaenera had a soul. He must have.

Kaenera cackled and urged his men forward. "I want him!" He pointed at Mav, and his Dybbuks charged.

Chaos surrounded them as the Heavenly Host engaged the dybbuks and halted the charge. Fallen dybbuks disappeared in a puff of dust, and as each of them passed through Mav, he instinctively deflected them. The guards of the Heavenly Host glanced at each other warily, then at the dybbuks and then they charged again.

Julius rushed up behind Serenia, reached around her

with a knife in each hand, and calmly slit her throat. She collapsed to the floor as Mav released her, limbs twitching. Julius stood over her until she stilled.

Serenia passed through Mav, kicking and screaming in death as she had in life. He had to get rid of her; he could not cope with having her clawing at him from the inside.

Julius observed her body for a moment longer and then looked at Mav. His expression was empty—no joy, no relief at killing the woman who had murdered his partner in life. "Stop wasting your time on her and deal with Kaenera."

"I will. I just need to do something. I'll be right back." Mav transported himself to the rose gate.

"Solanji has retrieved Felather and Bailey. They are in the heal-erie," Oji said.

"Alive?"

"Yes, though there are some problems. Bailey seems stuck inside Felather; he's keeping him alive."

"Ah, yes, he told me."

Mav didn't stop but walked through the rose gate and let his shadows unravel as he released all the soulless he had collected.

He exhaled as the pressure eased and he could breathe easily again. Serenia was gone. For good. He squared his shoulders and strode back through the gate, his shadows writhing around him. Now, it was just Kaenera.

But there was one more thing he needed to do first.

"Shandra?"

"Mav?" Shandra replied immediately.

"You need to pass Sero's gift to Bailey," Mav said. *"He's doing something cherubic to keep Felather alive. But he says he got himself stuck inside Felather. Sero's memories may help him figure out how to get out."*

"He doesn't look right, Mav." Shandra's voice quavered. *"It's like his body is frozen. How do I pass them to him?"*

"I have no idea. Ask a cherub." Mav exhaled. He could do no more for his oathsworn. His job was to stop Kaenera.

Returning to the Crossroads, Mav realised nothing had changed in the few moments he had been gone. He flared his wings. Black feathers glinted with silver, and strands of shadows streamed around him as he strode towards the thickest density of dybbuks. He knew Kaenera would be hidden within.

Dybbuks parted as he approached, horror on their faces as the Angel of Death walked towards them. Whatever they saw in his expression made them dropped their swords and run.

Adriz fought beside Julius. They moved in unison, each defending the other. Dybbuks disintegrated all around them, coating them in their dust.

Kaenera straightened, his eyes ablaze. He glared at Mav and claws extended from his fingertips. He pointed at Mav and then curled his fingers into a fist and disappeared.

The shadow linking them tightened, and Mav smiled.

59

RYVALIN – DOVETON, EIDOLON

Ryvalin crouched in the undergrowth and peered at the encampment. The stone mansion was located in the centre of a compound. Wooden barracks stood in regimented ranks on all sides. She exhaled in relief. The layout was just as Vern had described, though seeing the size of Kaenera's army was daunting. Dybbuks moved from one building to another like busy ants mindlessly following orders. It was indicative of how they had ignored what was actually happening to the people of Eidolon.

The compound quietened as the dybbuks disappeared into buildings. They must have arrived at some changeover or something. Water dripped on Ryvalin from above, and she shivered as the droplets trickled down her neck.

Crouched beside her, muttering under her breath, Ziriel, Amaridin's Captain of the Host, glared at the scene. Ryvalin was surprised that Ziriel had led the division herself. "Ziriel, take your division and go to the north. We'll crush them between us. Xylvin's first pass is the signal."

Ziriel gave her a vicious grin. "It will be my pleasure,"

she growled and snapped at her cohort leads to follow her silently.

Ryvalin waited. Her officers spread out, following the plan without her having to intervene. She smiled grimly. It was good to have well-trained troops around her again.

Inhaling the damp aroma of soggy green vegetation and listening to the drip of water off leaves, the sudden concern that everything would be too wet to burn flashed through her. Thankfully, Xylvin's flame was draconic and could burn anything.

"There are no patrols," she murmured, shocked at Kaenera's arrogance.

"Ziriel is in position," Xylvin said a few moments later.

Ryvalin snarled under breath. *"For Averdeus and Sero,"* she said.

"For Averdeus and Sero," Xylvin repeated and then swooped down on the unsuspecting encampment and roared as she breathed fire over the timber structures. The wood erupted into flames, and screams pierced the air as dybbuks tumbled out of the burning buildings in disarray.

"Archers, release!" Ryvalin ordered, and a flight of arrows curved through the heavy sky and thudded into unprotected bodies.

"Second flight!" Ryvalin yelled, knowing Ziriel would be doing the same. No matter which direction the dybbuks ran, they would run into a similar barrage. She shook her head as she watched the chaos. This was too easy.

More dybbuks rushed out of the main mansion as the roof blazed, and deep, booming explosions detonated one after the other.

Ryvalin raised her sword. "For Averdeus!" she screamed and ran forward. The Heavenly Host charged with her, their swords glinting in the flames. The Host cut through the ranks, and Xylvin set fire to the structures.

Xylvin roared overhead as more dybbuks ran out of the barracks.

The Host battled on, ignoring the way the dybbuks collapsed into dust as they struck them down.

Ryvalin peered upwards as Xylvin banked and swept back over the mansion. *"Focus on the buildings,"* she said as she parried a strike and forced the soldier back. She thrust her dagger into his gut and blood spurted. The man staggered and dropped to one knee. Ryvalin faltered, expecting the man to disintegrate, but he wasn't a dybbuk, he was a soulless.

Tugging her blade out, she kicked the body aside and, ignoring the blood, ran after her men. They swarmed across the training yard, cutting a swathe through dybbuks and soulless alike.

When Solanji received word from Kerris that they had found Bailey and Felather, Ellaria transported them to the small cell under the stone ridge. She paused at the sight of Bailey kneeling over Felather, frozen in place. His skin was salt white and tinged with blue, his eyes were closed and his lips were a pale grey. The boy was barely breathing. His hands were locked on Felather's chest, which rose up and down beneath him.

"What is he doing?" she asked as she crouched beside Bailey.

"Don't touch them!" Kerris exclaimed, grabbing her arm. "He's keeping Felather alive."

"But if we can't touch them, how do we get them out of here?"

"This should not be possible," Kerris murmured and scrubbed his palms down his face.

Ellaria peered closer. *"I can move them as one,"* she said. *"I'll have to come back for everyone else, though."*

"Transfer me first," Kerris said, "so I can warn the healers what's happened. We don't want them charging in before we've separated them. I don't think either of them will survive it."

Solanji nodded slowly. "Good idea. And call Shandra when you get there. She has some of Sero's memories for Bailey, though she doesn't know how she is supposed to give them to him."

Ellaria curled around Kerris, and they disappeared. She was back almost immediately. After carefully embracing Bailey, she wrapped her tail around Felather, and they all disappeared.

Solanji gripped Muntra's shoulder. "Are you alright?"

Muntra stiffened, his eyes wide and fearful. "What if… what if we can't separate them?"

"Don't go there. We will. We have to."

Ellaria returned and transported the rest of them to the entrance hall, calopes included.

After a shocked moment, Solanji and Muntra rushed up the stairs to the healerie, leaving Vinial to manage the animals. The healers were gathered around the beds where Bailey still knelt over Felather, and Kerris was talking very, very fast.

Instructions flew back and forth. Blankets already warmed by the fire were wrapped around them, and hot rocks were placed at their feet to try and defrost them.

A bag of blood was connected to one of Felather's arms, and a bag of fluids to the other. The healers couldn't find any injuries on Bailey except for the contusion on his head, so they just connected the fluids and concentrated on warming him up.

"The cold slowed the bleeding, but we need to remove

the blade," one of the healer's said. "The wound is infected; the blade's been wedged in his back for too long." The healer met Solanji's gaze. "This is going to be extremely painful."

"For both of them," a melodic voice said as an unfamiliar cherub appeared in the healerie. His golden wings fluttered as he hovered in the doorway. He looked just as young as Sero had, though his curls were a more burnished red-gold. "Bailey is keeping Felather alive. He is using personification, a very rare ability which allows you to control another's actions. In this case, he is breathing for Felather, but he is in so deep that his life is now connected to Felather's.

"What Felather feels, he will feel. I doubt his blocking skills are up to that. If we lose Felather, we lose Bailey as well. Their lives are linked, and we can't unlink them until they are both conscious."

"And we can't force Bailey into unconsciousness because Felather will stop breathing," Kerris murmured.

"Unfortunately, that is so," the cherub replied. He flew closer and dropped onto the chair next to the bed. "My name is Tevo. I was a friend of Sero's." His lips tightened for a moment. "I can't block Felather's pain, because I'll get sucked into this"—he waved his hand at them—"connection, and then you'll have three lives at risk."

"So, Bailey will suffer what Felather suffers?" Muntra asked.

"I'm afraid so if he isn't blocking. Until we revive Bailey's body, I can't help him return to it." Tevo scowled at Bailey. "Idiot boy. Why do they always have to do it the hard way?"

Solanji gave him a grim smile. "Because they care." She rubbed her temple. "Is there anything at all we can do to alleviate some of the pain?"

"Whatever you can get them to swallow, but that probably won't help much."

"How did you get here?" Solanji asked.

"The Oblivion Gate spoke to the citadel, who spoke to Amaridin, etcetera." Tevo waved his hand. "And here I am."

"Shandra was with Sero when he died," Solanji said. "He gave her some of his memories to give to Bailey. Would that help Bailey get out of…" Solanji pointed her finger at Felather and Bailey.

Tevo shook his head. "Bailey needs to be conscious, but that is good news that not all of Sero's knowledge has been lost. He was our elder, the most knowledgeable cherub in the citadel. You can't imagine what losing him means." Tevo blinked away tears.

Clearing his throat, he scowled at them. "There's far too many people here. I think you should leave. All except you." Tevo pointed at Kerris. "You can see what is happening here. You'll need to help us unravel them."

Solanji was surprised to find herself and Muntra on the other side of the healerie door. She ran her hand through her hair. "We'll wait in Mav's study. Oji will keep me informed." She led the way up the stairs to join Shandra.

***

Mav's shadows were still connected to Kaenera, and wherever he went, Mav followed.

Mav appeared in the middle of the battle of Doveton.

He ducked as Xylvin roared overhead and breathed a swathe of flames into the dybbuks.

Kaenera shrieked in fury, his eyes wide as he realised his dybbuks were surrounded and the Heavenly Host were grinding them to dust. The buildings were on fire, and thick smoke filled the air, making visibility poor, but the Heavenly Host were relentless.

"There's nowhere to run!" Mav shouted, and Kaenera

spun and disappeared. Mav followed, and they appeared in the abandoned mine. It was deserted, the cell was door open, and the prisoners were gone.

"How?" Kaenera snarled.

"I took a lesson from you," Mav said with a grin. "Distractions are such a useful tool."

"No!" Kaenera howled and disappeared again. Each jump was taking its toll. Mav knew Kaenera wouldn't be able to keep this up.

They appeared back at the Crossroads. The Oblivion Gate was now visible to the east, its tall stone towers reaching for the clouds, the connecting walkways gleaming in the weak light. Kaenera screamed at his dybbuks, and they swarmed around him. The balance of the fight undulated as the dybbuks retreated.

Mav advanced on Kaenera. "There is nowhere you can go that I will not follow," he said, allowing his aura to roam free.

The dybbuks swayed and took a step back, and then they charged towards Mav. He raised his hand and brushed them away. His anger fuelled his shadows, and they were implacable.

He summoned Wenson; it was time to end this.

More dybbuks rushed him, and Julius stepped in front of him, swinging his sword.

Wenson appeared in the middle of the mayhem, and he shrieked as he ducked a flailing blade and then scrabbled back towards Mav.

"Master Demavrian! Please don't get me killed."

"Apologies, Wenson. It's a bit chaotic."

"A bit! Why am I here?"

"I need you to draw Kaenera towards the tavern. I need to separate him from his men."

Wenson scowled at him as he hugged a box in his arms. "Then why didn't you make me appear over there?"

"Because he wouldn't have seen you and as he's watching me, he's seen you now, so off you go." Mav waved him away.

Wenson straightened and then said, "We will be having words, Master Demavrian."

"I'm quaking in my boots already. If I survive this, I will gladly have words with you."

"Then I expect you to survive, sir." Wenson stalked out of the melee and made his way towards the skeleton of the tavern. He had barely reached the shelter of the tavern porch when Kaenera appeared beside him.

"Wenson, well done." Kaenera's voice was a purr, and yet Mav still heard him over the noise of the ongoing battle. As Kaenera went to seize the box, Mav extended his shadows, wrapped them around Wenson and Kaenera, and they all disappeared.

"*Oji, open the Main Gate!*" Mav yelled, as he transported himself, Wenson, and a distracted Kaenera through the slowly opening doors.

Wenson landed with a thud and without breaking his stride, stomped forward into the darkness and placed the chest of sigils on the floor.

Kaenera chased after him. "Wenson, where are you going? Give those to me."

"They are all yours," Wenson replied and stepped back.

Mav's stomach dropped; this was not part of the plan. "No, Wenson! What are you doing?"

"You should stand back, Master Demavrian. This could get a little noisy."

Kaenera knelt beside the box, oblivious to the fact that his robes were beginning to disintegrate and fade away. He scrabbled at the fastenings and opened the lid. A sullen red glow illuminated his face, and he reached inside.

"Get further back, Master Demavrian," Wenson said, pushing Mav backwards. How had he moved so fast?

"What have you done?" Mav whispered. "That box was supposed to be empty."

"What we set out to do," Wenson replied, still pushing a reluctant Mav back. "Please, Master Demavrian, you need to be out of the blast zone. You must get out."

"Blast zone?" He stopped resisting and let Wenson push him back. His shadows writhed, reaching for Wenson, pulling him with Mav.

Mav stiffened as Kaenera lifted out a glowing bar. Kaenera's expression was one of awe until he noticed his fingers beginning to disintegrate. He spread his other hand in shock and watched his fingertips disappear one by one. Grabbing a second sigil, he lurched to his feet.

Mav's shadows wrapped themselves around him so tight he could barely breathe. Wenson's form began to thin and waver, expanding to form a shield around Mav.

Kaenera spun, registering where he was. He had been so intent on the sigils that he hadn't noticed.

"No!" Kaenera wailed. "I won't go alone! You'll be coming with me." He smashed the two sigils together and disappeared in a brilliant explosion that rocked the Oblivion Gate and lit the swirling grey mist with an eerie red glow. Wenson tried to shield Mav, but the compression blast flung them both into the tall doors, which Oji had closed again.

Stunned, Mav slid to the ground. Grit bit into his cheek as he tried to assess his injuries. Everything hurt. He couldn't tell if he had broken every bone in his body or if he was a pulped mess on the ground. All he registered was a burning agony consuming him, and he was grateful when his greying vision consumed him and he lost consciousness.

The Oblivion Gate rocked as an explosion rumbled through the building. Crockery smashed to the floor. Somewhere glass shattered, and Solanji gripped the end of Mav's desk with both hands.

"What was that?" Shandra asked as she clutched Muntra. She gathered the papers that had fallen to ground and placed them back on the desk.

"Oji?" Solanji called as Ellaria appeared beside her. "Where is Mav?"

"Master Demavrian is on the other side of the Gate. He will return shortly. Kaenera has been passed through the gate and is no more."

Solanji's stomach dropped and heart rate sped up. An internal monologue of "Oh, god, no. Oh, God, no" began running in her mind. She licked dry lips and forced the words out. "And why is Demavrian within the Gate?"

"He had to transport Kaenera there. The Aeora sigils exploded and are also no more. If you could excuse me a moment, I need to check on him." Oji's voice cut off.

"What? And Mav was in the vicinity? Is he alright? Oji! Is Mav alive?" Solanji reached for Mav but found nothing. When she looked at Kiara and Shandra, they were both just as horrified.

"I can't reach him," Shandra said.

"I'll go and check the Gate." Kiara winked out of view.

"I'll kill him if he's done something stupid."

"Oji said he would be back soon," Shandra said trying to be positive. "And Kaenera is gone. That's a relief."

The building trembled again as it settled, and everything solidified, becoming just a little bit sharper. Solanji moved over to the window to check where they were. "I think we're on the other side of the Crossroads."

Oji's voice came from the ceiling. "There are injured, and we have healers."

"Who are looking after Felather and Bailey," Shandra snapped.

"We have enough healers to spare one. Felather is being stabilised, and I've just let Adriz enter, so she is with him. Tevo is trying to help Bailey, though I'm not sure I understand what is happening. I need to wake Mav up. They need him. If you'll excuse me."

"Wake Mav up?" Solanji repeated, her stomach churning. "Oji, tell me exactly what has happened to Demavrian."

Why had he allowed the sigils to be used? Bile rose at the thought that Mav could have been killed. "Oji? Is Mav alive?" Solanji demanded. It would be a wonder if he hadn't died. They would be having a discussion about acceptable risks.

Oji was silent for a moment, and then he said, "Mav is fine, just not awake. Although we shielded him as best we could, he has gone deeper into Oblivion. I'm having trouble reaching him right now, but I assure you he will return soon. Please don't worry."

"Don't worry?" Solanji screeched, and Ellaria hissed as she extended her wings.

"We have other things to concern us," Oji said. "Julius is at the door. Could you greet him for me? Shandra, could you help Kerris set up the triage for the injured? He has selected the rooms and the equipment he needs."

Shandra patted the fuming Solanji on the shoulder. "What about Kaenera's men? Are there any injured we need to help?"

"No," Oji said quietly. "With Kaenera's death, there is nothing to hold them here. They have all passed on."

"Is Mav injured? You said he was unconscious? Was he hurt by the blast?" Solanji asked as she walked through the halls to the main entrance.

"I'm sorry, Solanji," Oji said, his voice tense, "but I

wasn't able to completely shield him from the explosion. It's just taking him a little longer to wake up. But I swear he's alive."

"Mav promised no more risks," Solanji said as she ran her fingers through her curls. "What was he thinking? Oji, you tell us the minute Mav wakes up."

"Of course, Solanji."

Solanji wasn't sure if Oji was contrite or worried. Neither reassured her.

Oji opened the tall doors, and Solanji walked out and observed the remains of the battle. It was eerily quiet. A few groans drifted in the air as Julius's men helped their injured colleagues to a clearing on one side.

Solanji inspected the area. There were not as many crumpled bodies lying on the ground as she had expected, though swords and axes were littered all around.

By nightfall, Solanji knew most of the weapons would be gone if Julius didn't clear them away. She was quite sure the audience stuck in the tavern would find a use for them, one that Mav might have to deal with later.

Julius stared up at the building with wide eyes, his hand still extended as if to knock, but frozen in place, his jaw hanging.

"Captain Teravin? Julius? Are you alright?" Solanji asked.

Julius let his hand fall and closed his mouth. "It's not every day that you see a huge building appear out of thin air," he said faintly. He waved his hand at the entrance. "Mav explained, but seeing it yourself is a different matter. Even the sight of a dragon wrapped around a fountain is more normal."

Solanji laughed, and some of the tension in her chest eased.

"Kerris has set up a triage in the halls. Bring the injured inside; the healers will help them."

Julius nodded and started issuing commands. "You heard her. Take the casualties inside." His men helped the walking wounded to their feet. One of the healers came out of the building and began checking those who couldn't rise.

"Julius, could you make sure all the weapons are collected and stored in the Gate," Solanji said. "I don't think we want that many flooding the nearby villages,"

Julius scanned the battlefield and grimaced. "It was weird. Those dybbuks just going up in puffs of smoke or whatever it was. I've never fought a battle like it."

"The weapons?"

"I'll deal with it."

Solanji watched the fallen being lined up along the side of one wall and exhaled. They would call Amaridin later, once they knew all of their own were safe.

60

___

KERRIS – OBLIVION GATE

Whatever Bailey was doing was beyond Kerris' comprehension. It shouldn't be possible. To his normal sight, Bailey's hands rested on Felather's chest, but Kerris could "see" that his hands actually cupped Felather's heart and gently squeezed it in a regular rhythm, which, he realised with a sinking feeling, matched Bailey's own heartbeat.

The cherub was right. Bailey was using his own heart to help keep Felather's beating, and just watching him was exhausting.

Kerris moved closer, squinting as he followed their lines of connection. There was something else Bailey was doing, but he couldn't figure it out. "This shouldn't be possible," he muttered.

"No, it shouldn't," Tevo replied from beside him. "I've never seen a personification so..." He twirled his fingers, struggling to encapsulate what he wanted to say. "So deep," he finished.

"He's matched Felather's heart rate to his own, but there's something else going on."

"You can see it?" Tevo asked.

"Bailey's hands are inside his chest, but there is a shadowy connection between them, a sharing of some sort, maybe?" Kerris frowned. "Would Felather know what Bailey is doing?"

Tevo shrugged. "Difficult to know, but from his condition, I doubt it."

Inspecting Felather, Kerris winced. Felather's whole body burned with infection, a virulent orange that was streaked with flashes of red pain. Muscles protested, nerve endings shrieked, and he had no defence. Exhaustion was draining him. Only Bailey's transfer of… Kerris stiffened. Bailey was sustaining him with his shadowsoul.

Calming green infusions from the healers tried to sooth the raging battle within Felather but they were not enough.

Adriz hovered behind the healers, her face pale and strained. Kerris knew she was torn between supporting Felather and getting in the way.

Bailey was feeding his shadows into Felather to the detriment of his own life. Shadows swirled around Bailey's body and flowed down his arms and into Felather. The shadowy connection thickened as Kerris watched.

Kerris grabbed the arm of the healer next to him. "Can you sustain Felather if we separate them?"

"We are trying to stabilise him, but the infection is well ingrained."

"Bailey is dying. He can't keep Felather alive much longer."

Tevo frowned at him. "What can you see?"

"Nothing good. How do we separate them?"

"We need to get Bailey to respond to us."

Kerris carefully gripped Bailey's shoulder. *"Bailey? You need to stop now. The healers are here."*

Bailey didn't respond.

"How do we wake him?" Kerris asked, desperation churning in his stomach. *"Felather? Can you hear me? You need to tell Bailey to stop. He's killing himself to keep you alive. The healers are here now."*

Kerris wasn't sure if he imagined the brief stutter in the flow of shadows, but a moment later, Bailey whimpered.

"Bailey?"

"No," Bailey whispered.

"The healers are here, Bailey. You can stop now."

Bailey's eyelashes fluttered.

"Tell him to think about his own body," Tevo said. "If his heart fails, he'll kill Felather."

"Bailey? You have done really well, but the healers need to take over now. You are draining yourself to the point where your own body will fail, and then Felather will die. You need to let go so the healers can work on Felather."

"I can't," Bailey said, his voice a shaking whisper.

"You can," Tevo said, infusing calm authority in his voice. "Imagine you are releasing a bird into the air. Flex your fingers and release."

Bailey shuddered, and the flow of shadows slowed. The healer's infusions increased, a veritable tidal wave swamping the sullen glow that was Felather. Bailey fell back with a gasp, and Kerris lurched forward to catch him.

"I've got you. You're safe now," Kerris murmured over and over as he hugged Bailey tight.

The healers swarmed around Felather, and Kerris carried Bailey to the next bed. Bailey wouldn't release him, and he shook so violently that Kerris sat in the chair instead and continued to hold him, murmuring constant reassurance and feeding him tendrils of his own shadowy healing power.

Tevo dropped a blanket over them and tucked it around Bailey. When Bailey didn't stop shaking, he found another one and tucked that around them, too. He patted Bailey on the shoulder and crooned under his breath, his worry a tangible presence.

Kerris concentrated on soothing Bailey, trying to ignore the increasingly frantic healer's voices.

61

SOLANJI – OBLIVION GATE

As the days passed after the confrontation with Kaenera and there was no word from Mav, Solanji's despair increased. Oji became alarmingly quiet and would only say Mav was sleeping.

Solanji found solace sitting in the library, staring at the oil painting of Demavrian and Athenia.

She was often accompanied by one or other of the oathsworn, or Julius on occasion. They had stopped trying to get her to leave or give her false hope.

She had tried to go through the Gate, but neither Oji nor Kiara would open it for her, no matter how much she shouted at them. The small rose gate had disappeared, as if Oji knew she would try and sneak through it when he wasn't looking.

Solanji was glad she had been banned from the healerie. From the sight of Tevo's ashen face when he joined her for dinner, treating Felather's injuries hadn't been pleasant. After that, it had taken a week for Tevo to help Bailey truly untangle himself from Felather.

Felather's progress was slow and concerning. Removing

the metal blade had sapped what little of his strength had remained, and he was existing but not improving. The healers' said he had overstrained his heart and it would be a long and slow recovery, if he even recovered. Only time would tell if his body would regain enough strength to function and fight off the infection.

Bailey was confused and having trouble sleeping. He kept thinking he was Felather, as Felather's psyche had tangled with his own. Every time he slept, he woke up screaming. Tevo recommended that they did not add Sero's memories just yet. It would only confuse Bailey further.

Unsurprisingly, the healers insisted on keeping them both in the healerie. Adriz held Felather's hand and read books to him while he slept, and Muntra was at his wit's end, trying to remind Bailey who he really was.

The Oblivion Gate was heaving with people, staff, guards, and oathsworn, but the one person who held them all together was missing. "You promised me," Solanji whispered as she stared at the painting. "You promised me you wouldn't leave me."

While looking at the painting, she had a sense that Mav was in the room with her. When she had said that out loud, the only person who didn't look at her with concern was Julius. He said the same thing about Athenia.

The painter had caught their likenesses extremely well. Demavrian's amber eyes glinted with life and intention. His youthful air of confidence dominated the image as if there was nothing in the world he could not overcome.

Tears gathered as her throat tightened. Could he really survive the Aeora sigils exploding? The sigils were capable of destroying a planet, of killing gods. Why would Mav be able to survive that? Oji wouldn't say, only that he was asleep, and Oji couldn't wake him.

Asleep, unconscious, or dead?

The library was quiet, a reminder that they had lost Wenson as well as Mav. A very subdued Oji had told her he had died defending Mav. The grumpy wraith was missed, even though they hadn't known him that long.

Solanji tilted her head as she inspected the painting once again. Athenia extended her hand towards Mav, a slight smile on her face as if she knew something they didn't. She was an exquisite young woman. Her strawberry blonde hair fell around her shoulders like rivulets of liquid gold, but her expression was sad as she reached for him.

Her robes were that of an archangel, rich and golden. Mav wore the regalia of an Archdeus general. He looked so youthful. It was painful to realise how much he had aged. Solanji frowned. He was Deus now, a god. Why hadn't he removed the signs of ageing?

Solanji rubbed her eyes; maybe it was time to sleep. But she hated going to an empty bedchamber. She now understood why Julius had been driven to chase Mav for all those years. You needed something to fill the void inside you.

Searching for Mav, catching his beloved's killer, had been the only thing that had kept Julius sane and given him a purpose. As soon as he had found out his mistake, he had hit the bottle, trying to drink himself into oblivion.

Solanji shuddered. It was a slippery slope she could find herself on if she wasn't careful.

Her gaze was drawn back to the painting. She rose and walked closer, narrowing her eyes as she peered up at Mav. Was he wearing two vendetta stones around his neck? The cords were partially disguised by the fur collar of the cloak he wore. That wasn't possible. This painting had been commissioned centuries before Athenia's death.

She reached up to touch the frame, and a vibration rippled through her. "Athenia?" she whispered. Her stomach roiled. Had she been in the painting all this time? Sheltering with the man who had tried and failed to save her life?

Solanji dragged the table closer and then, with some difficulty, heaved a sturdy chair on top of it.

"Ellaria?" she screamed silently as she climbed on the table and then onto the chair. She peered at the painting. They were vendetta stones, one red and one blue!

Solanji looked more closely at Athenia. Her expression wasn't joyful; it was sad. She was sure it had been joyful the first time she had seen it. Athenia's gaze pierced Solanji. Her vivid blue eyes gleamed as if covered in a film of tears. Who was she crying for?

Ellaria appeared in the library, her wings flapping in concern. *"Solanji! What are you doing?"*

"Look. Look at the painting!" Solanji said.

"Solanji! Be careful!" Tevo said as he flew into the room, closely followed by Julius and Adriz.

"Solanji, get down now before you do yourself an injury." Adriz's voice was sharp with fear, and Solanji felt a moment's guilt for adding to the burden of concern weighing her down.

"Look at the painting. Mav is wearing the vendetta stones, but this painting was painted years before Athenia died." Solanji cringed. "Sorry, Julius."

Julius waved away her apology. "Doesn't mean you should try and die, too," he said.

"No, don't you see? This painting has changed since it was first painted."

Tevo fluttered up beside her and peered closely at the canvas. "She's right. He's wearing the vendetta stones."

"And Athenia looks sad. She was joyful the first time I saw this in the citadel library. I remember how vibrant and full of life she was and how young Mav looked."

"If you get down, I'll see if I can retrieve the memories," Tevo said.

"I think Athenia's soul is in the painting. I think this is where she has been sheltering all these years. You need to be careful, Tevo. We don't know what you'll find, and we can't afford to lose you, too."

"Dear child, I could say the same for you," Tevo said. "Now, get down,"

Julius climbed up onto the table and helped Solanji down from the chair.

Adriz assisted her to the floor and hugged her tight. "Please don't scare me like that. I can't take any more," she said into Solanji's hair.

Solanji hugged her back. "I'm sorry. I didn't mean to worry you."

Julius remained on the table, staring at the painting. His fingers hovered over the surface as he reached towards Athenia.

Tevo fluttered beside him. "Her expression is different," he murmured.

"How did I not notice?" Julius asked. "How could I not know?"

Tevo patted his shoulder. "I don't think finding Athenia here was something anyone would have considered until Solanji suggested it."

"Could she really be in the painting?" Julius asked.

Tevo laid his fingertips on the canvas over Athenia's heart and he froze, his tiny golden wings stopped fluttering and as he dropped, Julius lunged for him.

"Tevo!" Solanji screamed and both she and Adriz dived forward in an attempt to catch him.

Ellaria swooped in, and grabbed Tevo in her claws, and lowered him to the ground.

Solanji cupped Tevo's cheek as she bent over him, striving to control her fear. Mav had said a cherub would be battered by their emotions as well as the memories he was dealing with. "Tevo?" she whispered. She was so glad the little cherub had chosen to stay in the Gate and help Bailey. When he had been told about Sero's death, Bailey had withdrawn and gone silent. Since then, Tevo was the only person who seemed to be able to reach him. It was quite possible that they had all substituted him for Sero. They all missed the little cherub so much.

Tevo's lashes fluttered, and his eyelids moved as he processed all the memories. Then he exhaled, long and deep. He opened his eyes and gazed up at Solanji. "You were right," he said.

"About what?" Solanji asked.

"Athenia is in the painting, but I don't think she is ready to come out."

"Why not?"

"Because Deus Demavrian has the vendetta stone, and that is what will release her."

"Does she have to leave?" Julius asked, his gaze once more focused on the painting.

Solanji's heart ached for him. "Julius, I am so sorry, but Athenia did die. If she chose to stay, it would be a half-life, not real; it would not be the same." She didn't think that would help him move on.

Julius' glare cut through her. "If it was Mav, would you say the same?"

Solanji flinched, and Adriz hugged her tight. "We are not doing this," Adriz snapped. "Mav is not dead, and it will be Athenia's choice if she stays or goes, so don't be an idiot and decide for her."

Julius flushed and looked at his feet. "I'm sorry. That was uncalled for."

"No, Julius, you are right," Solanji said. It is not so easy to let go, when there is the possibility of holding on."

Tevo sat up. "Alright, enough maudlin talk. I need a drink."

"What about Athenia?" Julius asked.

"She's not coming out today," Tevo said, "so we all may as well go get a drink. I'm sure Deus Demavrian has a nice basinthe that has my name on it."

Ellaria picked the little cherub up in her claws and disappeared.

Solanji stared at the empty space. "I guess Ellaria agreed with him," she said with a small smile.

62

DEMAVRIAN

Mav slowly regained consciousness. He wasn't sure he wanted to as pain flowed down his limbs. His joints ached, deep in the bone as his body started waking. He rolled on to his back with a groan. Sharp-edged pebbles poked into his skin, and he levered himself up on his elbow and opened his eyes.

Inky-black water lapped on the pebbly beach. He was surprised at how stale the air smelt; the air lacked the sharp tang of minerals and water. Grey stones, leached of colour, lined the river, which curved away. There was nothing else, just darkness lit by the eerie glow coming from the stones.

A wooden row boat appeared on the water, and a shadowy form stood in it. "Really? Is this how you see death?" The voice was empty, devoid of expression.

Mav stared at the image until it faded. Was he dead, or was he hallucinating? Mav rubbed his temple. At least he felt solid.

"Oji?"

There was no answer, only a deep, velvety silence that said he was all alone.

He drifted, just existing as his mind tried to wrap itself around what had happened. What had he been doing?

Mav sat up, and his empty surroundings morphed into his library at the Gate. He was seated in a comfortable armchair with a book on his lap. A crystal glass of basinthe sat on the small side table, and a lot of darkness still surrounded him. He picked up the glass and sipped the amber liquid. Smooth deliciousness slid down his throat and warmed his innards.

"Am I dead?" he mused. "I should be dead." Remembering Kaenera exploding the sigils, he patted himself down again, but he seemed whole. When he lifted his hand, he froze. He could see straight through it. Was he a wraith, then? Lingering because he didn't want to leave his family?

He rotated his hand, and it solidified again. Back and forth, he rotated his hand, mesmerised as his body faded and returned. Could he be half-dead? Was he a dybbuk?

Had he succeeded in destroying Kaenera? And also himself? He had underestimated how lost he would feel; it was much worse than losing his soul. He owed Kiara an apology—he had left her to overcome her emotional chaos on her own.

Something warm was leaning against his leg, and he dropped his hand to his side and felt soft, velvety fur. He forced himself to look down and met the doe-soft eyes of a black vemlow, which was looking up at him in absolute adoration.

The vemlow was warm, soft, alive! As was he, he realised. His skin was warm. He had a pulse. He lived!

Where was he? He didn't remember how he'd got here.

A vague conversation with a semblance of death drifted through his mind. No, *he* was death. Wasn't he? He stiffened. Maybe he was just going mad. He knew Kaenera had died, even though he had never passed through Mav. There had been no need; he was already within the Oblivion Gate. So how was Mav still alive when the sigils could destroy gods?

Memory slowly returned. *Wenson* had protected him. But Wenson was a wraith, wasn't he? But if he was a wraith, he should have passed over straightaway. So, what was he? How had he been able to enter the Gate with Mav and keep his form?

"Oji?" Mav said out loud.

Silence.

Mav had entered the Gate with the intention of protecting his family, of sacrificing himself for them. His shadows had protected him. He remembered them swirling around him, as had Wenson. Was Wenson part of Oji? An extension or some other form of the Gate? Because Oji hadn't been with him. Once he'd passed through the Gate, Mav was the keeper, not Oji.

Kaenera had intended to maim and destroy. He'd had no thought of protecting himself or others. He'd had no protection against the destruction he had wrought.

Anguish roiled through Mav, and he clutched the vemlow. The warmth of the vemlow's body was comforting, the only thing holding him there. Had the Gate and all his family been destroyed? Had he failed them?

A faint echo caught his attention. He strained to hear what it was saying, but it was too muffled.

He stroked the vemlow, still surprised to feel its soft fur, the warmth of its body. If he was dead… No, that wasn't right. He wouldn't be able to feel things if he were dead. But if he was death, then what did that mean?

He was the Keeper of the Shadows. Yes, that felt right.

He was a wraith; he was comprised of shadows. That was true as well.

He was the Oblivion Gate.

He was the Gate Keeper.

He was an Angel of Death.

He was also a god. He had one foot in the living world and one foot in the shadows.

He was heartsworn to Solanji and oathsworn to many people depending on him.

He was many things, and not all of them were in the shadows.

Surrounded by absolute darkness, Mav waved his hand and met more nothing. The atmosphere was heavy and weighted, and he felt a sense of expectation. Something was waiting. Who or what, he didn't know.

Closing his eyes, he listened intently, straining to hear the slightest movement. There was nothing, no movement, no sound, no sensations.

He started walking, his senses questing. The vemlow trotted beside him.

Kaenera had offered his people no peace at the end of their lives, just an infinite cessation of being.

His heart rate jumping, Mav stopped walking as he realised there was no bond; he couldn't feel Solanji, or Ellaria or his oathsworn. Was this Oblivion? Absolute absence of anything? No light? No air? Nothing?

Wenson had been telling the truth when he'd said there was nothing behind the Gate. Mav would have to take his words more literally in the future. He hesitated—that is, if Wenson had survived and Mav had a future.

He started walking again.

Did it have to be nothing? he wondered.

Imagining blades of soft blue grass sprouting in freshly turned soil, and a sturdy, magenta leaved tree, he sat and leaned back against the trunk. He wriggled to get comfortable and opened his eyes. A soft white glow surrounded him, illuminating the grass, him, and the tree. He threaded his fingers through the soft blades of grass, smiling as they joyfully tickled his palm.

The smile felt strange on his cheeks as if he hadn't smiled in a while. He supposed he hadn't, as he'd been riddled with guilt at his failure to protect his people, his fledglings. Failure to redeem anyone ripped through him and clawed at his intestines, weighing him down. No, it wasn't the guilt weighing him down; it was all the pieces of shadows he had collected.

Staring up at the impossible leaves, he observed the spirals of shimmering pink fronds. Mav sorted through his shadows and selected a small strand of matter. Was this what it came down to? One dark shadow to represent a whole person's life? He held it between his fingers and then closed his eyes.

Images flashed through his mind, a person's whole life in a matter of moments: their joys, their regrets, their loves and losses, their demise. It sat heavy in his mind, a miasma of misery that would drown him if he let it.

"What is it you want?" he asked.

For it all to end so I can rest in peace.

Mav considered this for a moment, and as his glow extended, a mountain range appeared to his left, majestic peaks of grey stone rising towards a pale green sky. He gazed at it and then planted a slender silver pine tree on the sloping flank of the nearest valley. He nestled the shadow within its roots and selected the next shadowy strand.

After a life full of happiness and regrets had flashed before him, he asked, "What is your final wish?"

To run free and never be caged again.

A grey and purple striped rabbit jumped over his legs and stared at him inquisitively with large black eyes. Its nose twitched. Mav tucked the strand of shadow inside. "Go play," he said and smiled as a gentle snore drifted down the slope from the pine tree.

He pulled out another shadow. He had been collecting these last requests since he had entered Eidolon. For centuries, Kaenera had been ignoring them, so they had gravitated to him instead, and he had unknowingly welcomed them in.

Another request: *Let me die and end this agony.* Mav transformed it into a golden pebble and gently laid it on the beach next to the iridescent waters of the river now meandering across the plain.

A harsh request made him falter. *Leave me be. I want nothing from you.* Mav released them, and the shadow dissipated in the soft breeze.

He continued until there was a forest of snoring trees, a plethora of excited creatures, banks of exotic flowers, and a graceful waterfall descending onto an iridescent lake filled with red-scaled fish with golden barbs trailing through the water. A new world.

Mav frowned and felt his face wrinkle. He touched his face, and fingers ran over smooth skin, threaded through soft hair. He existed. Therefore, he was. He patted his body, and he solidified under his fingers.

Sudden doubt rocked him. How? Shouldn't he be dead? Shouldn't the sigils have killed him as well? He leapt to his feet and spun around. Kaenera! Was he here as well? He tensed for another attack, but there was only silence. Except for that faint voice. Calling. Calling him? What was his name? Did he have a name?

The vemlow whined and pressed against his leg.

He was death. He existed. Therefore, he had a name. A purpose. He rested his hand on the vem's head, and it settled, leaning against him.

"Mav?"

Was that what the voice said?

"Demavrian? Please. Can you hear me? You need to wake up."

Was he asleep? Was this all a dream? Mav cleared his throat. "Who is that?" But his voice was rough and croaky as if he hadn't used it in a long time.

"Demavrian?"

The voice was getting louder and more insistent.

Was he Demavrian? "Yes?" he said.

"Oh, merciful lord. Mav? Are you alright? Are you hurt?"

"Who are you?"

"I'm Oji. Remember? The Oblivion Gate? You are my Gate Keeper."

Mav stepped back from the vemlow, and the voice fell silent. That's right; he was a gate keeper. He remembered the gate. He had passed through it with Kaenera and the sigils to protect his oathsworn.

He was death. A wraith. A god. Keeper of the Shadows. One foot on either side. He was one with the Gate. He was the Gate. The litany ran through his mind.

Solanji! His family! Memories flooded back, and his heart stuttered as he remembered Bailey's terror and Felather dying.

"Is Felather alive?"

There was no reply.

"Oji?" he said as me the vemlow pressed against him.

"Mav?"

"Oji? Is Solanji alright? And Felather and Bailey?"

"Solanji is well. She is mourning your absence. Felather and Bailey are not well; they are struggling to heal. They need you. You need to come back."

"Back?"

"Back to us. To me. To your home. Our family is waiting for you."

"I'm not sure I can. I…I'm not what I was."

"Of that I have no doubt," Oji said. "How could you be after what you have done? You survived the sigils, protected your family, and removed the threat. But it's time to return." His voice grew more persuasive. "Your oathsworn need you. I need you. You are missed."

"And Kaenera?"

"You passed him through the Gate."

"I did?"

"Yes, both him and Serenia. They are gone now."

Mav began walking again.

"It's time for you to return, Mav."

"I'm coming."

As Mav walked, the mist around him glowed and then began to dissipate. The vemlow trotted beside him, its tail wagging. Rolling plains of violet and blue grasses appeared out of the mist and spread out before him. A vibrant green sky arced overhead.

Oblivion was whatever he made it. Feeling much lighter, he walked through the peaceful landscape. The soft glow followed him, lighting his immediate surroundings and casting what was out of reach into the shadows, allowing them to slumber until he returned. All would rest in peace while he was its overseer.

The sudden need to share it with Solanji and Ellaria rippled through him. He reached for their bond and imagined his beautiful wife and her exquisite dragon at the end of it, and he embraced them, opening himself to their love and concern, which flowed back towards to him. Anything was possible here in Oblivion. It was his creation, his world.

Smiling, he thought of the small rose gate, and all the

buds bloomed; their soft perfume filled the air as the wrought-iron gates swung wide open. His Oblivion would not only be a final resting place but also a place for joy and celebration, and on that uplifting thought, he walked towards the archway.

63

DEMAVRIAN

av stumbled to a halt as he saw Felather approaching the rose gate. The faint glow around him brightened, revealing the path to the gate. He took a deep, steadying breath as his heart started to race. *Please, no*, he thought. *Not another one.*

"What do you think you are doing here?" Mav asked, trying to remain calm. His joy at discovering Oblivion was replaced by sheer terror. His chest tightened, and breathing became difficult.

"I'm tired, Mav." Felather came to a halt before him, and Mav inspected his face. Felather looked exhausted. Deep lines grooved his skin, his eyes were unfocused and blood-shot, and his shoulders drooped, but otherwise, he appeared uninjured. The healers must have healed his physical wounds; it was the mental exhaustion, the strain on his heart that had brought him here.

Guilt speared through Mav, almost bringing him to his knees. Felather deserved so much more from him. He should have been by Felather's side, encouraging him to live, not maundering through his memories and settling other folk.

No, that wasn't fair to the soulless, either. Everyone deserved to be heard in their final moments.

"Still, you should be knocking on the citadel door, not asking to go through the Gate."

"I think you may have influenced me over the years." Felather frowned. "No, it was Bailey. His shadows were sustaining me."

"Ah."

"You are my angel."

"And you are my scribe."

Felather shrugged. "I guess you gave me a shadow soul. However it happened, I had a choice, and I chose to come here."

"Have a seat," Mav said, settling on the onyx bench lining the hallway.

"Where do these benches come from? Normally, it's only the gate with the roses." Felather twisted his lips. "Though I know you hide it most of the time."

"The benches appear when needed. They are not always here, and I wouldn't want anyone to go through the Gate by mistake."

"I suppose not," Felather replied, stretching out his legs and sighing out a long breath.

"Do you remember the first day we met?" Mav asked.

Felather chucked. "Of course. How could I ever forget that? Adriz had you in a headlock, and you were so stubborn that you wouldn't surrender."

"If you hadn't wandered by with that bag of Dewberry Delights, I'd probably still be there. The scent of those sweets made my mouth water, and I suddenly realised I was starving."

"Adriz can be just as stubborn as you."

Mav cast Felather a glance. "Do you really think she'll let you leave her?"

Felather's face fell, and the lines on his face deepened as he dropped his chin to chest. "I am so tired, Mav. My mind is willing, but my body has had enough. Without Bailey helping me breathe, it's too draining. I don't have the strength to continue."

"Can't you last a little longer? I'm trying to find my way back."

"I don't think I can." Felather dropped his head in his hands, and Mav rubbed his back.

"I never meant to leave you to struggle on your own."

"You didn't. You took out Kaenera. It was never going to be easy."

"It wasn't me. It was Wenson. He brought the Aeora sigils through the Gate with us. I suppose it was a way of getting rid of them, but at such a huge risk. The whole Gate could have been vaporised."

Felather exhaled. "I've been lost for a while. I couldn't find you no matter how hard I searched."

"I'm here now, and you are not lost. Adriz is waiting for you, and the rest of the family has lost too much already. They won't survive losing you as well."

"They'll be fine when you return. It's you they are missing."

Mav shook his head. "You undervalue yourself." He leaned forward. "Which I would never do."

It was silent in the healerie. Too silent. Everyone was waiting, Adriz realised. Waiting for Felather to die. Adriz had been listening to Felather's tortured breathing for turns. It had stuttered on occasion and then resumed, slow and crackly.

They were waiting for him to stop breathing, for his body to fail him even if he didn't choose it.

Adriz stroked his hand, which was cold and still, and then lifted it to her lips and kissed it. She sent her love down their bond, but nothing came back.

Solanji sat on the other side of Felather's bed. There was always someone; it was like they took turns. All except Mav. It was excruciating, enduring their grief, their loss on top of her own. No matter how she willed it, she could not breathe for Felather.

Bailey had tried, almost to the detriment of his own health, and she would love him forever for trying.

She suddenly realised it truly *was* silent, and she lifted her head. No!

Adriz gripped Felather's shoulders and shook him. "Don't you dare. Felather, don't you dare leave me!"

Solanji stood and leaned over to feel Felather's neck, and Adriz batted her hand away. "Don't! He's not d-dead."

Solanji backed away, her eyes filling with tears.

Adriz ignored her. Pulling Felather into her arms, she began rocking him. "Sweetheart, please. There is something you don't know. You have to stay so I can tell you." She hid her face in his neck and tugged their bond. She inhaled the scent of his skin. It didn't smell like him, cool and impersonal, medicated. It was like he had already left.

"Adriz…" Solanji began.

"Don't say it," Adriz said, her voice muffled in Felather's neck. He lay limply in her arms, and tears welled as her heart broke. The pain made breathing difficult, and her breath stuttered. Her throat tightened, and tears stung her eyes.

She tightened her grip. It couldn't be true. Mav would never let him die. Would he? If only Mav were here. He could have saved him. If Averdeus had been here, he would have done something. Adriz screamed out her pain, her agony, her anger. She didn't care who heard her. Raw pain engulfed her, and she lifted her face and screamed in defiance. Her screams echoed back as if to taunt her. She wouldn't allow it. Felather was hers. He was supposed to live with her forever.

Demavrian rose from the bench and watched Felather as he jumped to his feet.

"Is this it, then?" Felather asked. "A last walk down memory lane and a quick goodbye?" He looked around. "Not what I was expecting."

Mav smiled at him. "You haven't passed through the Gate yet. Who's to say how you will perceive what is beyond."

Felather cocked an eyebrow and grinned. "You mean to say everyone's oblivion is different?"

Mav shrugged. "Depends on what you choose."

"That is so you." Felather laughed. "Always a choice."

"Usually," Mav agreed. "But on this occasion…I'm sorry, but I'm not ready to let you go through the gate."

"What?"

"Your request is denied."

Felather's jaw dropped, and he stood frozen in disbelief.

Mav chuckled and then punched Felather in the chest. Felather flew across the alcove, crashed onto his back and slid down the corridor into the halls of the Oblivion Gate.

In the healerie, Adriz exhaled and dropped her forehead onto Felather's chest. Her arms ached from holding him so tight, and her throat hurt with all the screaming, but nothing had changed except that she was exhausted. Her lashes were heavy with tears as she closed her eyes and existed for a moment in a world without Felather.

Her head bobbed as Felather's body jerked, and she stiffened as his chest rose and deflated under her cheek. She sat up, staring at him as he breathed.

She rested her hand on his chest and watched it rise and fall, felt the slow and steady thump of his heart beating beneath her fingers.

"Solanji? Are you seeing what I'm seeing?" she croaked. Her voice was worn out; only a gravelly whisper remained.

"Adriz, please—" Solanji's voice cut off abruptly. "Oh, my God," she whispered. "He's breathing."

Adriz leaned over Felather and gripped his shoulders. "Felather, don't you ever do that to me again."

Felather's lashes flickered open, and he stared at her. His eyes were glazed, and Adriz's heart clenched as she realised he couldn't see her. "He punched me," Felather whispered. His voice was so low she barely heard him.

"What was that, sweetheart?"

"Mav wouldn't let me through the gate."

Adriz flinched back and gazed at Solanji. "Mav wouldn't let him pass through the Gate."

Solanji leaned forward. "Felather? You said Mav wouldn't let you through? Where was he?"

"He said my request…was denied…and he punched me. Hurts." Felather's hand flopped as he tried to rub his chest.

"Adriz?" Solanji gasped, lurching to her feet.

"Go." Adriz stared at her, hope blooming in her chest. "Find him. Make sure you drag him back here."

64

DEMAVRIAN – OBLIVION GATE

S haking his hand out, Mav stepped into the hallway and reassimilated his body's physical mass. He paused for a moment, flexing his shoulders against the tension that tightened his muscles, the weight of substance that grounded him. His hand ached.

He rotated his wrist, and his skin looked normal. He exhaled in relief. At least on this side of the Gate, he wasn't a wraith, just the Oblivion Gate Keeper. When he passed through the Gate, he became a wraith, the Keeper of Shadows.

The vemlow barked, and he looked down. He could see through the animal. His fur was now a silver grey, and he was completely translucent. Mav's hand passed through him, and the vem barked again and then scampered back through the open gate. He would be waiting on the other side anytime Mav visited.

Weariness impinged on Mav's senses, and he suddenly wondered how long he'd been away. Glancing at his hands, he realised how useless they really were. His mind was much more powerful. He grinned ruefully; punching Felather had been more symbolic than necessary. Mav could have restarted his heart with a thought. He shivered. Or he could stop a heart just as easily.

A need to see Solanji surged through him, and as he reached for their bond, he tripped over a pile of blankets and bedrolls on the floor. His hand slapped the wall to keep him upright, and the stone shimmered, dissolving beneath his fingers. He snatched his hand back as he steadied. Curling his fingers, he stared at the mural infused into the wall. He didn't need a gate. He could find Oblivion whenever he wanted.

The mystical landscape rolled off into the mountain range in the distance, a burst of colour and unusual foliage. He smiled at the range of colours and shapes; they all blended beautifully. That was his vision of Oblivion.

Untangling his feet from the blankets, he headed down the corridor, reaching for Solanji and his oathsworn.

"Mav? Oh, my God, Mav? Where are you? Where have you been? Are you alright? Oh, my God. Oh, my God."

"Breathe Solanji. Asphyxiating won't help you get to him any faster!" Ellaria said as she materialised beside Mav with a wriggling Solanji in her claws.

Ellaria released her, and Solanji shot into his arms, almost bowling him over. He grabbed the doorframe next to him and held on. Pulling Solanji closer, he returned her frantic kiss. He deepened the kiss, aware she was patting his body as if she wasn't sure he was real, and then she cinched her arms around his waist. He clasped her tighter in return. Had he really been gone for a long time? He would have to be very careful about time spent in Oblivion.

When Solanji finally released him, she peppered him with questions. "Are you alright? Where have you been? It's been weeks! Oji said he couldn't wake you."

"I couldn't," Oji said. "Welcome home, Gate Keeper. We are very relieved to have you back."

"Understatement," Solanji muttered under breath, and Mav squeezed her tight.

"Thank you, Oji. I'll explain all, or as much as I can, once you tell me where we are and how everyone is." Entwining his fingers with Solanji's, Mav tugged her towards the healerie. "I think I need a chat with Felather."

"Oh, Mav. Did you really deny him entry?" Her breath caught. "He died in her arms. Adriz was distraught."

Tears rose, and recent grief tinged their bond. Mav hugged her to his side. "So, he remembered our conversation?"

"I don't know. When he said that you had refused to let him through the Gate, I came running and left him with Adriz."

"How is everyone?"

"We're all fine except for Felather and Bailey. You know about Felather, and Bailey is confused. He got all tangled up with Felather, and he can't find himself. He won't sleep; he's afraid he won't wake up again. Everyone else is fine and around somewhere. We found Athenia's soul, but she won't speak to us; we're hoping you'll be able to coax her out. We relocated back to the coast because it was too busy at the Crossroads, and we got fed up of being gawped at."

Mav tried to assimilate everything she was saying, but Solanji ploughed on.

"We were planning on taking Bailey outside tomorrow. The fresh air will do him good. Most of Julius's men have recovered. A few linger in the healerie." Solanji paused and shrugged. "Xylvin likes swimming, and we like the sea."

Kerris' voice came from a nearby room, and Mav changed direction. He was grappling with the fact that

Solanji had found Athenia when he paused in the doorway. Mav frowned at the sight of Kerris lying on a table and Kiara hovering over him with a dagger in her hand.

"Wait," Kerris held his hand up. "What if I go to Solanji instead, and she gives me my soul back? Then, if I enter the Gate, I'll be able to come back, won't I?"

"If we could do that, Solanji would already have gone looking." Kiara rolled her eyes and shook the knife at him. "You are the one who convinced me to do this. I am fast changing my mind; if all you can come up with are excuses not to go through the Gate, then I think you shouldn't go."

"You shouldn't," Mav said, "but you would be very welcome should your time ever come."

Kiara spun, almost slitting Kerris' throat, and he shrieked as he fell off the table.

He bounced up off the floor, frantically checking his throat and was visibly relieved when his fingers came away blood-free.

"Where have you been?" Kiara bounded into his arms and hugged him tight. "You've been gone so long we thought Kaenera had managed to find a way to kill you. Solanji is a mess. You are in so much trouble!"

"Solanji is right here, and I'm fine," Solanji said dryly.

Mav kissed the top of Kiara's head as he hugged her back. "Maybe you should put the knife down. I thought I said no playing with pointy, sharp-edged things?"

Kiara blushed and sheathed the dagger in her belt. "It's Kerris' fault. He was trying to find you."

Raising an eyebrow, Mav tilted his head towards Kerris. "And why did you feel the need to sacrifice yourself on a proverbial altar to find me?"

Kerris pushed Kiara out of the way and buried his face in Mav's chest as he hugged him. "We thought we'd lost you." His voice was muffled, and Mav rocked him gently as he realised the dampness on his skin was Kerris' tears.

Holding him close, Mav murmured apologies in his ear. "I didn't realise I was away for so long. Time is deceptive behind the Gate; I thought it was just a day or so."

"A day or two!" Shandra exclaimed from behind them as she skidded into the room, closely followed by Ryvalin. "We've all been so worried."

Mav cringed as he met Ryvalin's indignant gaze. He would be explaining for the rest of his life. "I am sorry, but Kaenera used the sigils, and they exploded. It took a bit longer than I realised to recover from that."

"He did what?" Ryvalin's exclamation was drowned out by Shandra's: "Thank goodness you are alright!" And Solanji's: "Mav, you could have died! What were you thinking?"

Everyone spoke at once, and Mav let them vent.

Their obvious concern for him, the love that poured down their bonds, melted the remaining sense of isolation and loss. He relaxed as he realised that he was home with his family and the threat that had been hanging over them all was finally gone.

"I need a moment," Solanji said as she dragged Mav into a side chamber. She stared at him for a moment and then slowly reached out to touch his face. "Are you really here? Or is it my imagination?"

Mav placed his hand over Solanji's. "I am really here."

She placed her other hand on his chest. "Are you alright?"

He sighed. "Define alright. If you mean, am I recovered, then yes. If you mean, am I unchanged, then no."

Solanji stepped nearer. "How are you changed?"

"I embraced death. Maybe I died; maybe I lived. I have a feeling that I'll never really know. What I do know is that I straddled the divide between life and death, and I chose to be alive here in the Oblivion Gate with you."

"Wise choice," Solanji said as she slid her arms around his waist.

"I hoped you might think so."

"I know you need to speak to everyone, reassure them all, just as I need reassuring. But you've been missing for nearly two weeks. It felt like a lifetime. I'm not sure I'm going to be able to let you out of my sight, even though I know I'll have to, and that's after two weeks. I have no idea how Adriz and Felather functioned for fifty years. I am in awe of their resilience, their belief."

"The only reason I am here is because of all my oathsworn. Your love tethers me here, calls to me, draws me home."

"Shut up and kiss me."

Mav was very happy to do as he was told.

Once Mav had managed to reassure his oathsworn, and promised Solanji and Ryvalin that he wouldn't go anywhere without telling them, he paused at the healerie entrance, his heart beating faster.

Felather lay on his side, facing the door, propped up by pillows to keep him from rolling onto his healing back. Adriz sat beside him, her hand in his, her head resting on the bed as she slept.

Mav walked over to him and bent to kiss his forehead. He smoothed Felather's golden curls off his face and whispered, "You have never failed me, dear heart. And you won't fail me now. You will hold on to me, and I'll never let you go."

Felather mumbled in his sleep. "I found you."

"That's right. You never gave up on me, and you found me, and I thank you for it every day. Hold on to me tight." Mav blew away the lingering taint of death hovering over Felather, and Felather sighed.

When he realised Bailey was watching him, Mav smiled, and Bailey's pale cheeks flushed pink.

"Aren't you supposed to be asleep?" Mav asked.

"I can't."

Mav nodded and walked around to the chair by Bailey's bed. He sank into it with a low groan and exhaled as he rested his head against the back of the chair.

"You should sleep," Bailey whispered. "You look exhausted."

"Mmmm."

Bailey crawled out of his bed and into Mav's lap, bringing his blankets with him. Mav hugged him close and whispered, "I am so proud of you."

"Even though I got stuck?"

"Because you got stuck. You did everything you could to save Felather, and I am forever in your debt."

Bailey squirmed in embarrassment, and Mav held him tighter.

"I hear you have a book you should read backwards."

Bailey gave a burst of laughter before muffling it in Mav's chest. "Sero was so angry."

"No, he wasn't. He was worried and scared for you. Just as I was. But you did brilliantly. We have much to thank Sero for. We were fortunate to call him family. You will always remember every lesson he gave you."

"Yes, Mav."

Mav laughed and hugged Bailey. "I would be honoured, my dearest boy, if you would be my oathsworn."

Bailey sighed in happiness. "I thought you'd never ask." He concentrated on aligning his heartbeat with Mav's, slow and steady, a soothing beat. Mav's love and that deep connection that now tied them together, he sheltered within his heart, similar to Felather, a treasure to be protected and all his. A small smile curved his lips, and his cheeks were flushed with colour as his lashes fluttered shut.

Mav's breathing deepened, and they both slept.

65

DEMAVRIAN – OBLIVION GATE

av woke a few turns later, his arms full of a sleeping cherub. He smiled as Bailey's golden wings fluttered in time with his deep breathing. They glistened in the dim light, drying as they flapped, forming as he slept. That would be a surprise when he woke. A nice one, Mav hoped. They had much to talk about; Mav was sure of it. Getting stuck within Felather's body must have been frightening. It was not surprising Bailey was afraid to sleep.

Carefully, he shuffled forward, and once he had enough leverage, he rose and placed Bailey back in his bed. "Sleep well, my cherub," he murmured and Bailey sighed as he snuggled into the sheets. Mav tucked the blankets around him, kissed his head, and left him sleeping.

"Mav? Is that you?" Felather's voice was low and full of longing. Mav hurried to his side.

"Shh, don't wake Bailey. I'm here."

"I'm sorry."

"For what?" Mav cupped Felather's cheek and sent a wave of love and healing through him. "Felather, you have nothing to apologise for. If anything, I should apologise to you for leaving you all so vulnerable."

"But…"

"But nothing. If not for Bailey, I would have lost you. I would not put either of you through such an experience again. You need to get better. Shandra is planning the ball so we can celebrate our amazing family."

"Everything is already better now that you are home."

"Well, I promise I'm not going anywhere. Now, go back to sleep and concentrate on healing. I'll be back to see you both tomorrow."

"Good." Felather squinted around Mav at Bailey. "Has he…?"

"Yes. A nice surprise for when he wakes, don't you think?"

Felather chuckled and pummelled his pillow as he made himself more comfortable. "I can hear the shrieks now," he said and closed his eyes.

Mav laughed and left him to rest.

Walking through the silent corridors, Mav smiled as the wraiths, one by one, showed themselves and waved. Kiara was the only one who glided up to him and hugged him tight. "Don't you ever do that to us again," she whispered fiercely. She kissed his cheek and then flitted off again.

"You were missed," Oji said softly.

"I think that is a theme," Mav agreed. "You should have warned me about what you intended. I would have been more prepared."

"Wenson did not tell me," Oji said.

"But he was part of you, wasn't he?" Mav asked.

"I think he was once, but he acted independently."

"The only reason I'm here is because of him, but I'm not the same." Mav thought of his alter ego. He was not only the

Gate Keeper; he truly was the Keeper of Shadows now. He wondered what Solanji would make of that.

Oji sighed. "I don't think he meant to put your life at risk."

"But he did, and everything is different now."

"I know," Oji replied. "But it doesn't have to be."

"I can't ignore the shadows."

"Nor would I expect you to. They are part of you. But that doesn't mean your objectives for Eidolon have changed."

Mav was silent as he headed back towards his rooms.

Solanji met him in the corridor and snuggled into his side. "You need to come to bed."

"Yes, dear heart."

"Tomorrow, you'll be bombarded with demands. Tonight is for us." She pushed open their doors and pulled Mav through.

He shut the door behind them and smiled when he heard the lock click. Oji would guard their privacy for tonight.

Mav was surprised when all Solanji wanted to do was hold him as if she still didn't believe he was back. The depth of her distress brought home how much she loved him. He held her close, wrapping himself around her so she could feel nothing but him, and he murmured how much he loved her over and over until she fell asleep in his arms.

The next morning, Mav didn't comment on the previous evening, only kissed Solanji awake, washed her back in the shower, and held her hand as they walked through the corridors to find some food. Even as they sat at the table in the dining room, Mav didn't release her hand. He kissed her knuckles and said, "I'm not leaving your side ever again."

Her brilliant smile alleviated some of his growing guilt. "I *will* hold you to that," she replied.

Adriz stayed long enough to eat. She cast a searing glance over Mav and gave him a joyful grin before saying, "I'm so glad you're home, Mav. I'm sure Solanji won't let you out of her sight, so I'll sit with Felather. Make sure you visit him later; you need to make sure he stays with us." She waited until he nodded, and then she said, "I'll see you later," and flitted out of the room.

Mav stared after her until he was distracted by Shandra. "Now that you are home," she said, "we can plan the oath-swearing ceremony and the celebration ball. We want the world to know you're ours and we're yours," Shandra said.

Mav smiled as all his oathsworn bonds resonated with their agreement. He was well and truly snared by his family, and he couldn't be happier. His shadows rippled, caressing Solanji and Shandra, who were sitting either side of him.

Kerris and Muntra sat opposite, with Kiara beside them. Only Bailey was missing, and Mav was determined to rectify that as soon as possible. Ryvalin was grinning, fit to bust, and Xylvin was crooning in Mav's head.

"Where is Julius? Isn't he joining us?"

"Julius is…" Oji's voice faded. "Umm, he hasn't left the library since we found Athenia's soul in the painting."

Solanji squeezed Mav's hand. "Athenia wouldn't speak to us. I think she's waiting for you."

"You're the SoulBreather, not me."

Solanji shrugged. "You're her best friend, and you're the one with the vendetta stone."

"Has she spoken to Julius? He's the one who loved her."

"Loves," Solanji said. "He still loves her."

A pulse fluttered under Mav's eye, and he rubbed his face. "He does realise she died? Her soul has to pass on. The only reason she lingered is because she couldn't."

"I think he's ignoring that fact. He thinks she'll choose to stay, like Kiara."

"Could she stay?" Kiara asked.

"I have no idea," Mav replied.

"Then you need to speak to her and find out," Solanji said.

Mav silently groaned. He had a feeling this wasn't going to go so well.

Mav found Julius seated in the library, staring up at the painting. His uniform was wrinkled, and his hair hung limply around his face. His eyes were red-rimmed and heavy.

"Haven't you slept?" Mav asked as he closed the door behind him. "Or showered?"

Julius lurched to his feet. "Mav! Solanji said you had returned, but I wasn't sure I believed her." He gestured at the painting. "Athenia's soul is in the painting. Tevo said so. Mav, she's here!"

A small spike of pain jabbed Mav in the chest at the casual mention of a cherub who wasn't Sero, but he ignored it and nodded. "So I've been told, but if I persuade her to come out, are you sure you want her to see you like this? You're a mess, and you stink."

Julius looked down at himself and winced.

"Go get cleaned up while I figure out how to contact her."

"You won't let her leave without speaking to me first?"

"I swear it."

Julius hesitated, torn between leaving and staying.

Mav grasped his arm and gave him a shake. "I promise, if I can persuade her to leave the painting, I will ask her to wait for you."

Julius nodded and reluctantly left.

Mav sat in the chair and stared at the painting much as Julius had. He tugged the red vendetta stone out of his shirt and rubbed it between his fingers. "Hey, Athenia, I think it's time to redeem your stone."

There was a moment of stillness, as if time had stopped, and then there was a whoosh of air, and Athenia's slight form shimmered in the air in front of the painting. The cord around Mav's neck released, and the red bead fell into his palm.

"It's time," Mav said and held out the bead.

Athenia drifted closer and stared at the vendetta stone. Then she lifted her gaze. "I'm so sorry for what I did to you, dearest," she whispered, tears glistening in her beautiful eyes.

"It was not your fault," Mav said, his throat tightening. "I'm sorry I couldn't help you."

"That was not your fault, either. Serenia was deliberately thorough. I wish I could have told you, but at the end…"

"I know," Mav said. A shiver rippled through him as he remembered his inability to speak as he'd bled out on the marble floor after Serenia had attacked him.

"But Julius, he hated you, for decades. Because of me."

"We have resolved our differences. He's been waiting for you."

"I know, but there is nothing I can give him."

"You are in the Oblivion Gate. You have a choice."

"A choice to do what?" Athenia perched on the edge of the table without realising it, and Mav smiled.

"To stay or pass on."

"To hide in a painting forever?"

"There are wraiths living in these halls, bound to me and the Oblivion Gate. They are dead like you, soulless, but they chose not to go through the Gate. They chose to serve the Gate."

"And you would have me bind myself to you as well?"

"No," Julius said from the door. "I would have you bind yourself to me."

Athenia's translucent form rippled, and Julius crossed the room. His hair was still wet, his shirt open at the throat. He had dressed in haste, and his boots were still in his hand. He stood in his bare feet, dishevelled and desperate, completely vulnerable, and Mav's heart ached for him.

Athenia rose from the table, and Julius swayed towards her, flinging his boots aside. They clattered into the corner and were ignored.

Athenia smiled and reached for him. "Beloved," she whispered. "I am so sorry."

Julius hauled her into his arms and kissed her.

Mav turned to inspect the bookshelf, smiling to himself. Julius' all-consuming love had grounded her. If Athenia chose to be bound to Julius, she would exist in the Oblivion Gate with him. A souled wraith. Would she be a wraith? Or something else? Mav didn't know and didn't care.

Mav cleared his throat. "Umm, does this mean you're staying with Julius, Athenia?"

Julius swung her around, his gaze never leaving her face. "Of course she is," he said.

Athenia's radiant smile was only, and would only ever be, for him. She ran her fingers through Julius' hair and then stared at the moisture on her fingers.

"I can feel it. I can feel you," she said in wonder.

The red vendetta stone crumbled to dust in Mav's fingers, and he brushed the remnants away.

"The library needs a librarian. You could stay here while you decide what you want to do," Mav offered as he smiled at them both. He shook his head. They weren't listening, they only had eyes for each other.

Mav wasn't sure how that would work, but that was their problem to solve. He left them to their reunion.

66

OBLIVION GATE

Felather groaned at Bailey's shrieks as he bounced on his bed, twisting around to see his golden wings. Felather plastered his pillow over his head as he tried to block out the noise.

Rubbing his chest, he frowned at the ache but also at the ease with which he was breathing. It wasn't a struggle to breathe. He slowly sat up, and Bailey froze and then fell off his bed.

Bailey scrambled up, rubbing his elbow. "Felather?" he whispered in shock.

Felather frowned. "What?"

"You're awake!"

"Of course I'm awake. Why wouldn't I be with the racket you're making?"

"You-you've been unresponsive ever since Tevo separated us. I thought I'd done something wrong."

"You kept me alive, Bailey. If not for you, I would be dead. You did nothing wrong." Felather's confusion deepened. "Tevo? What is he doing here? Where's Sero?"

"Umm." Bailey sat on his bed, his shoulders drooping.

"A lot happened after Kaenera's people attacked us. But Kaenera is dead."

Felather stared at him and slowly nodded. "Nice wings," he said, somewhat bemused.

Bailey laughed. "I'm a cherub. I'm actually a cherub."

"Congratulations."

"Felather?" Adriz's voice interrupted them as she stood in the doorway. She stared at him in amazement. "You… you…" She didn't seem to be able to form a sentence.

Bailey chuckled. "You died yesterday. She totally freaked out. You have a lot of apologising to do." He grinned. "I'll leave you to it." Bailey hopped off his bed and grinned at the shocked look on Adriz's face as he passed. She twisted and followed him as he walked down the corridor.

"What happened to him?"

"He got his wings," Felather said. "Be prepared for many more shrieks."

Adriz shook her head and entered the healerie. "How are you feeling?"

"Much better," he replied with some surprise. "My chest aches, but I feel…I don't know, lighter."

Adriz smiled and leaned over him. "I am so glad to hear it." She traced his cheek with a gentle finger and kissed him on the lips. Felather cupped the back of her head and pulled her down on top of him.

"I've missed you so much," he whispered.

"I know. I've missed you. I have a lot to tell you, but first, I have some news I hope you'll like." She braced herself above him and licked her lips as she hesitated.

Felather gripped her arms. "What is it? You know you can tell me anything."

"We're having a baby," she blurted out.

Felather gaped at her and then the broadest smile spread over his face. "We are?"

Adriz nodded.

"Oh, sweetheart, that's amazing." Tears filled his eyes, and he pulled her into another kiss. "You are so amazing," he whispered, and she relaxed into his embrace.

"I thought I'd lost you," she said sometime later.

"If it hadn't been for our brand-new cherub, you would have," Felather admitted. "I was fortunate Mav knocked some sense into me."

"We couldn't lose anyone else," Adriz murmured.

Felather stiffened. "Who did we lose?"

Adriz sighed. "There is no good way to say this, so I'm just going to say it. Averdeus and Sero are dead."

"No," Felather whispered as he clutched her, the ache in his chest spiking.

"There is much to tell you, but we have plenty of time for that. Shandra is preparing a big shindig to celebrate Mav and Solanji's being heartsworn, a memorial for Averdeus and Sero, and the fact that all Mav's fledglings have sworn their oath to him." She smiled. "Our family grows."

"And Mav?"

Adriz sighed. "Too early to tell. He was lost to Oblivion for a good two weeks. We almost lost him, too. I've not had the chance to get all the details about what happened. All I know is that he took Kaenera and the Aeora sigils through the Gate and they exploded, killing Kaenera and Wenson and driving Mav deeper into Oblivion. I think we are fortunate he found his way back."

Felather was silent for a moment. Then he said, "Well, I think once you tell him about our news, maybe it will set his mind on a course for life instead of death, and maybe Solanji can step up and make sure he stays here with us."

Adriz sighed into his chest. "I hope you're right."

A month later, the Oblivion Gate had undergone a remarkable transformation. It was adorned with garlands of golden flowers and green ribbons. The towering structures stood proudly next to the shimmering sea, and the salty air wafted through the tall, open doors and into the bustling corridors.

Extra canvas tents had been set up around entrance doors, and lines of folding chairs filled the grassy space in between. A sense of expectation hung in the air. More colourful pennants fluttered along the edges of the marquees which had been raised around a temporary marked-out courtyard to the side of the building, extra space to cater to all their guests.

Mav and Oji were still wary of opening the doors fully and decided to allow access only to part of the ground floor, mainly the entrance hall and the ballroom, which were similarly decorated with fluttering flags and swags of material.

Oji, with his usual resourcefulness, had created guest rooms in yet another wing. Mav was taken aback by the Gate's newfound vibrancy, from once silent halls to corridors teeming with excited people and wraiths, all working together harmoniously. Julius' men, after their initial surprise, had grown fond of the wraiths and, over the last month, had begun to treat them as equals.

Shandra had been driving everyone to complete her plans, hounding oathsworn, guards, and wraiths alike to distraction, until Mav had said enough and declared an evening of rest for everyone. If it wasn't done now, then it wasn't going to be.

Mav tightened his grip on Solanji's hand as they strolled along the beach, their bare feet sinking into the soft grey sand.

"Is there a reason there is so little colour in Eidolon?"

Solanji asked, gazing around her at the grey sky, sea, and land.

Mav followed her gaze and shrugged. "I suppose Kaenera drained the place of everything. Doesn't mean it has to stay that way." He watched Xylvin breach the sea's surface and trumpet water high in the air. She rolled, a flash of iridescent scales as the spray fell around her. "It will just take a little time."

Xylvin floated on her stomach, her head nearly submerged and her faceted eyes watching them walk on the beach.

Mav stared at the sandy bay that curved off into the distance. "I think this should be our home." The steel-grey sea rippled in the breeze. Tall grasses covered the rounded dunes which edged the beach, flattening into a grassy plain. Behind him, the imposing green stone walls and towers of the Oblivion Gate rose into the grey sky, they pierced the clouds and continued unseen.

"You like the water?" Oji asked, his voice resonating in Mav's mind.

"I find the sound of the waves soothing," Mav replied.

Oji was silent for a moment. *"So do I!"* he said with surprise.

Xylvin rumbled deep in her throat as she walked out of the surf, her glorious wings stretched wide. Mav smiled when she shook herself like a vemlow and then leapt up and over the sandy dunes, landing near the tents. *"You need to get ready,"* she said as she stalked between the tents and settled at the bottom of the steps leading up to the open doors of the Oblivion Gate.

"Yes, we should," Solanji said, tugging Mav towards the dunes.

They struggled through the sand dunes, laughing as they

staggered in the sucking sand. Mav wrapped Solanji in his arms, rolled her over, and kissed her.

"Mav! Stop it. I'll never get all the sand out of my hair."

"I'll help you."

"People will be watching."

"Let them," he said and deepened the kiss.

Solanji melted beneath him, and her arms snaked around his neck, drawing him closer. When they came up for air, she chuckled and kissed the edge of his mouth. He smiled at the soft tickle.

"Ready, dear heart?" Mav asked.

"To let the world know I love you? To welcome our family home? Definitely."

"Then, let the ceremony begin," Mav said, pulling her to her feet. "I want the world to know I love you. I want them to know that I am the happiest man alive. I want them to know the Oblivion Gate is awake and watching and that Eidolon may be a land of shadows, but it is a land of opportunity, too."

Ellaria appeared beside them. Her golden scales glistened as a narrow ray of sunlight pierced the thick cloud cover. *"Then, I suggest you get a move-on before Felather changes his mind about performing the ceremony."*

"Demavrian?" Felather stood at the top of the steps and then yelled again. "Solanji?"

Mav laughed, and wrapping his arm around his wife, they hurried towards their home and their waiting family.

The ceremony was perfect.

Demavrian and Solanji stood before Felather and stared into each other's eyes as they exchanged their vows in front of their oathsworn and friends. Bailey stood within Muntra's sheltering arms. His joy at becoming a cherub had replaced some of his recent fears, and Muntra's calm and steadfast love grounded him. Kerris and Shandra stood next to them with huge grins on their faces, and eager to celebrate swearing their oaths. Kiara hovered with Athenia, Julius, and the wraiths within the entrance hall, peering excitedly out of the door. Adriz, Ryvalin, and Xylvin took up the other side of the small area. Amaridin and Valerian sat with other select guests and smiled as they watched, their hands linked and still planning their own ceremony.

Demavrian twisted his lips as he felt his bond with Solanji tighten. Since the "final confrontation", as it was called, all his oathsworn were concerned he would walk through the Gate and not return. He didn't understand why they didn't trust him, but he let them bind him tight, and he bound them tight in return.

Every single one of them swore their oaths again, and he welcomed them into his heart. His joy was overflowing as his family was confirmed, and their joint happiness overflowed as Adriz and Felather shared their baby news.

Demavrian wouldn't allow the memorial to his father and their friend, Sero, to be sad. They laughed through their memories and embraced the love they had felt for each other. Bailey stood on the steps to the Oblivion Gate and shared one of Sero's memories from the first time he'd joined them in the Gate. An empty jam pot featured prominently in the tale.

Shandra's ball continued into the early turns of the next morning.

EPILOGUE – A MONTH LATER

Exhaling, Demavrian rose and walked around his desk. A dull glow lit his window, and he scowled at the grey view. It was time he did something about that.

He slid the blue vendetta stone on the cord around his neck back and forth, an unconscious habit that was now a permanent feature. Since his father had died, he would never know his father's intent for Eidolon. Instead, Mav would work to bring his own vision to life. If that meant he would wear the vendetta stone forever, then so be it.

Strolling out of his office, his hands digging deep in his pockets, he debated about how far to change the climate.

It was always such a delicate balance. Much of Eidolon flourished in the gloom and the shadows, an important part of this world that he didn't want to damage. But he also wanted to introduce a touch of colour; a soft blush to the sky, a deeper blue to the rivers, a vibrant green in the gorse bushes, and a variety of colours to clothe the trees. He wanted to give his world depth instead of this flat, misty grey canvas.

His Oblivion was bright and vibrant, full of possibilities even if it slumbered when he wasn't here. He wanted to share the odd sparkle his own shadows exhibited, that depth of existence that meant, no matter what, you lived your life to the full, taking every moment as it came and embracing the opportunity. His people had become downtrodden, reviled, and forgotten through no fault of their own. It was time to reinstate their pride, their drive for life, their belief that they deserved to live the life they wanted, not what someone else dictated.

He was here to give them that opportunity. It was up to them what they did with it. And it would all start by giving the sea a silver sparkle to shimmer in the distance and catch the eye and by thinning the clouds enough that the sun could peek through and reveal some of the wonders of nature shyly hiding in the gloom.

Their site by the sea was in a surprisingly populated area. Mav had scoured the maps in the library and Oji's awareness of the area, which had revealed that he had chosen the deserted end of the double-crescent beach. The east end hosted a large fishing village, and some sparsely populated hinterlands which bled into some rich farmland, and peat bogs which supplied the surrounding area. The west end was starker, with sharp rock barriers and grey-shingle beaches. But the stark beauty and relative peace enticed Mav.

The Oblivion Gate didn't need to be in a busy city like Puronia. In fact, he was glad it wasn't. His Host would spend more time in the depths of Eidolon than in the Gate, ensuring order was restored and the lawless were punished.

With Kaenera gone, his suggestions and persuasions were lifted, and good people were able to return to the lives they had been leading before they were unfortunate enough to have crossed his path. Even the young man planted as a mole in the OblivionGate turned out to be an innocent victim who, after a few days of confusion, reverted to the person he was supposed to be.

There was so much still to learn, and so much to fix that the peace was a solace to his busy mind and soothed the need to be always doing something, to be always stressing over unexpectedly complex or life-threatening situations.

Standing at the top of the beach, looking out over the sea, Mav inhaled the salty air and concentrated on thinning the clouds. He encouraged some of them to coalesce into denser, fluffier clouds and then persuaded them to drift over the fields, which needed the water.

The remaining clouds, he thinned, and he lifted his face as the sun struggled to penetrate the wispy barrier. The grey became more yellow, a pale hint of colour. Inhaling, he enjoyed the clean, fresh scent and exhaled.

"You shouldn't be out here on your own," a woman's voice said from behind him.

Mav turned and smiled. "I am just admiring the view."

"It's not safe," the woman insisted. She was grey-haired and thin, with beady blue eyes in her lined face. She clutched a wicker basket in her bony fingers. The basket contained a paper-wrapped package and two apples.

"You're out here," Mav said.

The woman huffed. "I ain't got nothing for them to take" —she glanced at her basket— "'cept my dinner, but you..." she gestured at him. "You scream money."

Mav stared at her in surprise. He wasn't dressed in anything particularly special. "What about me screams money?"

"No patches," the woman said. "Nothing's been mended. None round here can say the same."

Mav was silent for a moment, shocked that such a simple

thing was noticeable. "If you could change one thing in Eidolon, what would it be?" he asked, staring back out to sea.

"I want to live in my home in peace, to be safe. I'm fed up with having what little we have stolen or ruined just because some bully boy says so."

"And who are these bully boys?"

"Wastrels, dybbuks, those who think they can just because they are stronger."

"How often do they visit?"

The woman sighed and came to stand beside him. "What does it matter?"

A single ray of sunshine penetrated the clouds, and the woman gasped, turning her face to meet the weak warmth.

"It matters because I say it matters," Mav said, inspecting her more closely, recognising the worn and faded clothes, the lined face and tired eyes. He gently tucked her hand in his arm. "My name is Mav. What's yours?"

"Celine."

"And where do you live?"

"In a homestead out yonder," she said, vaguely gesturing into the hinterlands.

"Would you show me. I would love to see what you've done with it."

The woman smiled. "Very little, but it is home."

Unsurprised to see Solanji and Ryvalin striding across the heath towards him, followed by the duty guards, Mav offered Solanji his hand as she approached. "This is my wife, Solanji," Mav said as she stalked up to him. She stopped in surprise as she saw the woman. "Solanji, meet Celine. We are going to visit her home."

Solanji flicked Mav a questioning glance and smiled at the woman. "I am very pleased to meet you."

"Did you really think you could go anywhere without an escort?" Xylvin murmured in his head.

"I wasn't intending to," Mav replied.

"Do you think I really believe that?" Ryvalin asked as she arrived. *"You're about to head off into the gloom with a strange woman, and you didn't tell us."*

"And yet, here you are."

Mav grinned as Ryvalin snorted in his head.

"See, I am not out here alone," Mav said to Celine. "Do you have family at your homestead?"

"Just my husband. He does most of the work. That's what makes me so angry. He does all the work, and they destroy it."

"Then, maybe we need to ask them to stop," Mav said.

"Ask?" The woman stared at him as if he were mad.

"A peaceful solution is always preferable."

Shaking her head, Celine said, "What world do you live in?"

Mav grinned. "The same one as you do."

Tutting, the woman led him along narrow trails through low bracken and gorse bushes. Mav was aware of at least three guards following behind them. Ryvalin must have brought in reinforcements, and he smiled as he kept Celine chatting about her home.

Solanji's fingers entwined with his kept him grounded, and the constant ebb and flow of love and comfort through their bond reminded him how lucky he was. He was safe and surrounded by his family. Many of those living in Eidolon were not so fortunate, and he was determined to change that.

They topped a small rise, and her home lay spread out before him. His chest tightened for a moment when he saw it was very similar to Shandra's old home. The dilapidated house had a veranda running around it. Wicker chairs were scattered about the veranda, all jumbled together as if someone had tossed them about. One even lay in the yard.

Celine stiffened when she saw a calope tied up to the

veranda rail. "Visitors are rare and usually not good." She tucked her basket behind a gorse bush and strode across the yard to the house.

Mav and Solanji followed, with Ryvalin and her guards close behind. Raised voices came from the house, and Celine dashed inside, surprising Mav with her agility. He rushed after her. "Celine, wait."

Inside, the room was dim, but after a glance around the room, Mav could see the damage that had already been wrought on these poor people's home. The table and chairs lay in splintered piles of wood, good for nothing but the fire, and two scrawny men were forcing a third man against the wall.

"Let him go, you bastards!" Celine screamed, grabbing a piece of wood off the floor and charging at them.

Mav seized her and transported her beside Solanji as one of the scrawny men swung around, and a blade flashed in his hand.

Celine yelped as she landed and almost swung her piece of wood at Solanji, but Ryvalin took it off her.

Mav concentrated on separating the men. He transported the man he assumed was Celine's husband next to her and pinned the two scrawny men against the wall, all by just using his mind. When their blades inexplicably heated to a red-hot glow and burned their hands, they yelped and dropped them. Ryvalin's guards kicked the knives away and bracketed the two men so they had nowhere to go, not that Mav intended to allow them to flee.

Behind him, Celine fussed over her husband, who had a stunned expression on his bruised face, and Solanji tried to reassure both of them, her voice low and soothing.

Mav inspected the men. Scruffy and destitute, they appeared to be common ruffians, but he needed to make sure. He let some of his aura leak as he peered into one of the men's minds and hastily retreated at the constant stream of resentment and hate he found there. After a moment's thought, he planted the suggestion in both men that they wanted to tell him all about their recent activities.

"Who are you, and what are you doing here?"

"I'm Reg, and he's me brother, Ted. We ain't got nowhere to live, so those that do give us food and money."

"You mean you take it through force instead of accepting what they can give?"

"They give us nothin', so we has to."

"We've got nothing to give," Celine snapped.

"But the more you destroy, the less they have, so how can you expect them to help you another time?" Mav asked. "Wouldn't a day's good work for a meal and a bed be better than destruction and fear?"

"What if they don't give it after we done the work? That's a mug's game," Reg said.

It saddened Mav that such thoughts existed, such distrust and hatred towards one another. "Where do you come from? How did you end up this far south?"

Reg shrugged and straightened his shoulders. "Used to have a business outta Traxa, a bit o' carpentry. Fell on hard times. Couldn't pay our bills. Both of us got carted off to Eidolon without having a chance to negotiate terms we could fulfil."

The man's speech improved as he spoke of better times, and Mav realised their fall from grace had impacted them more than losing their business. Their self-esteem, their personal pride, had been destroyed as well, leaving them destitute and desperate in a hostile country. From there, it had taken little for the resentment and ill will towards others to fester and grow. How many others had resorted to this type of behaviour? Ideal fodder for Kaenera's whims.

"Well, you will not threaten or destroy ever again. You

will work hard and repair or replace every item you damaged. Celine and her husband will provide you with one meal, and allow you to sleep in the hayloft for the night." Mav held the men's eyes until they sheepishly nodded. "When you are finished, you will be escorted to the Oblivion Gate, and there, we will discuss how you can put your carpentry skills to better use."

The men's faces paled. "Don't kill us, please," Ted pleaded. "We never meant no 'arm. We never murdered anyone, just roughed 'em up a bit."

Mav wanted to roll his eyes. "Which bit of 'put your skills to better use', translated into being put to death?"

"Oblivion Gate," Reg whispered, his eyes still wide with fear. "Once you go in, you never come out."

"Go get them cleaned up," Mav said to the guards. He released his mental hold on the men, and they both sagged with relief. "While Celine and her husband make a list of jobs for them to do."

"We would pay them fairly for a good day's work," Celine's husband said, "but we have little ourselves. We trade our honey at the market, but the bees don't always give us much, and times can be hard, especially when the likes of them come along and destroy the hives."

Mav transported a jug of hannoe and five mugs out of the Gate's kitchen, and they hovered in the air. "Take one," he said as he grabbed the jug and a mug, drifting the other mugs into the shocked couple's hands.

Solanji rolled her eyes, muttering, "Cook is going to be so mad," and Ryvalin grinned, grasping hers as Mav poured out the steaming liquid.

"H-how did you do that? How do you create things out of nothing? Who are you?" Celine asked, taking a step back.

"He is Deus Demavrian, and he is the new Oblivion Gate Keeper," Ryvalin said somewhat grandly.

Celine's jaw dropped. Mav poured her some bannoe. "I didn't create it. I stole it from Cook's kitchen, and he will no doubt try to clip me around the ear when he finds out."

Celine's jaw snapped shut, and Mav grinned. "I'm no better than those poor men out there, but at least I am stealing from myself.

"Let's sit on the veranda. I could replace your table and chairs, but those men need to replace them for you. I will provide some good timber for them to use. They need to pay their dues before we get them back on track."

After leading the way out to the veranda, where one of the guards was busily turning the chairs upright, Celine sank into the nearest one as if her legs could no longer hold her up. She sipped her bannoe and sighed out her breath as she closed her eyes.

Leaning against the veranda railing, Ryvalin watched the yard, her alert gaze flicking around checking on her men. She jerked her head at the guard, who took up a sentry position by the steps.

Mav sat opposite Celine.

She opened her eyes and inspected him. "Now, this isn't scalable."

Mav raised an eyebrow. "Scalable?"

"You can't personally visit every home and sort out everyone's problems."

"I have to start somewhere and I need to know about the problems I face before I can solve them. And I need advocates like you. No one is going to trust me. They don't know me, and they only remember Kaenera. You saw those men's reactions to the Oblivion Gate. I expect you feel much the same."

Nodding thoughtfully, Celine drank her bannoe. "Then, you need to show them how you are different."

"Which is why Solanji is returning souls."

"Returning souls?"

"Yes, we are performing a census, registering everyone so we can try and match them to the souls in the citadel," Solanji said as she sat beside Mav. She rested her hand on his leg, and the heat from her palm warmed Mav's whole body. "It will be a long job, but one day, we hope to return all the souls."

"Our souls still exist?" Celine asked in wonder.

"I hope so," Mav said. If they couldn't find the souls, then, if necessary, Mav would give them a shadowsoul. Everyone within Eidolon would have the same freedom as those who lived in Angelicus, to live wherever they wanted to. "If you give us your details, where you came from in Puronia, what happened for you to end up here, we'll pass them to the SoulBreather."

"There's a new SoulBreather?" Celine's husband breathed.

"That's all very well, but this is a very important thing you are doing," Celine said, leaning forward to tap his arm. "You need to make a show of it and then send runners telling everyone about it. Build excitement, interest. Otherwise, you are shouting into a wilderness of suspicious people."

"Runners?"

"Youngsters need the coin, too."

"I see," Mav replied.

Celine sat up. "I used to teach before we became beekeepers. Let me tell you what you should do."

Mav grinned as he leaned back in his chair and let Celine instruct him on the best way to teach others. He drank his bannoe and paid close attention, topping up her mug as she spoke. The people of Eidolon would learn how to help themselves, and their lives would be better for it, but most important of all, with the help of Solanji and his family, they would be safe under his watch.

The End

GLOSSARY

Deus

Veradeus (v-AIR-ad-ay-us) God, father of Demavrian and Amaridin

Demavrian (duh-MAV-ri-un)

Angels

Amaridin (a-MA-RI-din) Archdeus

Valerian (Val-AIR-ian) Archangel - Amridin's partner

Malena, (Mah-Lain-ah) Veradeus' Wife

Kaenara (k-nair-a) Veradeus' brother

Serenia (s-REN-i-a) Archangel

Athenia (a-th-eh-ni-a) Archangel, SoulBreather

Golaran (go-law-ran) Archangel

Julius Teravin (t-air-a-vin) Captain of the Heavenly Host

Sero (s-air-ro) Cherub

Tevo (tee-vo) Cherub

Kyrill (k-i-rill) Seraphim

Mav's Oathsworn

Solanji (so-lan-j-i) -SoulBreather, Demavian's wife
Eladriz/Adriz (el-a-driz) Cherubim
Felather (fell-a-th-ur) Scribe
Ryvalin (riv-a-lin) Captain of the Heavenly Host
Xylvin (SHIL-vin) Dragon
Ellaria (Ell-ar-ree-ah) Dragon

Mortals

Brennan/Bren (bren-an) Solanji's younger brother
Georgi (j-or-gi) Solanji and Brennan's elder brother
Xabier - (Sab-ee-ay) retired custodian

Fledglings

Kerris (k-air-riss) Orphan
Shandra (sh-an-druh) Orphan
Muntra (mun-truh) Orphan
Bailey (bay-li) Orphan

Wraiths

Kiara (key-ar-a)
Liam
Jessica
Wenson- Librarian
Cecil - Cook
Laurel
Clarence

Creatures

Calope - four legged domestic animal to ride, like a horse
Freller - a rodent
Vemlow (vem) - wild hunting animal, like a wolf

Locations

Angelicus (an-zh-el-i-cus) country

Puronia (p-roh-ni-a) Capital city of Angelicus
Bruatra (bru-ar-tra) Town in south Angelicus
Eidolon (Eye-d-oh-lon) Country

Apologia (ap-o-low-gee-a) Formal process to prove innocence of charges or forfeit life.

ACKNOWLEDGMENTS

It is with some amazement that I write that the SoulMist series is complete. A trilogy in the end, though I was unsure for quite a while if there would be three or four books in this series.

A bittersweet moment for sure. I have been writing the SoulMist series for the last four years and inevitably, the question arises: What next?

Well, I hope you'll be glad to hear that there are new epic fantasy series in the offing, if I can decide which one to focus on and complete.

Thank you to my editors, Maddy Glenn and Jefferson for making me think long and hard about this book. Thank you to Michael, my alpha reader who has been on this journey with me from day one, offers unstinting support, and is always ready to read another one of my books.

My wonderful team of ARC readers continues to grow. Thank you to each of you for joining me on this journey, I really appreciate all your support, comments and feedback. Click this link to sign up to my ARC team if you are interested in reading my books early.

I love my cover. Seeing my characters brought to life is such a great feeling. The cover was designed by the Ukrainian creative company MiblArt, who have continued to support their authors through very difficult times.

Thank you all.

Helen

ABOUT THE AUTHOR

Helen Garraway is the USA Today Bestselling author of the award winning epic fantasy Sentinal series which was first published in 2020, followed by the first book of the fantasy romance SoulMist series, SoulBreather, released in 2022 as part of the Realm of Darkness boxset. Both series are now complete and you can also find some of the books in audio.

An avid reader of many different fiction genres, a love she inherited from her mother, Helen writes fantasy novels and also enjoys paper crafting and scrapbooking as an escape from the pressure of the day job.

Having graduated from the University of Southampton with a Degree in Politics and International Relations, she remains an active member of their alumni. You can find out more at www.helengarraway.com.

<u>Patreon</u>
Join Team Arifel, Team Darian or Team Sentinal and get access to the first chapters of my new books first, free bookish downloads, polls, early sneak peeks.

ONE
THE SENTINAL SERIES

SENTINALS AWAKEN

HELEN GARRAWAY

SENTINAL SERIES

Want to read more? Interested in my epic Fantasy Sentinal series? Find out more at www.helengarraway.com
Available in the format of your choice.

- Audiobook
- Ebook
- Paperback
- Hardcover

Remargaren is a vibrant, ancient world. With Goddesses, Sentinals, Rangers and Ascendants all trying to protect or attain that which is important to them.

Join me on the journey, as we meet Jerrol Haven, a King's Ranger, who is destined to become Lady Leyandrii's Captain. A role lost in the mists of time after her last Captain spectacularly disappeared with her when she sundered the Bloodstone and banished all magic from the world.

Throw into the mix some magical creatures, magic seeping back into the world, an insidious disease affecting the

Watches of Vespiri and the tall sentinal trees, the only reminder of the Lady's Guards, her faithful Sentinals, and we have the Sentinals Series.

We travel deeper into the world of Remargaren as Jerrol grapples with the expectations of goddesses and kings, and tries to stay alive long enough to figure out how he can wake the ancient guards sleeping in their tall trees. They are his only hope to help him protect their world against the wild magic of the shadowy Ascendants.

Start with book one, Sentinals Awaken:

https://Books2Read.com/SentinalsAwaken

Sentinals Awaken is the first book in the award winning saga of Remargaren, a vibrant, ancient world of high fantasy suffused with magic and adventure.

As a three thousand-year-old threat reemerges, only one man has the power to awaken the world's greatest protectors and restore order to the realm. He just doesn't know it yet. When Jerrol Haven, a captain in the King's Rangers, discovers treason at the highest level, he knows immediately that the knowledge puts his life at risk. And indeed, though he expected the ailing king to shield him, the ambitious Crown Prince sentences Jerrol to death.

What hold does the Prince have over his weakened father, and who or what is he protecting?

Now, with signs that her veil is weakening and the Ascendants are creeping back into power, the goddess, Leyandrii, has returned and is in dire need of Jerrol's help. For though he doesn't know it, Jerrol possesses a rare gift: By chance, he touches a revered Sentinal tree and awakens Birlerion, one of the Lady's personal guard who have been sleeping in the strange, tall trees since they were last called to battle. Aided by Birlerion, Jerrol flees and begins his journey to help Lady Leyandrii save Remargaren once more.

But time is running out: As it was with the king, the old guard lords are everywhere being usurped, attacked, and assassinated. Jerrol must unravel the mystery of the Ascendants' return, stop the sinister force that is dividing good families through bloodshed and betrayal, and rescue the king—and his troubles are only just beginning.

Ideal for lovers of The Witcher, Tad William's Shadowmarch or David Eddings' Belgarion series.

Global Book Award Silver Medal, Wishing Shelf Book Award Bronze Medal, Readers' Favorite Finalist.